Dean Scott was born in Dumfries, Scotland in 1978. He now lives in Edinburgh with his family. Nocturne in Bleu is his debut novel.

Dean Scott

Nocturne in Bleu

LIPSTICK PUBLISHING

A Lipstick Paperback

First Published in Great Britain by
Lipstick Publishing 2005
This paperback first edition 2005

Lipstick Publishing
West Knockenbaird Croft,
Insch, Aberdeenshire.
Scotland AB52 6TN

A CIP catalogue record for this book is available
from the British Library

ISBN: 1-904762-23-9

www.lipstickpublishing.com
admin@lipstickpublishing.com

Printed and bound by Antony Rowe Ltd, Eastbourne

The author greatly appreciates the opportunity to thank Sarah and Lois, David and Jacqualin, and to devote this effort, and all efforts besides, to Alison.

The wee Kirkcudbright centipede, she was very sweet.
She was very proud of every one of her hundred feet.
Early every morning, her neighbours came to glance.
She always entertained them with a beautiful little dance.

Matt McGinn

The sky is grey,
the sand is grey,
and the ocean is grey.
I feel right at home in this stunning monochrome,
alone in my way.
I smoke and I drink,
and every time I blink,
I have a tiny dream.
And as bad as I am,
I'm proud of the fact that I'm worse than I seem.

Ani Di'franco

The Last Weekend

A certain amount of reverie is good, like a narcotic in discreet doses. It soothes the fever, sometimes high, of the brain at work, and produces in the mind a soft and fresh vapour, which corrects the too angular contours of pure thought, fills up the gaps and intervals here and there, binds them together, and blunts the sharp corners of ideas.

But too much reverie submerges and drowns.

Victor Hugo

1

She opened the tall baroque doors and lent out over the terrace, the warm May breeze penetrating her nightdress, her eyes heavy with drink. Lifting a glass of dark rum to her lips, she hesitated as the tinny smell filled her nose, and then wincing, swallowed a deep draught. The sad, weary garble of Edith Piaf drifted up in the night from a nearby music hall. Stretched out before her, pierced by the Eiffel Tower, the occupied Left Bank landscape seemed below the blanket of stars unchanging, somehow innocent and oblivious. That it would survive seemed certain; it had done so before. The endurance of its current populace, however, from her lofty perception, appeared more dubious.

After a second gulp, licking a spilt drop from her chin, she lit a harsh cigarette.

She was waiting. She had waited for almost twelve hours and yet, while contact had been assured by noon and it was now nearly midnight, Alison did not mind the wait; such things were often a matter of guesswork and she had become a patient woman. Pause allowed reflection. Not that reflection was always a good thing, but it did at least permit absorption.

Patience in her previous life had been rare. Each night, the wait until her husband, the schoolmaster, arrived home from work had seemed like individual eternities. Waiting out the long nine months of pregnancy had nearly driven her out of her mind, although in hindsight the waiting was preferable to the stillborn infant. Worse still were the helpless and tedious months while John was away fighting the war. But no measure of hard-learned patience would ever bring John home. Like his baby, John was dead.

She often heard him inside her head. Of course, she knew that it was her own voice, but it spoke John's sentiments, and with the lack of a physical body to hold, a comforting voice sufficed.

Ease up, sweetheart, it said now. Think of your liver.

Alison Gorry ignored the advice and drained her glass.

Four floors below, on the ancient lane connecting Boulevard St-Germain and Rue St-Dominique, an open-top Citroën cruised the cobbles. Alison felt the familiar fear rise, growing like a choking weed as one of the three dove grey-uniformed Gestapo officers lifted his head to inspect her, seeing from his low position, she immediately realised, everything she had to offer. His cap's deathly skull emblem radiated yellow under the streetlamps. Swallowing the fear down with rum, Alison became Violette and smiled through a puff of cigarette smoke as the car rolled on out of sight.

Violette Rodin, thirty-seven years of age, a French national, had been Alison Gorry's principal alias for almost a year. Identity papers explaining that Violette, the wife of a French Army officer taken as a prisoner of war under the Franco-German armistice, lived quietly on her private family income were exceptional and would pass - had passed - the very closest inspection. Violette Rodin, after all, was not a work of fiction; she was everything the papers claimed. They simply failed to mention that Violette Rodin now lived in England, replaced by the woman from the Special Operations Executive.

The apartment's floorboards creaked softly as Alison crossed on bare feet to pour another dose of rum. She settled with the glass in her favourite armchair, closing her eyes to wait.

She dozed. She dreamed briefly of John. She was running, dragging him by the hand, but he could not keep up. Naked, pursued, they fled through streets ruined and ablaze, shards of glass piercing their feet. It was a familiar dream, pleasant in its own way, interrupted by three slow, gentle taps on the apartment door.

'Oui?' Alison's eyes remained closed.

The voice came in a whisper. 'Je suis venu de l'opéra.'

Alison crossed Violette's modern white apartment, threw open the door, turned, and sat back down with her glass.

Major Philip Scott, wearing a dinner jacket and tie, was a British war hero. He had led three successful recognisance missions during the Great War into the very heart of Germany and had walked ever since with a cane. An unremarkably built man approaching his fiftieth year, the Major was not yet to be underestimated; he was said to have the reflexes of a cat. Yet, three years in occupied France had left him drained. His eyes said it, his entire demure agreed. Major Scott was exhausted, body, mind and soul. Into the room he limped, met by the perfumed, alcoholic smell, and began immediately in his nasally taut English, firmly but quietly:

'There's been no contact with Madeleine for two days, Violette. She's gone. It's a fucking disaster. We're looking everywhere, we've sent out flags, we've…hell! Two bloody days! Fuck.'

Alison took this in, eyes wide, noting:

'Philip, you're very tense. Would you care for a drink?'

'You're drunk, Violette! Did you hear me at all? Madeleine has vanished.'

'I heard you. Take a seat.'

Blinking his red eyes several times, the Major leaned his weight on his cane, swallowed a deep breath, and his weariness got the better of him.

'I'm sorry,' he breathed. 'You're right. You're entitled to get drunk. I am very tense, but I don't think it's any bloody wonder. The waiting is driving everyone insane.'

'I understand,' Alison whispered. 'Have some patience and sit down. Please.'

The Major slumped down in the lined baroque chair opposite Alison, holding his cane across his knees, his face set in a helpless scowl, almost a cringe.

'Will you please find out about Madeleine?'

'Of course.'

'But be careful. At this stage, Violette, we cannot afford to lose...' The sound of an approaching siren interrupted them and both sets of eyes turned instinctively to the open terrace doors. As the sound began to disappear, they shared a forced smile.

Alison sipped her rum, rolling the liquid around her mouth before swallowing, and then lit two tailor-made American cigarettes from her case simultaneously. One she gave to the Major, the other she hung from her bottom lip.

'I assume you're not here because of Madeleine, sir.'

'That's correct.'

'Is it Overlord?' Alison could not disguise her eagerness. 'Do you have some news? I hear that England is overrun with Americans.'

Before he could stop himself, the Major snapped bitterly:

'Yes, that's right, and where were the bastards four years ago?' He tapped ash from his cigarette into the ashtray. 'Sorry. That's unfair.'

'Is it?'

'Eisenhower has finally agreed on the fifth, weather permitting. The final BBC codes will be transmitted then. Bombing has severed Normandy from the rest of the Nazi army, but because of the fictitious radio traffic, Rommel still expects the attack to come at Calais, and even if they discover the rouse, there have only fifty-nine German divisions in France and the largest coastline they have ever had to defend. Besides, the army of the Master Race is less than pure these days. France is occupied by Russian prisoners armed with sharp sticks, and anyone else the German's could coerce into their uniform.

'Liberation in the south has already begun, Violette. The local resistance simply refuse to wait any longer for the Allies, which, despite the losses, is a jolly good thing because we suspect that Eisenhower, after Paris, will push straight to Berlin, leaving the rest of France to fight for itself. However, as I said, Overlord will truly begin in two weeks time.'

Having said this, exhaling smoke, the Major was surprised to see Alison's eyes wet with tears. 'This will really be the end,' she said.

'Yes, I think it will, though it'll take time. But that's not why I'm here. One must think, as I'm sure you can appreciate, Violette, in the long term. A problem has arisen concerning the aftermath.'

The Major lifted an eyebrow. 'What I'm about to ask of you has been sanctioned by neither Churchill nor Chamberlain, who have not only the Nazis and the French to fill their heads but also the Poles, the Czechs, the Norwegians and the Communists. And it goes without saying that should we succeed, neither Stalin nor Eisenhower will know of our actions. Nor, I suspect, would they much care.'

3

Crushing out her cigarette, Alison studied the Major and lent forward with her elbows on her knees, holding her glass with both hands, either unconcerned or unaware that her short nightdress barely concealed her embarrassment.

'An attempt is to be made on the life of General Charles de Gaulle,' Major Scott stated. 'We don't know when or by specifically whom, but we have no doubt that the threat is real. The intelligence came from Marius.'

Marius was a double agent installed inside the Reichstag, and since the detection of his last such agent, Admiral Wilhelm Canaris, and Hitler's subsequent abolition of the Abwehr, the German military intelligence organisation, Major Scott was very protective of such information. He would not have proffered even the name of Marius to any of his other staff.

Alison's eyes became sober. In her head, she saw her mother's parents, the Bouvier's, native Parisians lucky enough to have died of old age before Occupation. But there was no time for such dreaming.

Léon Blum became in 1936 the first Socialist premier of France but was arrested as a Jew by the Vichy government in 1940. The text of one of his leaked letters had become an adage to the Gaullists. He wrote:

'The future government can only be built around one man, around one name, General de Gaulle. He was the first to arouse in France the will for resistance and he continues to personify this spirit. He will be therefore the indispensable man, or rather, the only possible man, at the hour when the idea of the Resistance and the fact of the liberation will form the bond between Frenchmen.'

French support for Charles de Gaulle had not always been so apparent. Just after Paris fell, fearing that the French fleet at Mers-el-Kebir in North Africa was about to surrender to the Nazis, the British tried to force the fleet to defect to de Gaulle, who was in London at the time of the Petáin's armistice, and who the British recognised as a member of the last legitimate French Government and therefore the leader of the Government in Exile, the Free French Forces. The French fleet in Africa made no such recognition and refused to defect, and so the British sunk the ships. De Gaulle's hope of widespread support in France went down with them. However, by 1942 the brutality of the occupying Nazi regime had convinced most Frenchmen that de Gaulle had been right to reject the surrender.

'You understand the implications of what I say?'

'I understand that without de Gaulle the Communists will have more than a fair chance at Paris after the war,' Alison said.

'Precisely, Violette,' the Major pronounced. 'And I want you to…'

Annoyed, Charlie lifts her eyes from the page and hisses:

'Pardon?'

'I said,' Stan Hume smiles, 'Good Morning.'

'I see.'

Two straight-back armchairs, a carved low table and three overflowing bookshelves, one of which is in fact an obscured upright piano, leave the waxed rosewood floorboards of the high-ceilinged room otherwise empty, but such is the compromise, tight, crammed shelving and a small mounted television afford no hanging space on the walls. Around the room, there are eleven various lamps. The large ornamental panes of the grand corner window, three stained in the style of the Arts and Crafts movement, flood the room with rising sunlight. One pane is set ajar.

Perched upon one of the two armchairs with her book, wrapped tightly in a soft kimono, Charlie is three years shy of thirty, half a stone too thin for her small size, and sickly pale. She has freckles and a small, slightly upturned nose. Her hair is a thick crimson web of wilful curls that when wet stretches to the base of her spine but otherwise, as it does now, maintains a tightly coiled natural shape above her neck. Rarely does it deviate. Its texture is of wire.

She presses gently on her eyelids and feels the breeze from the open pane pleasing across her white legs. Pollution is the compromise. Outside, four floors down, the rapid river of Leith Walk, cars, taxis and maroon Lothian buses, spews noxious fumes and noise upwards.

'Have yie been up long?' Having only been awake for a matter of seconds, Stan appears completely lucid.

'An hour.'

'What time did yie get in?' he asks.

'One. Yie were asleep.'

'Skunnered?'

'Mm hm.'

Opening her eyes - Charlie's eyes are grey, the core of an uncompromising and frank expression - she watches unblinking as with noticeable difficulty her companion lifts his long legs down from her coffee table, which contrasting with the practical manner of the room is a single lump of carved, hollowed and warped rosewood finished in oil, onto the floorboards with a thud. Slouched into the armchair, caked in creased khakis and a stained t-shirt, he clasps his fingers across his stomach, inhales deeply and smiles, appearing to Charlie, simultaneously tranquil and alert, like an otter floating on its back.

A fresh joint, six inches long, as thick as a pencil, tapering out slightly, and twisted closed at the end, waits in a clean ashtray. Charlie lights it, tilting her head to reduce the risk of igniting her hair as well, and tokes deeply, holding the brutal smoke inside her tender body. Her entire, tiny body convulses, but she does not cough.

Neither does she converse. Her gaze falls back down to her book.

Motionless, Stan listens a while to the symphony of sound in the air, the traffic outside, the purring of an unseen cat, Charlie's breathing. Recovering from a three-month bout of flu that blocked his ears something hellish, he is eager to make the most of his cleared hearing. Indeed, breathing easily despite the smoke, and feeling the coloured sunlight on his face, Stan feels altogether splendid.

Charlie lifts her grey eyes. Her nose comes up, and nostrils flaring, she takes a keen, expert sniff.

'Stan,' she scowls, 'what in God's name is that reek?' She sniffs again. Fainter than the scent of her burning joint and the plants around her home but more powerful than Stan's natural smell, she recognises the alien scent immediately. 'It's...'

'Vomit, I ken, but dinnae worry, it isnae on the chair. Some fat fuck fae Fife regurgitated his chicken bhuna over me last night in the pub. At least I think that's what it was. It might have been a biryani. I dunno who the cunt was or why I was speaking tae him, but I remember he was saying something about swallowing dodgy pills, and, I mean, the way he was talking I assumed he meant last week or some other time, but he actually meant right then. And I dinnae ken what happened, really. I think...'

Unsurprised to find that he is talking to himself, Stan stops the account. Charlie is reading. Charlie is, when she wants to be, impenetrable.

Almost.

'D'yie have a busy day today, Charlotte?' he pronounces.

The question irritates her; the very interruption irritates her, as does the use of her given name. Her grey eyes dilate. But she reacts with a strange gesture, the very last thing Stan expects.

She smiles. At least, the making of a smile cracks in the corner of her thin lips. Her voice, although always soft, now comes with a surprisingly metallic rasp as she says:

'Yes, quite busy. Am I to assume then, Stanley, my friend, that since yie're here, yie failed yesterday to meet the electricity man for a second time, and are therefore without power in yir new house for the weekend, even though I reminded yie twice, *dipshit*?'

Exhaling smoke across the table at him, she watches Stan's cheeks flush with colour. His eyes widen. He sits up properly in the armchair, furiously crossing his legs. A furious otter, Charlie thinks. Loathed to answer her, manners insist.

'Correct,' he grudges.

Charlie loves to drive. Her present car is an overhauled 1989 Ford Cortina with lowered suspension, tinted windows, alloy wheels, suede bucket seats and a transplanted V6 engine that sounds like a sleeping tiger. The bodywork is the crimson of her hair. From Picardi Place, along Queen Street and up to George Street, the journey is infuriatingly brief. There, she parks, feeds the meter and concludes the journey on foot.

Concealed by an elegant neoclassical fascia, and squeezed between two lesser buildings, No. 39-43 North Castle Street was constructed in 1793 as apartment homes while Edinburgh's New Town, a solution to the filthy, medieval old one, expanded rapidly westward. Once home to such Georgian dignitaries as Sir Walter Scott, its units now home commercial properties. Charlie settles against the building's railing, wrapped in a thick duffel coat, long scarf and a woolly toory, where leading down to one of the two basement units, a simple, shiny brass plate announces:

RESERVE

Christmas shoppers, abundant up the hill on George Street, do not venture down Castle Street, so she is able to smoke her second joint of the day openly, watching a homeless man further up the hill, wrapped in filthy blankets and shaking with cold, struggle with the effort of rolling a cigarette. Beyond him, framed by Pink Fashions, Starbucks and a huge council Christmas tree, Edinburgh Castle sits high on its frosty rock. Eventually the beggar does manage his cigarette, but it seems to Charlie a small triumph.

The sky is the colour of slate. Swallowing smoke, she tries desperately to savour these last moments, imagining herself as just another Christmas shopper out to spend a fortune, have lunch and go home. She attempts to enjoy the fresh wind, the stillness of the street, the fleeting beauty of the moment. But the effort is hopeless. Her mind has already shifted gear.

Exhaling smoke into the winter gloom, she kicks her roach into the gutter and wearily begins the worn stone steps.

In browns, oranges, yellows, and with an entire wall faced in glazed Persian-blue bricks, Reserve's interior is striking, highly stylised in the curvilinear and whiplash imagery of art nouveau. Tables and tall chairs to seat sixty embellish a large mosaic floor, while clever glasswork, mirrors and hanging lamps invent an impression of light and space in the windowless basement. A non-smoking environment, the dining room smells of lilies and of burning logs on the open hearth. Much discussed by both restaurant patrons and the envious city art establishment is Reserve's collection of paintings. Amid the numerous prints, drawings and oils of the *nouveau* period hangs a Winslow Homer seascape, a Lu Yüan print on silk and a village scene by David Wilkie. There is a huge Lucian Freud. Reserve, it is often said, is aesthetically without competition. As for its food, while several restaurants in the city have a Michelin star, Reserve is the only restaurant in Scotland to have a pair.

Heels clicking on tile, Charlie uncurls her long scarf, weaving amongst the busy workforce, her gaze lowered to avoid eye contact, particularly that of

7

Fanny the maître d', who in a lilac Gucci suit is clicking on a hand held computer and screaming piercingly at some poor soul.

By the long bar, passing an enormous Christmas tree decorated tastefully with baubles and tinsel that Charlie looks upon slightly contemptuously, she arrives across a pair of subdued lovers.

'Good morning.' Her voice is warm and kind.

From the dizzying heights of a barstool, the male of the pair, Tom, is a muscular twenty-four, with thick curly blond locks and dark stubble. All of his concentration is engaged in the act of studying the racing odds of a Saturday tabloid newspaper, which does nothing to divert his mind from the shudders of nausea passing through him. Three concentric woolly jumpers fail to prevent his shivers. He turns his head to Charlie but not his twitchy, red-rimmed eyes, croaking in an Australian voice:

'I shall need forty pounds from you, brother. Before ten, please.'

Evelyn's welcome is more civilised. In the uniform orange and brown of the waiting staff, tall and waif-thin with faultless posture, her long honey-coloured hair held in a butterfly clasp, Evelyn is twenty but has the haunting, ageless eyes of a marble statue. Her beauty is shrill and brooding. Her powerful scent is of aniseed.

'Good morning,' she says in a similarly Australian accent.

'Good?' Tom scratches his armpit. 'Yeah, good for polar bears. I hate this fuckin country.'

'No, sweetheart, you don't. You only hate the weather. It's like Billy Connelly says,' Evelyn slips heeled shoes over her feet, 'there's only the wrong clothes. Cold is a point of view. Remember the Fjords last winter?'

'I remember I had icicles on my cock, hunny-bunny,' Tom's pained expression eases into a smile. 'I was scared to take a piss.'

On her feet now, Evelyn grips Tom's yellow curls in her hand, turns his face to her own and says:

'Smile more, handsome man.'

They kiss, looking to Charlie like big cats licking each other. When they are finished, Evelyn says:

'Catch you guys later.'

'Have a good day, hunny-bunny.'

Gliding away into the swarm of waiting staff and cleaners, Evelyn retorts with a single finger. 'Har-de-fucking-har, asshole.'

Charlie unbuttons and removes her duffel coat, springing - such is her smallness - up into Evelyn's warm stool. It is Charlie's habit to select clothes not as an aesthete but as a functional sensualist. The silk shirt beneath her sleeveless jumper is soft against her skin and pleasingly tight around her tiny waist and not-so-tiny 32C chest. Her corduroys, too, are tight, but taper out wide over her healed cowboy boots. As a rule she wears neither jewellery nor cosmetics. She pulls off her toory, releasing the smell of anti-bacterial shampoo and her wiry hair into its natural shape, and settles perfectly still, looking down at her clasped hands.

A lovely moment of peace passes, which Charlie spends breathing in the scent of the open fire, until she feels the atmosphere stiffen. Gloom descends. Tom's head ducks down low to his newspaper and even Fanny's shrieking voice diminishes, though does not stop completely.

In a shining-smart waistcoat and open-collar shirt, with a fine head of raven-black hair and a not unattractive angular face, Reserve's manager, Gavin, appears behind the bar. Gavin is a few years older than Charlie, and is clearly in a foul mood. Bloodshot eyes glowering, he demands of her:

'What the fuck happened last night?'

'Pardon me?'

'Yie said yie were coming up the toon wae us, eh?'

'Did I?'

'Yes, yie fuckin well did! I waited an hour in Paddy's, stood like a spare prick until two o'clock this morning.'

'Man,' Charlie sniffs with evident frostiness, 'please dinnae burst ma heid. Any normal person would be sick of the sight of me.'

The manager drops a thick bound ledger on the bar top with a dull thud and from a marked page produces a small forest's worth of loose paper. 'That's scarcely the point. Manners cost nothing. D'yie want to know what's happening today?'

'I ken what's happening today, Gus.'

'D'yie want tae discuss it?'

'I do not.' Charlie's eyes, as she lifts them for the first time to Gavin, clear despite the two joints-worth of cannabis in her blood, appear quite black. 'But I do have some good news, Gus. To cheer yie up, eh? I know how you like the weekend.'

'What is it?' he asks. More than her eyes, Gavin finds Charlie's stillness disconcerting.

'I want yir paperwork before three this afternoon.'

'Fucking hell! But...'

'It's only Saturday, I ken. I have a busy day tomorrow, so I want it today, Gus, okay? Gimme the waste figures, stock invoices and margins since the first of the month, the staff hours and wages with deductions, the VAT, an idea of the staff yie'll need for Christmas and Hogmanay, and yir ideas on bonuses, thank you kindly. Before three, mind. Dinnae make me chase yie.'

The manager's pained eyes narrow further. 'Why before three?'

'Because I'm off tonight.'

'Yie're fuckin what? But who? It isn't...'

'Vincent.' The trace of a smile flutters across Charlie's thin lips.

'Fucksake.'

'Pardon me, Gavin?'

9

Disgruntled, muttering curses under his breath, Gavin strops off across the tiled mosaic in search of heads to gnaw. Charlie watches him go, and then returns her gaze to her lap.

'Wanna see your picture?' Tom asks, his head coming back out from his newspaper like a tortoise from its shell. 'You're in here.'

'If it isnae horrific.'

Forgoing his racing odds, the Australian thumbs his tabloid backwards to the colourful centrespread, where under the bold legend of *Celebrities, Out and About*, placed between images of Travis' lead singer Fran Healy, and the First Minister Jack McConnell, a larger photograph shows Charlie exiting the steps of the Royal Balmoral Hotel in a thick woollen shawl, corduroy trousers and her usual cowboy boots. Loose, blowing freely in the wind, her hair hides her eyes entirely. Clinging to her arm, in a kilt suit and easily a foot taller, the Irish actor Colin Farrell presents his familiar smile for the press.

'It was a successful night,' the Australian reads croakily, 'for Edinburgh's award-winning Reserve at the 2003 Scottish Culinary Industry Awards, hosted last week by Marco Pierre blah blah... Creativity award and the coveted Best Chef award collected for the second year running by twenty-seven-year-old local renowned bachelorette, Charlie Brown. With Reserve's manager, Gavin McFly, Miss Brown also collected the Best Restaurant award again... the rest is boring.'

Indeed, Charlie yawns, covering her mouth with her small hand. Then after a damp cough, she asks:

'What kind of word is bachelorette? It sounds to me like some kind of manicured poodle, or mibbae a type of holiday caravan.'

'What would you prefer?'

'Charlie Brown, eminent spinster.'

'Good grief,' the Australian snorts, returning to his racing odds. 'You might need to wait a few years, chef.'

'Ah, Tommy.' Charlie's face and voice remain expressionless as she wonders if there is time for a last joint. 'That's just what people said about my Michelin stars.'

Pushing through the swing doors in a fresh chef's jacket and red and green checked trousers, with her hair securely fastened under a headscarf, Charlie eases into kitchen clogs, tosses a clean towel over her shoulder, and advances. An arched stone vault deep underground, filled with stainless steel cooking ranges and refrigerated storage, Reserve's kitchen is already a hive of industry.

Charlie's priority, after dispersing a few sharp staff directives, is her stock. She knows without looking exactly what has come in, but Charlie is very particular and always makes a point of looking, burrowing deep into the various crates, sniffing and poking, able to heave heavy boxes and canisters of liquid nitrogen out of her way for a closer investigation; Charlie's strength, quite disproportionate to her smallness, is remarkable. She tastes sorrel and kale, wild garlic and black winter truffles.

None of Reserve's stock comes via the city's usual channels. Vegetables do not arrive in damp cardboard boxes, left to rot on the doorstep. Meat does not come from a warehouse. There is no cash and carry run. Nothing is frozen. Bought and delivered fresh from source four times a week, Reserve's organic stock is for quality incomparable to the vague, genetically tweaked produce offered generally to the city that is often no better than the drivel found in a supermarket. Stalk vegetables, cabbages and greens come from a dedicated farmer in East Lothian; root vegetables from a farm just outside the city. Everything is local, seasonal, fresh.

Charlie's true passion is seafood, and she spends fully ten minutes poking through the seven iced crates of fish, shellfish and roe, satisfied only after inspecting each item individually.

Finally content, she washes her hands and settles against the back wall. Charlie likes to watch. She is, admittedly, something of a voyeur.

Her sous-chef, Viola, is originally from the Greek island of Crete although she has lived in Edinburgh for some twenty years. Her cheeks flushed, her expression taut and unwelcoming, she quietly fashions sheets of fresh pasta into delicate, ornate shapes, while beside her, Nigel, trainee chef, restaurant supervisor and all-round culinary prodigy in his final year at Telford College, barks persistently to three commis chefs. Known at Reserve as 'Tony' because of his reverence for Tony Singh from Oloroso across the street, he is gangly in pristine black kitchenware, his expensive spectacles balanced on his hooked nose. His knives are Japanese carbon-alloy imports. Together, Viola and Tony are an excellent team, complementing and anticipating the needs of one another, creating a whole stronger than the sum of its parts. The reason for this is simple. Viola and Tony viciously abhor each other. Like chalk and cheese, Viola is a self-taught veteran of the trade while Tony, twelve years her junior, is educated to the teeth with molecular chemistry and gastronomic history. Sparks often fly.

Tom, on the other hand, dressed now in a butcher-stripe overall and what can only be described as a floppy tartan chef's bonnet, works better alone. The Australian is the newest member of Charlie's staff, having served less than six months, but in that time he has shown himself to be a chef and butcher of quite remarkable stature. Unlike Viola, he is flexible. Unlike Tony, he is tolerant. Delving through the meat delivery, ripping out what he needs for now and storing the rest into fridges, his hangover remains, as do his tabloid racing-odds. He mutters inaudibly. He is merely concentrating.

Unseen, Arthur and his staff work in the cold kitchen, creating the smell of baking bread, which fuses with the other smells.

And then there is Vincent, an entity entirely unto himself. Entering through the swing doors, offering smiles and jokes all around like Christ offering de-

11

liverance, he makes his way towards Charlie at the back of the room. The journey seems to take an age.

Vincent Dussollier, the great French chef, is world-famous, a multimillionaire, and at fifty-six, lean and entirely bald, still very much a handsome man. Instead of kitchen whites, he wears an expensive, Regal-purple silk suit that resembles, at least to Charlie, Picasso's pyjama suits. Yet, despite the lavish dinning room upstairs that bares testament to his indulgent nature, Vincent is not at all, as the press would have it, pretentious. He is an unassuming man, gentle and subdued.

And this morning exhausted. Peppercorn eyes peer out from his drawn face. Settling with Charlie, towering over her, he sucks up a deep whiff of roasting geese, thin nostrils flaring, and asks:

'How many of the fuckers is it today?' His voice, tightened by fatigue and fifty cigarettes a day, his inherent Parisian twang annihilated by twenty years in London and ten in Edinburgh, is a melodic, soft and convincingly local sound.

'Hundreds,' Charlie half-smiles.

There was a time in Vincent's life, he vaguely recalls, when the knowledge that his restaurant was crammed to capacity would have filled him with an enormous sense of well-being. But this is no longer the case. Not that it displeases him; it simply does nothing for him. Expect for the annoyance of promising to work today.

'I am shagged,' he pronounces. 'I truly am. I've been up all night with Chloé and I would go for a sleep now except that Amanda wants me to…' The sound of an old French opera, Vincent's mobile telephone's ring tone, interrupts, and without checking the caller ID he answers:

'Hello, pretty lady. Aye, of course I remember, nappies and dry-cleani…but…what? Hells bells, Amanda! Fine. Aye, okay, fine. Love you, too.'

He ends the call exhaling a weary sigh.

'Mon dieu. I'm apparently taking Amanda's mother to Ikea. There goes the…'

Grey eyes narrowing, Charlie snaps more crossly than she intends:

'Yie are helping today, eh, Vincent? Yie promised.'

'Actually, Charlotte, that's what I wanted to…'

'Vincent!'

'But…'

'If yie arenae here by a quarter to one, Vincent,' Charlie coldly states, 'I swear to God I'll smash up yir new Ferrari. Is that clear?'

Vincent's bottom lip protrudes. 'Yes, chef.'

'Good.'

'I dinnae promise I'll be any use, though.' The great Chef has a great set of teeth and a smile, regardless of fatigue, he fully commands. Implementing this device now, silk flapping, he is gone.

Charlie's workstation, in the centre of the kitchen beside the service lifts, consists of eight gas burners, an oven, a grill, two fridges, a magnetic rack loaded with pans and various implements, one small preparation surface and a shelf, her only dry space, used for spare towels. The station, like the entire kitchen, is surgically clean. Charlie lights her burners with several pleasing popping noises and sets the clean blue flame low for the meantime. She actions the noisy ventilation system and then, slightly reluctantly, the intercom that floods the kitchen with the uninterrupted, torturous sound of Fanny and Gavin screaming viciously at one another. With the flick of a final switch, thin plasma-display monitors attached to the arched stone ceiling above each workstation fizzle to life.

Amid the toil, Charlie takes the time to stretch, contorting her small, supple body into three different positions, and yawns.

She closes her eyes and presses firmly on her eyelids, wishing there was time for a last joint. The business of the day, above the usual Saturday trade, is two-hundred corporate pre-Christmas lunches and the prospect is not a happy one. But there is light at the end of the tunnel. Tonight, for the first time in twenty-three weekends, Charlie has the night off, her Saturday night all to herself. She draws strength from this.

But there is the day to get through first.

2

Detached, an enormous gothic palace constructed at the turn of the twentieth century in red Dumfries sandstone amid the pale neoclassical New Town, the Scottish National Portrait Gallery advertises its temporary *Faces of the Enlightenment* exhibition on enormous, flapping, vertical banners. Across Queen Street, upon a bench dedicated to the memory of *Old Jock, who was often tired*, Stan waits, sitting comfortably despite the lateness of his appointment, inexhaustibly fascinated by the gallery's construction. In the north-east tower, the point of the building directly facing him, mounted between John Hunter the surgeon and Viscount James Dalrymple the lawyer, Stan ponders Henry Raeburn, rendered by James Pittendrigh Macillivray in a trim, tapered dress-jacket with paint-board and brush, the only one of the thirty embellishing exterior statues held in place by nets to prevent a nasty compensation claim who was painter of portraits or even a painter at all.

Stan does not mind the gale from the distant Forth as much as the roar of brutal traffic around him. Fumes catch in his throat. Stan does have a driving licence but does not like to drive, preferring to walk or cycle, resorting to public transport only in rainy weather, and has never owned a car of his own. Nor does Stan condone the use of so many private motorcars, all burning fossil fuels and pumping out toxic reek.

A while more he waits, some thirty minutes more, until finally, baring the reason for her tardiness, a Harvey Nichols' shopping bag, Stan's appointment arrives without apology.

Striking, thin and equalling Stan's six feet in height, fashioned in a long sleek winter coat and open-toe shoes, her copper hair cut short at her unpierced ears, Rose Mackenzie is forty-seven. The only piece of jewellery she wears is a simple wedding ring.

'Beautiful morning.' She allows Stan her cheek.

'Isn't Stuart coming?'

'Ha! Dinnae start me, Stanley. Apparently there's been some kind of crisis that nae other bugger in the whole city could manage. So I've been shopping for Jimmy Choo's.' Rose lifts an eyebrow. 'A girl, after all, wants to look her best for the First Lady and her husband.'

'How much?'

'Yie're so fucking crass, Stan.' She stands on her cigarette, exhaling smoke. 'It's not attractive.'

However, willing to neither justify nor apologise for the wealth she certainly did not win in a lucky bag, she lifts her chin.

'In my own opinion,' she admits, 'they were reasonable. Want a Polo mint?'

Stan and Rose stroll through the twentieth century exhibition room, talking quietly and comfortably, their low voices dampened further by deadening artificial walls. Although their interest is purely amateurish, Stan and Rose, at an interval of twenty years, both came to the city to study paintings and hold similar qualifications from the University of Edinburgh. They are apt to share their Saturday mornings at one of the city's galleries or museums. However, today is the last such jaunt. Rose's husband, Detective Inspector Stuart Mackenzie, will tonight receive commendation for his efforts by both Lothian and Borders Police and on behalf of the government, the nation's First Minister. A week today, Stuart begins a new position in a quiet anti-terrorism department based in Wales. The Mackenzie's have just bought a thatched cottage in the Welsh countryside. After thirty years Rose is not sad to be leaving the city. Neither is she sad to be leaving the fine galleries in which she sat a lifetime ago sketching, or any of the paintings she has seen a hundred times before. The prospect of investigating the unknown-to-her galleries of Wales more than compensates.

She settles at Harry More-Gordon's *The Secretaries of State for Scotland*, a pallid, pre-devolution watercolour in elongated landscape, portraying the ministers somewhat awkwardly from Willie Ross to Donald Dewar in Bute House, where she is dining tonight. Rose is fond of More-Gordon and indeed owns a couple of his paintings. Yet, something in this particular effort makes her abruptly weary.

'Did yie ever have to pay the poll tax, Stan?' She slides her arm through his. 'Rather than the new council tax.'

'Nah. I was a student. I remember my parents cursing it, though. I also remember my grandmother defending it.'

Rose nods, smiling, and asks:

'Do yie want a filing cabinet?'

'Eh?'

'I'd prefer to keep it to be honest, but it isnae possible to keep everything. It's beautiful and very practical, and I'd rather it went to an appreciative home. Think of all the space you have to fill, Stanley.'

'You've already given me too much' Stan spreads his palms. 'The book-shelves, the plates…'

'Shhh,' Rose purrs, brushing her copper hair from her eyes. 'Stan, yie have no idea how much the idea of being your benefactor pleases me. Stuart will bring it in the car during the week.'

'Thanks.'

Mounted alongside his caricaturised Connelly and Coltrane, and his much larger Frank Zappa-like *Self Portrait in Flowery Jacket*, John Byrne's drawing of his wife, the actress Tilda Swinton, as it always does, holds Stan's attention. Done quickly in orange and black chalks, the feathery orange hair, the tip of the nose just so, the frankness of the rough composition, reminds Stan of Charlie.

'Do yie have electricity in the palazzo yet?' Rose asks. 'The man was coming last night, yes?'

'Auch, dinnae bloody ask.'

As a rule, Rose does not smile; rather, her lips curl.

Like herself, Stan has also recently bought a house, his first home, No. 24B Lee Crescent, Portobello, and while she has been buying and selling houses for twenty years Rose can still remember the thrill of the first time. She pictures Stan wandering around his new quarter-villa, opening and closing doors, repositioning himself for a different view of his property, a fresh perception. She is able to imagine this particularly accurately because she knows the interior layout of Stan's new property well. She sold it to him.

Rose has never lived alone, and she wonders now what it would be like. But she is unable. After a childhood in a house with over fifty residents, and having lived for twenty-seven years with her husband, she could easier imagine living on one of the moons of Jupiter.

Upstairs in the darker medieval rooms, the *Cobham Portrait* is not an original work, neither is its creator known. It is a 1578 replica of Pierre Oudry's earlier portrait of Mary Stuart, Queen of Scots. The classic Mary, *En Devil Blanc* by Francois Clovet, minute by comparison, also hangs, which Rose prefers. But Stan prefers the mannerist Cobham.

From the Italian meaning stylishness, Mannerism was a reaction against the harmonious and idealised naturalism of the High Renaissance. Mannerist figures often have graceful but queerly elongated limbs, small heads and strange facial features, their poses contrived. While Renaissance paintings are harmonious, portraying Christ as angelic, a painting by El Greco or Parmigianino portrays Christ as pale and weak. Thus, the Cobham Mary is not as pretty as expected, and not quite as young. She is wary and sterile.

Stan believes Rose is a Mannerist portrait of sorts. She depicts the same sterile quality, though subtly. Indeed, Rose and Stuart are without children.

'What'll be the first thing yies do in Wales?' Stan wonders.

'Decorate! Like yirsel. Stuart and I are old hands by now so it shouldnae take long. Then I might try to paint a picture, which I have not done since 1982. I could never think of anything to paint. I was like the man in the Amélie film with brittle bones who never left the house, painting the same Renoir repeatedly. Sad as a lily. So I stopped. But I've been saving up my ideas.'

Stately claret and green in arrangement, the *Faces of the Enlightenment* temporary exhibition contains no other visitors, which may be accounted to the four pounds per head admission charge, despite an initiative by the Scottish Executive decreeing that Scotland's Galleries would be free for all. Planting herself in the centre of the room, clutching her Harvey Nichols' bag behind her back and holding her weight on one leg with the other curled behind like a ballet dancer, Rose commands:

'Enlighten me!'

'Eh?'

'Pretend I'm some girl yie've brought here to impress, like I dinnae ken anything. I only want to listen, Stan. I think yie owe me that much.'

An incomer to the city, Stan's speech, accent and choice of words are after ten years of practice nearly perfect. Adapt or perish: Mother Nature's cruel simplicity. But rather than altered, his natural voice is merely repressed. Usually with Rose, he is apt to speak in a less altered voice, but now he drops the pretence completely. The result is a polite, distinctive Western Isle twang.

'Modern Britain as we know it,' he begins, 'in terms of law, tax and political hierarchy, took hold of Scotland in seventeen-oh-seven with the Act of Union, a devil's deal made with the English to secure foreign trading rights and remedy the critical economy after a botched attempt eight years earlier to colonise the New World. In the grandest aspirations of all things Scottish, alas, the Darien Scheme amounted to a clumsy idea poorly executed, and worthy of note is that that no fiscal lessons were gleaned from it because years later, during English rule, construction of the humble Regent Bridge at Waterloo Place, which allowed cart access to Calton Hill without having to begin at the bottom, almost ruined the city once again. But I digress. My point is that London bought the political heart of Scotland, and Edinburgh became a subsidiary of the mighty English Empire, sold by its privileged for a handful of beans, that cheap instant fix so commonplace today, and not for the last time either.'

Delighted, Rose's lips curl. Stan finally breaks eye contact to enjoy the paintings. There are perhaps twenty-five large oils of the usual Enlightenment suspects, from James Craig through Adam Smith to Joseph Black, some of which Stan has never seen before, though a meagre amount, he considers, for the admission fee. Watercolours, drawings, engraving plates and a trove of curious miniatures below glass pad the exhibition out. His favourite portrait, a tiny anonymous work of poet Robert Fergusson, usually displayed permanently in the gallery for free, looks out with the devilish gaze of either genius or craziness, appearing sorely out of place amongst the other larger, more regal works.

'Most of these paintings are by Allan Ramsey, himself painted there by John Smibert. Ramsey was the most fashionable Scottish portraitist of his day and eventually the resident portraitist of King George of England. Ramsey detested abstraction,' Stan explains. '*No analysis can be made of abstract beauty*, he said, *nor any abstraction whatever.*'

Although the execution is not too bad, Ramsey's subject matter is not at all to Stan's taste. Exclusively the elite of the day, powerful aristocracy portrayed in ruby robes and frilly lace, he looks upon them with near distain, preferring the softer, more humble work of Catherine Reid, Scotland's first professionally trained female painter.

'The union did fuel an awakening, so the old myth says,' Stan continues, tearing his eyes from a political drawing featuring the English Lion chewing the Scottish Thistle but not quite eating it, 'but in truth the Age of Reason had already begun and was spreading around the world like wild heather. Science was properly born, accurate maps printed and dusty principals questioned.

'In the middle of the fuss stood Edinburgh, the Athens of the North. In seventeen-forty-eight, the year Charles Edward Stuart landed in Scotland, worldwide interest was renewed in the ancient and near forgotten classical style of the Greeks and Romans with the discoveries of Pompeii and Herculaneum. The resulting contemporary art was representational, calm and ordered in construction, emphasising reason, balance and restraint, what we now call the neoclassical style. Hence, all the square buildings in Edinburgh.

'The Enlightenment marks the point in history when reason as a concept replaced religious faith as western man's common denominator, the last time being the prime of the Roman Empire.'

Four large oils of the same man, rendered at various stages of life and weight by different painters, heads the temporary exhibition. Stan gives them a brief look, slips his hands into the trouser pockets and arrives upon his principal topic.

'Sometimes known as the Untroubled Sceptic, David Hume was born in seventeen-eleven and lived for sixty-five years during which he worked amongst other things as Secretary to the British Embassy in Vienna, Turin and Paris before becoming Undersecretary of State for Scotland at the Home Office.

'An accomplished historian, economist and by all accounts delightful fellow, Hume is principally remembered as one of the most influential philosophers in Western history. In his own time, however, it was his elegant, lucid and, considering the Act of Union, shrewdly conceived six-volume History of England that made him truly famous and wealthy. From the Invasion of Julius Caesar to the Accession of Henry VII, the work shunned the traditional and somewhat Tory-minded chronological account of wars and deeds of state for an impartial evaluation of political decisions in their proper context. It was a classic for many years.

'Hume's philosophy considered humanity, goodness, passion, tragedy, morality, benevolence, happiness, politics, wealth and taste. His first effort, *A Treatise of Human Nature*, published anonymously, later rewritten and ultimately renounced by the author as juvenile, is nevertheless regarded today as one of the truly great theoretical works on the Human Condition. *Can I be sure*, he asked, *that in leaving all established opinions I am following the truth?*

'In a constant search for truth untainted by perception, although not a faithless man, Hume all but declared war on Christianity, scorning metaphysics and proclaiming the dominance of human reason over spiritual faith in an age when it was dangerous to do so. Hc did this in the belief that it was better to teach people to gear their lives to the pursuit of happiness in the world of common life rather than pursue the uncertain and imaginary joys of happiness in a life hereafter. Atheism, of course, was not without its problems. His beliefs kept him from the chair of Moral Philosophy at Edinburgh University, and similarly at Glasgow. In fact, Hume never held an academic post. Even as Keeper of the Advocates' Library, he suffered a plot of excommunicate by the zealots. His dissertation on *Suicide and Immortality of the Soul* was threatened with legal action, and his *Dialogues Concerning Natural Religion* went unpublished in his lifetime because it contained a scolding critique of the notion of miracles.

'Not that such things troubled Hume, so buoyant and mild of disposition was he. Upon finding that he had intestinal cancer, Hume prepared for his death with the same peaceful optimism that characterised his life, cheerily arranging the posthumous publication of his most controversial works. By the end of his life, still a bachelor, he had become an A-list celebrity, knocking back glasses of claret in both the British and French royal courts.

'David Hume was one of the great philosophers of western empiricism, believing that knowledge comes exclusively through experience. While John Locke claimed that the mind has ideas caused by material objects - *Material Substance* - and George Berkley thought that there were no material objects, only the minds perception of them - *Spiritual Substance* - Hume's particular brand of empiricism did not even support the constant of the mind. He believed in no essential *I*, that we have no knowledge of self as the enduring subject of experience but rather bundles of perceptions with no underlying harmony, and that reason and rational judgments are merely habitual associations of distinct sensations or experiences.

'*I, therefore*, he said, *am always becoming something else.*'

'David Hume, Rosemary, regarded life as a journey through which we stagger and bump rather than walk, which was hardly surprising considering the vast quantities of claret the man swallowed.'

'And David Hume,' Stan Hume concludes, 'is my direct ancestor. Eight generations separate him and I.'

The most remarkable thing about this tale in Stan's opinion is that it is absolutely true. David Hume never married and it was not common knowledge that he had fathered a child. In his forty-ninth year Hume had a daughter, Jacqueline, to a woman named Mary Barclay, who was basically a friend of a friend. He never denied the child, providing Mary and Jacqueline with a handsome living, a beautiful house in Dumfriesshire, and visited whenever he could. Jacqueline Hume grew up to be a splendid miniaturist, and was Stan's grandmother's great-grandmother's great-grandmother.

Yet, Stan feels no kinship with the man or his work. There is no family resemblance. The fact remains, simply one of those things.

It comes as no surprise to Rose. She has known Stan for five years, since he was, in her opinion, a child. Now a man, she regards and examines him with a keen eye.

From a distance, Stan is physically ordinary. He is twenty-seven, tall and slight, and has clean, non-descript dark hair, with long and slight shaggy sideburns. Two commas at the corners of his mouth make Stan's smile either mean or kind, depending on his mood. He wears a brown tweed coat over a maroon t-shirt, flaring jeans and trainers, stylish in understatement, manner and colour, worthy she believes of aesthetical approval. But unlike her, as a matter of policy Stan does not wear brand names.

Close up, perception changes. Even after five years as work colleagues and friends, Stan's eyes disarm Rose. They are large and somewhat melancholic and, most notably, his irises are olive green and seemingly translucent.

Rose will not miss Edinburgh or its galleries. But she will miss Stan's transparent eyes.

'Bravo,' she says, and she means it. 'Thank you, Stanley.'

Stan takes his bow.

Moments later, they cross the gothic Mural Balcony together, past the Battle of Largs, their footsteps echoing across the hard tile until they reach the carpeted stairwell. On the ground floor, passing the monument to John Ritchie Findlay, once owner of the Scotsman newspaper and anonymous donor to the original construction of the portrait gallery, Rose stops in the Great Hall to enjoy William Hole's frieze one final time, turning a full circle on her heels.

But it is not the frieze that catches in her throat. It is a much more humble piece of art, a small bust positioned by the main doors. She grips Stan's arm tightly, her spine stiffens and her face becomes a mask as her eyes meet the stony, lifeless gaze of Donald Dewar. As with the More-Gordon watercolour earlier, Rose's stomach sinks.

Cursed by talk of his well-meaning legacy, the Holyrood Parliament building, once hailed as a hero, Dewar is now discussed in scoffing tones. Another great hope, Rose thinks bitterly, dead and defaced. Another good idea poorly executed.

Her eyes fill now and the damn threatens to break. But it does not. Instead, her lip curls as she pronounces, though not to Stan:

'Cheerio, pal.'

She collects her sleek winter coat, buttons it up and for the last time, she and Stan exit out onto the cold of Queen Street and go their separate ways.

3

Many of Reserve's corporate pre-Christmas lunch bookings are several years old. Ten sittings in all are staggered across three Saturday afternoons, and the present sitting is the last of the last. In the lavish stillness of the dining room, amid a wealth of art, elegant waitresses tend to BBC executives, Historic Scotland trustees and twenty ranking civil servants from the Executive, while below in the kitchen, Viola, Tom and Tony dance feverishly around a production line that compromises the majority of the workable space, the ancient stone walls acting in the fashion of an underground kiln.

Viola coordinates the effort, calm despite the pace, presenting a range of potatoes and vegetables across the current batch of beautiful glazed plates that hang precariously on every available flat surface, employing only strictly necessary movements, conserving strength, keeping as much out of the way as possible.

Tom follows less gracefully with steaming, tender slices of beef, mutton, pheasant and goose, stopping at intervals to carve, slicing tenderly but ripping out bones with his fists. Scalding goose fat clings to him. Sweat pours from him. His eyes ache, as do his fingers, but the Australian is a professional and takes pride is his ability to work through the pain.

Finishing the batch under his hooked nose with the cold touch of a perfectionist, Tony rearranges, garnishes and drizzles velvety claret and chestnut gravy, all the while barking constantly to the commis chefs who load finished plates into the service lifts, ferry breads and deserts through from Arthur in the cold kitchen and maintain in the manner of engineers the Christmas lunch line. Two more scurrying bodies, pot-washers bearing replenishment plates and pans, grabbing anything that needs washed, could be invisible except that they are constantly in the way.

Reserve's usual Saturday afternoon trade is typically as heavy as a Saturday night. Today, albeit with limited space, is no exception. The work for Charlie is a pleasure, an unexpected delight overlooked in the planning of the day. Rarely does the opportunity arise to drop her head and cook mindlessly, selfishly, as she does now, high with an adrenaline buzz that completely overpowers her nicotine and cannabis cravings. She weaves rapidly and effortlessly around Vincent's surer gait, coordinating an assortment of simmering pans, tasting continuously and mindful always of hygiene regulations. Cleanliness, after all, is next to godliness. Not that Charlie is a religious woman, although she does have a keen fondness for stained glass.

In terms of her gastronomic and managerial disposition, Charlie works as she always has in very much her own palette. She has little time for her tem-

21

peramental, egotistical colleagues in the trade and despises the pretensions attached to professional cooking as utterly passé. Because of this, the awards she so frequently wins, her pair of Michelin stars and the fact that she achieved them without any official training at all, Charlie is deeply resented in the industry at a national level. Such things are unimportant. The judgements and praises of critics and rivals alike mean nothing to her. She cooks only for her customers.

Her responsibility is seafood. Sole soufflés sell consistently, as do monkfish risottos, parcelled baby mackerels and her nippy salmon broth. Exclusive to Reserve, crappit heids - boiled haddock heads stuffed with a mash of its liver and oatmeal then boiled in water - are fast achieving cult status.

Fish special today is a small whole sea bass served with sorrel velouté. The fish are poached individually in kettles in her usual court bouillon of dry white wine, fennel, shallots, carrots, orange zest, lemon juice, unpeeled and wild garlic, salt, black peppercorns, thyme, basil, parsley, a bay leaf and an anise star. There are presently nine cooking, at various stages of readiness. The court bouillon is reusable thrice, but the process of preparing a fresh kettleful is one of the tiny jobs of the day that never fails to form a thin smile on Charlie's lips. She also makes the velouté to order. Shallots are sautéing in clarified butter before dry white wine and vermouth are added, then the mixture is reduced by half, which means that most of the water is cooked off, not only thickening the sauce without the addition of agents such as flour, but also intensifying its flavour. She adds fish stock - pots of fish, beef, chicken and vegetable stock simmer constantly in the kitchen - and again the mixture is half-reduced before chopped winter sorrel goes in, then cream, and finally a knob of butter to give a glossy sheen. The finished velouté is poured over the fish and served with a rösti potato and lemon chunk. Each portion takes twenty minutes. Seventeen have sold in the last two hours. The customer price is less than six pounds.

That she is constantly preparing a tide of oysters, grilled lobsters, steamed mussels and of course her own signature dish of pan-fried scallops with spaghetti and a kale, caper and scallop roe sauce enters only passively into Charlie's consciousness, so impulsive is the process. Every finished plate of food, however, she scrutinizes thoroughly under her grey eyes.

Beside her, whisking egg yolks into a béarnaise sauce, Vincent is less enthusiastic, in starchy kitchen wear and neckerchief. Beads of sweat trickle down his bald head. Today's shift is the first he has worked since the pre-Christmas lunches last year, and three hours into it he is weakening badly. Which was to be expected. Just as his presence today is a matter of courtesy, Charlie has made every effort to ease his burden. Tony's kale-wrapped pigeon terrine requires only lightly sautéed foie gras and a mushroom dressing to serve, and his winter broth only needs topped with pieces of crispy duck. Tom has prepared a range of meat cuts that are ready to hit the pan. Charlie and Viola pre-chopped vegetables, prepared individual lasagnes and gratins, and even slightly reduced the menu.

Even still, Vincent's joints ache. With too many years behind him to feel an adrenaline buzz, he lets out a deep, lingering, animal yawn, scratches his growing potbelly and examining the face of the commis chef beside him, asks:

'Who are you?'

'Lynn, chef.'

'Well, Lynn,' he says gently, 'why dinnae yie leave what yie're doing and go and fetch an old dog an espresso? Better make it a big one.'

Born the only child of eminent French jazz trombonist, Jean-Luc Dussollier, and prolific Scots author, Megan Poe, Vincent's privileged childhood occurred in the countryside just outside Paris in the fifties. But after completing his formal training at Le Cordon Bleu, world famous Parisian culinary school, with distinction, Vincent relocated to London and rapidly attained a reputation as the youngest, hungriest and hardest chef on the Soho scene.

Educated in the traditional French Cuisine Bourgeoisie but practised in Nouvelle Cuisine, Vincent's resulting blend of the rustic and the sophisticated aesthetic - he did work in a refined, decorative manner to an extent, and did thicken by reduction, but he also thickened sauce with beurre manié, a kneaded mixture of butter and flour - is now universally imitated in the contemporary restaurant industry. Not as commonplace, but central to his professional philosophy, Vincent could never abide pretension. He has always cut his onions not with obsessive-compulsive perfection but rather by simply chopping them into pieces.

Known as the Jackal because of his ability to detect the scent of death in his competitors to the end of stealing their clientele and staff and buying their equipment, Vincent was, at his peak, generally regarded as the most successful restaurateur in the world. His seven 'shops' from London to Tokyo fed the rich, the famous and the powerful.

Success, however, was not easily afforded. In 1981, only months after the purchase of his very first restaurant, The Bishop's Place, Knightsbridge, favoured by Lady Diana Spencer in her Mini-Cooper days, Vincent's wife of two years, Gillian, died in childbirth, taking the infant with her.

The subsequent years are regarded as the prime of his career. They were spent drunk. Well-documented is the great chef's alcoholism. That he spent ten years wallowing in the denying depths of it, abusing staff and friends alike, is a common tale often heard across Reserve's dinning room intercom. Less well publicised is that the Jackal was prolifically addicted to heroin.

A heart attack at forty finally gave pause for thought. Still living and working in Soho, and for the cost incurred still very much a successful man, Vincent took the initiative to liquidate. He sold all seven restaurants. Many of the paintings that decorated them he sold cheaply to loyal cooks and staff. To one woman, a faithful employee of ten years, he gifted a painting by David Hockney.

At the dawn of the nineties, it was the achievement of Vincent Dussollier to break his addictive lifestyle. His doctors demanded it. Any chance of sustained life demanded it. He achieved the deed alone.

In 1992, Vincent relocated to Edinburgh, his mother's birthplace, and published *Leçons dans la Cuisine* the same year, a colossal collection of traditional and contemporary French recipes, highlighting the importance of three ingredient cooking. Although originally published only in France, the book became a best selling hardback for five years in eleven countries, redefined the art of modern restaurant cooking and made Vincent more money than he has ever bothered to count. Most notably, *Leçons* is a witty, self-effacing read, accepted inside and out of the industry as a modern-day reference manual, a classic master cookbook.

Reserve has been Vincent's only restaurant since his jaunt into the literary world. Clean and sober for more than ten years now, it seems ridiculous to him that so many years of his life were lost to addiction. No longer does he crave attention or success, nor do any promotional work as he once did. He has never attempted to write another book and does not plan to.

At the turn of the new millennium, Vincent married Amanda, a local chef, and they are very happy despite an age gap of twenty-five years. Amanda and Vincent have a baby now, Chloé, who in her third month of life plainly refuses to miss any of it by sleeping. Hence, Vincent's exhaustion.

Charlie has worked for Vincent for four years and so accustomed is she to his ways that as she removes perfect soufflés from the oven, she anticipates his words even before they form in his mouth.

'Chef,' his bottom lip protrudes, 'are you sure yie wouldnae prefer to work tonight? I know how yie value routine.'

'Quite sure, thank you.' A glance to the order screen above her head shows Charlie that an order for two special sea bass has been placed, and without thinking she organises the necessary fish kettles and a pan for the velouté. 'Table three?'

'Ten seconds. But look at me, chef. I'm totally shagged. I'm a fucking liability. There isnae any way I'll last 'til eleven the night. Go'n dae an old dog a favour, no?'

'No!' Charlie's rasp is startling against his soft tones.

Lynn returns with Vincent's espresso, which he exchanges for a rare chateaubriand in whiskey sauce and a braised fennel bulb. His final attempt, the great chef pronounces without shame.

'Name yir price.'

'Up yir fuckin arsehole!' Charlie plates a risotto. 'I have plans, Vincent, so dinnae gie me nae fuckin shite, eh? Yie make ma heid hurt. Just try to suck in yir gut to let folk squeeze past and yie'll dae fine. *Table three now, I'm waiting!*'

Wise enough to appreciate any further protest as futile, Vincent swallows his espresso in a single gulp, produces a roasted pheasant for table three and says no more.

Nor does he bother to turn his head when, from across the room, a piercing, startling howl comes, followed by a succession of smashing and a barrage of cursing.

Assuming that Tom has either burnt or stabbed himself, neither of which would surprise her, Charlie's head snaps round and immediately registers the wound as an incision because blood pools on the work surface and stains his overall. Viola works faster to compensate, dumping the bloodstained food in the bin, and offers the clumsy Australian an efficient kick in the shin. A pot-washer scrambles around on the floor, cleaning up food and the fragments of at least four broken plates.

With wonder-filled eyes, Tom examines the three-inch cut in the ball of his thumb, dangerously close to his wrist. But his fascination lasts only a second. He quickly cauterises the bleeding with a hot pairing knife and covers it with a sticky plaster from his supply. Such things are a common occurrence.

Spectacle over, he lifts his guilty eyes, scratching heat-rash below his yellow curls.

As much as Charlie hates the clichéd notion of temperamental chef's verbally humiliating their staff, she is occasionally willing to take their example. Not often does Charlie shout or even raise her voice, but when she does the result is memorable.

But she is not unreasonable. Tom has worked like a mule for nine hours today, doing the work of two high-end chefs, and will work another nine before the day is over. More importantly, breaking a plate or two is not the same crime as not listening or repeating the same clumsy mistake three times. Besides, Charlie knows precisely, down to the beef-fat-waste-per-hour percentile, that while Tom breaks Vincent's expensive plates, the handless Australian is still a cost-effective chef. There are boxes of spare plates.

Returning to her pans, berating herself for taking pleasure in the fear in Tom's eyes, Charlie asks over her shoulder:

'What time are yir horses racing, dipshit?'

'Twenty past four, chef.' Tom realises only now he has adopted a schoolboy stance, his tartan bonnet in his hands. 'It's a sure thing.'

'That should pay for the plates then, eh?'

Precisely seventeen minutes before midnight, Alison Gorry took position in a filthy alleyway off Rue des Abbesses in Montmartre. Dressed entirely in black, with British army-issue boots, incognito she was not. Discovery would mean death, but such were the perils of the profession. She unscrewed a flask of rum and lifting her eyes towards the unchanging stars, swallowed a deep dose.

She was waiting, allowing her mind to wander, wondering at how much her life had changed in the last years. Her homeland, which was a word only three years earlier she would not have properly understood, seemed so far away, so very long ago, her cottage in Ayrshire nothing more than a romantic notion. As for the woman she had become, Alison wondered if she recognised herself at all. Certainly not by her actions. Alison abhorred her actions, necessary though they were. Nor was her physical appearance familiar. An unkind war service had rendered her, while maintaining reasonable fitness and health, deathly thin. As a younger woman she had never been fat, curvy perhaps, but definitely never thin. Her radiant face of old was gaunt and drawn. The flowing hair that was the pride of her youth sat cropped above the ears. She had become a stranger, the remnants of her former life unravelling one by one. Above all, Alison Gorry wondered exactly how she had come to be crouched in a filthy alleyway with rats in occupied Paris, more alone that the stars in the sky, more drunk than sober.

Commissioned in reaction to Henri Pétain's signing of the Franco-German armistice in 1940, known in the field as Churchill's Secret Army, the Special Operations Executive was a British Secret Service department responsible for fostering resistance amongst the civilian population of Europe and promoting sabotage and subversion against the occupying Nazi force. Alison Gorry first encountered the Secret Service in early 1940, when a British army officer came to her home in the Ayrshire town of Largs.

Mortar debris, Alison learned during the conversation, killed Private John Gorry during only his fourth week on the front line, yet in that brief time her husband had been well received in his unit. It was explained that John's dry wit had eased many a long hour, and that he had talked often of his wife and of holidays spent in Paris with his mother-in-law. Private Gorry had also spoken of the child he and Alison lost. Once the tears dried, the visiting officer suggested to Alison, over shortbread, that she might like to help.

Parachuting from a Whitley bomber into Auvergne in late 1942, just after the complete occupation of France, Alison toiled initially in Toulouse and Marseilles with local résistance groups doing mostly sabotage work. Her true talents did not reveal themselves until one bitterly cold December morning in 1943, when Alison Gorry, with neither forethought, fear, nor any assistance at all, did the unthinkable.

Some agents had been arrested, locked in the local Gestapo headquarters. Locked with them was vital supply routes information. Alison stormed the local Gestapo headquarters, killing nine Nazis including a woman, rescued five agents from torture and saved the integrity of the intelligence.

It was rumoured within the Allied Forces that all SOE agents were assassins to some degree, but that was merely a rumour, a matter of propaganda. There were many skilled military marksmen of course, but marksmen, ultimately, were not assassins. Assassins required a range of diverse skills, skills that in Alison, once exposed, seemed to hone themselves at an astonishing and frightening rate. And so a new life began.

It was by way of these skills that she had arranged during a meeting the previous day with Frédéric Trépont to be standing amid the rats on Rue des Abbesses at seventeen minutes before midnight.

At twenty-three, Trépont was a schoolteacher with the keen if somewhat clouded eyes of a man of fifty. His lips were chapped, his pallor weak and emancipated. His suit was nearly threadbare. Yet, Frédéric Trépont somehow bore the insinuation of propriety, his hair brushed neatly to one side, his long legs crossed just so as he sat alone in a street café on the Île de la Cité under the shadow of the cathedral, mulling over his newspaper. He had not always lived such a delicate existence. Four years ago the Trépont's had been amongst the wealthiest and more respectable city bourgeoisie, but Frédéric had become the sole survivor. His inheritance stolen, left to adjust to life in the working class alone, the schoolteacher had succeeded admirably well. He was still alive, at least; no small matter for a résistance fighter, particularly one Jewish.

'Je dois savoir,' Alison had begun the meeting, but a single word whispered by Frédéric was enough to stop her, to steal the breath from her, to confirm the dread in her belly.

'Madeleine,' he said.

'Yes.'

'Dead.' Frédéric turned his newspaper page. There was distance enough between the tables to allow the use of English, which he had learned admirably well in the last six months. 'She was hanged.'

Although she did not move, other than to lift her coffee cup as one is expected to do in a café, Alison's eyes seemed to catch fire, burning a deep violet in a cool marble face.

'What?' she hissed over the rim. 'What!'

'I found her myself, Violette, or I wouldn't have believed it either.' Frédéric folded his newspaper, allowing Alison to absorb the shock; while life often made some people hard, it had made Frédéric only prepared. A nostalgic accordion player filled the silence.

'We know that she was picked up only two hours before,' he continued. 'She was taken neither to Foch nor Fresnes. I doubt she was questioned as there was no evidence of torture. Ask me where it happened.'

Alison asked with her eyes.

'L'église Sainte-Marie-Madeleine. Midway up the third column from the left, stripped naked. Madeleine was…'

Alison interrupted, her eyes glassy and distant, focused on the patrol boats on the river.

'Brenda,' she said.

'Pardon me?'

27

'Madeleine's name was Brenda, Frédéric. She had a husband and two daughters.'

Frédéric acknowledged this with an appropriate pause, grimaced, and then continued:

'I'm sorry for her and her family, you know that. Tactics are changing Violette. She was killed to show that information is no longer the Nazi principal objective.'

Alison agreed. 'They just want to kill us.'

'Yes, all of us, which means they are scared and that's our strength. What news on Overlord? If it's going to happen, it has to happen soon. Everyone is waiting and the waiting is killing everything. A thing like this needs momentum. In the south, I hear...'

'Patience,' Alison said. 'It's begun. The Major will give you the information, but for now there's something I need from you. It's dangerous.'

The young Frenchman laughed. To onlookers it seemed a natural gesture, a light moment in an otherwise gloomy morning. The request did not surprise him. After all, he had been summoned here.

'Living is dangerous,' he commented. 'I only hope it's worth missing my lunch for.'

'I need some people.'

'How many?' Frédéric frowned.

'Ten.'

'Ten, no problem. Why not take one of my eyes or perhaps a finger, and what about the clothes on my back as well, do you want them? You don't ask for much. Next, you'll tell me you want these ten souls for open warfare.'

Open Warfare was a term used loosely by the résistance for any kind of physical combat where the 'soldiers' were put directly in harms way, rather than more covert operations.

'That's right,' Alison said.

Frédéric swallowed hard. His brow darkened. 'Explain.'

'All my people are jailed or dead, and I can't do what I need to do by myself.'

'Which is what?'

'I need to see Claude Blancpain.'

Face flushing, Frédéric became livid. 'No,' he hissed. 'Why even ask such a thing? The old vulture is watched constantly. Why waste my time like this? Violette, I do what I can willingly and to the best of my ability, but I will not commit suicide and I will not expose that danger to so many of my people. I missed my lunch for this shit? I have essays to...' And then his eyes narrowed. Alison saw the gears in his mind change. 'Violette, you have the entire resource of the Allied force at your fingertips. You have more than enough people. Why come to me for this? Unless... ah, I see.' The schoolteacher sat back, arms folded. 'They don't know what you're doing, do they, your High Command?'

'I'm working alone,' Alison allowed.

'To what end?'

'I can't tell you that.'

'But you will,' Frédéric said. 'Because of Madeleine.'

Alison accepted this. 'I wouldn't go as far as to use the term power struggle, but let's say there are too many conflicting agendas inside the Allied corridors. Definite results require definite action. They are a long way from you and I, my friend, as is their war from ours,' she said.

'What are you doing exactly? Speak plainly, I have papers to mark and I'm hungry. Look at me, I'm wasting away.'

The Scottish SOE agent smiled across the table to the Jewish résistance fighter.

'Is the life of de Gaulle important enough to miss your lunch for?'

After brief contemplation, Frédéric's expression eased and his usual even temperament returned. He brushed a displaced tress of his hair back into place, crossed his legs and leaning across the table with a charming smile, asked in a muted voice:

'Did Moses part the Red Sea?'

An explosion shattered Alison's reverie, bringing her harshly back to the present. Rue des Abbesses was ablaze. Immediately following the first, a second stationary car ignited, aided by canisters of diesel inside. Moments later, a half-dozen bewildered Schutzstaffel officers burst from two doorways on opposite sides of the road, an arsenal of guns levelled as they began the confused charge towards the inferno, shouting furiously. They realised simultaneously their mistake and the ambush too late. From the top floor windows on both sides of the street, machine gun fire rained down.

Quickly, silently, offering a grateful prayer to Frédéric and his men, Alison made her move. Inside No. 54, a pale, ivy-covered sandstone tenement, she crept to apartment 5C, knocked twice on the door and listened with her ear against the wood. As the internal sound of shuffling stopped - the flat's singular and no doubt panicked inhabitant about to look out through the view hole - Alison shifted her balance, recoiled and then lunged her shoulder against the door with amazing force, shattering it clean from the hinges.

'Bonsoir,' she said, walking over the door. Reaching down, she grabbed Claude Blancpain by his filthy hair and dragged him, kicking and screaming, through the hall into the main room, where she threw him into the corner like a sack of vegetables.

A profiteer of occupation, a once reliable seller of Nazi information to the résistance who now sold résistance information to the Nazis, Claude Blancpain was a scrawny, vile man with the yellow skin and brown teeth of a hermit. His smell was a fusion of decomposed mutton, fresh faeces and death. His home mirrored his personality, although amid the filthy clutter, Alison was amazed to see hanging on the damp wall two paintings, originals she correctly presumed, by Monet and by Lévy-Dhurmer.

Blancpain was amazed to see the revolver trained on his head. Alison's principal gun was a large six-shot revolver that looked like something used in the American frontier era a century earlier. It was old and heavy, but well cared for and accurate. When Alison fired a gun, she liked to feel a certain power in the release.

'Who are you?' the old man spat. 'Why break down my door?'

'Get up off the floor and sit down,' he was commanded, the revolver indicating the chair by the window overlooking the carnage-strewn street. In the distance, approaching sirens were audible.

'Speak clearly and succinctly,' Alison instructed. 'Do not make me repeat myself and do not try to lie. Do as I say and I offer you an outside chance of being alive when I leave.'

'The Nazis will kill me anyway,' Blancpain hissed. 'Their men are dead out there on the street. It makes no difference if they think I've talked to you or not. And I won't talk to you, spy, so shoot me now.'

Alison seemed to consider this, nodding thoughtfully. 'Then perhaps we should make a bargain.'

'You have nothing with which to trade, spy. Shoot.' The traitor's lips curled back in a sneer to reveal his jagged teeth. 'Can't you do it? I don't think it's in you to shoot me. I see fear in those pretty eyes.'

As Alison cocked the trigger, the click was considerably louder than the gunfire below on the street, at least to the old man.

'Don't judge so hastily,' she said. 'Patience is a virtue, monsieur Blancpain. But since we're acquainted now, I wonder if you would mind me using your real name, *monsieur Leblanc*.'

Watching these words take effect, seeing the old man's eyes snap shut and a thin stream of urine run down his trouser leg into a dark stain, Alison helped herself to a bottle of gin from the sideboard but not one of the dirty glasses and swallowed a deep, soothing swig.

'The difficulty we had in finding your real name, sir, is both a tribute to your cleverness and to what money can achieve. Your papers are almost as convincing as my own. Once we had this information,' the assassin continued, 'it didn't take long to learn that in early thirty-three you had your daughter and granddaughter hidden in Switzerland, where they are still, living in Neuchâtel.' She paused to give Blancpain-Leblanc a chance to speak, which he chose to forgo.

'Do I have your full attention now?' Alison smiled. 'Understand that it would bother my conscious to slaughter your family, but I will do it. It's merely business. I'm sure you understand.'

Opening his eyes, hands clenched into fists, the old man shook with rage. 'You'll die for this, spy,' he spat. 'Like your friend, Madeleine.'

Alison did not allow herself to react. Through the window, she could see the stars and that helped.

'No doubt,' she said. 'But you shouldn't look so sad, my good man. This is a great night for you. I have come with an opportunity to repay the nation and the people that you have so badly betrayed. For all the Jews and sympathisers you have denounced, for every man and woman you have betrayed and for every child you have helped send to military brothels, for the résistance you've hampered at every turn in the name of profit and self-survival, for moral principles you care nothing about, tonight, monsieur Leblanc, you make amends with France! Doesn't that make you happy?'

No response.

'It certainly makes me happy,' Alison smiled. 'Let's begin with de Gaulle.'

'What of him? I know nothing of such things.'

'The other option, instead of going to Switzerland myself, one supposes, would be to lead the Nazis there, and while your daughter would certainly be raped and shot, the best you could hope for your eleven year-old granddaughter would be that she was only sodomised once before they slit her throat.'

'Alright! Alright. De Gaulle is to be... *studied*.'

The assassin stepped closer. 'Quickly!'

'Shot. De Gaulle is to be assassinated. A man came here two days ago waving his gun about just like you. I'm only an intermediate. I know nothing of his intentions, just that he intends an attempt. He only wanted a name.'

'A name for what purpose?'

'An intelligence mole.'

'To what end?'

'I don't know. I swear. I'm a businessman. It's not prudent to ask questions!'

Time was fleeting. On the street below guns fired sporadically and sirens grew dangerously close. About thirty seconds remained before Nazis would be coming up the stairs. Alison could see that through his fear the old man was thinking exactly the same thing, hoping that to delay would offer him a better chance. She squeezed the trigger, watching with fascination as the old man's shoulder exploded, coating the valuable Lévy-Dhurmer in a fine mist of red spots.

'Let me hear your best guess...

Reserve's lower-floor emergency exit leads up into a narrow, cobbled service lane, hidden away from the surrounding streets. High walls decorated by steel fire escapes and a scattering of glowing windows enclose the space, some of them the backs of George Street's buildings. Refrigeration outlets drone but otherwise there is silence. Darkness has fallen. Beneath the dim glow of a single bulb, atop an industrial refuge bin, Charlie lowers her book to roll a cigarette. With her chef's jacket in a heap beside her, she wears only a sweaty vest.

Sitting on a milk crate on the cobbles, Gavin sips a seven-pound glass of Pieddé Blanc with a vacant air, sleeves rolled up, his waistcoat hung carefully from a hanger on a drainpipe. To mention nothing of the typical day's work behind him, the last three hours spent completing paperwork for Charlie have left him weary, and the night ahead offers little inspiration.

The stillness is a blessing. Gavin's rapport with Charlie, even before Reserve, has much to do with an ability to share snatches of mutual silence. Even after so long, however, her near-preternatural physical stillness unnerves him. Particularly when he lifts his eyes to finds her staring at him, her eyes reflecting light like those of a cat.

'Yie look tired,' he says.

Charlie exhales tasteless smoke and admits to fatigue by a nod, even managing a half-smile. To be leaving early on a Saturday night feels unnatural to her, grating completely against her instincts. But not unpleasantly so. Suddenly, untying her headscarf to release her curls into their natural, wilful shape, the cold air sublime on her scalp, she ties them back again with a band from her wrist in a seamless fluid movement.

'Try this.' Gavin offers his wine. In his limited spare time he often guests on BBC Radio Scotland to wax-lyrical on the joys of the grape. Reserve's wine list offers over seventy bottles.

Charlie accepts the glass, enjoying the coldness of it in her hand, sniffs the wine with her sharp nose well inside the glass, and then passes it back.

'It smells nice,' she admits. 'Like raspberries and cinnamon.'

Although this seems like an excellent description to the expert, he frowns, running his finger through his black hair. 'Taste it! A sip'll no kill yie. Consider the biblical Noah, chef. He drank wine by the arc full and it was all he could dae to live to be nine-hundred and fifty.'

Refusing with a half-smile, Charlie lifts her knees up to her chin.

'Gus, are you coming out tonight after you lock up?'

'Aye, wae you, I thought. Or is that next week? I get muddled up.'

'Tonight, Gus. Will yie do something for me?'

The question is superfluous. It is merely politeness. For four years, Charlie and Gavin have together run Scotland's most popular restaurant and to deny that a certain bond had grown would be folly. Above this, Gavin is professional enough to appreciate that Charlie is his direct employer. He is bound.

'What do yie need, chef?'

'I want yie tae keep Tom amused.'

The manager's eyebrows meet above his nose. 'What dae yie mean?'

'Yie ken what I mean, Gus.'

'I see.' Not entirely pleased by the mission, Gavin swallows the last of his Chardonnay with a wince. 'Nae bother.'

'Much obliged.'

Speak of the devil. Into the nippy, northern-European winter, Tom emerges, filthy, bloody, muttering something about the arctic wilderness, and farts loudly in Gavin's face, beaming with joy at having achieved such a thing.

'Mingin cunt.' Had he the energy, the manager would inflict bodily pain unto Tom. 'What time's yir race?'

The butcher rolls a cigarette, although a nasty open blister reaching across three knuckles, not to mention the wound in the ball of his thumb, render the act of smoking it problematic. Still, with his usual buoyancy, he perseveres.

'Brothers, I fuckin love Christmas,' he muses. 'I must admit to feeling very sentimental. Homesick, y'know? I've been thinking all day long of my gran's fruitcake. Tasty as it is, old Arthur's just isn't the same.'

'Never fuckin mind Arthur's fuckin fruitcake!' Gavin becomes irate. 'What time's yir fuckin race? Where's ma fuckin money, fuckheid?'

The Australian calmly produces a thick roll of cash wrapped in a betting slip from his crusty kitchen trousers and peels off more than a dozen twenties for the restaurant manager, peeling them straight onto the concrete. Scratching the heat-rash in his crotch, he says with a smile, though colourlessly:

'Have some faith, brother.'

The money immediately puts Gavin in a better mood. He even smiles as he gathers up his prize. 'I think yie're a bloody genius, Tommy.'

'Sono un artiste, fratello,' the Australian retorts, Florentine accent faultless, accompanying hand gestures theatrical.

'A piss artist,' Charlie counters with a smile. She considers Tom's non-culinary talent just as remarkable as his kitchen skills. In exchange for the forty pounds he requested this morning, he now hands her back two-hundred and seventy. How he achieves such a thing, other than the broad notion that it is something to do with horseracing, she has no idea, and certainly does not question him. She remembers the wee old men back in the pubs of Kirkcudbright, unable to fathom the price of a half and a half in the fangled decimal money, but mathematical piranhas around the domino table.

'Buy yourself something nice, chef. Or better yet, buy me something nice for Christmas,' Tom grins guiltily. 'How much do I owe for Vincent's plates?'

'Dinnae be dim, Tommy.'

'Sure? Thanks, chef.' Tom's appreciation is genuine. He is very fond of Charlie.

Charlie listens for a while as Gavin and Tom recount in fantastic detail last night's rampage of beer and Class-A drugs, only moderately interested. Gavin goes out drinking after work nearly every night, usually with Fanny, Tom and Evelyn, and is, surprisingly for a wine connoisseur, the drink to get drunk type. Rarely trying anything he has not already, his stories tend to be quite repetitious.

Last night, apparently, after waiting vainly for Charlie until nearly the middle of the morning, Gavin met the usual suspects and together they went to party in the Hilton hotel rooms of Americans who dined at Reserve earlier in the evening, including a famous film director. But the story, off to a promising start with talk of prostitutes, huge bags of cocaine and hand held digital cameras, quickly tapers off into tedium, forcing Charlie to stop listening altogether.

She has a surprising notion to buy herself something to wear tonight. This is not common practise for Charlie because she rarely has the opportunity to wear anything new, with the exception of the occasional awards ceremony. Nor is it an easy task to find something in her size without having to look in teenage departments, where there is usually little accommodation for large boobs. Tonight she is thinking of a particular dress in the window of a boutique round the corner on Hill Street and has an inkling that it might just fit. At five hundred pounds the dress is certainly not cheap, but money has never been Charlie's principal motivation.

'Listen, brothers!' Tom voice is suddenly serious. 'I need to know, do we work Christmas Eve here?' Rather than Reserve specifically, by *here* it is assumed that he means Scotland or perhaps Great Britain.

Either way, Gavin scoffs. 'Fuckin right we do!' Then to smooth the blow, 'But not Hogmanay or New Year's Day. You get double time for the twenty-fourth and we only work until ten instead of eleven.'

The Australian considers this. 'Can I take the night off?'

'Away 'n boil yir heid.'

'But, I mean, like, I'd assumed we'd shut up shop after lunch like everywhere else in Europe. Y'know, the very suggestion of working on the night Mary and Joseph searched for an inn in some Italian towns is enough to cause a riot.'

'Couldnae gie a fuck,' Gavin remarks.

'But I've made plans!'

'That's no the restaurant's fault,' Gavin explains quite rightly.

The final plea from Tom comes with sincere eyes:

'*Please*, brothers.'

'Hmm.' The manager considers for a moment, looking into his empty glass. 'What tae dae then, my immigrant friend,' he muses, 'is write yir grievance down on a square piece of paper, fold it up three times and go'n gie it tae some cunt who *gies a fuck*!'

'But, this one time in Germany...'

'Tom, you will work it,' Charlie puts in, finally annoyed by the noise, the metallic rasp in her voice prominent. 'I'll gie yie double time and yir fat bonus, which I will not gie yie should yie not do as we ask. In fact, Tom, if yie're no smiling when you arrive here for yir shift on Christmas Eve I'll fire yir arse and yie can go'n fry Mars bars for a living. It's entirely up to you. *Brother*.'

Defeated but taking none of it to heart, the Australian fixes his eyes on an enormous rat peering out from a crack in the alley wall. Its eyes are red, its teeth like razors. Swiftly and with utter precision, he catches the beast, like a kitten in his hands, wrings its neck and throws it into the gutter. Frustration vented, his bright mood returns.

Again, ripping the stillness, the fire-door opens, this time to Evelyn. She wears a long woolly cardigan over her uniform and her honey-coloured hair in a bun. Both the stillness and the relative darkness she finds heavenly. She lights a tailor-made cigarette, balances it on her lip and glides like a swan to her lover, wrapping her arms around his greasy neck.

'Did we win, hunny-bunny?' she asks.

Tom's chest swells with pride. 'Sweetheart, of course we won. Is there not a single soul with faith in me? I'm a genius, remember.'

'Ah, yes, I forgot,' Evelyn exhales.

'Will yie pole dance for us again, Eva.' Gavin stands, slipping on his waistcoat. 'I enjoyed that tremendously last night. Use the drainpipe there, or possibly I could hold a mop shaft.'

Evelyn's face falls. Horrified, truly insulted by the very suggestion, she looks as if she might actually burst into tears. But this is merely Evelyn's act. Fixing her statuesque eyes on him and inhaling a sharp hit of nicotine, she says:

'Sure, I'll dance, boss. But not for free this time. If you give me and my hunny-bunny here the night of the twenty-fourth off, I'll dance for you, suck your cock and Tom will take a photograph while I blow bubbles with your sticky mess.'

Tempting as this sounds, Gavin is a professional and not to be swayed.

'No.'

'Wanker.'

'Aye, yie're mibbae right, Eva.' The manger straightens himself up before heading back inside, taking his clothes hanger with him. 'Dinnae be too long, eh?'

Ignoring him, the Australians console each other with a deep, lingering kiss.

The sight is too much for Charlie. She finishes her cigarette, puts on her chef's jacket, gathers her tobacco pouch and her book and jumping down from the bin, disappears with the words:

'Nae rest for the wicked.'

4

In recognition of the Nazi effort in Europe, the Staatsoper Berlin, much refined in the eyes of the Reich since the cleaning of the companies Jews,
toured for almost three years under the renowned baton of Robert Heger,
roaming the dangerous empire with a protective Schutzstaffel entourage.
When the interval of Strauss's *Elektra* began that particular evening just before nine, the audience filtered through Garnier's grand neo-baroque palace,
its marble friezes and lavish statuary, to drink, smoke and gossip, the sheer
terror installed by a uniformed Nazi presence decently although not entirely
repressed.

Amongst the crowd was Édith Thiéry, an art dealer and a familiar face in
the Parisian social scene, moving effortlessly, her sleek white satin dress a
perfect cut, her long auburn hair rousing approving murmurs. The barman
served her usual glass of burgundy and received his usual handsome gratuity,
paying the transaction no particular attention.

'Merci, Madame,' he said simply, unaware that ten hours later he would
recount the brief exchange over thirty times under Gestapo interrogation and
that, because of his ignorance, would be dead by morning.

Known to be the widow of an expired industrialist, Édith's singular presence at the Opéra was not uncommon and attracted that night no more than
the usual impressed acknowledgement. From her velvet and gold leaf seat,
she sat perfectly comfortable amid frescoed cherubs and nymphs, occasionally lifting her eyes from her programme to grace a familiar face with a warm
smile, or even share a word or two, but not often.

Madame Thiéry, however, was not under the proper circumstances unap-
proachable. Franz Wetzler knew this. He had made enquires, drawn records
and had surveyed the woman personally for many months, albeit from a distance. Forty years of age, Wetzler, a Schutzstaffel clerk regarded by his colleagues, wrongly, as a man of neither importance nor influence, had never
been confident with women. His passion was for the arts. Yet, tonight was
different, had to be different. He was out of uniform - in itself a remarkable
occurrence - and scheduled to leave Paris the next day without expecting to
return.

Summoning all the courage available to him, Wetzler drained his brandy,
excused himself from his company, crossed the room and struck.

'Madame.' He affected a charming smile.

'Monsieur?'

'I beg your pardon,' Wetzel's French was broken and uncomfortable, 'but I
could not help noticing you studying the performance details, as I have seen

you do before. I wondered if perhaps it might interest you to know Wilhelm Pfeil, tonight performing the role of the nurse, is a direct blood relation of Herr Wolfgang Mozart!'

Édith smiled with intrigue - *ah, the German obsession with bloodlines* - as she studied the perfect Arian in his perfect suit. 'How delightful.'

'Yes, Wilhelm and I studied together. He doesn't like to perpetuate the fact because he wants to succeed on his own. He composes, too, you see. But the fact remains. My name is Wetzler, Madame. Franz Wetzler.'

Édith's eyes flickered with recognition. 'Mine is Édith Thiéry, Herr Wetzler. I love your suit.'

'Thank you,' Wetzler blushed. 'Reputation precedes you, Madame. It's said that you studied with Picasso.'

Wetzler pronounced the name with hidden distaste. As the painter of *Guernica*, criticising the Luftwaffe's bombing of the Spanish Basque town in 1937, Pablo Picasso had survived for as long as he had in Paris only because the Führer wished not to make him a martyr.

'Briefly, yes.' Édith sipped her burgundy. 'I was a silly young girl at the time. But surely that is nothing to a man who studied under maestros Weingartner and Strauss.'

Delighted, Franz bowed to the compliment. 'That, also, was a long time ago, Madame Thiéry.'

'Édith, please.'

'Édith.' Franz kissed her extended hand. 'Are you enjoying Herr Strauss this evening?'

'Schlüter is sublime in the lead role. And of course the Staatsoper orchestra is wonderful, but one expects no less.'

Ten years ago, Franz Wetzler was the assistant house conductor of the Staatsoper Berlin. Indeed, he still held a great deal of influence within the company. But the current motivational tour, somewhat understandably he believed, was not up to the usual high standard; nor, although he would die before admitting such a thing, had he ever been particularly keen on the work of his old mentor, Richard Strauss. Steering the conversation away from specifics, he enlightened his new acquaintance with the fact that:

'In Berlin, under Herbert von Karajan, the Staatsoper recently pioneered the very first stereo recording in the world. It's a wonderful achievement for the Reich.'

'You must be very proud,' Édith smiled indulgently. 'I wonder, may I confess to you a secret, Herr Wetzler?'

'Franz, please.'

'Franz.' A disarming smile formed on Édith's rouged lips as she lit a cigarette, flicked her auburn waves over her shoulder and leaning close enough for Wetzler to smell her seductive scent.

'Let me admit to you that I, Franz, simply cannot stand Strauss. I appreciate him, of course, please don't misunderstand me, but I must admit that I find him quite puerile in parts. It's simply a matter of taste.'

This equally delighted and confused Franz Wetzler. He smiled and then frowned. 'But, why did you come?'

'To get out of my empty house.' Édith exhaled smoke. 'One can live neither in the past nor within ones own narrow frame of reference. Life must continue and it must do so by expanding its perceptions.'

Somewhat touched by this simple though sincere sentiment, Wetzler said, in a soft voice, lying:

'If you'll forgive me, Madame, I know that you are a widow. I, too, have lost my beloved, who was killed by a British air strike on Bremen.'

'My God, how terrible!' Édith was appalled. 'This war is truly awful.'

'Yes, it is. However, as you say, Madame, life must continue.'

The theatre bell rang, signalling simultaneously the end of the interval and Wetzler's last chance. The large crowd of people around them were moving. For the second time, from deep inside himself, feeling his bowels loosen, Franz summoned all the courage available to him, and said:

'I hope you won't find it inappropriate of me to ask but I still have a headfull of information to impress you with and I wondered perhaps if you would care to join me for a drink after the performance.'

Édith drained her burgundy, a thin smile on her lips.

'Herr Wetzler,' she said. 'I have no desire to endure the rest of this ghastly performance. Do you have a car?'

As the sun began to lose its sheen in the late evening sky, Wetzler's Citroën car took the busy avenue de l'Opéra, through the grandiose scenery of the Second Empire, and at the Louvre turned onto Rue de Rivoli, coming finally into the smaller streets of Le Marais. The driver would later testify that neither Édith nor Wetzler spoke during the drive.

In May of 1944, many parts of Paris, barracked and fortified, truly resembled battlefields, while some areas managed to retain a semblance of past dignity. From the early seventeenth century, once home to Cardinal Richelieu, the writers Bossuet and Hugo, and the esteemed courtesan, Marion Delorme, Place des Vosges remained during the years of occupation at its finest because the large pale-pink stone townhouses had been split into apartments that to a large degree were occupied by ranking Nazi officers.

The car stopped at the arcade outside No. 20. Inside the top floor apartment, the tall German ex-conductor admired the well-furnished room, hands clasped behind his back, suit shining, as Édith Thiéry arranged some light Bach on the gramophone.

The room was a visual feast. It still had its original windows. Wetzler saw several interesting paintings in stark contrast to the style of the room. One in particular, by von Stuck, delighted him, and he wondered if the proper authorities knew of its existence.

The Schutzstaffel, known and feared throughout Europe as the SS, was the elite paramilitary organization of the Nazi Party, created originally to protect Adolf Hitler at the early National Socialist meetings, and as such was not supported financially by the Reich. From three-hundred members in 1925, under Himmler the Schutzstaffel swelled to half a million souls who all needed equipment and food. Looting, therefore, became the means by which it self-supported. From the seventy-thousand homes plundered throughout Paris, little of the confiscated art was of any real interest to the party and was sold immediately to Switzerland to raise funds, but finds of German origin were rare and invariably liberated to the motherland. In fact, it was the second time in less than a week that Wetzler had come upon hidden booty; he had been equally surprised to find the Monet and the Lévy-Dhurmer, lesser works of course, being French, in the informers' filthy home. Tucking away the von Stuck in his mind, he turned to receive a flute of chilled champagne.

He felt his confidence grow. He could sense Édith's sudden nervousness. It was in the way she spoke, the subtle manner in which she moved around the room, straightening a cushion here, aligning a chair there. Wetzler knew this because, professionally speaking, Franz Wetzler was not at all what he seemed. Posing as a middle-ranking and sometimes clumsy administrator, Franz Wetzler was in fact an intelligence officer highly trained to read body language. Over his glass, he watched Édith glance - just a small glance, but easily perceptible - to a photograph of her dead husband on the wall.

Finally, she turned to him.

'I'd like you to know,' her voice was a whisper, 'not that you will believe me, I know, but I don't make a habit of bringing... I'm not...I have never done a thing like this before.' She cast another glance to the photograph. 'Nobody has ever been here.'

'I do believe you,' Wetzler said, not at all convinced that he did, and then smiled. 'Just relax.'

'Relax, yes. I'm sorry.'

'Don't be sorry.'

'Yes... I mean...'

What happened next took Wetzler entirely by surprise. Dropping her shawl, Édith walked to the couch, stood for a moment regarding him with a solemn expression, and then hitched up her satin dress to her hips. Wetzler had no time to speak before she straddled him, pushing him back against the couch.

Unzipping him with one hand and with the other pulling her own underwear aside, Édith guided Wetzler wordlessly, effortlessly inside. He was larger than she had taken before, his impaling size momentarily shocking and then delicious. She pulled his hands up to her breasts, squeezing her own hands roughly over his, causing Wetzler to sound a moan of primitive animal release as she began an easy rocking motion.

An interlude occurred as Édith slid to her knees on the floor and with her clasped hands behind her back, lent forward to seize Wetzler's cock in her mouth, swallowing him as deep as she was able while forcing a stiff tongue down the throbbing underside. Sucking firmly, she resisted the urge to bite. Then she was on him again. Rocking became thrusting; thrusting soon enough something more intent. Édith pounded her hips down upon the German, feeling release grow. Their kissing became rough, messy, their moans vulgar, and after only a moment Édith could tell by his breathing, his heartbeat, that Wetzler could not last much longer. She whispered something quickly into his ear but by the time Wetzler had translated the French words, understood their meaning and realised what was about to happen, it was too late.

The first knife slid through his shirt and his chest, entering between the third and fourth ribs and piercing the heart. The second knife garrotted him, releasing a flow of blood and any chance of a scream.

Then, as the Bach reached its peak, as Wetzler expired with a final shudder, Édith's orgasm came, quietly, forcing her eyes closed and her body to contract and release three times.

After a moment, looking deeply into Wetzler's dead eyes, Édith caught her breath. She climbed off the corpse, smiling to herself at its comical expression, and wiped herself and her knives.

She stood motionless, appraising her work. The moment, though deeply erotic, was a sad one for Édith. With the death of Wetzler came her own death. She knew she could not survive such a thing, knew she was expendable and accepted it fully. She had served her purpose, been nurtured for it - without knowing what specifically it might be - for years, and now it was done.

Édith Thiéry was all but dead.

She looked around the apartment for the last time, stripped off the dress, and then washed the visible blood from her face and hands. Blood covered her entire body, but that was not a priority; it could be concealed.

She would not hide Wetzler's body. It was to be found exactly as it was. *Almost* exactly as it was. If the Gestapo wanted to send messages through their kills then they must to be prepared to face the consequences.

With the removal of her make-up and her flowing auburn wig, Édith Thiéry became Alison Gorry, who stood naked with a razor sharp blade in one hand and in the other, Wetzler's….

Furious, Charlie lifts her grey eyes. 'What?' she snaps.

'I said,' Stan pronounces, looming over her with a pair of socks in his hands, 'yie've sat there for an hour, Charlotte. Please go and get ready.'

'I'm gaun now.'

'Mo chreach!' Stan declares, translating from the Gaelic as *Goddamn!* or more literally *My Ruin!*

Naked but for underwear, her pale body slick with moisturiser, Charlie grudgingly uncurls in her armchair, marks her page by an elegant fold and tosses the book onto the carved table. Her hair rests in its natural shape, smelling of shampoo and tea tree conditioner. Mellow is the light thrown by the variety of lamps around the room. Sublime is the contemporary folk music. Four consecutive joints Charlie has smoked, and there is certainly time for another.

Approximately nine grams in weight, chocolate-like and still tacky, Charlie's nugget of hashish is the illegal resin derived from the dried flowers, known as marijuana, of the Indian hemp plant, Cannabis Sativa. The drug comes only from the female of the species. The main chemical released by smoking hashish or marijuana is tetrahydrocannabinol, which via the blood, binds to protein receptors in the brain, influencing pleasure, memory, reason, concentration, sensory and time perception and coordination. Charlie's hash is of Pakistani origin and pleasingly potent.

To begin: she employs three fine-weight rolling papers to make the skin of the joint, two attached together for a longer structure, the third as a strengthening bridge. She burns a corner of her hash over the flame of her lighter until it blackens and then carefully crumbles it generously along the length of skin. Normally, Charlie would repeat this after adding tobacco to the joint, but this time she does not use tobacco. Instead, she uses marijuana from an air-sealed plastic bag. All the same, she crumbles on more hash.

Deftly lifting the filled skin to her lips in her thumbs and index fingers, Charlie licks the glue and skilfully teases the joint into the correct pen-like tapering shape. Instead of ripping random pieces of card off her cigarette paper packet, or worse, as once was her habit, book covers, Charlie prefers a booklet of hemp cards cut perfectly for the job, which she rolls into a tiny tube - a roach - and slides into the thinner end of her joint.

After a final inspection, she lights the joint, mindful not to light her hair as well, sucking smoke deep into her lungs, and sinks back into the armchair, listening as a clarinet and a violin flirt in thirds above a stark acoustic guitar.

Snoopy's claws, as he eases down from the back of the armchair, hungry for the tangy smoke and some attention, are pleasurably painful on Charlie's skin. The semi-feral beast has been her housemate since she rescued him from the Cat and Dog Home when he was a baby. He is four now, twenty-eight in cat years, a year Charlie's senior. Dutifully she checks him for tics and fleas and tickles his distinguished white beard. Snoopy, though, appreciates neither the benefits nor the smell of skin moisturiser and has soon had enough.

Charlie is apt to surrender entire evenings to the act of self-maintenance, at least when she is not at the restaurant. Kitchen heat-rash is unavoidable and she is prone to chapped skin and lips in the winter months. She particularly loves clipping her toenails. Preening is to Charlie a sensual act, often climaxing in masturbation. But not when Stan is looming.

'Charlotte!'

'Man, please dinnae shout at me,' she whines. 'I said I'm gaun.'

'But yie're no,' Stan all but pleads.

'I am. I'm gaun now.'

Winter herbs grow on the kitchen sill, gently scenting the air. There is a small breakfast table with one chair. One wall is tiled and painted with Hellenistic imagery in fine details, but other than this Charlie's kitchen is purely a functional room, warmed constantly by an aga. She sets her ashtray with her joint on the bunker and bundles her reeking dirty work underwear, until now abandoned on the floor, into the washing machine, noting without surprise that Stan's vomit-stained t-shirt is inside, unwashed.

Domestic duties are an important part of Charlie's life. After an exhausting day at the restaurant she is never too tired to tidy up, iron clothes or wash dishes. It is a matter of habit. Since fleeing her mother's home in Kirkcudbright some ten years ago, Charlie has had seven homes of her own in Edinburgh to maintain, all of which she is able to picture and smell clearly; three shared leases, three single leases, and this her first home.

Stan has also lived in Edinburgh for ten years. He and Charlie met as housemates. But while Charlie lasted only a matter of weeks in that particular three-bedroom residence on Gordon Street, at the bottom of Easter Road, it was Stan's achievement to survive there for ten tears, until only last week. Now Stan is a homeowner too, and of No. 24B Lee Crescent, Portobello, the top-left quarter of a Victorian villa, Charlie finds herself unexpectedly green - positively furious - with envy.

'Stan,' she projects loud enough to carry through as she snaps on rubber gloves and begins the few dirty mugs in the sink, 'when's the man coming to connect yir electricity? Yie did mind to phone today, didn't yie?'

'Monday night at six o'clock. Go'n no let me forget this time.'

'I asked Dave to come for dinner on Tuesday for a look. Yie can cook,' Charlotte scoffs.

'Charlotte!' Stan appears in the kitchen doorway, a furious otter. 'Is there any need to be standing there nearly naked doing the dishes at this precise minute? Please go and get ready. Please, man.'

Charlie shrugs. The dishes are already complete. She drains the water and hangs her gloves over the basin. Collecting her joint, taking the time to re-light it and swallow a deep dose of smoke into her lungs, her tiny back arched, she knocks shoulders with Stan in the doorway and hisses nastily with a puff of smoke:

'I'm gaun now.'

Stan chokes on the smoke.

Back in the living room, he experiments a while with different lamp combinations, considering each for a moment from various positions in the room before deciding on a format that pleases him. At the window, opening a second stained pane for fresh air, he looks down on the busy river of Leith Walk and across to Elm Row, which looks like a voyeuristic Avril Paton painting. Charlie's flat is on the forth floor, the highest in the Gayfield Place sandstone terrace, offering an excellent view. Small crowds move around the street, some already falling-down drunk, most merely merry. It is early still.

Tonight is a big night for Stan. He wears his favourite cocoa-toned, flared corduroys, heeled boots and a clinging, brown shrunk-silk shirt - £1.25 from eBay plus £2.12 postage and packaging from France - off of which he picks cat hairs. His own hair and sideburns are neatly styled with wax and he is unshaven. He feels butterflies in his belly and realises he is pacing the floorboards.

Towering piles of books around the shelves threaten to topple down upon him. Charlie's major expense in life - in fact with the exception of hashish, Charlie's singular expense - is reading material. From period romances to surrealist horrors via feminist poetry and modern crime mysteries, several thousand novels clutter the flat, not necessarily printed in English, all second-hand, all arranged with the care of a person who gives small regard to inanimate objects. She particularly likes political thrillers but will read almost anything except westerns. Similarly, reference books are acquired second-hand, ranging from Scottish history, ancient Greece, chemistry, back problems, the French revolutions, sociology, mechanics, DIY, accountancy, sleep problems, hairdressing and cats. The only novels bought new are the Alison Gorry spy novels written by Vincent's mother, Megan Poe.

The cookery books, however, behind protective tinted glass, are something altogether different. Charlie owns rare and expensive copies of *Hors d'œuvre*, *L'Art Culinaire*, *Larousse Gastronomique* and Mrs Beeton's *Philosophy of Housekeeping*. She owns a second-edition *Grande Cuisine* by Marie-Antoine Carême. Her first-editions include Escoffier's 1903 *Guide Culinaire* and 1934 *Ma Cuisine*, Mrs Glasses' *Art of Cookery Made Plain and Easy by a Lady*, published in Edinburgh in 1747, and her most recent acquisition, bought by telephone bid from an auction in Paris, an 1825 *Physiologie du Goût* by Anthelme Brillat-Savarin. The thickest book in the room is *Leçons dans la Cuisine* by Vincent Dussollier.

Nervous and anxious to get going, Stan lights an imported incense cake and sits down with the newspaper to wait.

Fully an hour he waits, reading the Saturday Scotsman from cover to cover, all its supplements and a good dozen pages of an Anne Rice vampire novel before he rises again, as is his nature to do when a lady enters a room.

Standing there, he forgets to breathe.

Charlie's dress is long and sleeveless, simple, cinnamon, oriental in style, holding firm a taut cleavage. She wears pointed, heeled shoes. The mass of her scarlet hair is moulded, twisted and gripped away from her neck in an impressive catwalk style. She wears no jewellery, but breaking with tradition

43

she wears deep blue paint on her upper eyelids and green on the lower, all lined in black pencil, creating a flash of colour and something of a spell each time she blinks. A joint hangs from her lip, curling smoke around her face.

'Early Christmas gift,' she says. 'Do you like it?'

'What?'

'The dress, idiot.'

'Who from?'

'From me!' Charlie scowls. 'Do you *not* like it?'

Stan does not answer immediately. Under terrible scrutiny he allows himself a long examination of the overall vision. Finally, he answers:

'I love it. It's beautiful. It's very you.'

This obviously pleases her. In the free armchair she sits, toking her joint, slowly exhaling smoke. Stan reclines back into his chair, folding his fingers across his stomach in his usual otter position.

The music has ended. In silence they regard one another, her grey eyes burning into his olive green, seemingly transparent ones. Stan expects to see her painted eyelids when she blinks, but she does not blink. She is almost-frighteningly motionless.

But then, in a quick fluid movement, she hands him across the highly reflective surface of the carved table her joint.

'Go'n take a wee shot of my marijuana cigarette,' she smiles, laying the local twang on thick.

Stan sold cannabis for many years and made a great deal of money in the effort, though there is certainly none left now. But he does not smoke cannabis. Stan does not smoke at all; he never has. Yet, so surprising is the poisonous offering that he accepts without debate, toking deeply and without coughing, which is a painful effort for him.

Immediately, his olive eyes dilate. A flush of colour rises in his cheeks. After a second draw, coughing now, he passes the joint back and sits back into the chair, holding firm eye contact.

'What did you do today?' Charlie asks in a small voice, her Edinburgh accent suddenly gone.

'Spent the whole day painting.' Indeed, there is paint under Stan's fingernails.

'And what did you paint?'

'The ceilings, the skirting, cornices and a small Madonna and Child. I love your hair like that. Not any more than I usually love it, of course. Less, in fact. But it's beautiful nonetheless.'

So unexpected and delivered in such strange tones, these remarks quite disarm Charlie. She feels her strength drain. With detachment, she feels her mouth open but hears no words escape.

'What time's Dave coming?' Again, these seemingly innocuous words come in a tone so odd that Charlie's voice returns in a sudden blurt. She sucks deeply, nervously on her joint.

'Why?'

Stan smiles gently, mischievously, eyes narrowing, falling on the cinnamon dress. 'Just wondering.'

'Said he'd phone when he's about to get here.'

'Well, I…'

The telephone rings and Charlie nearly jumps out of her skin.

The Doonhaimer is a modest, low-lit and poorly ventilated public house hidden in the depths of Leith, entertaining its weekly peak of twenty crammed punters by means of a female singer with an acoustic guitar and more amplification equipment than seems strictly necessary. Her face contorts with passion as she performs a tender, wistful adaptation of Iron Maiden's *Can I Play with Madness?*

Behind the bar Larry maintains patient and witty banter with the locals but presents no pretence of a smile. She is twenty-six years old, tough and astute, with porcelain skin, a shorn head and shocking dark lipstick. However, at the sight of Stan, the facade falls completely and a warm smile illuminates her face.

'Same again?' she asks.

'Thank you very much.' Stan leans his elbows on the bar top. 'And a packet o' yir finest pistachios.'

'Still managing tae keep clean, I see.'

'If anybody pukes over me tonight it'll be myself, Lorraine, which is actually quite likely.'

'Nervous?'

'Mildly.' He smiles dryly. 'Are yie sure yie'll no come wae us? Fake period pains and yie'll probably still get paid for the shift.'

It is no easy thing for Larry to refuse Stan. She is drawn helplessly by his pale eyes. Indeed, his eyes have drawn her several times before.

'My period was my excuse last week, remember? I doubt it'll work again. Anyway, I'm working up the road twenty minutes after I leave here.' When she is not a barmaid, Larry is an exotic dancer.

'Until when?'

'Probably four.'

'Poor thing. Where's Ruby-doobie the night?'

'Wae her faither, believe it or no. And please dinnae call her that, Stan. It makes me say it. Listen, will yie be here for the quiz tomorrow night? I need a partner, and more importantly I need the money.'

'Sorry, pet-lamb. I'll still be away.'

'Prick. Where are yie gaun?'

'Visiting the folks.'

'In the Hebrides?'

'Aye.'

'Prick. Here's yir change. Go and teach me some more rude Gaelic words.'
Stan thinks for a moment before pronouncing slowly and patiently:
'*Bheir mi araon de do shùilean as na 'n Nach eil deoghaill anns mò ball.*'
Larry repeats the phrase three times and then asks:
'Which means?'
'I'll poke both yir eyes out wae it if yie dinnae suck it.'
'*Pòg mo thòin!*' Larry works the electric till. 'What's blowjob?'
Stan wishes he had not begun such charged banter. '*Ith Bod* is literally to eat cock, or you could say *Obair-Shèididh*,' he explains. 'But yie'd actually say *Smuasaich Bod*, Larry, which is to deepthroat, more appropriate for yirsel.'
Larry winks. 'I'll bring yir drinks over.'
'No, it's nae bother, Larry, I'll…'
'Stan!' she hisses. 'I'll bring yir drinks over.'
'Oh, I see, right, aye. Thanks. Can I take my nuts, though?'
Regardless of the marker-penned sign inviting patrons not to smoke above the pool table, Charlie lights a cigarette that is a poor substitute for another joint, and with a harsh crack pots two yellows from the break. She has not removed her duffle coat or scarf. Although Charlie does drink, occasionally enjoying a glass of Guinness to boost her blood iron, for now she sips fizzy Irn Bru from a champagne flute, enjoying the bubbles up her nose and the bizarre tangy taste.
Beside her sits Dave Quinn. Dave is a slightly round man in his early thirties wearing an expensive grey velvet suit, an open-collared shirt printed in an Indian design and leather sandals. His skin is the colour of charcoal and while his hair is also dark, grey flecks his stubble. His eyes are naturally calm and sleepy.
As it is for Charlie, to be out drinking is a rare occasion for Dave. He is a family man, and, besides, has no desire to go out drinking more than twice a year. Tonight he is happy. His face is set in an easy smile. Dave, in fact, is rarely without a smile.
'Did yie bring oot any hash?' he wonders.
'Just a taste,' Charlie smiles. 'I thought yie'd stopped.'
'I huv. I havnae smoked a joint for six weeks.' Dave's sleepy eyes widen at the noticeable lack of drinks in Stan's hands, and he says, purposefully making a fair performance of crossing his legs, alas to no avail:
'Stan, it's only fair to tell yie that Charlie and I are sceptical.'
'Sceptical about what?' Stan shares around his nuts.
'We're worried that there willnae be enough room for everyone on Christmas day,' Dave explains in a soft hybrid of west coast and east. 'Of course, I admit that I've no been fortunate enough tae be invited tae see yir new house wae my own eyes yet, but thirty people consume a massive amount of space, aye?'

46

Potting a particularly tricky double-bounce shot, Charlie adds, cigarette balanced on lip:

'A lot of turkey, too.'

'There arenae really thirty people coming, eh?' Stan appears thoughtful as he chalks his cue. 'Sounds an awful lot when yie say it like that, eh?'

'You fuckin invited them, bawbag! So yie see our concern?' Dave hits Stan between the eyes with a pistachio nut and again crosses his legs without acknowledgment. 'It's all very well arranging yir seating plan but folks arenae just going to sit on their arses all day long. They might want to move around a bit. Be *reasonable*.'

This is the worst insult known to Stan of the reasonable Hume's, but he takes it on the chin. 'Reason is and ought to be the slave of the passions,' Stan quotes his ancestor. 'So it's a good job I bought such a big fuckin house. And go'n dinnae be whining that yie've no seen the place yet, because I hear yie're coming for dinner on Tuesday night, which is good timing, my friend, because yie can help me finish painting.'

'Aye, nae bother, but Victoria has athletics on Tuesday's, mind, so I'll need tae be away by quarter to nine.'

'Crafty bastard,' Stan remarks.

'Howz it gaun, Dave?' A passing woman asks this.

'Gaun fine, Rhonda. Yirsel?'

Rhonda answers with only a mischievous smile, and Stan's green eyes follow her pert buttocks as he asks:

'Who was that?'

Dave shrugs noncommittally. It is Dave's ability to command the eyes of passing women, and even men, ranging in age from twenty to sixty. Charlie and Stan have never known Dave to be anything other than a single man; they met seven years ago by which time Dave and his wife where already estranged, though they are still not divorced. Their daughter Victoria, who is ten, lives equally and happily between houses, considering herself to have, rather than a broken home, two homes.

'Here, Stan, man, yie like ma sandals?'

Looking at Dave's feet, Stan fails to see what is glaringly obvious. 'Aye, I dae. How, are they new, like?'

Charlie shares a smile with Dave as she pots yet another yellow ball.

'Look closer, dipshit,' she says.

'Eh?'

After a twist and an audible snap, Dave's left foot, still in its sandal, comes cleanly away below the ankle, and he hands it to Stan. But even then, Stan registers nothing unusual.

Then his eyes grow large. 'Oh, for fucksake, fatman; it's yir new foot! I wondered how yie kept crossing yir legs, I thought yie'd bother wae yir bladder. I didnae see. I'm sorry, pal.' Stan carries the foot, as he would an injured bird, to the pool table's bright lights for meticulous investigation.

'Outrageous, Stan,' Dave remarks. 'I'd notice if you had a new appendage.'

Anatomically and aesthetically correct, the prosthesis is tailored precisely to match Dave's tone and build. A lifelike 'skin' conceals the latest in shock absorption, energy distribution and propulsion technology. The foot is Dave's Christmas present to himself, bought to order from America, and it is, after the constraints and actual pain of its clunky NHS predecessors, nothing short of a genuine Christmas miracle.

'I'm nervous about the night, eh?' Stan apologises. 'I'm impressed, though, buddy. Feels like a real foot, wae tendons and muscles. Dae yie no need tae break it in?'

'It isnae a fuckin shoe!' Dave snatches it back. 'Anyway, it's too late to be enthusiastic now. Yie can go'n throw shite at yirsel, my friend. But listen, dae yie really want me tae drive yie tae the airport at nine o'clock in the morning? Or are yie fucking kidding me on, man? I'm supposed to be playing golf.'

Tomorrow is the fourteenth day of December, Archie Hume's birthday. Tradition determines that Stan's father will blow out his candles at exactly three o'clock, and for this Stan's presence is expected. The problem is one of geography. Doris and Archie Hume live in an attractive stone maisonette on the edge of Stornoway in the Western Isle of Lewis, where they have lived since the death of one of their twin sons twenty years ago. Stan has a deep connection with the island that was his latter-childhood and adolescent home. He thinks of it entirely fondly. But he has no need to go there. Since returning to attend university, and including those before his brother died, Stan has lived on the mainland for sixteen years now, while on the island only eleven. Balance has shifted. Stan is a city man now and the journey is a nuisance.

'And collect me at midnight, aye,' he says.

'Away'n boil yir heid! How can yie no get a taxi? In fact, if yie can buy such a big house, how can yie no buy a car?'

'I cannae afford a taxi, Dave, never mind a car. Anyway, think of the environment. Think of the ozone layer. Think of yir daughter's future!'

'Charlie, can yie no get him? Help me oot here. Yie'll just be finished yir work then, eh?'

'Dinnae inveigle me,' Charlie sniffs. Her hairstyle is uncomfortable, pulling on her scalp, but there is nothing to be done about it now.

'How old will Archie be tomorrow?' Dave asks, resigned.

'Fifty-three,' Stan wonders. 'It's difficult to believe. I can remember when he turned thirty-three and he was an auld man then.'

'Ho! Watch yir mouth, sunshine.' *Dave* is thirty-three. 'Did yie buy him something good?'

'Did you buy him anything at all?' Charlie furthers.

'Flying lessons.'

'Wow.' Dave is impressed. 'That's an excellent present.'

'Aye, I ken.' Stan is nonchalant. 'That's how I'm so skint. I'll be eating cauld porridge for a month.'

As Charlie pots the final yellow ball and without hesitation the black, the singer ends her cover to a brief flurry of applause and begins a faster number, louder, stamping her foot in time. Stan racks his unused cue.

Larry arrives with a creamy pint of 80/- and a martini, and smiling at Stan, perches herself on Dave's knee.

'Is that yir mobile phone I can feel throbbing?' she asks.

'I havnae got a mobile.' Dave takes his pint. 'Howz it gaun?'

'Gaun fine, Dave. The usual bother of lap dancing, fighting wae the Working Families' Tax Credit people, my mother's pish, Ruby's faither's pish, general pish and Christmas. Yirsel?'

'Aye, top form, sweetheart. I've come oot the night to look after the bairn.' By a nod of his head Dave indicates Stan. 'Yie ken the bother he gets into when he's by himsel.'

'I ken well enough.' Larry gives purposeful eyes to Stan, handing him his gin martini. Stan is very specific about his drinks. He likes one part dry martini added to two and a half parts Bombay Sapphire gin with neither fruit slices nor ice, in a wide, stemmed glass. Needless to say, Larry's is just right.

'Thanks,' he says, trying not to encourage her.

Charlie is still picking at her hair, now entirely regretful of the endeavour. She rubs blue pool chalk from her left-hand fingers but has less success with the black stain on her right thumb and index finger from crumbling hash. Larry gives her only a cursory glace. Indeed, just as Charlie settles, Larry stands up, but not before she passes a cigarette paper wrapped around a small column of pills to Dave, reminiscent to Charlie of a packet of Parma Violets.

'Larry, I'm sorry yie huv tae work,' Dave says.

'Well, yie ken where I'll be for a freebie.' Larry says this to Dave but she is looking at Stan. And then to everyone: 'Have a guid night, folks.' Over her shoulder, she adds:

'Dave?'

'Aye, Larry?'

'I like yir suit, man, but it's no as nice as yir new foot.'

Beaming from ear to ear, Dave hits Stan square between the eyes with a pistachio and declares as less option than fact:

'We'll invite Larry and Ruby for Christmas dinner, eh?'

Stan becomes livid. 'But yie've just hud a fuckin go at me cause there willnae be enough room!'

'Auch, Hume,' Dave sighs, wearily, like a father speaking to a demanding child, 'gonnae no be such a sourpuss, eh?'

Twenty minutes later the three occupy a corner table in the Waterhole on Leith Shore. The restaurant is owned by Charlie's sous-chef, Viola, and her husband, Alfredo, and is a world away from both the Doonhaimer and Reserve in its style, hitting a happy, calm and civilised medium. The meal is enormous and excellent; platters of meatballs, marinated pork, octopus, sardines, rice and pasta that Charlie devours with a vigorous appetite, rolling her eyes to Dave as the waitress repeatedly makes blatant eyes at Stan. For an hour and a half they eat, talk, share stories and laugh riotously as only close friends can. The conversation invariably returns to the Christmas family party.

After the coffee - Stan has lemon tea - Dave turns his attention subtly to Larry's drugs. Not only an experienced narcotic user, Dave is in fact a qualified chemical engineer. He received his diploma from Glasgow University twelve years ago.

Methylenedioxymethamphetamine in Ecstasy, a manmade hallucinogenic stimulant developed in 1913 as an appetite suppressant and later used extensively in psychotherapy, derives from the amphetamine family. The drug produces prolonged and overwhelming hours of euphoria for less than the cost of a pint of beer, depending on the supplier, by increasing serotonin production in the brain and blocking its reabsorption. Although Executive statistics wrongly estimate the figure significantly lower, well over a million Scots swallow an Ecstasy pill at least once every weekend, causing an average single biannual death. Often said of the drug, as is often said of all drugs, and indeed almost all marketable commodities, is that it is not what it once was. This is certainly true. Made in clandestine laboratories that are always keen to cut manufacturing costs, Ecstasy pills are typically supplemented with dust, talcum powder, aspirin, chalk, salt or even washing detergent.

Across the years however, Larry has earned Dave's full assurance, and a quick, sly glance tells him all he needs to know. Larry's pills come from Amsterdam and consist of a pure white, densely packed powder, defined by hard edges and an intricately engraved dove logo. To expect further reassurance of any Ecstasy pill is naïve and foolish.

He crunches the tablet between his teeth to increase its surface area and therefore the initial high, washing down the powder with beer, all the while watched by Stan, who does not take drugs.

Charlie is hesitant. The input of chemicals into the body is not a subject about which she is ignorant. Food, after all, is the worst culprit of all.

Life, and therefore most food, is composed of molecules that in turn are constructed of atoms. Powerful ionic forces link atoms in the same molecule together firmly, while the forces between two neighbouring molecules are less strong. When ice is heated, the energy of the heat weakens the links between the water molecules, thus creating a liquid where, although still forming a coherent mass, the molecules are not held together. Similarly, boiled water evaporates because the heat energy is enough to sever the neighbouring molecules completely. The transformation, therefore, is physical and not chemical. Each molecule, a single atom of oxygen linked to two atoms of hydrogen, is still a water molecule.

However, most cooking ingredients are not so simple, and cooking requires a mix of ingredients. The most common cooking reaction is the Maillard reaction, named after the chemical engineer who documented it early in the twentieth century, which is central to the development of colour, aroma, flavour and texture of cooked foods, in essence creating the brown colour that occurs when food is sautéed in oil. When heating food to even a moderate temperature, molecules collide and by haphazard reactions between sugars and amino acids or proteins eventually form divalent bonding, creating altogether new substances. A baked potato, for example, can produce over four hundred and fifty new molecules. Those in cheese, with a highly intricate biochemical structure, combine with themselves in a multitude of ways when heated, but cheese and potato cooked together - hardly sophisticated cookery - produce tens of thousands of 'new' reactions.

Maillard hoped to recreate these new chemicals artificially for industrial kitchen use and so began the work of proving that there would be no detriment to human health. In fact, he proved quite the opposite. Maillard was able to isolate only fifty 'new' molecules and many turned out to be peroxidizing, antioxidizing, toxic and even mutagenic, meaning liable to damage cell nuclei and prompt cancer. He then abandoned his work.

Used in every kitchen in the world, the Maillard reaction effectively creates endless chains of ketones, esters, aldehydes, ethers and volatile alcohols that are innumerable and still unfamiliar. More than once it has been suggested that the development of diabetic complications, inflammatory processes linked to neurodegenerative diseases, and the acceleration of the aging process are direct consequences.

Charlie grinds the whole Ecstasy pill twice between her teeth and swallows the bitter residue dry, forcing herself not to gag.

She comes up - one of the many idioms used to describe the initial high from an ecstasy pill - in a black taxi heading into town on Regent Road. It happens, although the sense of anticipation is lost across the years, furiously, like an orgasm. Ignoring the grandstand view of the Old Town over the edge of Calton Hill, she closes her green and blue painted eyes, floating, and a thin smile forms on her lips. She sorts through the symphony of audible sound and isolates that of the taxi's tyres on the road, like a cat purring.

Stan has the fold-down seat opposite Charlie and Dave, hand clasped on his lap, olive eyes fixed out the window towards the unoccupied Royal High School of Edinburgh, which, based several years post-enlightenment and somewhat loosely by Thomas Hamilton on the ancient Athenian Temple of Theseus, is a particularly gloomy building, an obsolete heirloom. His expression portrays concern. From his duffle coat, he produces a packet of Polo mints and offers them around. Wide-eyed, Dave takes one eagerly, but Stan has to place one in Charlie's hand for her to notice.

'Stan, do you still want that furniture account on Monday?' Dave asks.

Stan appears to choke, glancing quickly to Charlie, and then nodding, gives Dave the evil eye.

Down Waterloo, over Regent Bridge and on past the Royal Academy's Degas café scenes exhibition the taxi races, skilfully avoiding the death-wish drunks and the traffic lights. There is no conversation, only a comfortable, eager stillness.

The mint refreshes Charlie's palette. She listens rapt to the powerful diesel engine beneath her, climbing in revs as the driver downshifts to accelerate past slow-movers.

Finally, at the taxi rank outside the Caledonian-Hilton Hotel they disembark into the frosty night. Leaving Stan to pay the driver, Charlie leads the way, unbuttoning her duffle coat, heels clicking across the night. Stan swallows the cough of the traffic fumes and watches Dave follow her lead towards the curved structure of the Rutland Bar.

Around the corner, wedged in a dark nook between the Rutland Bar and the first building in the terrace of Shandwick Place, in a particularly beautiful structure used previously as both a church and a casino, the entrance to the nightclub Hubba Bubba is little more than a door guarded by four mountainous fellows in black. Despite the long, freezing queue, Dave talks with one of the stewards, sharing a laugh, and as the door opens, a brief flare of house music marks his disappearance. Charlie is already inside.

Still at the taxi rank, Stan sees nothing of this. Suddenly he is not so eager to follow. He lingers, enjoying the fresh nip in the air, his breath crystallising. After ten years in the city he has not yet begun to take it for granted. The old and new coalesce around him, the elegant, the gauche and the plainly brutal. The dapper door-attendants of the red-stone Caledonian-Hilton set against the grey, semi-gothic of St John's, the sharp steeple of St Cuthbert's and the majesty of Castle Rock contrast sharply with the scaffold-covered Frazer's building, itself an unattractive 1930s monster, the beggars in every visible crevice, and the hordes of falling-over drunks. People are brawling up on Lothian Road. Such is the city of Edinburgh. Such, Stan tells himself, is society.

He remains. Beyond the nerves, he feels suddenly Christmassy. Naturally, nostalgia follows. He thinks of his family, his parents and sister whom he will see tomorrow, and his heart fills. But mostly, Stan thinks of his twin brother, Henry.

Although the twins were only young children when Henry died, Stan has several vivid memories of his brother. One such image is of Henry standing exactly where Stan stands now, out on a cold expedition with himself and their father for a Christmas gift for their mother in 1983. After what felt like an age to Stan, a simple piece of marbled glass from Jenner's was finally selected and suitably wrapped in crêpe paper. But Henry would not live to see the paper opened. Henry's twenty-year anniversary occurs on December eighteenth, Thursday coming.

Stan crunches the last of his Polo mint and a different thought comes to him. Past the elegant dome of Register House, Rose and Stuart Mackenzie are drinking wine with the First Minister in Bute House, and Stan wonders with a grin if he should go and knock, presenting himself as a friend of the Mackenzie's and a descendant of the great David Hume. But there is no time for such nonsense. There is a job of work to do. Summoning his wits, moving one foot in front of the other, he bids the Hotel doormen a cheerful Good Evening as he passes.

Hubba Bubba's interior is labyrinth-like and mostly underground. Past the initial lobby, cloakroom and the first of the bars, snaking downward passages lead to different rooms and dance floors, each styled individually, in deep woods, in industrial steel, in plastic, in velvet. Deep underground, the principal auditorium holds around a hundred and fifty dancers. Laser lights cut through dry ice, reflecting back from an enormous glitter-ball. Huge visual projection screens display bizarre and colourful imagery.

Charlie moves anonymously in the heaving crowd with an icy flute of fizzy Irn Bru. Without her coat she enjoys her dress, its revealing, clinging nature, its softness against her skin. The fact that she is not wearing pants significantly increases the sensation. Indeed, her chemical amplified senses run amok, drawing her into a tangle of sounds, colours and smells.

Moving in the crowd, she feels the usual resentful glares of women, to which she is much accustomed, although tonight it is less a matter of personal achievement than simple appearance. As the only cook in Scotland to have achieved two Michelin stars, Charlie has also attained, whether she likes it or not, a fair degree of celebrity. Only last month she appeared in a four-page article in the Scotsman's Spectrum magazine, featuring several beautiful black and white photographs that hid the paleness of her skin and the contrast with her hair. Tonight, however, with her distinctive mass of curls moulded away, her dress and her distracting make up, Charlie is all but unrecognisable. For a refreshing change the indignant looks are not personal.

Charlie loves to dance, but it is not a thing she does often. Nor is it an innate talent; Charlie is by nature clumsy and shy. She remedied this years ago by attending Wednesday dance classes until work commitments interfered, and she can now waltz, jive, tango and salsa with confident precision. Of course, a man is necessary. And one is at hand. He is large, dark and muscular, Mediterranean perhaps, two or three years her senior and already engaged with a blonde woman. But he allows himself to be led. He has little say in the matter.

To the booming house music, he and Charlie thrust and heave without spilling their drinks. He matches Charlie steps, often mimicking her. But in the hazy, sexual funk of the moment, it does not take him long to understand who is leading who.

The old ex-church, as Stan descends through its narrow bowels, affords just as much interest to him as his destination. He marvels at elaborately carved stonework, which as it never did in its own day shakes with a pulse, a growing heartbeat, and seems to reverberate with the roar of an ocean.

Pressing deeper into the din, past billposters and Coca Cola crates, the smell of mouldering beer is overpowering. Soon there are other people in the corridors, all in uniform, some speaking to Stan, or rather at him. One person, an undernourished young woman wearing black and a microphone headset, exchanges his coat for a tasty-looking gin martini.

The last corridor Stan travels alone, arriving finally upon a door with a carved Gothic arch. There he waits, sipping his drink under a cold blue wash of light. An image is visible on the stone wall. Done in two colours of thick chalk, distorted, twisted through planes and angles, the drawing is of an elderly couple waltzing. Both figures, in cubist fashion, share a single head. But there are two smiles.

The pounding music lessens, diminishing to little more than a hypnotic drumbeat. The sound of the ocean fades to the recognisable roar of a crowd, which in itself fades to an anticipating silence.

Now, a thought occurs to Stan, unsought and unappreciated, barging into his mind, removing all others. His forehead creases, his eyes narrow. He tries to push the thought away but it resists, growing in clarity, round and round and round, dizzyingly:

Did you feed the fish?

But there is not time to consider, because then, in the silence, quite without warning, a blasting chorus, Carl Orff's *O Fortuna*, nearly shakes the building apart. Only the introductory, recognisable refrain plays however, and an absolute, sudden and eerie silence follows, pierced only by a few whistles and screams.

And at this point, after brushing a few cat hairs from his corduroys, Stan steps under the Gothic arch and slips into blinding light.

He has always enjoyed entertaining. Primary school dramatics led to high school rock bands that in turn led to Stan Hume in his seventeenth year - his last on the Isle - compeering the annual Stornoway Christmas charity concert, an honour usually reserved for an older, more deserving Islander. But Stan had been a tremendous success, well rehearsed, relaxed, engaging and with a confident sense of wit that both astonished and frightened his parents.

Study replaced entertaining upon relocation to Edinburgh, except for a brief spell as a theatre producer. His first set of turntables and at the same time the initial idea of being a DJ came to him less than eight months ago as a birthday gift from Charlie.

The crowd roar is thunderous, like a crashing wave. Stan climbs hazardously onto the ledge of the high DJ booth, further rousing the throng below and a few drops of martini fall over the edge. After a moment of basking in his personal ocean, nerves completely eliminated, Stan settles down, slips on enclosing headphones, selects a pair of records from the rack and with a gentle touch, the crowd already forgotten, he begins his work.

'I wasnae sure if I was supposed tae call her Your Majesty or Your Highness or what the fuck,' Charlie says, exhaling tainted smoke, 'so I just called her ma'am. She seemed tae like that.'

Looking into an estate agent's window on Shandwick Place, Dave and Charlie openly share a marijuana cigarette. Set against the drunken, brawling, screaming ambience they are the most inconspicuous souls on the street. Two police officers walk right past, offering friendly smiles.

'What was she like?' Dave asks.

Charlie considers the question and after a final toke of the joint, passing it to him, answers:

'Superfluous. Me and one other guy cooked her dinner and then it took three times as many people to serve her it.'

'Yie'll mibbae get a medal next year for service to the royal palette.'

This is not likely, considering Charlie's criminal record. She picks at her hair and scoffs:

'If I do, you and Stan can go to collect it.'

'She'd like me, the Queen,' Dave smiles, his perfect white teeth set in a black face. 'I'd remind her of Empire.' He inhales harsh smoke. 'Listen, what time's Stan's flight in the morning? He'll blame me if he misses it.'

'Nine.'

'Flying at nine?'

'No, check-in at nine. Gate Three. He cannae be late, Dave. It's the only flight to Stornoway the whole day. Come into the restaurant afterwards and I'll cook yie lunch.'

'Nice one.' Dave passes back the joint.

The cold air up Charlie's skirt makes her want to pee. Ecstasy generally encourages production of an anti-diuretic hormone that prevents the excretion of urine, but the fact remains that Charlie wants to pee. An Ecstasy high, in fact, makes the sensation of passing water somewhat pleasant.

She exhales, watching Dave admire his new prosthesis. While he is not to her own personal taste, it is undeniable that he is a fine looking man, physically and mentally rounded. His presence inspires trust and comfort. He wears his usual smile. Satisfied with his new foot, he retrieves the Ecstasy pills from his wallet.

'Want one of these? I got us two each,' he says. 'Might as well. It's Christmas, after all. Near enough anyway.'

'I will, but no just the now, thanks.' From inside her bra, Charlie retrieves a paper-wrap of flaky white powder. 'I admit that my Christmas spirit's been sorely lacking, Dave,' she explains, 'so I've brought this as an early Christmas present. It's such a long time since yie've come out wae us. I didnae bring my purse. Go'n gimme two credit cards, eh?'

The pleasant surprise of the cocaine leaves Dave quickly. His sleepy eyes open wide in mounting horror. 'Yie're no gonna dae that on the street, are yie?'

'Watch me.'

Extracted from the leaves of the Erythroxyloa Coca shrub, cocaine is a heterocyclic alkaloid that, when snorted, produces an intense twenty-minute high. Although Queen Victoria praised the properties of the substance, found then in the form of Vin Martini, a tipple to which even the Pope was partial, possession today could result in a term at Queen Elizabeth's pleasure.

Just as soon as Dave hands over his Platinum Barclay Card and his Organ Donor card, Charlie does indeed prepare the cocaine on the street, at least in the enclave of the shop doorway, blocked from the wind and from prying eyes by Dave's large and slightly nervous frame.

He spends the time perusing the estate agent's window. Property interests him, but only peripherally. He has no intention of flitting or buying a house ever again, at least not in the present seller's market. He lives in the basement flat on Leith Links he bought after his separation in 1995, for which he paid £84,500, when house prices were if not reasonable then not unreasonable. Now, the flat is worth £145,000. More amazingly, the semi-detached house he and his wife bought in 1993 has since nearly tripled. His eyes move over the panels of house particulars with detachment and he smiles in wonder, exhaling smoke into the cold night air.

He thinks of Stan's new house, feeling an unexpected rush of pride that he has finally moved out of his nasty rented, shared flat and bought a house, even if he did get a little help along the way.

They snort one large line each with a straw Charlie procured and cut earlier in the club. They lick a credit card each clean and Charlie puts the wrap back into her bra.

'Speaking of Christmas,' Dave says, wiping his nose, 'have you spoken to yir mother yet?'

'I have not,' Charlie states.

'Shall we just assume she'll come? She is yir mother, Charlie.'

'Ah, but that isnae to say she'll want tae see me.'

'When exactly was the last time yie did see her?'

'When I had my wisdom teeth out in January, which was the tenth time in the last ten years.'

'I wish I could say the same,' Dave signs. 'I've seen my mine eleven times this week. But yie'll phone yir Ma the morra, eh?'

Charlie mutters assent and presses gentle on her blue-green eyelids.

'Good. I like your dress, by the way. And I like your hair.' Dave smiles knowingly. 'Yie'd hardly ken it was you. Stan's in fine tune the night, d'yie no think?'

'I hadnae really noticed.'

'Want tae hear a joke, Charlotte?'

The irritating use of her given name narrows Charlie's eyes with suspicion. 'Go on.'

'Two ship-wrecked Scots,' he explains, 'Jock and Jim, had been clinging to the remains of their upturned boat for about twenty-seven hours in the middle of the North Sea. They were fishing, eh? It was a good idea at the time, but the weather had turned and the storm had all but sunk them. They were soaked. They were exhausted and starving and were both about to reach the end of their tethers.'

Charlie, whose father did drown at the hands of the unforgiving sea, sucks deeply on the joint.

'Jock had been for most of his life a wild lout, and realising that he now was most likely fucked began to recount his past misdeeds to Jim, and perhaps to God, and vowed that, should he be rescued, he would lead from then on an entirely different life. Clean, faithful and sober.' Dave pauses as he accepts the joint and tokes. 'When he was finished, Jock felt much relieved, but was surprised when, in a pale and engaging face, Jim turned to him and said:

'Haud on, Jock. Dinnae commit yirsel too soon!'

Charlie becomes livid. 'What the fuck's that supposed tae mean?' she snarls.

Dave merely smiles, easy and comfortable.

Try as he might, Stan can never fully lose himself in the business of mixing records. There is no spiritual detachment. He remains throughout the consummate technician, monitoring, executing and calculating with objectivity.

Rather than the customary twin-deck set up, he prefers to use three record decks because while he plays a great deal of new house, funk and hip-hop music, he also enjoys using older tunes that more often than not have weaker bass tones. The third deck allows him to underscore these tracks with independent drums and bass, leaving a deck free for the next tune. He employs this trick now:

As The Street's full-bodied *Has It Come To This?* nears completion, or more specifically reaches the point when Stan loses interest in it, he lines up on the second deck his next track, Nina Simone's *Funkier than a Mosquito's Tweeter*, and on the third deck an underlying bass track that he suspects will fit perfectly, both rhythmically and with tone. An exact beats-per-minute union with The Street's is essential for a smooth cross fade, and Stan achieves this in earphones before incorporating the new elements through the front-of-house amplifiers that control two-kilowatt bass woofers, sub-bass, midrange and tweeter speakers throughout the various rooms and levels of Hubba Bubba. Both the transition and the new blend are flawless, and Stan allows himself a small smile at the effort. Where the flow is going from here however, he has no idea. The endless possibilities and opportunities of creating a non-stop flow of music are as much a part of the joy for him as the actual implementation.

The only distraction is the cache of cigarette smoke in the club that rises to and lingers in the DJ booth. Air extractors and the booth's own osculating fan provide little reduction. Nicotine in tobacco, a poisonous alkaloid commonly used as insecticide, costs the National Health Service in Scotland over two hundred million pounds annually and is in terms of physical detriment simply incalculable. Regarding the recent Irish ban on smoking in public places, Stan is confident in his mind that Scotland will soon follow suit.

He feels a nip on his bum - another distraction - and turns to see Julie, Hubba Bubba's resident DJ smiling mischievously, leaning casually against the door frame.

'Stan the man,' she says above the music. 'Soundin guid. Lookin pretty guid, tae.'

The commas around Stan's mouth deepen into an unintentionally suave smile. 'No by comparison, Jules.'

In jeans and a revealing vest, despite the fact that she is ten years Stan's senior and steaming drunk, Jules certainly does look good, almost exactly like Shirley Manson. In her calmer moments away from the club, away from the scene, Julie is a self-employed cabinetmaker, although decidedly less so of late. She is the author of both the handsome coffee table than stands in Stan's new house and the curved rosewood one in Charlie's home, and she has come up to the booth for no other reason than to lay her eyes on Stan. Her lustful intention is obvious and without guilt. Recently separated from her long-term partner, Jules came to promiscuity late in life, but is endeavouring to make up for lost time.

'Plans for later?'

'I'd love tae,' Stan says, not entirely truthfully, but not completely against the notion either. 'But I need tae be up early in the morning. I'm flying tae Stornoway.'

'I'll get yie up, Stan the man, dinnae worry about that.'

'I'm sure yie would, aye.' He smiles. 'But I must decline, Jules. I need my beauty sleep.'

Jules takes rejection well. Maybe she is becoming accustomed to it. Maybe she is numb from drugs. 'Nae bother,' she winks.

After the interruption Stan tunes back into his music just in time to lift the needle on Nina Simone and drop in a track by Röyksopp with skilful and intended abruptness, which has the double function of increasing the tempo slightly and lifting the overall tone. He has unconsciously developed the habit, in this his fourth professional engagement, of pouting his lips a bit like a young Mick Jagger.

Dark and discreet, Hubba Bubba's private lounge is full to capacity. Visibility is low within, but from the balcony Charlie can look down clearly over the club's two lower levels. She sees amongst the crowd Dave dancing with a leggy blonde. From the lofty height she even looks down on the booth, where Stan's head bobs with his beat almost crudely. His composition has mellowed to a rich bass groove set against loose acoustic drums, headed by an intoxicating and melancholic female Arabic voice.

Charlie is waiting. Underneath the lounge's psychedelic lights, her drug-enhanced grey eyes collect and then refract all the colours of the spectrum. Her pale skin appears white. She curls her fingers around her Irn Bru flute, enjoying its coldness.

Then it happens. Like ink into water, the work crowd spill into the club. This is not to say staff specifically from Reserve but rather a flock of assorted restaurant workers from shops all across the New and Old Towns, East and West End's and Stockbridge, some fifty individuals bulking out the already tight crowd. Many of the trade's younger managers, chefs and cooks gather for their weekly binge - most do it more than once a week - fashioning the Edinburgh culinary underbelly. In ten years time the same faces will be the establishment. Still in her lilac Gucci suit, Fanny the maître dances with Escudo, Oloroso's new barman. Tony dances with Lazio's sous chef, Frieda, one of his current girlfriends. Usually competing enemies mingle freely, fighting only over who should buy the drinks. None mix with civilians. And in their midst, the group's elected leader, Gavin, thrives in his element.

Charlie studies her manager closely, expectantly. After working the entire day, seventeen straight hours with neither sufficient rest nor nourishment, he remains presentable, apparently having survived a night with Vincent admirably well. His raven-black hair looks clean and shiny, and thick stubble does him no ill. As always, his attire is immaculate, his waistcoat still fully buttoned. He moves through the crowd, shaking hands.

Finally, Charlie watches him buy a large glass of wine and then wince at its cheap taste. After a deep gulp, he slips effortlessly through the crowd to perform his final duty of the day.

Hubba Bubba's head of security, Amy, a pretty woman who seems tame but is not, staffs the staircase leaning up to the club's second and third levels, the third being the private lounge, her eyes trained on the heaving crowd of bodies like a lion staking gazelle. But Gavin distracts her in a second. She

turns on him with puppy-eyes. Their conversation is brief, its gist relayed to security staff throughout the building by means of a concealed microphone hidden up Amy's sleeve and is followed by a great deal of finger pointing by the security staff. The essence of the message is simple:
Tom shall not get near the stairs.
Alison Gorry, Charlie believes, must feel less sneaky.
However, this is only a precaution. Known and liked in the restaurant underbelly, the Australian is tonight a mess, his muscular torso supported by his friends, all of whom live in the same East End hostel and all regard Tom as a kind of God. Blond curls escape from below his beanie hat. His eyeballs are different sizes from drugs. His jaws grind.
Lifting her professional nose, Charlie smells Evelyn's aniseed scent even before she turns. She wears ripped jeans and a grungy top, looking tough and lean, and is much younger than Charlie is accustomed to in a lover. She is certainly appetizing. More than Evelyn's eyes now, her entire body seems to be that of a cold marble statue. Oval face set at an angle, her pouting expression is nothing short of decadent.
Charlie moves from the balcony and the women entwine harshly in darkness tinged by red and green flashes of light. Cigarette smoke trapped at the top of the building creates a haze. They press tightly against each other and delay the kiss until finally the moment is spine tingling. Evelyn has to bend her trembling knees slightly to reach her Charlie's mouth, and as she does, Charlie bites her glossed lip. She feels fingers moving down her back towards the strap of her thong.
'Rip them,' the Australian pants. 'Tear the fuckers off.'
With a spellbinding green-blue blink, Charlie says:
'Not here.'
'Don't tease.' This comes through clenched teeth. Evelyn's fingernails, like talons, break the skin of Charlie's arm. 'Do it. Please. I've waited for this... waited so...'
'I have a surprise.'
As if on cue, Stan's music changes, darkening, swelling, and altering the very air. Leading the mix is Jimi Hendrix's guitar solo from *All Along the Watchtower*, the wah-wah after the slide. And only now, Evelyn realises that in their solitude, she and Charlie are not alone. A genuine and delicious fright lights her eyes. Intrigue soon replaces it.
With twenty minutes to spare before starting her second job, and keen not to waist time, Larry steps from the shadows and slides her arms around Charlie's tiny waist, her shorn head reflective, her smile seductive.
There is no need of explanation. Evelyn has an instinct for such things, young though she is. She responds sharply, as she has been taught to do.
'Yes, chef.'

Stan realises as he manipulates Eminem into the Average White Band that his mobile telephone is vibrating. This is surprising on two accounts. Firstly, he had not intended to bring his phone tonight but realises now that as small and flat as it is, he simply had not noticed it in the back pocket of his corduroys. Secondly, and more pressingly, a glance at his watch reveals the time to be just approaching a quarter to two in the morning. Curious, flipping the phone open, he recognizes the caller ID immediately and his heart rate increases. He answers, shouting into the phone over the omnipresent sound with no trace of an Edinburgh accent:

'Doris!'

'Stan, I can hardly hear you! What's that hellish racket?'

'I'm in a club, mum. What's the matter?'

'Nothing's the matter.'

'But it's the middle of the night! Shouldn't you be in your bed?'

'Cheeky swine. I just got in from an Ann Summers party. Everything is blissfully quiet here. Your father, who is fifty-three now by the way, is sleeping on the couch, and your wee sister I presume is in her bed. I knew you'd still be up, though, and I was right.'

'Ann Summers?' Stan drops a Gene Krupa drum track into the mix.

'Don't sound so horrified, oh fruit of my womb.'

'And did you buy anything nice?' Stan asks, wishing for the life of him that he had not.

'Aye, just a wee something for your Da's birthday. Is that the Average White Band?'

Stan props the phone between his ear and shoulder, and rifling through the vinyl collection, looks down over the full club. 'It is.'

'I like them.'

'I know, mum. Listen…'

'Ah, cramping your style, am I, son? I shant keep you. I only want to know what time your flight arrives tomorrow. Dad wants to come and collect you.'

'It's only half a mile. I'll walk.'

'Stan, he misses you,' Doris says. 'Humour him.'

In the club toilets, resting her left foot on the bowl, Charlie stands in the cubical at ninety degrees to the usual angle, her spine straight, one thigh lifted onto the bowl as she would to insert a tampon, her new dress raised to her hips. She smokes a joint, drawing deeply, holding the smoke in her body for long periods before slowly releasing it. Brow knit, painted eyelids shut, she sips Irn Bru to wet her dry throat.

On her knees, Evelyn laps at Charlie's clitoris like a kitten, one finger inside the tight, tiny opening, her free hand exploring the raised leg. She is still something of a beginner at such things and acts with particular tenderness. Larry, however, is less gentle. Squat behind Charlie, her tongue attacks the anus with vigour, probing and delving. One of her hands teases Evelyn, the other herself. A glass of wine lies spilt at her knees on the unclean cubical floor.

Charlie exhales. The cliché of the situation - the three of them high on drugs, hiding in a toilet, swathed in indignity and shameful lies - is delicious to her and this only adds to the pleasure, as does the blunted vibration of Stan.

She lifts her chin, restraining herself, which only increases the sensations, and as the orgasm comes, almost without sound, Charlie cannot help but smile fully.

5

As night fell across the apartment, casting angular shadows, Alison lay in the bath, sipping rum. The water was cold and red.

She was waiting for the pain to release her, waiting to be plenty enough drunk, waiting to forget. With her eyes open she saw Madeleine hanging against the cold stone of the church and hoped against hope that her friend was dead before they strung her up. With her eyes closed Alison saw her own dead husband and her stillborn child. She did not think at all of the man who she had slain less than an hour ago, whose blood in which she lay.

When the tears came finally, in an uncontrollable flood, bringing no release at all, they were tears for neither Madeleine nor John, nor Franz Wetzler, nor even for the late Édith Thiéry…

Focus is impossible. Charlie lifts her exaggerated eyes to her own reflected gaze. In her soft kimono, and with her hair still up, she is brushing her teeth vigorously. Brutal is the comedown. The dull throb of lethargy, perhaps apathy, that follows so lush a forest of sensation is disorientating. Her reflection, distanced by drugs and an unusual hairstyle, seems alien, so she releases the restraints and her scarlet curls bounce immediately back into their natural shape, smelling of smoke, all the more wiry and wilful for an evening constrained. She is freezing cold.

Filled with plants, Charlie bathroom is jade green with white tiles, a high ceiling, ornate cornice and a claw-foot bath, upon the edge of which Snoopy sits, captivated by silhouetted snowflakes in the red stained glass window, poised to pounce.

In mid-nineteenth-century France, a small group of Parisians left their homes to take up residence, at least for a while, in the rural village of Barbizon. Their aim as painters, though they shared no particular values other than the abandonment of their academic tradition, was to attempt a *truer* representation of nature seen through a *less tainted* state of mind. The leader of the group was Théodore Rousseau, and his *Oak Trees in the Gorge of Apremont* hang on Charlie's wall, smartly framed in wood and glass. Although not original, nor is the work a printed reproduction, but rather a lustrous and exact oil rendering.

Charlie spits foam, rinses, and squeezing a precise line of fresh smokers' toothpaste from the tube, begins the process a second time. Charlie is very careful about the appearance of her pearly white teeth, although not through resolve; oral hygiene is a matter of nature to her, engrained in her subconscious by her lifelong dentist, Dr Elizabeth M. Brown B.D.S., who is also her mother, her only living kin. Yet despite this, since the painful procedure to remove her wisdom teeth at the start of the year, a damaged molar on her top left of her mouth has been shamefully neglected. The tooth has become little more than a shell that Charlie imagines black and repulsive.

Her thoughts involuntarily turn to her kitchen. Not that she is hungry. Ecstasy annihilates appetite, locking the stomach at the very notion. Rather, the particulars and practicalities of tomorrow's day of work, beginning in less than seven hours, reel unstoppably through her mind. She wonders if Vincent and Viola managed not to kill each other tonight, and if the kitchen was cleaned properly. She wonders how much stock is left.

Even with a mouthful of minty foam, Charlie can still taste Evelyn, and she is thankful that both she and Tom are off until Monday.

Changing from a backward-forward motion to a circular one, listening to the combined noise of Snoopy's resonate purring and that of Stan and Dave making a pot of tea in the kitchen, sadness blankets over Charlie, and though she is alone, she is forced to curtail her expression. Charlie is often overcome by such a feeling, particularly when tired. Charlie is often tired. She would cry if she could bring herself to.

But the remembrance that there is fresh linen on her bed is enough to ease the moment. Her bed, broken thing that it is, is her private sanctuary, and the thought of slipping into it, if only for six hours, is blissful.

She brushes her tongue hard, spits foam and rinses twice with antibacterial mouthwash.

As a matter of habit a fresh joint waits in a clean porcelain ashtray by the sink. Mindful not to light her hair as well, Charlie swallows the tainted smoke deep inside herself.

She holds the reflected gaze of her own perverted grey eyes. But she has little desire to see. To feel is plenty. She shuts her eyes and pressing firmly on her painted eyelids, smears the paint.

The Last Week

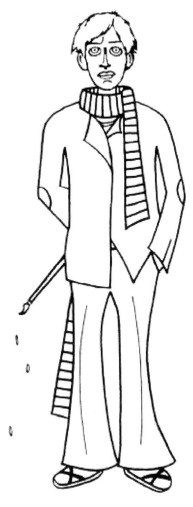

I found that the moral Philosophy transmitted to us by Antiquity, labor'd under the same Inconvenience that has been found in their natural Philosophy, of being entirely Hypothetical, and depending more upon Invention than Experience. Every one consulted his Fancy in erecting Schemes of Virtue and of Happiness, without regarding human Nature, upon which every moral Conclusion must depend.

David Hume

1

Behind his desk, spruce in his customary Harris Tweed office jacket, t-shirt and boot-cut jeans ensemble, and with the unseen benefit of thermal underwear, Stan's appearance deceives. His transparent, olive green eyes, however, which are utterly beyond his control, portray a more accurate and entirely hellish account of his present fettle; at least, they would if not for the fact that distracting thick-rimmed spectacles hide them. Nauseous fever courses through him, stinging like electricity with each breath. Burning, gagging bile lines his throat, tasting of gin martini. He imagines blood vessels bursting inside his brain and expects at any moment a trickle of blood to run from his nose or eyes. Clasped on his lap are his hands to prevent trembling.

Flashes of memory taunt him, abstract imagery trapped like a panicked wasp, bumping and making chaos of stillness. Other than that today is Monday, and that most of the nightmare that was yesterday is still unaccountable, of only one other fact is Stan certain:

Consequences are to be faced.

But more immediately, there is the day to face.

Situated in one of Edinburgh's oldest buildings but vaguely contemporary in design, the open-plan offices of G. W. F. Associates accommodates another twenty-odd drones, all busy on their PCs and telephones, all wearing what appears to Stan exactly the same High Street work suits. There is the dull hum of thirty computers, accompanied by the requisite peripheral clicking. Brand names - Coca Cola, British Airways, Gap, O2, Burberry - fill the room, on mouse mats, mugs, clocks, penholders. The room is a shrine to capitalism.

Checking the time on his thin computer screen against his watch, Stan hopes for a favourable disparity but is disappointed not to find one. 8:36AM. He sucks stale air up his blocked nostrils and resigning himself to the next nine hours and fourteen minutes behind his desk, lets it out again.

Upon his desk, the Scotsman's front page enlightens the nation of a remarkable development in the so-called Worldwide War Against Terror. The United States military has captured Saddam Hussein. The ousted dictator appears in photograph bearded and filthy in an orange prison suit; another features Paul Brenner, US administrator in Iraq, blatantly bragging. Since the Allied occupation of Iraq and the so-called liberation of its people, Stan has had conflicting feelings on the matter. Great-ancestor Hume wrote extensively on the topic of war, taking a variety of stances, but rather than the reasoning of the situation, the belatedly debated 'justifications for war', Stan is more concerned with the practical connotations of the occupation. A friend is presently serving his military rotation in Iraq with the Black Watch regiment and Stan has developed the habit, before devouring the bulk of the news report, of scanning its text for details of suicide bombings and military casualties with a semi-expectant wince.

On page five, below an article about twenty-four-hour drinking that makes Stan's stomach bubble, he finds a small piece concerning the Kyoto Agreement.

The greatest threat in the modern world, and indeed the greatest threat ever to face mankind, Stan Hume believes, is neither poverty, famine, disease, nor terrorism, but rather global warming. The fact of the matter is that modern society is ruining its environment at an unsustainable rate. It is a matter of rape. Since the Industrial Revolution the amount of atmospheric carbon dioxide has increased thirty percent, methane by fifty percent. Predictions suggest that by 2050, the millennia-old balance of the global eco-system will already be altered past the point of no return.

Widespread combustion of fossil fuel is the single largest cause, resulting in a marked increase in the natural Greenhouse Effect that traps solar rays inside the earth's atmosphere, responsible for the melting icecaps, rising sea levels, changing weather patterns and the fact that Alaska is rapidly turning into soup. On this argument all Western World governments concur apart from America, who produces a fifth of all human-produced emissions and still refuses to acknowledge the facts. The world's leading insurance companies predicted recently that climate change - specifically payouts made to people who have lost their houses because of land subsidence - will bankrupt the world economy within three generations. Even Lord Oxburgh, chairman of petroleum world leaders Shell UK, agrees that the situation is calamitous.

The only solution in Stan Hume's opinion, of which his great ancestor would be proud, is a worldwide progression of ideas. Civilisation must hold itself to account for its clumsiness and acknowledge that fossil fuels are simply no longer a viable option for energy production. The mass objections to wind farms in Britain would make Stan smile if not for the sheer stupidity of the situation. It seems that the Brits are more proud of their countryside than of their planet. It is classic small-mindedness, and the fact their children's children will be living in rafts seems to mean nothing. Stan, on the other hand, finds wind turbines particularly beautiful, an excellent marriage of function and the aesthetic. As a teenager on Lewis, he was apt to stand and watch the giant blades turning for hours on end.

Current world events, however, fail to add perspective, and Stan's pain remains, toothache on a molecular level.

For a while, unable to focus on his newspaper, he watches his workmates work.

Until in an elegant variety of violets, copper hair held to the side, Rose Mackenzie eases onto the corner of his desk, startling Stan into temporary focus. She is, as she always is to Stan, beautiful and elegant, gentle but at the same time hard. She does not immediately engage him but rather allows a moment, inhaling his subtle, sanitary aftershave, her eyes non-specific. When she finally does engage, she looks past Stan's glasses, directly into his deathly eyes.

'Tell me this and tell me no more,' she purrs. 'Was mother pleased to see her wee boy yesterday?'

Stan regresses...

Larry asks the question without judgement and then snorts an eighth of a gram of cocaine off the Doonhaimer's bar-top in one easy sniff. On the next stool, Saturday night's clothes somewhat soiled by this stage of the game, Stan is deeply drunk. Lights are dim, chairs upturned. They are alone in the bar except for Charlie and another man by the pool table, upon whom she is performing oral sex.

'Radge?' Stan smiles bitterly, commas at the corners of his mouth stretching. 'Larry, she'll be furious! I doubt she'll ever fuckin speak to me again. No that my faither'll be up nor doon, mind, and it was his birthday. My mother, though, well...' He scoffs, swallowing a mouthful of martini. 'However, Lorraine, there isnae anything tae be done about that now. Reason demands that we get pished. We did win the quiz, after all.'

'The philosophical Mr Hume!' Larry is not dancing tonight. Her head has a barely-visible halo of stubble. 'Ruby-dooby and I met Dave and Victoria in Harvey Nichols earlier. Dave said yie were excellent last night and that there was some kind of record company scout there, eh?'

'That's right.' Stan drains his martini and from over his shoulder hears a brief and swine-like grunt concluding Charlie's activities. 'But I soon gave the bastard the slip...'

A photocopier flashing repeatedly like a nuclear weapon breaks the reverie. At first, Stan is distrustful of this information, querying its placement within the frail shanty framework of other flashbacks and then reassessing the compete picture within in the context of the new information. His eyes dance in the middle distance as his fingers bind tightly together over his stomach. Producing an audible sound takes several attempts, resulting in a tone that is soft though not gentle, with a sullen reflection though without any attempt to gain sympathy.

'Didnae even phone, Rose. I still havnae. I'm a dreadful son.'

'But yie had a good weekend?' she asks, unsurprised.

'Is there any other kind?'

So half-hearted is Stan's lie that Rose feels something in herself quicken. She regards him, his deathly eyes, his mauve t-shirt bearing the words *Just Dinnae*.

'Want a Polo mint?' she asks. 'Stanley, yie look like yie waged a war, man.'

Feeling the minty freshness sooth both his throat and his stomach, Stan looks up into his benefactor's deep blue eyes. And then, amazingly, as the office hums and buzzes around them, the fog lifts and Stan experiences a moment of absolute clarity. He stiffens slightly.

'You didnae sleep last night,' he observes. 'What's the matter?'

Not often is Rose caught off guard. But she is now. With the exception of her husband, Stan is the only person able to see through her.

'I'm moving to Wales in five days, idiot. I'm retiring. I'm too exited to sleep,' she lies.

'Yie're a liar.'

Her expression hardens. She turns to a nearby window from which, in the beautiful crisp morning, the snow-powdered steeple of the Cathedral rises into the sky, and when she returns her gaze to Stan, it shows pain.

'A child is missing.' Her voice is small. 'Megan is her name and she's ten years old. She vanished from her own garden. That's why Stuart didnae come to the gallery wae us on Saturday morning.'

'Where?' Stan asks.

'Easter Road.'

'Jesus.'

'It'll be on the news tonight. Apparently there isnae another police officer in the whole of Edinburgh capable of dealing with such a thing,' she remarks, 'so Stuart had to give up his weekend off. I dinnae mean to sound uncompassionate, Stan, of course I feel for the parents, but it seems tae me very unfair giving this kind of thing tae a man on his last week on the job. He's already done enough.'

Rose is immediately conscious of the bitterness in her voice. She adds, to ease herself:

'The First Minister said so himself!'

Stan hits his forehead with the palm of his hand, which he immediately regrets as pain reverberates through his entire body.

'Fuck, I'm sorry, I completely forgot. The First Minister! How was it? Tell me all.'

'It was fine.' High praise indeed from Rose. 'Bute House itself was quite disappointing, actually. Stuart and I have nicer paintings. But the First Minister and his wife were lovely. He had all fifty of us hooting and laughing for an hour and only in the last ten minutes did I realise that he was talking about my husband. The food was excellent and I was fabulously drunk.'

Stan lifts an eyebrow. 'Jimmy Choo's?'

Rose pronounces with a sincere triumph:

'Not outdone.'

2

Alone in the kitchen, Tom respectfully examines each cut of the beef delivery with a keen eye, able to tell by the plumy dark flesh and creamy yellow fat that the pair of Galloway beasts yielded for today's consignment were reared lovingly on a purely grass diet, slaughtered at twenty-five months and their carcasses hung for the best part of three weeks. An enthusiastic butcher, and more importantly a chef who before several high-class establishments of Paris and Rome worked in many restaurants during his European travels where the incoming meat was already stiff, rancid and maggot-ridden, Tom handles his delivery with awe and a humbled sense of privilege.

He pays particular attention to his loin. From the lower back of the beast, tenderloin is the most tender and lean portion of a cow's carcass, and the most expensive although not most flavoursome, and may be either cut into steaks of filets mignons or châteaubriands - never to be cooked beyond medium-rare - or left whole to roast. The sirloin, from closer to the beast's rump, gets more exercise and is therefore tougher but slightly more flavourful. Tom inspects several boned small-end rib roasts. Kidneys and livers are vacuum packed separately; Tom uses a great deal of liver to thicken sauces. Veal, his favourite meat, is unfortunately out of season.

The source of the meat, the Logie Farm and game estate with in-house butchery, milking parlour and vacuum packaging facilities, is fast becoming a revered Scottish institution, its reputation for the direct supply of finest organic beef, pork, lamb and game. The Logie does not sell to supermarkets. Nor does it export, although it was recently made an example of the preferred manner in which to humanely harvest meat by the European Union. Today, in addition to the beef, dairy, pre-butchered mutton and a complete pig carcass, there are three dozen cleaned, plucked and trussed corn-fed chickens and a dozen similar ducks. There is boned venison, six skinned and cleaned hares and rabbits, and an assortment of grouse, pigeon, pheasant, turkey and gosling.

Reserve's treatment from the Logie is preferential, Tom's orders personally selected by expert eyes and left at his specific instruction in large slabs for fine butchery onsite. The delivery invoice comes at cost price, without mark-up or handling fees. The reason for this: Vincent Dussollier owns the Logie.

Tom crosses the kitchen to check his breakfast in one of the ovens, but although smelling heavenly it needs a few minutes more. Beginning the business of tidying away the fresh produce delivery, he sings, a decent tenor voice mature and powerful in the arched cellar, imitating fluently the twisting tongue of Edith Piaf:

70

'Non, Jien du rien. Je ne regrette rien…'

He stops abruptly, bashful to find an audience in Charlie. In jeans and a warm, high-necked woolly jumper, her hair tied tightly back, she leans against the kitchen doorframe, listening with ashen stillness. Her pained half-smile of welcome confirms this. Only her glassy, red-rimmed eyes seem animated, and the word that springs into Tom's mind is Vampire.

Without a word, he reaches into one of the tall fridges and pulls out a two-litre plastic bottle. One regional speciality the Australian has come to appreciate, though he had witnessed it before arriving in Scotland without finding the courage to put it in his mouth, is Barr's Irn Bru. Now he is hooked, rarely without the healing amber nectar.

With shaky hands, Charlie accepts the cold bottle, devours half a litre and then, quite disproportionately to her smallness, belches.

'I love yir voice,' she says. 'Yie should sing more. But not so early in the morning, eh? I must say I'm pleased to see yie rested and cheerful after a day off.'

'Ah, there's a good reason for cheer today, brother,' the Australian explains. 'I have favourable fillies. The two-twenty at Musselburgh and possibly a dog race at Ayr are going to make us a fair amount of money this afternoon, which is a very good thing because I'm buying my plane ticket home later today for an arm and a leg, and I haven't bought any Christmas presents yet. And you'd better believe that after four years away my mother will expect something damn impressive! Gimme thirty or forty pounds before noon, chef, if your game?'

Belching again, Charlie lifts her grey eyes. 'Yie ken me.'

In less than a month, Tom is leaving Charlie's employ and his departure is a tiny tragedy in her life, or at least a major nuisance. She is fond of him. But his fizzy ginger across her dry tongue does absolutely nothing to cleanse the phantom aniseed taste of Evelyn, even above last night's salty indiscretion.

Charlie is not without conscience. Remorse often overpowers her. But this is not to say that she is regretful. Guilt, for Charlie, is simply something to be borne. Besides, the memory of Saturday night's activities produce a warm tingle in her that does much to ease her alcohol poisoning, sleep deprivation and guilty feelings.

She is careful not to let her mind wander. Practicalities remain and focus is required. She is certain that at some point this morning Tom will ask why he did not see her at Hubba Bubba on Saturday night as planned, so in her usual frank manner she pre-empts him:

'I didnae see yie at the club on Saturday night? Did yies go somewhere else?'

'Search me.' Tom scratches the heat-rash beneath his blonde curls. 'Ask Gavin. I have no idea. I was pickled by the time we left here and then we swallowed some pills. I was actually about to ask if you'd seen me. Judging by my sore head yesterday I obviously had a good night. Not as good as Eva

71

though. She was sick as a dog yesterday. She puked over the side of Arthur's Seat.'

Charlie smiles thinly. She pushes off the doorframe, crosses the kitchen and as a matter of habit actions the air-vents, the intercom and the computer system. A few minutes she spends snuffling through the fresh seafood delivery.

Because of the irregular and inconsistent supplies of wild fish caused by severe over-fishing, sourcing quality fresh fish is rapidly becoming a nightmare. The intention of the Common Fisheries Policy has been since the beginning of the 1970s to protect the common heritage of fishing by guaranteeing equal access to communal European waters for all European Union members. But even with this year's rewrites, the policy is fatally flawed, permitting a hail of scams that the British consider themselves above. This is nothing new; the Dutch were fishing Scottish waters so heavily by the seventh century that Amsterdam, it was a commonly said, was built upon a foundation of Scottish herringbones. Today, the Common Fisheries Policy's quota system, with its practise of dumping dead fish back into the sea, has rendered several important fish stocks on the verge of collapse, cod the prime example. As more countries join the Union, industry spreads ever thinner and the outlook becomes even glummer. European ministers, in Charlie's' opinion, simply fail to address the blatant possibility that wild fishing may no longer be, as it exists today, a viable industry. Overhaul is essential in the interests of the marine ecosystem rather than those of industry. Charlie, however, bypasses the pantomime and potential disaster of sourcing wild fish in Scotland by obtaining hers from Piscivorous.

Piscivorous is a fish farm like no other in Scotland and possibly Europe entire. Established in 2000 in the extremities of an Aberdeenshire tidal bay, it has pioneered leading technology and practises in the field of humane fish breading and harvesting, offering an ever-increasing selection of fresh or saltwater seafood. Charlie's delivery of seven iced polystyrene crates packed with seaweed consists of halibut, cod, haddock, sea bass, rainbow trout, monkfish, John Dory, salmon, noisettes, sole and herrings, all staring tersely back at her with clear eyes. Roe from a variety of species is included, as are oysters, mussels, lobsters, langoustines and scallops. And as with the Logie meat orders, Reserve's tri-weekly seafood delivery receives preferential treatment at source. Harvested this very morning and then couriered to the restaurant at speed, the stock is of such superior quality that the fish look as if they are not dead at all. The reason for this privilege: Vincent owns Piscivorous.

Finally satisfied, Charlie is about to go and change into her kitchen whites when suddenly she is overcome - positively stuck dumb - by a notion as alien to her as it is consuming:

Breakfast.

Despite the wriggling cold fish in her belly, she craves a poached mackerel fillet with butter sauce. But before she can do anything about it, Tom thrusts a steaming, fragrant plate under her nose, demanding:

'Taste this, chef.'

Charlie's stomach flips. 'What is it?'

'Breakfast. I've made us one each. It's a kinky idea that came to me in a dream last night, or at least some kind of alcohol-induced stupor.'

Sniffing and poking, regarding the offering with half-shut eyes, she says not entirely enthusiastically:

'It's a bridie, Tom.'

'Exactly, chef!' The Australian has developed a powerful and consuming passion, referred to by some as an addiction, for the local delicacy of meat bridies. But his indulgence is not merely for pleasure. It is professional fascination. He intends to make both a reputation and a vast amount of money by means of the humble bridie back in Australia.

Australia.

The notion makes his mouth dry.

Tom has spent four years backpacking, effectively living from a single rucksack. He has seen the Pyramids of Giza, skied the Alps in three different countries, been drenched in a flimsy Norwegian cruiser by the salty spray from a whale's air hole, walked hot coals, butchered a stallion, taken in excess of twenty-thousand digital photographs. He has suffered, sweated and learned and his perception is all the broader for it. Grateful he is for the experience. But the idea is truly wearing thin. Tom's six-month stay in Scotland has been entirely compromised by the endurance of the same broken bunk in his hostel, its communal washroom shared by seventy mixed-sex Americans, Arabs, New Zealanders, Italians, Spaniards, French people and fellow Aussies, all freed entirely from the bounds of civilised behaviour, and all, at least in Tom's personal experience, thieves. He longs to be back home. More specifically, he longs for a home of his own. This is the crux.

Breathlessly, he watches Charlie nibble a small, reluctant bite of his creation, his eyes wide as she chews. The bridies texture is melt-in-the-mouth soft but with a substantial feel. The pastry is crisp, light, not at all oily. The filling, a combination of beef kidneys, oatmeal, onion, carrot and a variety of successful herbs, seasonings and garlic is cooked perfectly, a triumph.

'The secret ingredient,' he says, chewing, 'is…'

'Heart.'

'Yeah! Slow-cooked. You couldn't serve it with a knife and fork, though. It has to be the hands.' He exaggerates this gesture.

'I agree,' she decides 'It delicious. We'll put those on the menu today.'

Tom's eyes grow wide with disbelief. 'Serious?'

'Make fifteen. How much?'

'What d'yie mean, chef?'

'How much, dipshit,' Charlie chews, 'shall we sell them for? Money, Tom.'

'I dunno.'

'Well, why don't yie go and get the invoices and try figuring it out then. But finish yir breakfast first.'

Smiling at the noticeable spring in his step, Charlie devours the rest of her bridie in three easy, satisfying bites, aware that with one effortless compliment, she has made Tom's entire day. Charlie loves to feel benevolent.

But there is more to it. She recognises in her butcher the same determination and curiosity that have made her own career possible, and knowing all too well how difficult it is for an outsider, wishes him nothing but the best. She wants to offer him something for her breakfast, for his fizzy juice, and of course for the fact that she is having an affair with his girlfriend.

'What were you doing up Arthur's seat, Tommy?'

'Eva wanted to go up before we leave.' Tom is already studying the Logie invoice. 'You know what she's like, chef. She's got to try everything possible.'

'I've lived in Edinburgh for ten years now,' Charlie confesses, 'and I've never been up Arthur's Seat.' Neither has she any desire to. But she is unhappy with this statement and adds for balance:

'I've read a lot of Rebus novels, though.'

'What's a Rebus novel, chef?'

3

Marketing campaigns do occur on the Isle of Lewis but are largely redundant. Because the community is small, reports of new products spread like heather by personal communication and consumers are able to compare and judge for themselves which commodities, not unlimited on the island, they consider 'better'. But few communities remain so insular. Choice, in today's consumer society, has never been so time consuming; hence, the need to advertise.

Marketing is the activities that direct the flow of goods and services from the manufacturer to the consumer. The Scotsman newspaper reported recently that the average Scot involuntarily views over two and a half thousand advertisements in a single day, designed by expensive effort to psychologically condition and manipulate the mind. The archetypal industry maxim:

Sell the sizzle, not the steak.

Naturally, fundamentalists preach that marketing is a necessary force in a fair trade marketplace, maintaining low prices by encouraging competition, so eloquently explained by Adam Smith during the years of Enlightenment. Stan Hume, of the Hume's, however, remains dubious, clinging to the old whisper that it is all a ploy by the capitalists.

Despite this, marketing is the manner in which Stan achieves a living. He works for G. W. F. Associates, a New York City based company with offices in Britain, France, Germany and Italy. The Edinburgh office has the least staff, the least number of contracts and the lowest gross profit, but is of all eleven branches the most proportionately profitable. This, of course, in the international community is ascribed to good old-fashioned Scottish miserliness. Not much mentioned is that, in business terms, this means the same thing as good management.

The essence of Stan's daily pains, liaising between manufacturer and customer, he considers akin to those of a restaurant maître d'. His responsibility is to sell something to punters who nine times out of ten have already decided to buy something else. In the face of the classic beef stew, Stan attempts to shift the fish pie. His is a paperwork job. He has no interest in the visual side of the business. G. W. F. Associates has an in-house creative department of five designers who rarely come out from their dull, slightly smelly office into the natural light, grieved to leave their beloved Apple computers for any length of time. Besides, he considers their particular brand of digital art only a distant cousin of the true creative arts. This is a disputed point of view of course, but there is, as is often said, nothing as complicated as perception.

The bulk of Stan's present workload is a healthy eating campaign for the Scottish Executive focusing on primary schools throughout the city, but he has several less-intensive clients, including the Western Isles Cheese Company from Lewis - who have incurred and maintained massive success since the famous chef Charlotte Brown spoke highly of them during a newspaper interview - and an Edinburgh based recycling company that in conjunction with the United Nations provides clothing for over two million Third World children every year. While Stan is happy to work with these companies, proud indeed, his newest account is not so pleasing: Edinburgh Zoo. Stan does not believe in zoos, but while the moral compromise grates hellishly, he is willing to do what he is paid to do, at least until he can offload the client onto one his colleagues. Stan's greatest success in his four years in the trade - he prefers the term achievement - is the children's television programme *Shine*, which, originally broadcast across the Hebrides in Gaelic, is currently undergoing pre-production for a full UK release in the spring.

'Hume!'

Through his black-rimmed glasses, Stan lifts his eyes to the head of a polished oak table where John Whirrel the Accounts Manager, a physically frail though booming individual of sixty, heads the weekly Monday morning meeting like the figure of maturity in an Ages of Man painting. In her lilac ensemble, Rose is a vision of charm beside him. Together, they compromise Stan's immediate line management.

Stan's hangover is easing, which is both a blessing and a curse; the physical pain has stopped, but the memories of the disaster that was yesterday are all too complete. Amongst ten of his generic colleagues, in his neat jacket, he appears the epitome of lucidity and deliberation, but realises meeting John's gaze that he has not heard a word for quite some time.

'Yes, Johnny?'

'For you, sunshine!' John hurls a thin card folder down the polished oak. 'As you already know,' he explains, 'because of her departure, Mrs Mackenzie's accounts are being divided amongst us all. I know yie're busy enough as it is wae the Executive, but that's just tough.'

Leith Furnishings and Upholsteries, the thin file explains, are an independent local retailer of flat-pack furniture and occasional antiques, worth £2,500 per annum to G. W. F. Associates, less than 3% of the account's revenue. But none of this is news. Although he looks curiously upon the file through his glasses, thumbing its few pages somewhat condemningly, Stan's receipt of the meagre account was engineered above the head of his immediate supervisors with the aid of the office manager, and is the first move towards a larger and entirely self-serving goal. He feigns tapered irritation with newfound enthusiasm.

But the renaissance is brief, crushed by the weight of inexcusable actions. Yesterday, Stan awoke on Charlie's armchair precisely four minutes before the only flight heading to Stornoway left Edinburgh Airport. He remembers clearly the solemn, lonesome walk to the Doonhaimer and the six martinis he swallowed before lunchtime. Ignoring his vibrating mobile phone all afternoon was not easy, but not as difficult as the notion of facing Doris's rage. Not until the realisation penetrated his gin haze that, not being able to reach him, his parents would suspect the worst - possibly a plane crash - did Stan finally contact them. Fantastically drunk by then, however, instead of phoning home, Stan phoned Charlie at Reserve and asked her to do the deed. Shameful.

'Hume?'

'Johnny?'

'Raffle tickets!'

'Pardon me?'

'You are the only person here who hasnae yet parted with some cash in the name of charity!' John produces a plastic moneybag of coins. 'I suggest yie do it now.'

'That's not true,' Stan objects. 'I gave yie a pound yesterday.'

'And how many orphans will a pound feed? It's Christmas!

'I know that it's Christmas, Johnny. That's why I did gie yie a pound. Be satisfied, man.'

'Have a heart!'

'No.'

Indignant, John looks around the other faces. 'Susan, what about you? A mother yirsel, I'm certain yie'll no see the wee kiddies without a present to open.'

In her mid-twenties, her blonde hair parted into tight bunches, naturally pretty but four stones overweight, Sue is with the exception of Rose the only one of Stan's colleagues he has any fondness for. If she were a painting, she would be by Tamara de Lempicka. Five weeks ago, Sue's first weekend in the city after transferring from the G. W. F. Associates London office, Stan awoke in his then Leith flat to find Sue in bed beside him, the result of a work-related party the night previous.

'What's the prize, John?' she asks.

'Ask the miserable Mr Hume! He won last year!'

Stan's smile corroborates. 'It was a hamper, Susan. Very good it was too, certainly worth a pound. But what are the odds on me winning the thing two years running?'

'I'll take another fiver, John,' Sue smiles indulgently. 'When is it drawn?'

'Friday afternoon,' Rose says. 'And let me remind you, although I assume I need not, that every one of you is expected in the pub by twenty past two! Some of us are retiring at the weekend.'

This brings the first smiles of the day. But not for long. John Whirrel shifts uneasily in his seat and says with obvious reluctance:

'There is one other thing, folks. And it isnae a good thing.' He clears his throat and with the natural tact of middle management, distances himself from blame by saying:

'I spoke to Lafferty's this morning.'

Lafferty and Sons is the accounting company who handle the financial records for the office, and the statement brings disheartened groans from around the table.

'It appears,' John laments, 'there has been some kind of foul-up regarding the wages and commissions promised in time for Christmas, instead of the fourth of January, and while they assure me that every effort is being taken to ensure the funds are released, they have advised me to advise you, ladies and gentlemen, to made alternative arrangements. Okay?' He breathes a sigh. 'That's all. I shant keep yie back.'

John begins to rise but is stopped mid-stretch by the words:

'Pardon me?'

'Would you like me to repeat myself, Mr Hume?'

'Aye, I think yie'll need tae.' Stan rips off his glasses; his green, seemingly transparent eyes are clear. 'Because I think mibbae my ears are full of cotton wool!'

'I said, Stan, that although...'

'I know what yie said, Johnny! I'm just wondering: when Lafferty's told yie we should make alternative arrangements, did they mean, like, selling the family pearls or something? And when they said that every effort is being taken to release the funds, do they mean that they're making no effort because they've actually got some kind of overdraft kickback scam going with the banks, so they get a shady backhander on the overdrafts all of us are now forced to buy!'

'Stan, I know it's frustrating, but...'

'Frustrating? It's not frustrating. It's utterly infuriating. We have written evidence.' Stan suddenly produces the very piece of evidence and, standing now, throws it down the table towards his line management. 'Every single person here, including management I assume, received both an internal mail and postal correspondence from head office guaranteeing that we would be paid early. Some of us have been fool enough to make arrangements around that promise. My point is simply that it seems very late in the day to be telling us that, no, sorry, we've all getting fucked up the arse! Lest we forget, Johnny, is Christmas!'

More than one gasp rises from around the table. Gazes, however, remain focused on hands.

Horrified at the nastiness of his own tone, Stan understands that he is shooting the messenger and his anger defuses. Fortunately, however, his sceptical nature expected such a foul-up and he has already made alternative arrangements, which in fact lie inside the thin cardboard folder on the polished oak before him provided by the manager.

'It's indecent is all I'm saying,' Stan concludes, taking his seat. 'It's surely a violation. But I appreciate it's not your fault, Johnny. Beg your pardon.'

Rose is about to speak and gets as far as parting her curled lips before another voice overrules her.

'What's gaun on here?' it demands. 'Looks tae me like some kind of bother. Surely there isnae any bother in my harmonious office. No on a Monday certainly. I wouldnae like that.'

'No, nae bother, boss,' John says.

The figure of the office manager looms mightily over the oak table, one hand in the trouser pocket of an expensive patchwork suit, the other holding a thick slice of sultana and walnut loaf.

'Problem, Mr Hume?' he wonders, eyebrows lifted about his sleepy eyes.

Stan's queasiness returns in a flood. Nauseously he recalls the words spoken to him by the office manager on Saturday night:

'Dae yie really want me tae drive yie tae the airport at nine o'clock in the morning? Or are yie fucking kidding me on, man? I'm supposed to be playing golf.'

Chemistry, after graduating from Glasgow University in 1991 with first class honours, and then an equally distinguished year of teacher training at Edinburgh University, failed to maintain Dave Quinn's interest. In 1993, he entered into the world of marketing. Yet, Stan and Dave did not originally meet at work. The fact that Stan works in the office and in the world of marketing at all is entirely Dave's doing. Before his incarnation as a marketing agent, Stan was a restaurant maître d'.

Please, Stan thinks, please let Charlie have phoned him. Please let him not have missed his golf. Simultaneously he represses the bitter and childish reflection that Charlie is somewhat to blame for yesterday's circumstance since she left him sleeping in her armchair as she went to work.

But Dave's expression is unreadable. His grey weekend stubble is gone, as is any impression of joviality. He casts half a glance down at the Leith Furnishings and Upholstery folder in front of Stan, and although he says nothing, Rose sees his sleepy eyes widen only slightly.

'No,' Stan admits. 'Nae problem, boss.'

'Good!' With an enormous bite of his fruit loaf, the manager is on his way. But he stops to add, cheerily:

'I hope all of yie are buying plenty of raffle tickets, by the way. It's Christmas, after all.'

4

Vincent Dussollier's office occupies the entire subbasement of No. 39-43 North Castle Street, and the great chef is a man of great indulgence. The term eclectic does the room little justice. The desk is English Victorian oak. An eleven-drawer commode in original distressed white paint is from the time of Louis XIV. There are several art nouveau lamps. Two deep modern velvet couches finish the slate floor, arranged around two enormous woven old rugs. Three paintings hang amongst the multitude of framed photographs, all three works featuring drunks, by Jack Vettriano, John Bellany and Pablo Picasso. The entire building - Reserve's kitchen, dinning room and the five commercial units above - rests upon six gothic columns throughout the office. Bolted high up in the corner above the door, a carved stone gargoyle watches over all. Of course, it has been a matter of some years since Vincent truly required an office onsite, but since the birth of Chloé Dussollier three months ago, the space has established a new purpose. During her more unyielding times, it has become for Chloé's father, as it has equally her mother, Amanda, a sanctuary. Presently, the great chef dozes on one of the couches, snoring heavily, his regal purple silk suit crushed.

Cohabitation is a nuisance for Charlie. For years the space has been her own private sanctuary and she is only beginning to come to terms with the constant snoring of monsieur or madame Dussollier. The saving grace is that Chloé rarely visits.

Charlie sits on the floor, her hair held back and smelling of grease, engaging on several notepads the weekly accounts. Gone is her hangover, as is the pain of vomiting Tom's bridie back up. Only exhaustion remains, a disorientating, vacant feeling. She rolls a cigarette, allows her grey eyes to roam.

Many of the faces in Vincent's photographs are immediately recognisable, none more so than his own parents, Jean-Luc and Megan. Many of their photographs themselves are famous.

Jean-Luc Dussollier was at the time of the liberation of Paris a Free French combatant and occasional trombonist. Megan Poe was a Special Operations Executive spy who in later years would receive both the George Cross from King George V and the Médaille de la Résistance from Charles de Gaulle, and who loved the trombone. Well-documented is Jean-Luc and Megan's relationship. While Paris rebuilt, they courted, favouring the Opéra as well as the tattered cafés of the Latin Quarter. And perhaps Jean-Luc and Megan may have spent longer in this happy courtship of music if not for pressing tragedy forcing them to marry immediately.

Megan fell pregnant. But this was not the tragedy, which was the sudden death of Jean-Luc's father, Pierre.

Legendary is the Dussollier estate in terms of property, land, antiquities, political sway and hard cash in France. Vague are its origins. By Vincent's account, his ancestors, who have always been entertainers of sorts, were popular in the court of Louis XIV. In 1699, Philippe-Jean Dussollier, then family monarch, and a blind man, received from the King of France, by the pen of the chief designer of the Palace of Versailles, an enormous Baroque mansion outside Paris with a twenty-mile estate of wild fowl, lakes and ancient standing stones. With the estate came no official title. The precise reason for which this was done, however, has clouded with age.

Regardless, upon his father's death in 1945, Jean-Luc inherited the lot. But Jean-Luc was not a man to be steered. For the duration of his long and happy life, his interests remained steady: his wife Megan, his son Vincent, and his twisted brass horn.

For this, the musical firmament is thankful. While his American contemporaries cut their teeth touring with the bands of Louis Armstrong and Duke Ellington, Jean-Luc Dussollier studied his trade in the pit of the Opéra, immersed in Berlioz, Bizet and Poulenc. But as the 1950's began, although he never lived away from Paris, Jean-Luc Dussollier quickly emerged as a musician as influential to the world of jazz in his day as George Gershwin, Louis Armstrong or Gene Kruppa. A true master of melody, able to blend indeterminable tones with clarity at speed, and something of a conceptual genius, Jean-Luc brought to the fore in the age of the saxophone the trombone. One image upon the office wall, a small black and white photograph not immediately clear, portrays the great chef at ten years of age playing a piano accompanied by a bent-double-with-laughter John Coltrane. Unlike his friend Coltrane, however, Jean-Luc Dussollier never turned to freeform music. Melody was simply not a thing he could discount.

Jean-Luc Dussollier, unlike the majority of his contemporaries, was never driven, never a workaholic, though he did work all of his life. Nor did he drink, take drugs, live in America or England, participate in sexual affairs or sleep away from his wife a single night in his life. His favourite pastime would always remain taking Megan to the Opéra.

Given by the state, the funeral of Jean-Luc Dussollier in 2001 was a major national event in France, the boulevards of Paris lined five-deep by the truly bereaved, as commemorated on Vincent's wall by a Time-Life cover.

Hence, it was because of jazz music that in 1945, the day after Jean-Luc's father, Pierre, was lain to rest in the earth of the estate outside Paris, Megan Poe shocked all of France and most of Europe's upper-class by becoming at twenty-one the first woman, and foreigner at that, to assume entire matriarchal responsibility of the Dussollier estate, reigning over the far-reaching purse strings with an iron will, her husband firmly by her side, if slightly at an angle. The burden she supports still, now in her eightieth year and without her husband.

Megan Poe, who has always kept her maiden name, is the ninth most independently wealthy individual in France. She is a world-leading philanthropist in the fields of AIDS/HIV and cancer research, and world poverty. Dussollier House she has transformed across her term from a stuffy mansion into a world-renowned gallery and museum, free to the public and home to some of Europe's oldest art and sculpture, specifically in pre-Roman civilisations. Poe is a United Nations Ambassador for Peace and Fair Trade. Add to her legacy, twenty best-selling, semi-autobiographical Alison Gorry novels, portrayed on the big screen by both Audrey Hepburn and Susan Sarandon. Vincent's mother, it is often remarked, is quite a lady.

Charlie exhales tasteless smoke, looking forward to getting home tonight and losing herself in the latest and apparently last Alison Gorry novel. Reserve's Monday night trade is traditionally the slowest of the week and she plans to excuse herself no later that five. She is, she feels, badly in need of moisturising. And sleep.

The office's bookcase is a ragbag. In fact, most of the novels belong to Charlie. There are a few objects of interest, though, some Verne's and Zola's of note, as well as several nostalgic histories by Walter Scott, who for a while lived with his family and worked in an apartment above the restaurant. The only one of Vincent's books that really interests the collector in Charlie is his first edition Carême.

Born just before the French Revolution, Antonin Carême was sent away from his family at the age of ten by his father, allegedly with the words:

'Go my child, and fare well in the world. Leave us to languish. Poverty and misery are our lot and we will die as we have lived. But for those like you, with quick wits, there are great fortunes to be made.'

Carême's ambition, which he realised in *L'Art De La Cuisine Français Au Dix-Neavième Siècle*, was in his own words to publish 'a complete book on the state of my profession in our times'.

Vincent adopted the exact same tactic. *Leçons dans la Cuisine* is in the great chef's words, 'an effort in connecting the dots.'

Not only a complete history of French cooking, accessible to both the novice and professional, including over a thousand illustrated recipes and their variations, the book has a wine guide, a biochemistry section, a comprehensive guide to modern kitchen equipment and a treasure of plain facts about running a restaurant. Its dedication, which remains to this day, reads simply *For Redemption*. The only photograph of Vincent ever included in the book is of him at twenty-three, before what he calls the Dark Days, with his late and then-heavily pregnant first wife, Gillian. The real achievement of *Leçons*, however, and the reason for its longevity, was to strip away all past pretences about food and its preparation in favour of the simple facts. Vincent Dussollier, the great chef, sometimes known as the Jackal, snoring and dishevelled on the couch, is in fact the industry rule, the standard by which all is held to account.

Of all the photographs in the office, one in particular always grips Charlie's attention. Well-publicised is that Vincent studied at Le Cordon Bleu, the distinguished Parisian cookery school where his own literary effort is now part of the basic curriculum. Less well known, however, is that one of his flatmates hung himself shortly before graduation. Beside the Picasso, a grainy photograph solemnly laments the tragedy, if not the act itself. By the age of twenty-one, Vincent's winning smile has already developed, although his head of fiery red hair would not last many more years. Another face in the photographs is, like so many in the room, instantly recognisable. Eugène Bouveret is today the world-renowned chef and owner of the Duck's Breast on Paris's Rue Mouffetard, as well as an Assistant Dean at Le Cordon Bleu. The last face in the image, between Vincent and Eugène, chubby, nineteen years old and grinning broadly, is Bernard Spencer would leave no explanation for the dire action he enforced later that very evening.

Charlie hears Vincent wake with a sharp intake of air.

He climbs into slippers, rises to stretch and to use the bathroom, and before very long he is back on the couch, sitting upright now. An unsatisfying nap leaves his eyes like peppercorns and his face as creased as his suit. He spends a moment studying his long fingers, searching for broken skin and paying particular attention to the nails. Vincent is rightly proud of his hands; they have served him well over the years. Finally content, he steeples his fingers over his potbelly.

'What day is today, chef?'

'Monday.'

'Hells bells,' he groans. 'That means Amanda's mother is coming for dinner tonight. I dinnae think Amanda or me slept last night at all, so she'll be in nae fettle for Dot.'

Charlie smiles politely.

'Listen, about Friday,' he says, 'will yie do a nice menu. I really cannae be buggered.'

Friday night is Vincent's annual Christmas party, his last remaining public indulgence, a gesture of gratitude to loyal customers. Admission is by invitation of Vincent or Amanda personally.

'Of course.' Irritation simmers in Charlie. It is not her party.

Crushing out her cigarette and tuning back into her accounts, annoyed, she witnesses in her peripheral vision a stiffening in Vincent, slight but definite. She can feel his stare. She can sense his unease. She meets his gaze.

'Charlie?'

'I'm busy.' Charlie is aware that her heart is thumping in her chest. 'Is it important?'

Again, the great chef studies his hands and Charlie realises in his reluctant silence that he has never before looked so old to her eyes.

'Charlie...I...'

'Spit it out, man.'

'Chef, I'm closing the restaurant.' Then, to remove any ambiguity, 'I'm retiring, plain and simple. I sold the Logie and Piscivorous over the weekend, and I'm selling this building, too. To keep it serves no purpose. It'll be in the trade papers on the twenty-seventh unless I get an offer tomorrow, which I almost certainly will.'

Charlie nods, rallying all of her self-control to resist the urge of breaking eye contact to look up at a photograph of Vincent's mother.

'I see,' she says.

'I'm sure you do, chef.' Vincent speaks easier now. 'I'm too fuckin old for this. It's a nonsense. And of course, one must consider...' His face darkens in sadness. '... mother.'

The great chef lifts his tired eyes to his favourite of all his photographs. Although he is in the image, he has only a vague recollection of that particular day. He was a teenager at the time. He does remember clearly the porkpie hat worn by his father that night, but Jean-Luc is not in the photograph because Jean-Luc took the photograph.

In 1959, on the day the Fifth Republic of France was established, the image captures a lanky and spotty Vincent, awkward in a neat suit, shaking hands with Charles de Gaulle. But this is secondary to the composition, and slightly out of focus. The main point of interest, that which Vincent's father was attempting to capture, is Vincent's mother. She radiates light. Natural, beautiful, elegant, relaxed, all of these words are suitable, but Vincent has never been able to identify what makes the image so remarkable.

But Megan Poe, Dussollier family matriarch, legendary war hero and author extraordinaire, is young no longer. She is failing fast. Incontinent and bedridden, Megan has recently become blind and the knowledge that she will never be able to see her granddaughter is killing her more surely than any illness. Dussollier Mansion and the family estate of assets tangible and intangible are about to slip quietly - any moment now - into Vincent's hands.

He smiles at this unspoken admission with a silent and bitter devastation than nearly breaks Charlie's heart.

'I'm sorry,' he says.

Charlie closes her accounts ledger and, with her mouth hanging open, can think of not a single thing to say.

5

She walked from the boulevard to the river and crossed at Pont Neuf, stopped to watch the patrol boats and supply barges, felt the warm, early morning May breeze on her face. She wore an olive-green satin dress and a short, velvet coat of scarlet. A feathered hat pinned to her cropped hair matched her dress. Cosmetics reddened her normally pallid face. In true Parisian manner, Violette Rodin was a remarkably stylish woman, adhering stringently to her preferred combination of various reds and greens.

Looking down into the water, gears shifting in her mind, Alison Gorry easily recalled distant summers spent in Paris visiting her grandparents. She remembered their faces clearly, tangibly, their strange ways, their unfamiliar smells, her golden hair and his kind eyes. It was more difficult for Alison to remember her mother, Louise, who was still alive.

Violette lit a German cigarette and from the bridge, crossed the Tuileries gardens, where she saw painted crudely upon the base of a statute the Waffen-SS motto:

Meine Ehre Heisst Treue

The words were visible but hastily covered, replaced by the more elaborate and somewhat heartening Communist statement:

'To terror there is no other reply than a more powerful and more implacable terror. Assassination of any French patriot not immediately followed by the execution of those responsible is a dishonour for the résistance.'

From the gardens, Violette came to Place de la Concorde. Bombing had barely touched the city centre, although many of the industrial and too often residential suburbs lay in ruin; it was the numerous barricades like something from a Victor Hugo novel that were apt to lower a person's spirits. Neither did the tiresome business of showing identity papers at every second turn delight.

Coming finally onto Avenue des Champs Elysées, Violette felt with every step and from every direction a sombre, false serenity, a curtailed anger hidden from the watchful, obtrusive Nazi eyes. It was like invisible smoke in the air.

At the end of the avenue, close enough to the Arc de Triomphe to see the expression on Jean-Pierre Cortot's carved triumphant Napoleon, Violette Rodin bought a newspaper and found a street café in which to read and smoke. She was early but did not mind the wait. It was good to be out in the fresh air, good to be amongst people. She contentedly passed twenty minutes until, above her paper and her tenth cigarette of the morning, a familiar face emerged.

Major Philip Scott, experienced field agent and expert in the art of camouflage, could do nothing about his limp as he moved through the crowd. He was dressed according to his false documents in the universal tailored suit of the upper class, his cane made from bronze and ivory.

'Père!' Violette cried. 'Ici.'

The Major limped closer, smiling, and kissed both cheeks of his 'daughter'.

He ordered coffee from a dull-eyed waitress and after heavy consideration a strawberry croissant with fresh cream, feeling more than a tinge of guilt for the millions in the city who were starving and dying in poverty. He had witnessed two nights previous, on the same bourgeoisie street as his own house, one neighbour shooting another over a shovel full of coal.

The matter with de Gaulle was only one of Philip's many operations. His mind was ablaze. Overlord was his principal concern. The landing of five entire divisions on the beaches of Normandy took a degree of internal support and it was the Major's charge to land and apply the so-called Jedburgh teams as an aid to the résistance and his own en situ agents in the business of preventing German reinforcements from reaching the battlefield and in dismantling their communications lines. Sabotage was the name of the game.

Also, his captured agents grieved Philip mightily. Since the weekend, two more women had been arrested and taken to Fresnes. His staff was dwindling badly. As D-Day approached the pressure rose.

And yet, for the first time in years, the Major Philip Scott wore an expression that conveyed something resembling hope.

'I assume,' he began in hushed French, 'from the half-dozen unaccountably dead SS-men in Montmatre, the mutilated spy found in Place des Vosges and the general mass Nazi hysteria of the last few days, Violette, that we've made some progress in our objective, yes?'

'Oui.'

'Tipped our hand, wouldn't you say?'

Smiling, Alison waited until the same waitress served the Major's coffee and breakfast before she said:

'I hear from the papers that Gandhi has been freed from prison. I hear from the Americans that any day now Italy will fall. I hear from you that Overlord is to be a decisive success. You know as well as I, Philip, that this war is over. And you know that we deserve some amount of vengeance before we're all sent home to be court marshalled. Madeleine deserved that much.'

'Madeleine, yes.' The Major's face darkened. 'Frédéric gave me the details. Hanged, he said.' He thought involuntarily of every solider lost to him during his tender in France, some seventy men and women, and he almost vomited on the table. 'Even still, Violette, your temper is a terrible opponent. One must consider the long-term.'

'If you've come here to argue about my methods,' Alison said, 'then get someone else for the job because frankly, sir, I'd rather go home.'

'Any more of your carry on, my girl, and none of us will be going home. The Nazis are furious, Violette. More than the actual death of Franz Wetzler, they're furious to discover that he was something more than they thought he was. To his peers, Wetzler was just a mid-ranking officer with no particular skill, found dead, disembowelled, with his severed penis stuffed in his mouth.'

The Major stared hard as he said this, looking either for some kind of explanation or just to let Alison know that he knew; it was not clear. Either way, Alison merely smiled.

'He isn't anything now.' She sipped her coffee. 'They no longer need concern themselves.'

Forced to curtain both his voice and his temper, Major Scott said:

'But they are concerned, damn it. They're furious. Protect yourself is all I'm saying, because they are! Do not, mark my words, try to out-terrorise the Nazis because it is not possible. Besides, the war is not the only concern, Violette, as well you know. France needs a leader when the war is over.'

'You're right. I'm sorry.'

'Don't be sorry. Just be careful. You're valuable. Now, will you please tell me what the hell is going on exactly?'

'Franz Wetzler,' the Special Operations Executive assassin explained, 'once a prevailing conductor with the Berlin State Opera, was a clerk at the Hôtel Saint Marie, where he processed what my source called Transport Figures. Wetzler was also a spy. At the Opera, in 1934, he became a close friend of Brigadeführer Otto Abetz, but his commissions came directly from Himmler, usually via one other link, a captain I think in Berlin. Wetzler, sir, was the leading officer in Paris for your plot against de Gaulle. Even Abetz knows nothing.'

The Major had suspected as much. 'So that's it then?'

'No. There are others.'

This, the Major had also suspected. 'You know this from your source? Or is it one of your famous guesses?'

'It's common sense. It came from the source but it's also the way I would have done the job.'

'You're saying that we're too late, that Wetzler anticipated something like this and made arrangements for the job to go ahead without its coordinator?'

'Yes. And your source, Marius, must have known about this weeks ago. Mine did.'

'He's in a difficult situation.'

With a raised eyebrow, Alison could find no sympathy for the man.

'What about your source?' The Major bit into his croissant. 'How reliable is she? If Abetz knew nothing, how did she find out?'

'The German fascination for paperwork.'

'Ah. Is she a risk?'

'Not anymore,' Alison smiled. 'I shot her.'

Major Scott violently choked up pastry and managed the single word:
'What!'

'Don't worry, boss. She was a Nazi. I made it look like a domestic incident. The Nazis think the husband shot her. He's dead now, too, but I didn't do it.'

Incredulity passed across the Major's face. He smiled, frowned, coughed. He simply asked:
'Who are the others?'

'There were only three of them. Wetzler is dead. The other two are very soon to be. One of them I have yet to meet, but the second...' Alison's voice trailed off.

'Yes?'

Smiling pleasantly, Alison said. 'There's to be a party...

Annoyed, Charlie lifts her eyes to the sound of her front door banging shut, which momentarily wakes Snoopy on the back of the armchair.

In pants and a bra, her hair resting in its natural shape and smelling of antibacterial shampoo, she feels from an open windowpane the cold breeze pleasing across her legs, and presses her fingertips firmly against her eyelids. Absolutely still she sits in the dimness, listening to the faint symphony of otherwise ignored sound in the flat; creaking, heating, neighbours, ticking, and the relentless traffic noise from Leith Walk that also creates a gentle vibration. The loudest sound is the sink tap running in the bathroom.

After what feels like an age, she hears the toilet flush, and moments later Stan clumps through to the living room. Charlie regards him wordlessly, the violet hue of the single, soft lamp drawn to her eyes. Then she sinks down low in the armchair, balances her book on her knees and rolls a joint on her naked belly.

Still in his Harris Tweed but without his thick-rimmed spectacles, Stan is gaunt. That he has made it to the end of the day, that his body has endured, that he has neither ruptured nor bled, seems to him both miraculous and reason to be grateful. He is truly spent. He crumples into the free armchair and with a final effort and a groan, just manages to turn on via remote the Scottish evening news with Jackie Bird.

'...missing schoolgirl last seen by her mother in a neighbouring communal garden with friends on Edinburgh's Easter Road. Detective Inspector Stuart Mackenzie, who is leading the search, said earlier today...'

The small wall-mounted television screen displays the official photograph released by Mr and Mrs Gillies of their daughter. She is a blond girl, smiling, joyful, with a space in her front teeth. The photograph is not a static image, but rather an 'action' photograph of Megan helping her mother hang washing in the very gardens from which she was led.

But the Inspector's statement Stan does not hear because Charlie pulls out the television cable from the wall behind her chair. And, maddeningly, she is further interrupted from her book when Stan says, clasping his hands over his stomach in his familiar floating-otter position:

'Dave says tae remind yie tae phone yir mother about Christmas dinner. Yie've no tae forget, eh?'

Charlie considers this statement somewhat taken aback. It is, in view of yesterday, a bold one. But twisting her wiry hair in her finger, she decides not to say anything because he does look genuinely unwell. She says, instead:

'I brought home some bread and sliced beef for sandwiches tomorrow since yie're too poor to feed yirsel.'

'That's very thoughtful.' His appreciation is obvious. 'But I dinnae need sandwiches the morra. I'm gaun oot for lunch. The work's paying.'

'I see. How come?'

'Dull shit, man. I'm taking over one of Rose's accounts. It's nothing.'

So accustomed to Stan is Charlie that she can easily see his self-restraint. Although not lying per say, he is definitely holding something back, but again, she does not press the matter. Besides, the mention of Rose's name makes her seethe.

'Which reminds me: I've bad news about yir healthy eating campaign. Want it now?'

Stan signs a deep breath. 'Nah, man. I'm fragile. Better keep it for later.'

'Suit yirsel.' She spits these words.

Although tired, exhausted, drained, weary, bleary or even upset would be accurate words to describe Charlie's mood, Stan knows that the perfect word is *Thraun*, pronounce to rhyme with ran. Thraun is a word specific to Charlie, a south-western word. That he has never heard issued from another set of lips in his life. Apparently, it can mean stubborn or obstinate but Charlie uses it only to denote absolute pissed off-ness. And as surely as he knows this, Stan knows that the only way to fight fire is with fire.

'I've been wondering all day, man, whose cock yie were swallowing last night? Had yie ever met that chap before?'

Livid, her entire body emanating rage like angels supposedly radiate love, Charlie lifts her grey eyes from her book to meet Stan's over the carved coffee table, her expression pensive and frank, her mouth puckered.

Charlie's sexuality over the years has been a matter of constant fascination and wonder to her. One thing can be said with certainty: it is rampant. She has had sex with a near-uncountable number of men and women, enjoying equally penetrative and non-penetrative sex, vaginal, anal, oral, submission and domination. She has bound a sixty-year-old woman to a bed frame; she has penetrated a seventeen-year-old man/boy with a strap-on penis, and has more than once engaged in coital pleasures with Larry's Great Dane. The word Stan uses when he and Charlie discuss the matter - they often discuss it - is *Druisealachd*, which translates from the Gaelic as simply Nymphomania.

Of last night's episode, she has a perfectly lucid memory of everything but the face of the man she used. She did not ask his name. She remembers his timidity. There was no penetration; Charlie masturbated herself while fellating him, timing her own orgasm perfectly to his.

She remembers gagging. In both length and girth, he was too big, particularly for a creature of Charlie's smallness. Not that his size perturbed her; she managed to swallow an admirable portion of the cock, almost all in fact, forcing it down and breathing whenever possible. Her performance was simply a bit messy.

'At least yie got some vitamins,' Stan remarks. 'I dinnae suppose yie ate anything else all day yesterday.'

This is true. Charlie's comedown - one of the terms used to describe the dehydrated, dreary and disorientating state that follows heavy stimulant use - was evil. The seven hours she worked are almost without memory, the saving grace the fact that she was mindful enough to do her usual Sunday paperwork on Saturday afternoon. Eating did not rank high on her priorities. In fact, Tom's bridie this morning was Charlie first food since Saturday evening, the bridie she later regurgitated.

She looks at Stan hard. But then she does a strange thing, the last thing he expects.

She smiles, if somewhat cruelly.

'Stanley,' Charlie exhales smoke, inhaling again sharply, 'what did yie ask me to remind yie tonight, my idiot friend?'

Stan is loathed to admit:

'Dunno.'

But then by a sudden leap in his thinking it occurs to him that an electricity engineer will be arriving on his new doorstep in Portobello in about fifteen minutes with his toolbox.

'*Mo chreach!*'

Charlie returns to her book.

'I need to go now,' he says. Despite the inconveniences of having to dash the four miles to Portobello, the advantage of having electricity is decidedly tasty. He sighs, gathering himself up. 'Listen, are yie still coming round tonight to help finish painting? Yie said yie would, eh?'

The remembrance of this devastates Charlie. Charlie is, she is certain, her own worst enemy.

'Aye,' she groans. 'Better take the car or you'll be late again. But come back and get me. I'm no walking.'

'But think of the ozone layer!'

'Fuck yirsel.'

Stan is almost gone. There is nearly blessed silence, but there is not. His otter head pokes back around the doorframe.

'Thanks for phoning Doris yesterday, and for phoning Dave. Shall I cook dinner for us both?' he wonders. 'In my new shiny kitchen.'

Despite the gloat, and the implication that her own kitchen is in some way not shiny and clean, Charlie melts completely against her will, overcome by an enormous sense of well-being that, in fact, she confuses with the effects of her joint.

'That's exactly what I'd like,' she admits, the subtle change in her voice not inaudible to Stan. 'That would be perfect.'

She smiles a warm, genuine smile and lights up the room.

'Yie'll need to bring some shopping, then,' Stan says, and the bang of the front door wakes Snoopy for a second time.

6

Tuesday afternoons at Reserve are busy. Floor-staff in the uniform orange and brown weave gracefully and swiftly amid the art nouveau elegance caring for the fifty-odd diners, heels clicking across the mosaic floor, tableware tinkling melodically. In a burgundy Armani suit Fanny the maître d' coordinates the effort and maintains the ambience, its multitude of nuances with a professional authority that leaves her staff in terror and her patrons in awe, not from a desk or diary but rather a tiny palm-held computer. She is in perpetual motion. Fanny's iron authority, however, comes to her, as a film director lies at the mercy of his producer, via Gavin.

Immaculate as always, Gavin skirts the fringe of the room, watching with an owl-like intensity. His mood is foul, his expression no more than amiable. His mouth tastes of coffee, which is nothing more than a cruel imagining. Carefully he inspects Fanny's staff, judging their individual movements and expressions. They have already worked a particularly heavy lunch and Gavin understands exactly how far Fanny can push each of them before they become ineffective. Only then will he intervene, raining down cold drinks, praise and even, circumstances permitting, a cigarette break. It is the classic Good Cop-Bad Cop routine. Gavin and Fanny themselves passed the point of exhausted tears many years ago.

Gavin's mind is on the matter of Vincent's retirement. Charlie told him last night but none of the staff know. He wonders when to tell them, how much the information will disinterest them in serving food, if some of them will even bother to work the last few weeks at all. A healthy severance package is the answer, he thinks.

He smiles a few words with a liberal MSP before heading to the bar, but before he gets there Fanny thrusts a cordless telephone at him.

Without reaching for it, he shrugs. 'What?'

'It's Lechie,' Fanny spits, soiled it seems by the very name.

'So?'

'So he asked to speak to you,' the maître d' says flatly.

Gavin's eyebrows meet. 'And what does he want?'

'Didnae say, Gavin, other than that he wants you.'

Irritated, Gavin knows fine well. Ronald Lechie of Lechie Electronics in Wester Hailes, makers of electrical components, has become since the millennium and the subsequent re-recordable DVD explosion a dreadfully wealthy man. He does a great deal of his business at Reserve and buys wine literally by the crate, but selling in bulk is for Gavin neither profitable nor satisfying. He does not like to think of himself as a wholesaler.

And then there is the matter of taste. Ronald Lechie has none. He purchases superior wines - Gavin sells nothing else - typically the two Château Pieddé bottles, a dry oak-aged chardonnay, *Blanc*, and a rich cabernet sauvignon, *L'Obscurité*. Reserve is the only outlet in the world outside France for the Pieddé wines, which grown and bottled in the Loire Valley are regarded strictly and proudly as a local delicacy. Reserve gets its supply because Château Pieddé is Dussollier estate produce. Tasteless Ronald Lechie buys the label to astonish, for its wow factor, and Gavin would much prefer to sell a single bottle to a couple who enjoy it for its taste and the sheer thrill of spending a hundred pounds on wine. Until now Gavin has accommodated Lechie's needs because for the nuisance he creates, he has brought a might of business through the doors, but now in the face of Vincent's retirement and the restaurant's closure...

'Tell him tae fuck off.' Gavin pronounces this with a straight face, hiding his pleasure.

On a barstool, one long leg crossed over the other just so, Stan Hume waits patiently in his usual tweed jacket ensemble, comfortable with his newspaper. He is without his glasses today. On the left lapel of his tweed jacket, a small badge reads *Nuclear Power: the best of a bad bunch*.

Unlike the majority of the capital's eateries, Reserve is and always has been a cigarette-free environment. Fully recovered from his recent cold, Stan smells lilies and the burning logs and coal.

He is distracted from his newspaper, however, by two distinct sensations: hunger, naturally, as he inhales the heady concoction of food smells so familiar to him, and secondly, relief, massive and tangible, that he no longer works in the restaurant industry.

He is careful not to lift his eyes to Reserve's paintings. Although he has seen and inspected the works hundreds of times at his leisure, it is still easy to be hypnotised. All too easily might he find himself staring open-mouthed like an idiot. Of course, Reserve's paintings pale in comparison to Vincent's personal collection, which includes work by Monet, Canaletto, Moreau and Rembrandt. The last time Stan and Charlie went for dinner, Vincent had bought a Vermeer for Amanda. Similarly, Vincent's personal collection seems amateurish beside that of his family. In the summer, when Stan and Charlie went for the weekend with the Dussollier's to Dussollier House outside Paris, Vincent made for his mother a present of a recently discovered sketch by Desvallières made in preparation for his famous Salome. Even still, Reserve's humble collection is distracting.

Focus is required.

Stan's newspaper is a valuable part of his day. He consumes the Scotsman, the Herald and the Evening News, scouring every report, article and by-line, always with a pinch of salt. When forced to travel by bus in rainy weather, he also enjoys the free Metro.

Today, apparently, Saddam Hussein is a broken man who has 'given' vital information leading to the capture of two more of Iraq's most wanted men. But although the arrest of the deposed leader has dented the morale of his supporters, hardcore insurgents refused to be cowed. The Scotsman claims that eight people died yesterday following a suicide bomb attack on a Baghdad police station, including two American soldiers, while the Herald claims the death count as nine.

Also on the front page, accompanied by an altogether different photograph, the story tells that a massive search has begun for ten-year-old Megan Gillies, reported missing from Edinburgh's Easter Road area on Saturday morning by her parents, Jack and Sarah Gillies. The family has made no statements, but Detective Inspector Stuart Mackenzie, who is leading the investigation, said...

Gavin takes the stool beside Stan, leans an elbow on the bar and fixes his face into an already thoroughly bored expression that he is particularly pleased with, but which is entirely wasted because Stan does not lift his eyes. Rather, continuing to read, he turns his head perhaps half a degree in the manger's direction.

'When?' he asks, continuing a conversation that began quite some time ago.

'Three months ago, Stan.' Gavin tone is hushed. 'Yie're a real pal, eh?'

Turning his page, Stan retorts, causally yet markedly, lying:

'I never liked him, Gavin. And it probably serves him right. What happened?'

'Twenty-four half-gram bags of low-grade hash happened, to mention nothing of the fact that he was caught red-handed selling at Leith Academy's main gate, or the fact that it was his ninth offence, fourth before the same judge.'

'Saughton?' Stan enquires.

'Eight years.'

At this, Stan turns quite pale. He lowers his newspaper and shifting his entire body, truly engages Gavin for the first time. His voice is soft, his olive eyes wide. 'I beg yir pardon?'

'Eight years.'

'For selling half-ounce bags of hashish?'

'Aye, tae school bairns, Stan. The cunt's two bubbles aff centre.'

'Glaikit,' Stan agrees.

Stan and Gavin met eight years ago through the shared interest of Charlotte Brown but they have never liked each other. Their personalities are dissimilar. Gavin is proud to be a local while Stan is equally proud to be an incomer. Gavin is relatively renowned in the city of Edinburgh while Stan is not. Stan appreciates the restaurant's art while Gavin considers it only something to worry about. Stan's Harris Tweed jacket contrasts with Gavin's smooth silk waistcoat.

While Stan was a student, Gavin, older by three years and never a student, worked with Charlie in a noted Italian fish restaurant on Leith Walk and was already a cannabis dealer of local distinction. Despite their differences, Stan and Gavin quickly forged a business partnership, Stan offering a degree of boldness and vision to Gavin's more fundamental practises. The operation became a citywide concern, able, unlike their numerous competitors, to supply a variety of different hashish and marijuana at competitive prices, delivered to the door. The market in pre-rolled joints was for them particularly lucrative.

Derek Holmes was their minion. Unreliable, careless and only semi-trustworthy, Holmes at the time rented a room in the same flat as Stan. His incredible little-black-book with regard to the purchase of illegal resources in Edinburgh, narcotics or otherwise, was remarkable. Of course, after the establishment of connections, Holmes became dispensable, but Stan and Gavin agreed, in a gesture of appreciation and sheer goodwill, to keep him involved.

Holmes would be their downfall, although this appears less the case to Stan as time passes, and especially now. Now, he suspects that in greed Gavin and himself were equally accountable. That particular night, they went, as they often did upon Holmes' recommendation, to meet an unknown dealer in a Sighthill high-rise who had apparently only just moved to the city from Glasgow. In their greed it occurred to neither Gavin nor Stan to wonder why he had moved. In fact, the dealer was endeavouring to flee police suspicion. Upon leaving the flat, Stan and Gavin learned well enough that, enlightened by their colleagues on the west coast, local police had been watching the flat for quite some time in a bid to accumulate evidence for a secure conviction by means of questioning his customers. The evening's saving grace was that the dealer, who was a nice enough fellow called Geoffrey, did not have the amount of hashish promised. Expecting to buy eighteen ounces, Stan and Gavin left with only one, which turned out to be a blessing. It was disposed of before the police found it.

The only criminal charges that evening were brought against Charlie. Having driven Stan and Gavin to Sighthill, she was smoking a joint in the car while she waited. At fate would have it, that was the same day she received her first Michelin Star, and both incidents made the national newspapers.

Now, looking hard at Gavin, Stan thinks of Desmond McGhee, a primary-school teacher from the Isle of Lewis, found guilty last week at Edinburgh High Court of sexually abusing pupils in his classroom for twenty-eight years. One of the victims committed suicide in his early teens. Another did not wait that long. McGhee, in fact, taught Stan. And for his sins, Desmond McGhee received an eight-year prison term. Eight years for a dangerous, unrepentant monster and eight years for clumsy Derek Holmes. Not to condone the selling of drugs at school gates, the basic human error in this makes Stan's brow knit.

'I'm away,' Gavin says. 'Some of us huv tae work.'

But before he leaves, Stan asks with sincere concern:

'Howz Duncan?'

Anyone else asking this question would be fobbed off with a dull *fine* or *dunno*, but to say that Stan and Gavin do not like each other is not to say that they are not close. More important than the money they made together, they spent a lot of time together. At the mention of his little brother, the muscles in Gavin's face twinge involuntarily and for the briefest of seconds Stan sees him forget all about the restaurant. Attempting a weak smile, Gavin fails entirely and his eyes land on the cover page photograph of Hussein. He runs his fingers through his raven-black mop of hair.

'Still alive.' His voice verges on despair. 'I sent some shortbread and newspapers at the weekend. I wonder if he'll get them.'

'I'm sure he will.'

Born into a less than ideal parental unit, it was Gavin's achievement to raise his younger brother single-handedly, albeit within the framework of various council-operated foster homes. Gavin spent his entire youth in such depressing places, leaving at the age of eighteen, after having worked three hard years to save the money for his first leased flat. The day Gavin chose to move out was Duncan's sixteenth birthday, and they left together.

Duncan lived with Gavin for six years, until his twenty-second birthday, when around the time Stan and Gavin were dealing cannabis he enlisted in the Army. Since then, with the Black Watch regiment, Duncan has served as a mechanical engineer in Gibraltar, Cyprus and the former Yugoslavian states. Now he is a decorated captain, heading a communications task centre in Iraq. His rotation ends in early February. If he lives that long.

'His station took quite heavy fire last week and an American based with him lost his legs,' Gavin explains. 'He moves soon to Basra in the south. At least he has his regulation equipment now, which is one less thing to worry about.'

'Tell him I was asking.'

'Of course. Stan…'

'Table's ready, Stanley,' Fanny interrupts, clicking her palm-held computer.

'Excellent.' Stan hides his annoyance at the interruption, looking over Fanny's suit with an appraising eye. 'Francis, yie look wonderful. I hope Gus isnae whipping yie too hard.'

'Morse the pity. Yie dinnae look too bad yirsel, Stan.' She offers her arm. 'I'll show yie over.'

Taking his newspaper and his briefcase, Stan takes Fanny's arm and is about to leave Gavin without another word, when Gavin asks, knowing fine:

'How was Lewis, by the way? Guid to be back, eh?'

Walking away, Stan answers with a polite smile and an uncharacteristic single fingered gesture.

Despite the sheer drop of hundreds of feet, shielded from death by only luck and a flimsy steel railing, Charlie drives at fantastic speed, pushing her Cortina through the narrow, winding curves, rising and falling, and sucks harshly on a potent joint, her third of the journey. Her toory sits low over her head, trapping her hair, nearly covering her ruby eyeballs. Auden's *Night Mail* repeats in her head.

The Devils Beeftub outside Moffat is a natural basin sunk into the enormous Borders landscape, once used for storing thieved English cattle. Fog hangs, hiding the true depths of the basin, but the sun shines fiercely.

Charlie hates driving in the city. So infuriating are the numerous traffic lights, road works, multi-lane roads, ignorant bus and taxi drivers, and especially the other cars, that there is no enjoyment left for her at all. Out here, however, alone on the road, pleasure spills over her. The danger of the situation she barely registers, inhaling again, and as she slips down a gear, accelerates into a turn, she kills a pheasant on the grill.

G. W. F. Associates have represented Janet for eight years, but this is the first time they have invited her to lunch. Not that she is complaining. Since her husband died ten years ago leaving her Leith Furnishings and Upholsteries, retailers since 1928, Janet has becomes something of a self-taught gastronome, albeit for one, and the opportunity to enjoy a grilled trout in the handsome stillness of the great chef Dussollier's restaurant is simply too good to query.

'Yie arenae gaun too far, Rosemary?' she chews.

'Aye.' In a quilted grey satin office suit with eyehooks rather than buttons, her new Jimmy Choo's unseen, Rose smiles politely, feeling a headache form behind her blue eyes. 'Quite far, to just outside Cardiff.'

'In Wales?'

'Aye. To the town of Caerphilly, of cheese fame, although they dinnae make it there anymore. Tommy Cooper was born there.'

Janet shovels more fish into her mouth. 'If you meet a good Welshman, my husband used to say,' she spits as she chuckles, 'shoot him before he goes bad.'

Rose's smile is unwavering. Before her sits a delicious-looking plate of pan-fried scallops with spaghetti and a kale, caper and scallop roe sauce, but she has no appetite. She has moved the food around the plate for ten minutes. Lunch appointments were once commonplace within the industry, but in today's taut economic climate they have become less so. Dave arranged the present one as a leaving gift for her - Leith Furnishing and Upholsteries just happened to be the appointment - so she forces another mouthful. The wine is easier to swallow.

Rose has dealt with Janet for almost five years and is truly sick of the sight of her, weary of the sound of her croaky, cigarette-ruined voice, her refusal to accept change. To Rose she represents the epitome of commercial mediocrity. She is a dinosaur. She looks a bit like a dinosaur, a round, hunched woman with warty skin and peering black eyes set deep in an unwelcoming face. Janet buys her flat-pack stock from Pakistan, Taiwan and Vietnam through at least three of four merchants. But not for very much longer, Rose believes. Janet expects a place in her market without having to fight for it, appreciating nothing of the danger posed to her by such flat pack predators as IKEA. Rose believes that before long the dinosaur will be a fossil. She might be more compassionate - although probably not - if she knew more about Janet's circumstances; that while her husband was alive, she was happy to leave the business to him, trusting in him entirely, and that when she became a widow she inherited not only responsibility for business but also an unpaid tax debt to the Inland Revenue of £91,500.

'But dinnae worry, Janet,' she says, 'Mr Hume here'll take good care of yie.'

Enjoying Tom's pork cheeks, Stan takes his cue and begins in soft, polite tones, allowing Rose's aesthete eyes to wander. Although she and her husband have eaten here many times, the arresting flavour of the restaurant, its sheer authenticity to its art nouveau premise, never fails to catch her off guard.

A product of the arts and crafts movement with little historical development, the *New Art* style was originally a French expression against the machines and mass production values of British Victorianism, emphasising the ornamental quality of organic forms. British art nouveau began with William Morris, who would become its protagonist, and in Scotland, Patrick Geddes, a botanist. Morris and Geddes are both evident at Reserve in the cyclic wallpaper and hammered copper electrical fittings. The glazed brick wall is in the so-called Persian colours, turquoises, greens and reds, but predominantly blues, of medieval Islamic art, so influential upon Morris.

The entire room blinks with metalwork, glassware and ceramics. Rose picks out Gallé earthenware, which even from a distance she can tell is a century old. A Lauro mahogany bench with silk moiré of the same era sits impressively. But some of the furniture, particularly a very simple chest of drawers used for storing cutlery, is decisively older.

Of all the treasures - the restaurant is certainly a trove - it is to Rose, as it is to Stan, the paintings that are most remarkable. Hanging around the room are oils by Mucha, de Feure and Beardsley, prints by Toulouse-Lautrec and stained Glass by Grasset. There are three sketches by Stan's favourite artist, Gustav Klimt. The more modern work complements the style perfectly. The Freud is spectacular. Rose owns a Lucien Freud, too.

But of one image in particular, Rose finds herself unusually envious. Her lips curl. In radiant orange tones, A Paradox by Frances MacNair, done in

1904, is abstract, portraying wispy female figures, almost Celtic and almost oriental. Charles Rennie Mackintosh and Herbert MacNair met their future wives, the sisters McDonald, at Glasgow School of Art. Their collaborations, derived from the New Art, were treated with suspicion within the establishment, earning them the derogatory nickname The Spook School. Today, Spook work is as classically fashionable as Versace.

Rose watches a striking young waitress with the marble limbs of a Greek statue and the scent of aniseed serving soup to a High Court judge. She smiles beautifully, but her eyes do not smile at all, and Rose, who in her youth served her fair share of dinners, feels for her.

But her thoughts betray her. The pleasant reverie is smashed as she wonders how her husband is passing his day. But there is really no need to wonder. Stuart is undoubtedly sickening himself in the morbid and hopeless task of finding a dead girl.

Rose is instantly guilty at this thought. *Missing.* Missing girl, she thinks bitterly, sipping her wine.

'Hume, eh?' Janet's eyes sink further into her head. 'No relation I suppose to the great David Hume?'

She asks this not entirely seriously. Her tone is nearly mocking. But then Stan feels the small, round woman peering at his eyes. Not into his eyes, but at his eyes. Stan has his mother's eyes, as did his brother, Henry. There's no scientific term for the condition. Stan's seemingly translucent eyes are simply the consequence of freckles, the olive green pigmentation distributed unevenly across his irises, not connected in the manner that Rose's eyes are solid and clearly defined blue.

'Your face is familiar to me,' Stan's client muses. 'Are you local? Possibly I might know your parents.'

This is entirely likely. Doris and Archie Hume, before relocating to the Hebrides, were by all accounts well known and liked in Leith. The death of their son in 1983 is still remembered. However, Stan has little taste for discussing his personal life with strangers, even those who can benefit him. Politeness demands a response, of course, but this is not to say that Stan must respond truthfully. Affecting his usual courteous, patient and charming manner, he lies:

'No, I'm afraid. No relation at all. I think you recognise me, Janet, because for ten years I lived just across the road from your premises. I used to pass your place everyday.' This is true. Just off Leith Walk on Manderston Street, Leith Furnishings and Upholstery occupies one of the redbrick arched industrial units, squeezed between a brightly-coloured MOT garage and the MECCA bingo, across from where Stan did indeed live for ten years. 'But I live in Portobello now, near the beach. Please call me Sta…'

But Stan's words die with the expression of sheer terror that forms across Janet's face. Since the death of her husband, Rex, Janet has studied the pages of Leçons dans la Cuisine as some people might study Holy Scriptures. She has learned the Great Chef's recipes, his techniques and his variations. She has known him, his history, the problems he has overcome. She has all but loved him. Janet has eaten at Reserve five times in the past, always alone, and always with the hope that she might one day catch a glimpse of the great chef in person, which she never has.

Until now. Her pinhole eyes all but disappear up inside her head and she wonders if she has just wet herself. The great chef is less than ten feet away, in jeans and a jumper and with a baby in his arms. More amazingly, he is approaching her table.

Janet does not hear the beginning of the conversation that occurs between her new marketer and the great chef. She has gone deaf. She watches helpless as Vincent shakes Stan's hand and hands him the baby, who smiling broadly, Stan engages is a separate conversation of coos and baby-speak. Janet also sees the young and thin Mrs Dussollier speaking to other diners nearby and feels a flush of jealously. And at this, her hearing returns.

'What can I say, Stanley,' Vincent says, 'except that I'm sorry, eh? When d'yie meet the Minister?'

G. W. F. Associates are working on the Scottish Executive's Healthy Eating at School campaign in conjunction with two other agencies, and although Stan is working with several of his own colleagues too, he is, due to his 'connections', definitely leading the team. It is his job to compose publicity for the policies set by the Executive that the Council will implement, to which end he has secured the help of Scotland's finest chefs, including Andrew Fairlie, Nick Nairn, Martin Wishart, Tony Singh, Charlotte Brown and, until yesterday, the legendary Vincent Dussollier, who is at least half-Scottish but unfortunately will soon not be a resident. The policies, a fifty-million-pound investment allied with an effort to promote physical activity, are intended to develop positive eating habits and improve the health of a future generation of Scots by increasing nutritional standards. Presently, 20% of Scottish children are obese, compared to 15% of British children. Fruit will be given to all primary one and two children. Removing vending machines from dining areas and ensuring that where vending machines do exist in schools that they provide healthy alternatives, which seems a half-measure to Stan who would prefer to see all junk food removed. Stan has met several times with the deputy Education Minister, Euan Robson MSP, and the Civil Servant for Education, Mike Ewart, but after the New Year, a meeting is scheduled with Peter Peacock MSP, Minister for Education and Young People, and Councillor Lesley Hinds, Lord Provost of the City of Edinburgh, as well as many other councillors and civil servants, including the First Minister.

'But it's nae bother, Vinny.' Only Amanda and Stan call Vincent Vinny. 'Dinnae worry about it.'

'I feel bad, Stan. It's important, what yie're doing, and Amanda and I are sorry to be abandoning yie. I'm sure Charlotte will do more than enough, and tae be honest, probably none of the bairns would even ken my name.'

'Mibbae no the teachers either.' Amanda kisses Stan's cheek. 'Mr Hume,' she says, reclaiming her daughter and pulling her husband by the arm, 'yie're obviously busy. I apologise for the intrusion.' She smiles teeth to Janet and Rose. 'See yie Friday night.'

'Excuse me, Janet,' Stan frowns, faking annoyance at the intrusion. He opens a folder onto the table and eats as he talks.

'Janet, I've had a good look through all of this stuff here and I'm fairly sure that there is nothing that needs urgent attention. I like the radio adverts especially. I have no major changes to suggest...'

Stan stops himself, sips his water, smiles, and indulges in a quick mental account of the situation.

It has been made clear to Stan that Janet can be a difficult woman to work with, that she is *stubborn, not keen on change*, and he should make all efforts to *not make it harder than it already is*, especially for such a trivial account as hers. Only twenty minutes before, Rose reiterated these points, and Stan has come to appreciate that Rose's advice is always worth heeding. But Rose does not have all the facts. And there is nothing more important, great ancestor Hume once said, than having all the facts.

'However, Janet...'

7

She was running through the forest. Thorns and sharp rocks pierced her bare feet, sending with each step jolts of pain up her legs to the nerves in her knees. Her clothes were gone. Sharp branches slapped back against her naked skin, her breasts and her face. Blood clouded her vision, pumped hard inside her head. By the hand she dragged her husband, and behind him, throwing columns of illumination on the forest floor, the torches of their perusing executioners gaining, the sound of dogs barking and snarling angrily growing nearer.

As she hauled John on, Alison knew in her heart that he had not the strength to maintain. He was broken. Thin and drawn, his face had become grotesque, unrecognisably damaged by either gas or dire burning, she couldn't be sure which. His bulging eyes looked as if they might pop out any moment to dangle loose on their stalks. The right sleeve of the Wehrmacht uniform he wore flapped madly because there was no arm inside to fill it. Anger rose in Alison, a powerful fury. She wanted to scream: *Try! In the name of the child we lost, try harder!* Equally, she wanted to stop the chase and take him in her arms. She could do neither. She simply ran harder, dragging him harder. The hounds were gaining.

She saw the pair of rotted corpses on the forest floor too late and felt a shard of bone, pelvis she thought, penetrate and rupture her foot. Worse, she felt the jerk-reaction break her ankle and, in a spilt-second, she lost grip of John. He disappeared, and then she was falling, hurting, tumbling down a steep embankment.

She was hanging by the neck, thrashing her feet against the cold stone column of the church. Her fingers grasped at the noose to no effect; her weight pulled it tighter still. She could feel a stretching sensation and knew that the joints of her vertebra were pulling apart. Below, on the street, a crowd gathered to leer, parents with their children all laughing and pointing with blind staring eyes. Amongst them was Frédéric Trépont.

Her body swayed, weakening. She could no longer kick her legs, nor could she see, and with the realisation that she was truly dying, came a strange peacefulness. She ceased to fight. She could see herself in her mind's eye walking with John in the forest, talking and laughing happily. She was pregnant, her long, flowing hair hung below shoulders. She could smell fresh flowers.

Suddenly, panic flared in her. She was entirely aware of her situation, could feel the rope cutting her throat. And there was still a chance, there was always a chance! She tried to scream, but made only a choking sound that came from her throat with a knot of clotted blood. Life was running out of her, like her bowels through the tear in her stomach…

Violette Rodin opened her eyes, surprised by the reverie, and swallowed down a draught of rum. She lifted her face, which, except for blood-red eyes was chalk-white, to the waiter, wondering how long he had been standing there, and chose from the menu the veal cutlets, although the effort took more than one attempt to produce sound…

Presented in her customary spotless laboratory overall, as well as full make-up and jewellery, her blonde hair held tight in a sliver clasp, Elizabeth M. Brown B.D.S (Edi) lifts her eyes to find the source of the draft that disrupts the pages of her Alison Gorry novel. Not often in life is Margot surprised. She is a creature of habit. Her environment is controlled, ordered and predictable. But now, the vision standing in the coloured light of the non-figurative stained glass window steals the breath from her. Her soupspoon hovers in the air as her grey eyes move fitfully, amazedly. But Margot is not a woman to be thrown for very long.

'Darling,' she pronounces, and then swallowing down her broth, carefully marks her page with a leather marker. 'Ciao!'

'Hi, mum.'

Charlie's arrival in Kirkcudbright is timed precisely to coincide with the surgery's lunch hour and she is unsurprised to find Margot exactly where she has taken lunch alone for twenty years, looking out the window over the town square. The airy, clove-scented reception room is unchanged. Rather than magazines, laden bookcases display old penny-dreadful romances, National Geographic's and Burns. Wall-mounted, a beautiful image of a crimson-haired child baring her perfect teeth for the camera that could be an oral hygiene advert is in fact a photograph of Charlie aged seven.

Aged twenty-seven, Charlie pockets a new toothbrush from the display, enjoying the crinkle of its wrapper between her small, hash-stained fingers, and crosses to kiss Margot's cheek

'You look well,' she says, easily slipping into her natural twang.

Margot accepts the compliment and pointing her soupspoon, replies:

'There's tea if you want. It isn't cold yet.'

This, after almost a year, is exactly the welcome Charlie anticipated. No tearful embrace. No flattering complements. Just tea. She regards the uncomfortable chairs, her back stiff from the two-hour drive, and asks:

'Have you got time to give me a polish?'

'Darling,' Margot's plucked eyebrows lift, 'you look like you need one.'

In a room made famous by the fact that Robert Burns once conjugated in it and then immortalised the event by engraving a few lines on a wall, which is now protected and hidden, Charlie lies back into the surgery chair and curls her fingers over the armrests. Similar to the reception room, stained glass reclaimed from the town's now-destroyed Church of Saint Cuthbert illuminates the space in strange airy hues. Monk, missionary and allegedly blessed with the gift of healing, Cuthbert - not yet a saint in the seventh century - had a fondness for Galloway and gave his name to its largest county, Kirk-Cuthbert, which would become Kirkcudbright, although later in life he desired solitude and built himself a secluded hut on the shores of the Nor'loch at the foot of Edinburgh Castle, where today St Cuthbert's stands.

'I read in the Scotsman that you cooked for the Queen.' Margot finishes her tinned broth. 'What was she like?'

'Quite like you, mother, but patient and tolerant,' Charlie says. The tart antiseptic smell makes her feel small. 'I suppose she's like one would expect in that she does what's expected of her. She certainly cleared her plate. That was the second time I've met her.'

Margot dismisses the reproach. 'Did she ask for you specifically?'

'Apparently. I got a phone call the night before like something from a MI5 film asking if I could do it, and I got to Holyrood expecting to see loads of different chefs cooking for a big function or something, but it was only me. There wasn't a function or even a dinner party. I just cooked her dinner, which she ate alone. The Duke was abroad. Afterwards we had a cup of coffee, she showed me some of the old paintings of Mary Stuart. We talked about the parliament building, I gave her my opinion to which she made nice noises and gave nothing away. I made her what was effectively a fish supper, she told me she liked my hair, and that was it.'

'And Vincent? Still handsome as ever I expect.'

'He asked me to pass on his regards. He's retiring. He and his family are moving to France.'

'Open wide.' Margot snaps on latex gloves but not a facemask and missing the significance of Vincent's departures, says as she begins her examination:

'Old Mr Wyllie retired too, so I'm seeing practically all of his patients now. He retired on the Tuesday and he dropped dead on the Friday. Tragic, really. I have heard it said that some young Turk from south of the border is buying his surgery, but you know what this town's like for blether. I shant hold my breath. Still, one must live in hope. There's easily enough work for two, and in a town this size,' Margot's eyes narrow mischievously, eerily like Charlie's, 'fresh blood is always valuable.'

'If he'sh only oung, he ight need shome coaching,' Charlie remarks as best she is able.

Margot, expert in conversing with someone who has her fingers in their mouth, smiles drying. 'Or if I'm persuasive enough.'

But the smirk falls from her face and her expression changes to one of abhorrence. 'Charlotte!' She retracts her probe markedly. 'Is that nasty pulp of a thing that was at some point a molar not painful?'

'Not anymore.'

'You really should know better. All that smoking, darling.' She tuts. 'I'll remove it. Lignocaine?'

'No, thanks.'

After graduating from the University of Edinburgh in 1972 and forsaking a promising career as a concert pianist, Elizabeth Margot Cole accepted her first job as a qualified dentist with a small family practice in Kirkcudbright. Her parents, from Renfrewshire, had already succumbed to the family tendencies for cancer, and being an only child, Kirkcudbrightshire had seemed as good a place as any other. And it was. Two happy years passed in a blink.

Margot's life would change immeasurably, however, with the arrival in town of the new, fiery-haired General Practitioner, Dr Charles Brown, from London, who had shocking trouble with his wisdom teeth. They married almost immediately. Their daughter Charlotte inherited her mother's grey eyes and her father's wiry scarlet hair.

In the twenty years since her husband's drowning, Margot has come to appreciate that she was to all intent and purpose an awful mother, although not entirely; Charlie is after all the most successful chef in the country. Charles' life insurance allowed the purchase of the surgery from Margot's retiring employer and this was where she invested her energies, working, she had foolishly assumed, for the greater good. Detachment grew between mother and daughter, and then finally disinterest, until the only activity truly shared by mother and daughter was reading, which naturally they did in silence and more often than not in separate rooms.

Charlotte's needs, neglected by her mother, were satisfied elsewhere.

High School was a difficult time for Charlotte, not for the usual reasons of peer pressure, exam pressure or the fluctuation of hormones, but rather because Margot slept at least once with most of her male teachers. Margot's needs, too, as it turned out, needed satisfying. One incident from Charlie's third year at the Academy lingers in mind, a Christmas musical performance held in the Church of Saint Cuthbert to make money for a local old folks' home. Charlotte was asked to recite Chopin's Nocturne in B minor. She clearly remembers hunting for the requisite black skirt, typically, only hours before the performance and being able to find only one with a split side seam. She remembers Margot lecturing her about leaving such things until the last minute and then plainly refusing to mend it. Charlotte, being naturally clumsily, was handless with needles and thread. But she has always been resourceful. She mended the hem with masking tape that made a crinkly noise every time she moved, echoing in the church like a mouse in the rafters. Never had she been so thankful of her father's distracting hair.

The piano was a constant bone of contention in the Brown household. As a dentistry student, Margot played the piano extensively around the music halls and theatres of Edinburgh, often with the Scottish National Orchestra, which she did not only to pay her university costs but also for pleasure. Teenage Charlotte found no such joy; the lessons that blighted her entire childhood she considered excruciating, and would not learn to appreciate until well into her twenties. The grade-seven piano exam, coinciding with Charlotte's sixteenth birthday, marked a changing point in the mother-daughter relationship. Feeling pressured by her Higher Grade exams at the time, and a bit like Margot's doll rather than her daughter, Charlotte attended none of her lessons, refused to practise at home and just to spite her mother, passed the exam with merit.

Elizabeth M. Brown B.D.S (Edi) grips the decayed remains of Charlie's lower first-right molar between her thumb and forefinger and with a skilful twist of the chisel-like elevator, the rotted root comes away as cleanly as can be expected. Charlie makes no sound. With the forceps, Margot frees a last, niggling piece of bone and wonders in silence how her daughter fills her days, her life, though she has promised herself not to do this. Her husband's face, which had not grown much older than his daughter's has now, flashes in her mind and as she applies gauze to control the bleeding, Margot runs her fingers though Charlie's wiry hair, which is never an easy thing to do.

'Well done,' she says. 'Rinse.'

Charlie does so with warm, red mouthwash, spitting blood and tooth fragments into the vacuum drain, and then wipes her wet eyes.

'How's Stanley?' Margot snaps off her gloves. Stan always received his full name from Margot, not formally but rather intimately, in much the same manner she calls Charlie Charlotte.

'He's fine.' Charlie takes a moment to rinse and spit again and, standing, swaps her bloody gauze for a fresh one. 'That's why I'm here. Stan's finally bought a house and we're having a party on Christmas Day. It's like something from the Old Testament, actually. Stan and Dave have their families coming, so I won't have anyone to talk to.'

'You didn't drive all the way down here just to ask me that did you? You could have telephoned. We do have telephones down here in the sticks.'

'I wanted to see you.'

'Nothing to do with wanting that tooth out I suppose?' Margot looks hard at her daughter, remembering the wiry feel of her late husband's hair. 'Do you really want me to come, darling?'

'I wouldn't ask you if I didn't. You can bring someone if you want. It's Christmas, after all.'

Margot's smile does not falter. Charlie's father died at Christmas time, and this, although she was a small child when it happened and has very little conscious comprehension of the notion, is the reason that she dislikes the festive period. Of course, Charlie annually protests the increased workload, the corporate marketing manipulation and various other unpleasant aspects of Charlie, but Margot nevertheless understands the truth. She feels exactly the same.

And so Charlie's statement goes a long way to confirm Margot's initial suspicions: that despite her usual hint of a smile, her confident eyes, there is something very much the matter.

But she has learned by experience not to ask. 'I'll look forward to it,' she says honestly. 'Where's Stanley's new house?'

'Lee Crescent in Portobello.'

'That's near where I lived in my last year at University!'

'I know that, mother.'

Margot smiles. 'Well,' she says, 'things have a funny way of coming around, don't they?'

Charlie thinks about this for a moment as she fastens up her duffle coast, considering its possible meanings, and says finally and markedly:

'Go'n dinnae start, ma, eh?' she says.

'Talk property, Charlotte.'

Back out into the reception room, the clock is ticking. Margot's staff will be back from lunch in ten minutes time and Charlie does not intend to see them, particularly the receptionist who does everything but pinch her cheek and call her 'little Charlotte'.

'I'll phone to make arrangements about Christmas,' she says. 'What's your number?'

'Humorous.'

'Bye, mum.' Charlie kisses Margot's cheek. 'Thanks for pulling out the root.'

'Please take better care,' Margot says, and then, 'of your teeth, I mean.'

'I will.'

They face one another, mother and daughter, aesthetically like chalk and cheese, visibly related only by the shared colour of their eyes.

'Darling, listen, since you're here, there's something I've been meaning to tell you for a while,' Margot says. 'I think now's probably as good a time as any.'

Cancer is Charlie's immediate thought, the old family enemy. She finds herself stiffen, bracing for the news, but nothing could prepare herself what Margot actually does say.

'I'm very proud of you. So would be your father. I regret the way... things are between us.'

Somewhat overwhelmed by this statement, although not noticeably, and sounding more like Margot than she would have liked, Charlie says:

'Nothing to do with wanting to meet the Queen, I suppose?'

'Ye gods, no! Drive carefully. Ciao.'

Grinning, Margot turns on her high heels and walks away, but, her expression turning serious and honestly distressed, she turns and for a moment, regards the photograph of young Charlotte on the wall, and then her eyes fall to the Megan Poe novel, the self-proclaimed last of the chronicles which was released only last Friday.

'I've been reading Alison Gorry since I was a girl,' Margot says.

Charlie nods. She, too, has read Poe's novels since childhood. They novels were the principal topic of conversation in the Brown household for many years. While other pre-teenage girls were discovering masturbation in the bath, Charlie was in hers discovering Alison Gorry, completely unaware that years later she would work for the author's son and several times be invited to her home.

'Meg's eighty years old, ma,' Charlie says, and then stupidly, with utter thoughtlessness that horrifies her, adds, 'She misses her husband.'

'I sympathise.'

Charlie cringes. Because she has no substantial memories of her father it is near impossible to truly consider her mother a widow. Indeed, Charlie is apt to forget the fact and has, she supposes, no real concept of the word. She remembers telling Tom at the weekend that she preferred the term 'spinster' to 'bachelorette' and thinks now that perhaps she likes neither.

'Will she die?' Margot's tone in urgent.

'Poe?'

'Alison Gorry! Have you finished the book yet?'

'I haven't finished. I don't know if she dies.'

'But you have inside information!'

'I really don't know, mum. I assume that she does die, but why would I ask? It'd spoil the book.'

'Well, either way, darling, you know what it means, don't you?'

'Tell me.'

'You and I,' says Elizabeth M. Brown B.D.S (Edi), 'will have to find new common ground.'

Margot's surgery exits out onto Harbour Square, the heart of Kirkcudbright, which is actually a dismal car-park brightened by two terraces of family-owed shops, a community Christmas tree and the elegant ruins of Maclellan's Castle. On the banks of the estuary of the River Dee, Kirkcudbright was chartered as a Royal Burgh for trade six hundred years-ago, and trade - farming, fishing and the huge milk factory across the river - remains the lifeblood of the town.

With squinted eyes, Charlie believes, the town is quite beautiful. Guthrie painted here, as did Peploe, MacGregor and Oppenheimer, to name a few. Her mother owns a painting by Thomas Faed, a marriage gift from her in-laws. Charlie grew up without knowing any of her grandparents. Margot's parents died before their granddaughter was born, as did her father's mother. Charlie's father's father died when she was three and of course she has no memories of him either. But like his granddaughter, Cornelius Brown was a chef. At Claridges in London, he trained many a familiar name, including Brian Turner and Anthony Worrel Thompson. The present proprietor of Claridges, Gordon Ramsey, once showed Charlie a picture of her grandfather, the only photograph she has ever seen of him in colour, an 'action' picture showing him sautéing veal mid-roar, and, despite his sixty years, his wild scarlet hair.

Charlie is chilled to the bone. She stands a moment in the fishy air, pulling on her toory and feeling like an incomer, imagining herself easily distinguishable from the locals. She fastens up her duffle coast, wraps her scarf around and as she crosses the square with her hands deep in her pockets, begins to hum the Wee Kirkcudbright Centipede.

Memories fill her head but she easily pushed them away, feeling the breeze on her face.

She considers going home - Margot's home - for lunch but deciding against it, goes instead to the fishmongers to buy something to cook for Stan and Dave tonight.

Ten minutes later, armed with three reasonable trout in a parcel, she lights a pre-rolled joint openly and crosses Harbour Square. From the quay, without going too close to the edge, she can see anglers past the famed white harbour cottages who remind Charlie that until packing her life into one tiny suitcase ten years ago – for no other reason than to spite her mother - and riding the bus to the big city, she had liked to fish. She sees the factory where she worked briefly, up to her ankles in water, teeth chattering, shelling freshly landed scallops.

Two trawlers rest on their keels in the low-tide mud. In their shadow, Charlie arrives upon an old oak tree and a monument, a memorial, a simple polished black stone set into the knoll, and runs a finger over the indented white text.

> This community civically acknowledges the bravery
> of rescue crewmen George (Doad) Johnston and
> Dr Charlie Brown, who lost their lives to the sea
> saving seventeen of our sons.
> December 1983.
> In obliged memory.

Charlie exhales and begins back towards her Cortina.

8

'Let's you and I be clear, Mrs Mackenzie, just so there's nae misunderstanding. Yie ken how slow I can be at this time o'the day. What yie're telling me is that everything's away? Yie've sold the lot and kept nothing, absolutely hee-fuckin-haw? The Empire has fallen.'

Dave Quinn says this leaning forward with his elbows on his desk. He seems puzzled but is in fact only weary, ruined by a long, harassing day and a nightmare-pierced sleep last night. More than sleepy, his eyes are severe with exhaustion. Without the jacket of his patchwork suit, his unbuttoned shirt-sleeves hang loose, uncharacteristically untidy.

He confirms:

'That's what yie're telling me, Rosemary, aye?'

Perched on the sill by the darkened window in her sleek winter coat, her long fingers wrapped round a mug of hot herbal tea, Rose indicates by nod that this is indeed a correct précis. Her copper fringe falls across her eyes.

'Stuart wouldnae let me convert into diamonds,' she says. 'So we settled for cash.'

It is a common assumption, perhaps today more than ever, that the property market is a quick and graceful way to make a fortune, and that anyone who owns enough property is accordingly wealthy. Of course, both assumptions are laughable, but this is precisely the case of Rose and Stuart Mackenzie, who first conceived the notion some twenty-five years ago. Since purchasing their first home together in 1981 with the unexpected profits of a oil painting, they had until recently built an 'empire' of twenty-six private homes throughout the city, all of which have now been sold for a figure that even after taxation and lending repayments Dave can only imagine. Indeed, Dave considers, having only in the last few days completed the efforts of selling up and preparing to relocate to Wales, Rose is a remarkably composed lady. This does not come as a surprise, merely an observation. Rose is always composed.

But perhaps there is more to his concern. Dave and Rose have worked together at G. W. F. Associates for the better part of nine years and he has gotten to know both her and her husband as well as anyone knows them. He cannot help wondering, admittedly presumptuously, if in their childless existence their property business is the foundation that anchors the Mackenzie's to the ground, and he worries now it is gone, no amount of money will fill the hole.

Over her teacup, Rose plucks this suggestion from his eyes.

'Nah,' she purrs. 'It's like a great weight has vanished, a constant pressure that I equate to toothache, and now we can breathe again. It was never an anchor, Dave. It was just a great big heavy stone. Now we're finally free. Now there is only silence and cash.'

Through both internal and external protecting Perspex, the original tall windows of Dave's office look down over Princes Street Gardens, across to the Scott Monument and the festively-lit annual Christmas Euro-Market. In the centre of the vista, partially scaffolded, sit the galleries, the Royal and the National. Only the briefest of glances satisfies Rose. She has seen them a hundred times before. She rises, crosses the office and sits facing Dave, lifting her feet up onto his desk. She seems to debate herself for a moment, biting her lip, and then says:

'And let me tell you this, my friend, although I wouldnae tell many people: the thought of never again having to speak with another banker, non-English speaking tenant, social security scrounger or fuckin insurance man is almost as nice as the thought of never having to work again.' Unapologetically, gleefully, her lips curl.

'Ach, away 'n throw shite at yirsel,' Dave smiles.

'Want a Polo mint?'

'Aye.'

'Can I have one, too, please?' Stan asks this from the carpeted floor of Dave's office, scribbling on loose papers that surround him, despite the fact there is a couch. He wears his glasses but not his tweed jacket.

'Aye, if yie're gonna feel left out, Stan. Here.' Rose tosses the mint right into Stan's mouth, master feeding her pet.

The manager's office, though adequately sized and functional, is impersonal, arranged for its ergonomic value if anything. The only visual spark comes from a print of Saville Lumley's campaign poster: *Daddy, what did you do in the Great War?* Through the darkened doorway, the main office sits in abandoned darkness. But Dave realises with a shock that a figure stands in the doorway. And the figure has a gun.

'Nae cunt fuckin move!' The voice is strident in the stillness. 'Eh, this is a fuckin raid!'

In a sequence of swift and impressive police-like manoeuvres, including a dramatic forward roll, the intruder traverses the room and, finally, hands clenched in the shape of a gun, bends to kiss Rose's soft cheek.

'Cuffs?' she hopes.

'Later, ma'am.'

Having spent his morning questioning local paedophiles and his afternoon coordinating the effort to dredge the Water of Leith for the body of Megan Gillies, Detective Inspector Stuart Mackenzie maintains his usual fine fettle. Tall and athletic, although not as athletic as he once was, he wears a pale green velvet pin-stripe suit that makes Dave sick with envy. His brown leather shoes are pointy, by Vuitton. Ian Rankin's John Rebus he is decidedly not. He might be a Venetian art dealer. He sits on the corner of Dave's desk, smiling softly.

'Howz it gaun, troops?' he wonders.

'Gaun fine,' Dave says. 'Apart fae yie scared the shite oot o'me!'

'Good.' He turns to Stan on the floor. 'Howz Palazzo Hume?'

'I've got electricity now,' Stan says, scribbling still. 'Things are on the up.'

'I'm apparently bringing yie a filing cabinet the morra night. What time suits?'

'At yir leisure, inspector. I'll be in all night, thanks.'

'Huv yie met the auld dear below yie? What's her name, Rosemary? Jeanie?'

'Jinni,' Stan says.

'Jinni, aye! Stuart laughs. 'God bless her. She's a doll. She's about six-hundred years auld but she's better than a burglar alarm or a bloody great dog.'

'Aye, I caught her looking at me through binoculars when I was putting my recycling oot. I gather she's the Neighbourhood Watch.'

'If a rat farts in Portobello,' Rose says, 'Jinni's made a note of it in her book. Yie're in safe hands, Stan.' She rises, collects her Stella McCartney handbag and slips on her Jimmy Choo's. 'I'm fading away wae hunger, boys, so I shall see yies in the morning. I bid yies good evening.'

'Goodnight,' Dave says.

'Stan, have yie phoned yir parents yet?' she asks.

'Not yet.'

'Well, go'n no be an inconsiderate prick, eh?'

Hand and hand, Stuart and Rose walk to the office door, almost as if walking a catwalk, Rose's coat flapping. Watching them, Dave takes a deep breath, steeples his fingers over his desk and says:

'Stuart?'

Unsurprised, the Inspector turns and leaving his wife at the door, back-tracks to Dave's desk.

'David?'

Dave's resolve vanishes. 'Nah, forget it. Doesnae matter.'

Other than to slip his hands in his velvet trouser pockets, the Inspector does not move, and so taking a deep breath Dave admits:

'I saw the news last night on television, Stuart, and I didnae sleep a wink.'

Stuart nods. 'They're at the same school, eh, your girl and...' He winces at his clumsiness. 'Mine.'

This information hangs gravely in the room. Rose watches with glassy eyes, gripping the doorframe tightly. As a matter of policy, she prefers not to know the specifics of her husband's professional life, and now, enlightened, she feels selfish and cold. Stan, too, is taken aback. The news reports have said nothing of the school and neither has Dave.

Fatherhood is the defining principal of Dave's life. To imagine how it would feel suddenly to stop being a father brings him to a horrific mental place he can no more comprehend than bare. The sight of his ten-year-old this morning studying the newspaper reports with the expression of an adult between mouthfuls of Coco-pops is unshakable.

'Victoria's mother is friendly wae Sarah, Megan's mother,' Dave says.

'I ken.'

'I saw Sarah's picture on the front page of the Scotsman this morning while Victoria was in the bathroom and I vomited in the kitchen sink.'

'I can imagine.'

'But my concerns are purely selfish, Stuart.'

'I'm sure,' the Inspector nods. 'Yie need to know if there's a threat.'

This choice of words is hellishly perfect. 'I do,' Dave agrees.

Stuart's voice, disobeying his own strict orders, is sad and truthful. 'The truth is, man, I dinnae ken. I can tell yie that the girl, Megan, isnae just lost. Someone took her. I know that because we found both of her shoes in a litterbin in Gorgie and it seems unlikely that after finding her way out there from Easter Road by herself that she would take off her shoes by her own free will. And that, Davie-boy, is the sum of my intelligence. I ken it isnae what yie wanted to hear and I'm sorry.'

It does however answer Dave's question, and his mind swims with images of a prowling predatory paedophile.

'Thanks, Stuart.'

Stuart turns and says:

'Right, Rosemary.' He rubs his belly, which is not as slim as it once was. 'Serpico needs a fish supper inside him.'

9

No. 24B Lee Crescent, Portobello, is for Stan the realisation of a ten-year plan. On his eighteenth birthday, he began an endowment policy to provide a cash lump sum and increase his chances of one day being able to afford a nice flat, effectively a deposit on a mortgage. Stan went many times over the years without luxury and often necessity to pay the high premium, until the policy finally matured in August, returning just over twenty-two thousand pounds after tax. Dealing cannabis with Gavin also generated a healthy return; because Stan did not use his merchandise, he was able to work, unlike Gavin, on a purely profit-driven basis. After the bust, he walked away from the venture not only wiser but with eleven grand.

In September, with forty-seven grand saved, Stan spoke to various banks and building societies, all of whom offered him a first-time mortgage of around seventy-thousand pounds guaranteed on his salary and commissions, at varying rates of interest. In all his planning and dreaming, however, Stan failed to envisage the spectacular explosion in property prices of the last ten years. Charlie's flat on Gayfield Place, for example, has risen in value from the £104,500 she paid four years ago - no small achievement for a twenty-three-year-old self-taught cook, albeit a Michelin starred one - to a staggering £396,000.

Mortgage secure, Stan began the arduous and ultimately depressing task of property hunting. The first flat he looked at was a small, third-floor single bedroom affair on Great Junction Street selling for £89,000. The property set the trend for the next nine dreadful weeks of searching. From there he went to Easter Road, Leith Walk and Broughton Street before broadening the search to encompass Morningside, the Old Town and then the New. Never once within his budget was he inspired. Indeed, disappointment was beginning to weigh heavily, the acceptance that he had simply aimed too high. He had almost settled his mind on a two bedroom flat off Leith Shore for £102,000 that had the winning feature of a balcony overlooking the sea. The sea, to an Islander, is not to be neglected.

In early November, Stan's plans changed dramatically when Rose Mackenzie, casually, over the rim of a Starbucks coffee cup as if she was offering a Polo mint, presented Stan No. 24B Lee Crescent for £35,000: 'Exactly what Stuart and I paid for it in eighty-seven.'

Stan laughed in her face. Rose also laughed, heartily, holding her belly and wiping away tears. 'The joke is, Stan,' she explained, 'that having strived for twenty-five years to build and secure a property empire, watching ever penny and every pound, we've made so much money selling up that a couple of grand here or there means absolutely nothing!'

Stan's remaining savings bought suitable fittings and furnishings and a new fish tank, wall and loft insulation for the house and flying lessons for his father's birthday, which he failed to deliver. Now, however, he is penniless until his wages and commissions go into the bank on January 4th - not as promised before Christmas - and until then even buying food is a stretch. But the temporary strain is more than worth the prize.

This is how it happened that Stan Hume finds himself washing the dinner dishes in his first home, a remarkable Victorian quarter-villa not ten minutes from the sea, the week before Christmas in his twenty-seventh year, in the enviable position of being without a mortgage. Indeed, Stan has no debt at all.

The combined lounge and kitchen, its high walls toned in a variety of matt browns and yellows, is large and simply arranged, proportioned in the classical 'double cube'. Atop the rudely finished floorboards, two plain couches flank a huge wooden coffee table. While much of the furniture is new, sleek and cohesive, several pieces came from charity shops, auctions and eBay. The dinning table is black slate. Cabinet doors conceal a television and sound system. An acoustic guitar and a mandolin hang on the wall. The original hearth homes a spherical fish bowl. Stan has as many books as Charlie, although his are methodically arranged in sunken shelves and are almost entirely factual rather than fictional. New and old volumes of art history books sit rigidly with science books and books about politics and economy. Stan has a fetish for full opera scores, particularly for those of Puccini.

The most substantial problem incurred during the business of moving house was for Stan the choice of art, and after much deliberation and rearranging, the room displays only two principal works.

Russian by birth, Mark Rothko became one of America's most celebrated painters of the 1950s Abstract Expressionist movement, but because of the recent trend by high street retailers to punt nasty, scaled down, cheep prints of his work, Rothko's *Ochre and Red on Red* almost did not make it to Stan's wall. However, its yellow the only sharp colour in the room, Stan's reproduction is unlike any other he has witnessed, done like its 1954 original in oil, unframed and over seven feet tall. The work is not immediately obvious as a painting. It might be a part of the wall. Rothko did multitudes of similar paintings using different colours, until, poor and overwhelmed, he produced his final series of severe blacks against melancholic greys and then shot himself. But Stan's is not in this vain. To describe the mysterious and delicate equilibrium of *Ochre and Red on Red*, in itself a dark red rectangle with two smaller rectangles inside, one red and one yellow, is both impossible and futile. It is abstract, devoid of all meaning except to the individual.

The second painting is much smaller, behind glass and cased inside a thick wooden frame. From any distance, the image is a vague sandy-coloured mass with no apparent form, perhaps an ancient text or, depending on the viewing angle, a landscape. But a closer inspection, which can be disastrous for a person in a rush, reveals an entire ancient Egyptian civilisation in infinitesimal detail, hundreds of farmers, priests, pyramid builders and children busy with their daily routines. Done in acrylic ink, the work is by Stan's sister and is his favourite item in the tangible world. That is, except for his fish.

Stan is an expert fish keeper and breeder. There are eleven aquariums throughout the room, each a realm entire, all bubbling and purring softly and dancing with colourful life. Perception altered by the convex bend in the glass of the newest and largest tank, Charlie watches the few fish inside from a rug on the floor with immediate, unblinking fascination, deeply immersed in the act of smoking a joint. Music from wall-mounted speakers, a sublime, ambient sound, blankets over her. Incense burns. After ten years of cooking fish, her curiosity has not waned and she finds it impossible to resist the fantasy of eating Stan's beloved pets, sautéing them whole and serving him them with a nice peppery salad. Her lips are set in an almost-visible smile.

Dave has been gone for an hour. The faint smell of baked fish still lingers as Stan washes up the dishes, making more noise than seems to Charlie strictly necessary.

'Want cocoa?' he asks.

'Yummy.'

Stan finishes the dishes, dries his hands on a towel and sets a pan of milk to warm on the stove. He picks at the remains of Dave's cheesecake with a fork, a rich, succulent cake laden with thick cream cheese, about a million calories per slice but well worth the peril. He wears an ankle-length stripy linen kaftan, white and grey - £1.03 from eBay plus £1.99 postage and packaging from London - looking like an amalgamation of a post-impressionist painter, Moses and Wee Willie Winkie. Yet, he looks good, comfortable, at ease.

Whilst on his feet he enjoys for possibly the hundredth time tonight the view from his bay window, which is open to release Charlie's smoke. Lee Crescent is an elegant, concave terrace, each residence converted into two large flats, one upstairs and one downstairs; Stan's is the upper floor of the last building of the terrace, offering a view back along the street. The night is freezing. The only moving traffic is a Jack Russell leading a wee old man for a slippery walk. Charlie's Cortina wears a skin of frost.

At Stan's feet, behind the newspaper rack in the window bay, there is one final picture frame. During his University years, Stan was a keen member of The Pilrig Players, an amateur musical and dramatics society in Leith, and as his need to perform quickly matured into an interest in production, two of the Players' biggest successes were entirely down to his efforts. The first was Puccini's La Boheme, staged in Pilrig Church without electricity and with a twenty-nine-piece orchestra. In 1995, Stan produced an original three-hand play that ran as part of the Edinburgh Fringe Festival at the Pleasance Theatre, breaking a long tradition within The Pilrig Players by actually turning a profit. The only souvenir he has from this time in his life is a poster advertising Boheme, a simple ink illustration of an artist by his easel, which the frame preserves.

Walking back to the stove, marvelling at the warmth of the insulated room even in the dead of winter, Stan realises that there are lilies in a vase upon the black slate dinning table, although having already dined at it and failing to notice the flowers, he decides against saying anything now.

Settling on one of the couches, he sets the mugs of cocoa and his bare feet on the coffee table. Sinking low, hands clasped over his stomach complete the usual floating-otter position.

A week after the stressful relocation, the fish tanks are sparkling clean and there have been no fatalities. Stan keeps a wide variety of freshwater fish as well as dwarf frogs and snails. Two tanks are empty, specifically for breading, one as a base and the other as an anti-cannibalism reserve. The focal point of the room is a brand-new curved corner-unit tank that unlike the others holds no plant-life or ferns, only striking coral and bubbles. Amid its four-hundred litres of seemingly blue-lit water, only a few tomato clowns and yellow tangs swim. Stan's progression to marine aquariums is the culmination of six years learning, and a major step for him. This is where Charlie sits, fascinated, smoking.

Stan hears the music change from the ambient, pulsing modern sound to something completely different; Handle's *Ombra Mai Fù* from his 1738 opera, *Serse*. The stings and harp, warm and full, slow and comforting, fill the room with a glorious absolution, eventually giving way to the soaring soprano voice, tender and intimate.

His thoughts are a pest. He thinks of new billboards the Western Isles Cheese Company; of an upcoming conference with his recycling company; of the complex strategy for Shine's digital television release and the even more complex arrangements for the Government's Healthy Eating in School campaign; he thinks of the nuisance of the Edinburgh Zoo account and wonders how he can offload it onto one of his colleagues. And of course there is the Leith Furniture and Upholstery account. He pushes these things out of mind.

But the alternative is not much better. Stan thinks of his mother. It has been in his mind all day to phone and apologise for the disaster of Sunday, and now, underscored by the largo, he imagines her wrathful disappointment somehow diffused by the glorious sound. But this is fantasy. Maybe tomorrow, he thinks. Phone tomorrow. Or possibly the next day.

He moves his eyes from the marine tank to Charlie, wondering, his voice heavy:

'What did yie dae wae yir day off today?'

'Doctors in the morning,' Charlie says. 'Dentist in the afternoon.'

'Dentist? Which dentist?'

'Margot.'

'Yie went to yir mother's!' Stan sits up straight. 'When?'

'Today, Stan. I just said. I came straight here from there.'

'And?'

'I had a tooth out.'

'How was it?'

'Bled like a bitch.'

'Yir mother, Charlotte! I meant how was yir mother!'

'She was fine.'

'What does fine mean?'

'It means it was fine, Stan.' Charlie exhales smoke and her tongue finds the hole. 'Yie'll be pleased to hear that she says she'll come for Christmas dinner.'

Stan considers this. 'I am pleased, aye, but I'm more pleased yie went to see her. It's been a while, eh? Is she playing bridge tonight?'

'Pardon me?'

'It's Tuesday.'

'So?'

'Margot always plays bridge on Tuesday nights.'

'What the fuck are yie talking about, Stan?' Charlie inhales her joint, her grey eyes absorbing the colours of the aquarium like fleeting sparks. 'How the hell d'yie know what Margot does on a Tuesday night?'

'What do yie mean?'

'I didn't know that she plays bridge on Tuesdays.'

'Why not?'

'Never fucking mind why not. How do you know such a thing, Stan?'

'I dunno.'

'Think! When did my mother tell you she played bridge?'

'On the phone.'

'What!'

Stan thinks for a moment. 'Remember in the summer when I had the trouble with the abscess? I ran out of antibiotics and I couldnae get an appointment wae my dentist.'

'Aye?'

'I phoned Margot and she sent me some.'

Amazed, Charlie asks:

'Isn't that illegal?'

Stan shrugs. 'She was just away out tae bridge when we spoke. That's how I ken.'

'But... I mean... Stan, yie've never mentioned this before.'

'What's it go tae dae wae yie?'

'She's my mother!'

'Not noticeably.'

'Did yie phone Doris today, Stanley?' Charlie asks, turning back to the fish.

'Dinnae get pious wae me, Charlie Brown,' Stan smiles. 'Where shall I put the tree? I'm in a quandary.'

'Are you really going to buy a proper tree, with needles?'

'Of course.'

Charlie rises to her feet, stretches her stiff body into three different positions with audible snaps and settles on the free couch. Her hashish is wearing away into a not-quite round nugget, dusty and no longer moist, perhaps four grams in weight that will not last until the weekend. Likewise, her bag of marijuana is slowly disappearing. The low coffee table is a matter of interest to Charlie, made by the same woman who made her own, a DJ friend of Stan's; while hers is carved, warped and for its solid impression, delicate, Stan's is classically angular and solid. When the joint is complete,Charlie rises and Stan says nothing as he watches her disappear past the Rothko, past the slate table and out the lounge door, hips moving in graceful steps. Seconds later, she reappears with an already dog-eared copy of Megan Poe's latest book and then resettling on the couch with her legs crossed, lights the joint, mindful not to light her hair as well.

'Thank you,' she smiles, carefully gripping her cocoa in her small hand and exhaling smoke. 'Go'n shht. I'm gonna read.'

Lit only by a tease of moonlight, the small loft was desolate and damp, any hint of romantic decay destroyed by the stench. Peeling art nouveau wallpaper revealed budding branches of mould. A broken Christian Jesus hung on the wall above a flee-infested bed still with sheets. Ashes remained in the once-handsome fireplace. Clearly, the loft's inhabitants had, one way or another, simply vanished, and now in the May heat, the spiders ruled. The hovel's only redemption was the small window offering a splendid view of Hôtel Saint Marie, just off Rue La Fayette, not far from the church of Saint Vincent de Paul. Over the rooftops, the night stars were true and bright in the cloudless sky.

Alison Gorry stood by the window looking out, while on the grimy floorboards, Frédéric Trépont, hair brushed neatly, his long legs stretched out and crossed at the ankles, read, which was no easy task on account of the near-darkness. Yet, with his typical obstinacy and squinted eyes, he persevered. Back and forth, silently, the assassin and the schoolteacher passed a flask of rum that was rapidly running dry.

Initially requisitioned in early '41 as a Wehrmacht garrison, the Hôtel Saint Marie had since become a fortified Gestapo paper factory. But there was no administration occurring that night. Instead, a party raged. The entire structure seemed to shake, heaving and pulsing with life and music. Citroën cars brought a constant supply of wine and prostitutes. Schutzstaffel officers hosted representatives of the Wehrmacht, the Abwehr and the Luftwaffe, as well as Reichstag ministers, party propagandists and Italian ambassadors.

Bruno Melmer, SS-Captain in charge of stolen loot, had recently arrived with Raphael Alibert, Pétain's ex-Minister of Justice, the man responsible for the Statut des Juifs, consigning millions of Jews to death by either exhaustion in the labour camps or by methods more direct. On behalf of the present government, Pierre Laval, Pétain's Prime Minister, attended with Joseph Darnard, fanatical anti-Communist chief of Vichy secret police, the Milice, who hunted the résistance with the same fervour as the Gestapo, and were, like the Gestapo, willing to torture. It was a truly cosmopolitan ensemble.

Alison swallowed a draft from the flask and as she rolled the rum around her mouth, habitually surveyed the hotel's entrances, exits and possible areas of penetration. She saw automatic machineguns mounted not only on the roofs of the hotel itself but also on those of both neighbouring buildings. She counted, for the fifth time in an hour, eleven security officers, nine snipers and a small army of protective infantry in the shadows. Attack was impossible; siege would be suicide. But then again, she mused, had not once an experienced British officer said precisely the same thing about the Gestapo headquarters in Reims? Had she not achieved the task independently? Inside the Hôtel Saint Marie was a prize very much worth fighting for and she wondered…

Alison stiffened as she saw a lone figure turn off Rue La Fayette and walk casually the dark alley until he reached the guards at the hotel's main gate. Lean and lithe, with ink-black hair and the bronze skin of a South American, he moved with a noticeably light tread. His splendidly cut suit and overcoat gleamed in the moonlight, absent of any Nazi pomp. The holes that were his eyes reflected nothing at all. Alison gauged him to no older than herself.

Her perceptive instincts blazed. She was surprised to feel the tiny hairs on the back of her neck rise, which in itself was not an alien sensation; Alison fought a constant battle with her own manic paranoia. Yet, there was something about the graceful stranger, something perhaps to do with the way, as he exchanged a few words with the gate guards, he flicked away his cigarette. There was no immediate threat, of that she was certain, and as she watched the figure disappear inside, she told herself to have patience. Ideas occurred to Alison either complete or not at all. If it was not there, it was better to wait than to force the issue.

Danger, John's voice said inside her head. Be watchful, sweetheart.

Craving a cigarette, she denied herself. Cigarette smoke was the clumsy manner by which she was able to locate the Nazi sniper positions on the hotel rooftop. Instead, she swallowed more rum.

After reading Hugo's Les Misérables for nearly two hours, Frédéric was approaching the moment of Javert's suicide, but had not the will for it. Yawning, he marked his page, placed Hugo on the floor and watching Alison from the corner of his eye, retrieved from his coat pocket a paperback edition of de Gaulle's Vers l'Armée de Metier.

For three years, socialising had not ranked high in Frédéric's priorities. The assassin was in fact the only constant female comrade that circumstance had allowed him, and that she happened to be fifteen years his senior was irrelevant. Her thin frame clad tightly in black, her pale face and short hair, to mention nothing of her eyes, attracted Frédéric deeply, although while watching her, his expression was blank to the point of the macabre.

Quietly, his English tinged with the typical French cusp, he asked, as if the thought had just popped into his head:

'Why do you do it, Violette?'

Turning from the window, Alison made a puzzled expression even though the question did not surprise her. She asked it to herself every day, always without a satisfactory answer. In the beginning, loss had been her principal motivation, the loss of her baby and then only a year later, the loss of her husband. Later, rage became her fundamental inspiration.

'I do it,' she answered, more truthfully than intended, 'because I enjoy it. There's a certain thrill to it, I'm ashamed to say.'

An easy, disarming smile parted the schoolteacher's lips as he traced the Star of David on the floor with his finger. 'No, I do not mean the war, the fighting. I should hope those reasons would be obvious. No debate required. I meant the drinking.'

Now, Alison's face betrayed her surprise. It was easy to be loured by Frédéric, his comfortable way, his youthful optimism in the face of abominable things. His weighty manner somehow demanded nothing less than absolute candour.

'I drink for the same reasons,' she said. 'I enjoy it. The things I do are sometimes unpleasant.' After a pause, she added, 'I used to think that I needed it, that it made things easier, but of course that's not true at all. To be honest, I drink because there's nobody to tell me to stop.'

'Stop,' Frédéric said, smiling gently. 'It'll kill you.'

'The war will kill me.'

The certainty with which Alison spoke these words chilled Frédéric. It was his philosophy to find the strength necessary to endure his difficult existence by telling himself that the war would, on the contrary, not kill him. He wanted badly to argue the point but upon consideration found it difficult to do so. Instead, he stood to yawn and stretch his back with an audible crack.

'I wish you would tell me what we're doing here,' he said. 'I can be more use if I know what to expect. I'm not a child, although I do have school in the morning.'

'Patience,' Alison smiled, 'is a weapon better than any bullet.'

Frédéric threw his hands up in mock exasperation. 'Ah, yes, so you keep saying. But I think I would rather have a gun. Give me that flask,' he grinned. 'I'm parched.'

'I have some bread if you're hungry. It's fresh.'

'Is it kosher?'

'Don't be facetious.'

Looking at Frédéric, Alison was surprised to hear John's voice in her head. You like him, it said. And you want him. I don't disapprove, sweetheart. I'm dead.

'Violette, why are you looking at me like that?'

Alison smiled. 'I know I don't look my best,' she said. 'My ribs poke through my skin and my hair looks like a boy's. But I'm warm. And soft.' Doubting his interpretation of the sentiment, Frédéric's face flushed. But then silently, and with a confidence that thrilled Alison, he rose to his feet.

On the infested bed, protected from the parasites by Frédéric's coat, they made love, tentatively and tenderly, with their clothes peeled back only minimally. They nuzzled one another's necks but kissing seemed superfluous. To quell noise, Alison bit her tongue, and although she did not achieve orgasm, she was more than satisfied.

Afterwards, they finished the rum. Frédéric's gentleness, bodily and vocally, his buoyancy, soothed Alison, although of course she never lowered her guard. He talked of 'his' children and the day's lessons, omitting any mention of the distressing underlying current of Jew hatred amongst many of the children and the atmosphere of fear amongst his colleagues. One had to be very careful about one's words, particularly when living under an assumed identity. In general, he impressed Alison with his knowledge of literary history and his obvious passion for it.

But they fell surprisingly quickly back into silence, Frédéric reading de Gaulle, Alison resuming her watch by the window.

Twenty minutes later, three knocks on the loft door broke their silence, followed by a woman's whisper.

'Moineau.'

Alison opened the door. Escorted by a young Marlene Dietrich look-alike, Abbé Debienne and Claude Lemaître filled the loft to capacity. The woman, Juliette, was a Free French agent and had been in another life a gypsy. Awaiting deportation at Drancy internment camp in 1942, her mother bought a certificate attesting Juliette's value to the German fur industry for the entire family wealth and a sexual favour. Since then, her life had been the war.

'Merci de venir, messieurs,' Alison said.

After shaking Frédéric's hand firmly, Lemaître made a courteous bow to Alison and said in tone that was almost reverent:

'Madame.'

In addition to his strategic commander status within the Free French résistance, Claude Lemaître was an assistant schoolmaster who taught arithmetic in the classroom directly across the corridor from Frédéric. A malnourished man in his late forties with round spectacles and a respectable suit, a husband and father, Lemaître transferred to Paris last summer from a school in Reims to fill a position 'vacated' by a Jew, and it was in a similar manner that he was able to employ Frédéric Trépont, of course through an assumed identity.

In Reims, Lemaître and his wife had been involved in the aid and escape of Allied soldiers out of the country and the falsification of new papers. He had been the senior officer for Alison Gorry's first résistance posting, and he was - more significantly in his own mind - one of the people she rescued from the Gestapo headquarters.

Abbé Debienne was a different matter. A stocky, bull-like man without a neck, and a communist, Debienne's job was rather predictably to rally muscle. Panting heavily after four flights of stairs, he moved immediately to the window and considering the throbbing fortress across the street, released from his lips the mumble:

'Jesus fucking Christ Almighty.'

'I know,' Alison agreed.

'Violette, why have you brought us here?' he demanded. 'We've been told nothing! This is folly... to be here is folly! That place is a fortress. Look! See! If one of us sneezed too loudly, we'll all die here tonight. But not before we're... Jesus Christ, is that Prime Minster?'

A glance out the small window revealed to the band of résistance fighters that Abbé Debienne had indeed seen Pierre Laval vomiting in the hotel courtyard, steadied by his personal secretary.

'I'm leaving,' Debienne pronounced.

'Just be calm, Abbé,' Lemaître said calmly. 'Don't be so rash. Let Violette speak.'

'Abbé, you will stay here with Frédéric and myself. Claude, I want you to go with Juliette. She'll tell you what needs to be done. I'm sorry I don't have time to go through the details, but be assured that what we do tonight, we do not only for Paris but for France,' Alison said. 'I ask you to trust me.'

'You need not ask such a thing,' Lemaître said.

When Lemaître and Juliette were gone, Frédéric leaned back against the mouldy wall, folded his arms and looked to Alison expectantly. Debienne, however, paced the room, stopping only occasionally to look out the window.

'Well?' he hissed. 'What's so important for us all to lose our lives?'

'That,' Alison nodded towards the Hôtel Saint Marie, her arms folded, 'is a very big deal.' Her expression and voice were calm, which did not help Debienne's mood.

'Yes, I can see that with my own eyes, Violette! What the fuck is going on?'

'It's a social event more than anything. Laval's down there, as you've seen, and Melmer. Alibert. Darnard.'

'Darnard?' The communist had lost many comrades to the Milice.

'Yes, and Eichmann, too.'

Debienne jaw fell open. He stopped pacing, his square frame heaving with nervous energy. 'Adolf Eichmann! In Paris? I don't believe it.'

'I don't care if you believe me, Abbé. It's merely a fact.'

Frédéric was also astonished. That the Gestapo Lieutenant Colonel suspected to be responsible for the execution of so many Jews was so close turned his blood cold. His eyes burned. His hands became fists. He repeated the name in a surreal whisper.

'But guess who the guest of honour is,' Alison said.

With incredulous eyes, Abbé asked:

'Adolf Eichmann is down there and he's not the guest of honour?'

'No.'

'Then who is?' Frédéric asked.

'The Reichführer.'

Once a chicken farmer, Heinrich Himmler in fact looked a bit like a scrawny chicken. Schutzstaffel Reichführer since the thirties, he had by then, despite his neurotic social inhibitions, achieved the position of Minister of the Interior to become the second most powerful man in Germany.

Frédéric was sure he had misheard. He stared uncomprehending. His mouth fell open. He went cold. His legs buckled and he collapsed on the floor, cupping his heavy head in his hands, all sense of propriety gone from him.

Abbé was more composed. He asked for clarification in a clear voice:

'The Himmler is in that hotel across the street? Violette, you're sure of this?'

'I watched him go in myself,' Alison confirmed. 'I didn't expect him but he's been inside for almost an hour. I doubt he'll stay much longer.'

Debienne was talking, pacing again, but Frédéric had become deaf to the protest. He was remembering the April night in '41 when the occupying force tore down the door to the Trépont family home on Rue des Rosiers where he lived with his parents - themselves German immigrants - and younger sister. On that particular night, Frédéric had gone out with friends to see *Le Corbeau*, a film by native Henri-Georges Clouzot funded with German capital, staring Ginette Leclerc as the venomous, toenail-painted poison-pen letter writer. As fate would have it, Ginette Leclerc saved Frédéric's life.

From acquaintances made in the résistance circuits and specifically from Major Philip Scott of the British army, Frédéric later learned that more than three thousand Jews were imprisoned that week, his own family, like most of them, at the temporary Nazi holding station, the Vélodrome d'Hiver. The wealthy Trépont's went from there to the Drancy camp in the industrial suburb, and then in early '42, to the immense Auschwitz-Birkenau camp in Poland.

Misha Trépont, a naturally joyful girl, was eleven years old the last time her big brother saw her face, and eleven she remained in his nightmares.

Since those early days, there had been over seventy similar transports of French Jews. Frédéric Trépont, who had by then become on paper Michael Hugo, had witnessed many of them with his own eyes, watching what looked like cattle trucks filing through the broken boulevards. Of course, he was clever enough to understand that the Nazis were not singularly to blame. Pétain's lame Vichy government was equally accountable. It had aided, and aided still, the German cleansing efforts, consigning its own citizens to a life of slavery or to no life at all. Yet, Heinrich Himmler was the figurehead.

After a long time, Frédéric lifted his head, regained his usual composure and asked in a voice so stony it aged him thirty years:

'What are we going to do?'

'Nothing,' Alison said. 'We do nothing.'

'I beg your pardon?' Frédéric's eyes narrowed. 'What did you say?'

'I said we do nothing.'

'But that cunt cannot be allowed to live, Violette! If it is in our power to murder him tonight, then that's precisely what I intend to do. The devil's minion must pay for such allegiance. You and I, Violette, could each have fifty people here in less than half an hour. Abbé could have a hundred and fifty. I am not keen on the idea of death but I would gladly give my life to end Himmler's!'

'He's immune, my friend.' The assassin's voice was calm. 'Put the idea out your mind.'

Abbé Debienne sighed with deep relief, scratching his clammy forehead.

'Violette is right,' he said. 'A man such as Himmler is not within our reach.'

'But we could at least try! We could...'

'Frédéric, lower your voice.' Alison's face betrayed her disappointment. Watching Himmler arrive, she too had indulged the fantasy of presenting the Reichführer's head on a platter, literally, to Major Scott.

'But why?'

'Because of Heydrich!' Debienne hissed. 'Think, Frédéric. As well as passionate, we must be clever.'

Nearly two years previous, Lieutenant General Reinhard Heydrich, head of Reich Security and Hitler's heir apparent, the officer charged by the Reichführer himself with the Final Solution of the Jewish Problem, the first administrator of the concentration camps, was ambushed in his car just outside Prague by Czechoslovakian commandos. Heydrich died of the gunshot wounds he sustained while the commandos were sheltered in the town of Lidice by local residents. In retribution, Hitler annihilated the town, executing or driving out its entire population.

'If we took Himmler now,' Alison's voice was a whisper, soft, sorrowful and sincere, 'which I believe we could, then Paris would simply burn. The city and probably the entire country would pay the price, Frédéric, and it would be on our heads. We must have patience.'

'Patience!' Frédéric threw his hands up in the air, this time with sincere frustration, although he was mindful enough to keep his voice low. 'Fucking patience! But how many people will die while...'

The young schoolteacher's words died on his lips as he saw sense. Himmler, he realised, with his peanut-shaped head, would live this night. He would drink and indulge himself with whores and nobody could do a thing about it. It was a matter of playing the numbers. But with this realisation came another.

'Then why are we here?' he asked, feeling suddenly an uneasy tension in the loft. 'What are our intentions tonight, Violette?'

He turned from the window, first his neck, then his torso and finally his entire body, and the sight he saw him drained the blood that had only just returned to his face. He swallowed hard, finding his mouth dry.

Alison Gorry faced Abbé Debienne, her face set in a bitter smile, her revolver aimed directly at Debienne's head...

Annoyed, Charlie lifts her grey eyes and demands:

'What?'

'I didnae speak,' Stan says.

'Oh.' Charlie realises that the distraction is actually music. From the wall-mounted speakers she hears a simple piano line, stark but warm, instantly recognisable as the festive carol Good King Wenceslas. The volume is low enough to hear the fish tanks bubbling. But as the melody progresses, blending with a second line in the same middle register, a descending phrase that creates fleeting and sometimes abrasive disharmonies, the piece becomes, in fact, Nina Simone's Little Girl Blue.

Charlie exhales heavily as the sound deepens into a tumbling wave of scales and the dark, deep vocal begins.

'I thought tonight would be a nice easy, gentle night, man,' Charlie smiles sadly, 'with nothing to worry about and... and we could say things to each other. Nice things.'

Resignation crosses Stan's face, though he appears agreeable. 'But?'

'But there's too much gaun on. I'm stained, Máel, and ma heid's buzzin.' After his mother's father, Stan's middle name is Máel, by which Charlie is apt to address Stan for no other reason than she considers it a beautiful name and enjoys its feel on her tongue. She pronounces it ma-yell, more European than Gaelic.

'What's gaun on?' Stan voice is soft. 'Tell me.'

'Yie mean except for the restaurant closing?'

'Auch, big bloody deal.' Stan says this without condescension, but rather as a compliment. 'What else is gaun on?'

Charlie considers, turning her head back to the fish. 'I suppose I can't stop thinking about Megan Gillies. Dave looked hellish and it isnae even his daughter, and... that sounded unkind. I dinnae mean to be cruel. I feel for him and I feel for the girl's family. Imagine what they're going through, all of them.'

Saying nothing, Stan nods.

'Why that face?' Exhaling, Charlie realises immediately why, silently berating her thoughtlessness, and says:

'Oh. Are yie okay?'

'I'm fine.' Stan's green eyes follow a yellow tang on its hopeless journey. 'I cannae get it out of my heid that when my brother died, my parents were the age we are now.'

'It must have been just as bad. Will you put flowers on Henry's grave on Thursday?'

Stan smiles. 'I will, but I think you misunderstand my point. Doris and Archie, when Hen died, had already been parents for seven years. And yir mum, too, Charlotte, when yir father drowned, was exactly twenty-seven with a seven-year-old.' His eyes move around his new home. 'What I mean, if I'm honest, is that it makes me wonder what the fuck I've been doing with my time.'

This statement clearly amazes Charlie.

'To see Dave so passionate in his concern, even though it makes him so upset, fills me wae envy,' he muses. 'And of course, he's just as passionate when there isnae a crisis. To have that purpose, to have… God, I should phone my mother. She'll be furious. Anyway, that aside and forgetting the closure of yir restaurant, can we not still say things to each other?'

'I told you,' Charlie says, inhaling harsh smoke, 'my heid's buzzing. 'I'm stained. I'll read for a while.'

This said, she returns to her book. At least, she tries to.

'Can I ask one question?' Stan asks. 'Then I'll let you read.'

'If it can be answered briefly.'

'What are you going to do now?' His Edinburgh accent has completely disappeared. 'When the restaurant closes, I mean, it'll be a big change.'

Charlie lifts her stoned, tired eyes and meeting Stan's green, transparent ones, they dilate. She is particularly pale tonight, he notes, contrasting with the opaque grey orbs of her red-rimmed eyes.

'I dinnae ken,' she answers honestly, but then less so, 'I haven't really thought about it.'

'You should try to see it as a beginning, I think, rather than an end.'

Charlie's voice comes in her metallic rasp, her expression frank:

'But it is the end, Stan.'

The faint change in Charlie is easily perceptible to Stan.

'What dae yie mean?' he asks.

'Nothing. Ignore me. I'm stupid.'

'Do you want to dance with me, stupid?'

'No, I dinnae fuckin want to dance,' Charlie hisses without lifting her eyes. 'I'm reading! Leave me be. Please.'

'I finished that last night. Shall I tell you what happens and save you the bother? I know how little time you get to read.'

'Fuck off, Stanley.'

Charlie is faintly aware of footsteps as Stan crosses the room, but continues to read as she inhales smoke. The footsteps are followed by several indeterminable clicks and noises, but she does not concern herself, except to be annoyed. But by the particular hiss at the start of the recording, she recognises the music before it even begins, and she forgets to be annoyed, forgets even to breathe: the comical strumming squeezebox introduction to *Moon River*, Charlie's favourite interpretation of Charlie's favourite song, wordless and tender, recorded in 1976, the year she was born, by Jean-Luc Dussollier.

'Bastard,' she smiles.

But as the waves of the river lap against her face, it is too late. She falls helpless, drowning, and almost without realising, she is on her feet...

10

Fresh from the shower, wearing nothing but a cerise t-shirt bearing the words *Please & Thank You*, his tweed jacket waiting on a hanger, Stan tends his fish while enjoying a cup of black sugarless tea. The remains of his breakfast - eggs, cheese, sausages and herrings - lie on the black slate table. Aquarium regulation equipment bubbles soothingly, and the stark morning sunshine better suits his taste than the internal electric lights required at night. He feeds dry food to the freshwater fish and lettuce leaves to the saltwater ones, firmly reproaching himself that in the presence of the glinting marine corner-tank, the freshwater tanks must not be forsaken.

At one of the large tanks by the window, amongst angelfish, gourami, a clown loach and two dozen tiny neon tetras that reflect light like sparks, two oriental red fighting fish hover at the glass near Stan, seeming to jostle and vie for the master's attention. Smiling, he moves to tap the glass, but suddenly his sleepy eyes sharpen and his smile disappears. He stiffens to his full height and circles the tank in purposeful strides, considering each crevice from every angle, before, conclusively, and in a sullen desperation, he belts the side of the tank's hardwood casing with the palm of his hand, causes more pain to his person than ripples in the water.

A torrent of exited obscenities pours from him.

Startled, her crimson hair statically charged, Charlie sits up from underneath a blanket on one of the couches, her face aching from yesterday's extraction, her eyes bleary. Sleep clings to her.

'Stan, what's the matter?' she coughs. 'It's still early.'

Stan is livid, struggling for both expression and composure. 'One of these bastards,' he all but sobs, 'has gobbled up one of my fish! I think the females have eaten the male! Fuckin whoors!'

Barely has Charlie slept. Rarely does she sleep well. In white pants and vest she climbs across onto the other, cooler, couch, and a last cough clears her throat.

Quickly she rolls a joint on the coffee table, lights it, toking deeply, and her tiny frame convulses. She tries with all her will to remain focused on Stan and his cannibal pets, to enjoy the morning sunlight, to give herself time to adjust to being awake. But the effort is hopeless. Her mind has already changed gear.

11

Charlie spends the first few hours of her day cooking the books in the office. Self-taught in accountancy, she has been for eighteen months solely responsible for Reserve's financial records, enjoying the expression 'cooking the books' as merely a turn of phrase. She is meticulous in checking and musing over every invoice, comparing them with previous weeks and years, and is able to quote from memory - not that Vincent has ever asked such a thing - any figure from the tangled web of cost-per-unit, gross profit, tax, waste-percentile-per-unit, VAT, staff wages or leased equipment fees. She is also responsible for leasing the other four units of the building. Using her laptop computer for calculations, printing order sheets and emailing, she prefers to write out the final weekly books by hand. Of course, Vincent does have a licensed accountant, Maurice, a retired Royal Bank of Scotland director who comes in occasionally, but the act of handing him the complete record is for Charlie similar to filing copies away in a cabinet. Maurice's principal reason for the journey from Morningside is for a scone with jam and a blether.

Rather than in one of the couches or at the Victorian desk, Charlie works on a rug on the floor, under the cold gaze of the stone gargoyle, her back against a gothic pillar, her papers spread out in a wide arc.

As well as the usual business of running the restaurant, today there are the practical necessities of closing it to consider. She and Gavin must determine a timescale and make the proper announcements, both to the inside world and outside. Charlie's priority is the internal situation: her staff. Because of the nature of the beast, it is more than likely that she will work with many of them again in the future - certainly Gavin, Fanny, Viola, Arthur and several of the floor-staff - therefore she is keen to keep them on fair terms. To this end she spends an hour checking tax records, doing her best to make the transition easy for them. By hard experience she knows that in the upheaval of shutting down, restaurant staff are often neglected by the management, P45s forgotten, records left incomplete, wages and overtime unpaid. Then, after a dozen telephone calls cancelling supply accounts and equipment lease contracts she takes a full inventory of the various kitchen stores, satisfied only after physically counting all the stock twice.

The icing on the cake is the nuisance of Vincent's Friday night Christmas party, but Gavin, mercifully, has taken most of the responsibility.

At half past eleven, after a joint in the alleyway, Charlie changes from her combats into fresh kitchen wear, ties back her hair, and by noon the dinning room is heaving. The shift, though busy, is easily managed by Viola and herself with a pair of commis' and Arthur in the cold kitchen, leaving plenty of space to manoeuvre.

A glance to Viola is a pleasing if redundant action. With her usual leave-me-alone expression, the sous chef works with a professional technique that is graceful, mindful and in Charlie's opinion a pleasure to watch. Her station arrangement allows her to remain within arms reach of her pans, all her ingredients and a cool glass of sparkling water at all times. She is constantly fifteen steps ahead. It is a little known fact that the famous chef Brown's career began under Viola's wing.

With the benefit of hindsight Charlie believes that her decision a decade ago to withdraw from her HNC in Hairdressing and Beauty Therapy at Dumfries polytechnic college and to flee Kirkcudbrightshire was, like many of the big decisions in her life, taken quickly and without much thought. She has only vague memories of the move, her first week in Edinburgh flat hunting, or of the harsh words spoken with her mother, but she clearly remembers her first hours working in a professional kitchen. She hated it. She worked as a pot-washer in an Italian restaurant on Leith Walk. The job had the spectacular benefit of one free meal a day. One Tuesday in 1993, when the fry chef walked out of the restaurant in a rage, muttering under his breath, as Charlie would see often across the subsequent years, everything changed. Rather than hire another expensive and troublesome fry chef, the restaurant's owner, Freddy Four Eyes, a man so called because of his thick glasses and his uncanny ability to see behind his back, moved Charlie out of the washroom and into the kitchen. She was seventeen, untrained and worked cheap. At twenty-five and already a mother, Freddy's wife, Viola, was delinquent and disobedient, and hers would be a profound influence on Charlie. When that particular restaurant shut - over the next years many of Freddy's restaurants would do so - Charlie and Viola together migrated the Italian and Spanish restaurants of Leith and by the time Viola fell pregnant for the second time, Charlie's destiny, swayed by the entailing lifestyle of sleeping late, working late, sexual promiscuity, drinking and drug-taking, had been decided.

Like Charlie, Viola and Freddy Ritsos have done very well for themselves these past ten years, and for the same reasons: stubbornness and hard graft. They have become, finally, respected restaurateurs in the city of Edinburgh. But despite her independent wealth and success, Viola prefers to leave administrating the family business to Freddy, instead choosing what she considers to be working for a living.

'Chef, am I right in thinking that Vinny's selling up,' she asks, pealing steaming skins off boiled baby potatoes for gnocchi so nimbly that her fingers barely burn, 'and no leasing out the units? And that he'll sell cheap to sell quick, eh, since money means nothing to him.' After twenty-two years in Scotland, a touch of her natural Greek accent remains.

'I think there'll be folks living in this building by March, Vi.' Charlie plates two portions of her trademark scallops and a beef with oyster sauce,

131

allowing a commis to finish and load the plates into the lift. 'Unless you and Freddy make an offer Vincent cannae refuse.'

This is a joke, waved off with a dramatic gesture typical of Viola as she chops three garlic cloves into a near molecular state.

'Vi, what are the bairns getting for Christmas? Yie've already told me but I've forgotten.'

'Helen wants a proper painting easel and new brushes, so that's easy enough, and Luca wants a DVD player since he is after all four years old. Thirty seconds for table nine.'

Charlie rallies three of her eight pans. 'Marie?'

'Marie wants a tattoo. Freddy just about shit at the very mention and it took a great effort to explain that either she'll get it wae us or she'll go and get it by herself, eh? So where's the choice? I think it breaks his heart to see her grow up so fast. He grew up in a house of men, remember. He has nae point of reference. I dinnae really mind - no that it'd matter if I did, like - just as long as she gets something tasteful and no a Hibs badge or something.'

'What should I get them?'

'Books, chef. If Freddy and I buy them books they look at us like we're eejits, but they always read everything from good old aunty Charlie. What are yie doing for Christmas dinner?' Viola asks. 'Want tae come and eat wae us?'

'I would love that.' Charlie plates a lobster, a monkfish risotto and two crappit heids for table nine, which Viola meets with a chicken pasta and black winter truffle cannelloni. 'But we're having a party at Stan's new place. I told yie, eh? There's about thirty fucking people coming, all family.'

'Ah, yes.' Viola laughs. 'Sounds torturous.'

'You and Freddy should come. Yie could help me cook.'

'Aye, right. What's it like, Stan's new place?'

'It's the exact opposite of his old place, clean, spacious, stylish and generally lovely. But dinnae go near him for a week until he's finished painting, eh, or he'll have a gloss brush in yir hand.'

'Spacious enough for two, would you say?'

Charlie looks hard at her friend, her expression cold suddenly. 'What's that suppose tae mean?'

Grinning filthily, Viola ignores the remark and sets a sauté pan of baby squid alight with a loud whomph.

Time vanishes. Just shy of a hundred covers, lunch winds down, allowing chef and sous chef to go separately for cigarettes, although it occurs to neither woman to actually eat lunch. When Nigel arrives at two, Viola leaves to perform her domestic duties, which include collecting her son from nursery, feeding her family and doing homework with her daughters before Freddy takes over, allowing her to be back in the restaurant by seven.

Between Charlie and Viola there is love, but between Charlie and Nigel there is frost. This is not to say that Charlie is unappreciative. She respects

Nigel; she would not employ him otherwise. Above six nine-hour shifts for her, he works five four-hour mornings at college, and has never once been late for work. Under his hooked nose, the youngster painstakingly composes extraordinary terrines, pâtés, stocks and soups. He handles the afternoon trade single-handedly, snarling at the commis chefs and constantly sharpening his beloved carbon-alloy Japanese knives as if preparing for micro-brain surgery. He is a prize asset, a talented chef destined for great success. But for Charlie's taste he knows it far too well. His kitchen wear is the black of an assassin.

'Tony!' Charlie snaps.

'Aye, chef?' Nigel's tone is cold.

'Too heavy on saff,' Charlie judges. Saffron, the dried red-gold stigmas of the purple crocus, is the world's most expensive spice because of its labour-intensive handpicked yielding process and the fact that nearly five-thousand flowers produce only an ounce of product. Charlie's is Iranian and absolutely pure, and her concern it not financial but rather sensory. Nigel uses it to great success in his chicken and mussel soup, but his sense of delicacy is sometimes shockingly amateurish. He relies too much on sight. Taste, smell, texture and even sound are for him only backup senses. Charlie, on the other hand, can smell the soup's individual ingredients from twelve feet away.

Nigel hates such disrespect towards his food. He often suffers the same insults at college and is becoming practised at hiding his fury.

'A man,' he quotes the Scottish writer Norman Douglas, 'who is stingy with saffron is capable of seducing his own grandmother.' Quoting is but one of his annoying habits.

Charlie was at Nigel's age significantly less well endowed. It was then she ventured for the first time out of Leith into the pulsing, putrid vein of Rose Street, which exists to this day on its tourist and office worker trade, but is even considering the reputations of Niddrie, Sighthill and Craigmiller, the true gathering place of all the scum and diabolical life of Edinburgh. Eight months she spent working its multitude of indistinguishable bistros and back-alley holes, gliding mutely from one job to the next, and these months were not as she often considers wasted: she certainly enjoyed it. There are massage parlours about which she can tell a good story or two, although nowadays Charlie is loathed to set foot on Rose Street because it is simply filthy.

'Norman Douglas, Tony,' Charlie retorts, 'also said that education is a state-controlled manufactory of echoes. Dae as yie're fuckin told, eh!' She throws his soup into the bin, still in the bowl, which a pot-washer dutifully retrieves. 'And go'n put a smile on yir face,' she rasps.

The talented youngster considers retorting that being told the restaurant is for sale and he is out of a job is a good enough reason for a glum face, but thinks better of it.

'Chef,' he acknowledges without smiling.

As he is apt to be, Tom is twenty minutes late. When he does finally appear, looking like a half shut knife, Charlie is able to leave him and Tony to prep for tonight.

Back in the office, she takes her second shower of the day, scrubbing her pale body meticulously with strong carbolic soup and examining her feet - having worked ten years amongst the most gruesome feet of Edinburgh, she pays particular attention to her own - and then changes into fresh underwear and kitchen whites.

Settling in one of the couches, thankfully without the snoring presence of either Dussollier, she rolls a joint and finds her page.

Frédéric stood motionless, watching with enormous liquid eyes Alison cock the gun aimed at Abbé Debienne's head. He tried to speak but words failed him.

Debienne's eyes crossed as he looked down the revolver's barrel. 'What the hell is going on, Violette?' he demanded. 'Is this some kind of joke? This is going too fucking...'

'Your breath is already short,' Alison remarked conversationally. 'I suggest that you waste it no further. Put up your hands, stand against the wall and do not make me tell you twice. I'm in a foul mood already.'

Obeying, Debienne slowly lifted his broad arms, feeling as he backed up against the mould-covered wall an ill-timed revulsion and a spider web on his neck. It was not how he had envisaged the evening's conclusion. Forty-minutes ago he had been thinking about taking his wife to bed. Now he doubted that he would ever see her again.

'Monsieur Debienne, I'm afraid, that you have been deemed a traitor.' Alison took no satisfaction in the judgement.

Visibly overwhelmed, the communist stuttered the usual diatribe of injustice and innocence, recounting his escapades at Notre Dame where he shot six Nazis in a gunfight, ending with the factual statement:

'I have fought for my country!'

Although true, that earned him a bullet in the shoulder. The revolver's silenced report would be confused with the fireworks exploding from the roof of the Hôtel Saint Marie. Indeed, the 'bullet in the shoulder' had become something of a party trick for Alison. She had refined its intricate nuances over the last few months so that rather than absorbing the bullet, as sometimes happened in the cartilage, the tip of the shoulder literally exploded in a superficial haze of blood. The wound would not be life threatening. It was merely a teaser. Even before pain flared in Debienne's shoulder, Alison returned the gun's aim to his head.

'Try again,' she said.

'Yes, yes, I confess!' Debienne howled.

'Jesus, Abbé.' Alison laughed. 'I'd hate to see what the Nazis would get out of you.'

Frédéric was not laughing. His brow had grown dark and taut. Stood bolt-straight, arms folded, he appraised the situation with concentration. Alison's twisted smile terrified him.

'Has this nothing at all to do with Eichmann or Himmler?' he asked.

'No.' Alison winced. 'I'm sorry to involve you, Frédéric, but it was the only way I could persuade this swine to come here. I couldn't approach him personally. It had to be your people. I'm sorry I used you. Lemaître and Juliette are half way home by now, soon to be tucked up in their cosy beds. Abbé, keep your hands in the air. I know it hurts.'

Debienne's expression portrayed a sickening spectacle of pain, fear, rage, bewilderment and most of all shame.

Life as résistance fighter in Paris, particularly a communist one, had become a complicated and dangerous business. Propagated by Charles de Gaulle's initial BBC appeal from England in 1940, the original ideals of resistance had quickly sparked numerous factions so diverse that de Gaulle was later eager to call a second time for unity, again under his own leadership. 'It is desirable to avoid the proliferation of numerous, small organizations which could hamper one another, arouse rivalries, and create confusion,' he said.

Specifically, he meant the communists. Since the fall of Paris, they had been working nationwide in secret to publish a clandestine newspaper, L'Humanité, and to organise the resistance movement that would become in 1942 the Front National. Following de Gaulle's second call to unity, when the Armee Secrete, the Comté d'Action Socialiste and the Francs-Tireur, to name a few independent factions, were finally persuaded to unite, forming the Conseil National de la Résistance, the representative on behalf of the Front National at the first meeting was Abbé Debienne.

The Conseil National de la Résistance won the hearts and minds of the nation by publishing presumptuously and shrewdly a charter demanding a series of social and economic reforms to be implemented after the liberation of France, including universal suffrage, equality for all citizens, a minimum wage, independent trade unions, comprehensive social security and the extension of political, social and economic rights to colonial citizens. In Paris, however, de Gaulle's Conseil, like the communist Comité d'Action Militaire, was controlled by the Comité Parisien de Libération, which was not loyal to Gaulle's Government in Exile but because of its numbers, needed to be respected.

Outmanoeuvring his foes - something of a talent of de Gaulle's - he created the Force Française d'Interior, the only résistance movement that enjoyed the full support of the Supreme Headquarters of the Allied Expeditionary Force, under General Eisenhower. The communists, not only outfoxed, were in fact being murdered by the forces they once aided.

So it was then that Abbé Debienne had of late found that the business of freedom fighting and confused ideology often got too much for a person, and all that remained to do was please the only master one could: Oneself.

Abbé Debienne, the only résistance combatant Alison Gorry knew of any political persuasions who had actually met Général de Gaulle - serving with his Fourth Armoured Division as an artillery engineer at the start of the war - had been approached by undercover agent Franz Wetzler on the recommendation of traitorous Claude Blancpain, and had sold the movements and therefore the life of his ex-commander to the Nazis who despised communism as much as the Allies did.

Alison saw the plot against the General in Exile in its simple entirety and decided that Wetzler, who, except to use such an unreliable man as Blancpain in the first place, had done his job with the competence expected of the SS, deserved posthumous credit for more than just the exquisite orgasm his corpse had given her. She understood that the tall, dark Latino she had seen only moments ago with her own eyes was the gunman himself, if indeed a gun was the chosen method of execution. There were many alternatives. Obviously not a Nazi, the stranger was a hired professional killer, an assassin by choice rather than by circumstance like herself, and as such not in the business of signing contracts or advancing credit. Bound by an up-front payment, the assassin must fulfil his commission or face the wrath of SS-Reichführer Himmler.

Alison took the time to explain none of this to her companions. She was suddenly weary.

'Monsieur Debienne,' she wondered, 'have you ever cut a chicken's head off?'

Talk of decapitation did not inspire hope in Debienne.

'Yes.'

'Fascinating, isn't it, the way the body still reels? There's surprisingly little blood.' A twisted smile broke on Alison's lips. 'Abbé, Have you ever cut a man's head off?'

Sheer terror filled the man. His stocky legs threaded to give way.

'I don't know! I swear I don't fucking know anything! Please. Please have mercy!'

With amazement, in an eerie silence filled only by the sound of the party across the street, both Debienne and Frédéric noticed the profound effect the plea had on Alison. Her eyes seemed to cloud. Her lips curled inwards. The barrel of the gun dropped slightly.

'Yes,' she mused, as if in a dream. 'Mercy.'

But the dream ended quickly. Her eyes, briefly wistful, became two smouldering pieces of coal, and when she spoke it was with a bitter ferocity that chilled Frédéric.

'I require from you one only one thing,' she spat to her prisoner, 'and I, unlike Jesus up there on the wall, will not be denied. Rightly, you speak of mercy, and I shall grant it to you. I mercifully offer you penitence. Help me to right your wrong so that when this is finished you shall be received into the arms of our glorious Lord with forgiveness and compassion, instead of burning for eternity in the fires of hell! I need to know, in a good clear voice, sir, when and where de Gaulle is to be attacked.' Where this religious talk came from, Alison had no idea.

To hear his ex-commander's name spoken for he first time chilled Debienne.

'Or to be more truthful, I already know,' the S.O.E agent continued. 'I want conformation so I don't have to go running about like a ... headless chicken. Do you understand?'

'Yes.'

'Good. And I warn you only once, if you continue reaching for the knife up your sleeve I will cut off your balls and make you eat them, fucker, and you can forget about redemption. It'll be straight to the inferno. Or,' her eyes twinkled, 'the camps. So let's get to the point. I suspect that your man, at least Wetzler's man, based on information given by yourself, will make his attempt while de Gaulle travels from Algiers to London in preparation for the Overlord landings, yes?'

'Yes.'

'Where exactly?'

'I don't know. I know nothing. I... That has nothing to do with me, I swear!'

'It's okay, Abbé, I believe you.' Alison's voice was compassionate. 'Relax. We're almost done. When will it happen?'

'My information tells me that the General will arrive in London on either the third or the fourth of July. I don't know anymore! Nobody knows, not even de Gaulle.'

'By air?' This was an intentional lure.

'No, no! By sea. De Gaulle will travel under heavy guard with the British navy.'

'Very good, sir. And that's the information you gave Wetzler?'

'Yes.' Debienne closed his eyes.

Alison lowered the barrel of the revolver. 'Well done. That was painless, no?'

Frédéric, who until now had been merely watching events and reserving judgement, said in a soft voice:

'Was it for France, Abbé? For Communism? For the Nazis?' He faced the traitor for the first time, locking eye with him. 'Or was it for money?'

Swallowing a deep breath that did little more that aggravating his bleeding shoulder, Debienne pulled himself up and barked:

'I did it for my life! Your alliance cares nothing for my people. I have given endlessly and been offered nothing but the sight of my comrades shot by the same men they once helped. Or by women, of course.' He looked at Alison with contempt. But his tone softened. 'Frédéric, de Gaulle works towards his own ends, and we, all of us, are simply pawns, cannon fodder, while the man of the hour, who listens to no one, who steers the fate of France single-handedly, hides in Africa with his balls tucked safely up his ass. I did it, Frédéric, for the future.'

Amazedly, as if distrustful of his own mind, the young schoolteacher debated these words with a scowl. Alison did not complicate his contemplations by mentioning that during his army service, before being detained as a prisoner of war and his subsequent escape achieved by bribing a guard with almost eighty thousand Francs, and then concentrated his effort on the communist struggle against the Germans, Abbé Debienne, though a network of fellow servicemen in the French colonies of Laos and North Vietnam, headed a lucrative business selling opium. The armistice, of course, had restricted shipping and tightened port security, causing a striking hiatus in unauthorised trafficking, at least for non-military persons. By giving de Gaulle to the Nazis, Debienne had attempted to cut himself back into the market, his sense of nationalism bothered not at all by the fact that his future profits would be measured in Marks instead of Francs.

Allowing her lips to curl, Alison watched Frédéric emerge from his reverie, take two quick steps and then slam his fist into Debienne's face with astonishing force. Had the communist not already been against the wall, he would have buckled and fallen, but as it was his head smashed back into the wall, cracking both the skull and the wooden panels that covered the exterior stone. Debienne's left eye jammed back inside his skull and a thin spray of blood erupted, hitting the opposite wall, quite remarkably on the face of the crucified saviour.

Not that the schoolteacher noticed. He looked capable of cold-blooded murder.

'Frédéric, I have one more question before you kill him,' Alison said.

The communist's remaining good eye lifted to her as he spat three teeth out onto the floorboards.

Alison pictured in her mind the tall Latino. 'The hired gun, the one down at the party across the street, who is he? I should introduce myself to him. He's awfully good-looking.'

Only a stunned silence answered, so she took two steps across the reeking room towards the mess of a man, pressed the barrel of her revolver into the torn flesh of his ruptured face and repeated:

'I'm only curious. My professional nosiness is…'

A noise.

Like a cat's, Alison's ears pricked. Clearly, neither of the men had heard anything, but she was sure…

Again, the noise.

Feeling the familiar, choking fear rose in her throat like bile, searched her mind for the sound's likeness, she threw her eyes to Frédéric, finding him statue-still and suddenly very pale.

'Violette, did you hear something just then?' His voice betrayed his fear.

'Shht!'

And then she knew. The word that popped into her head and sent a shiver down her spine was:

Noose.

Like a rat, she had followed the bait and realised the trap too late. She was snared. Disbelief filled her, rapidly turning to anger, and she cursed harshly under her breath. How foolish she had been! How stupid! Her arrogance had caused her own death, along with that of de Gaulle, and, worse, Frédéric, who looked to Alison now no more than perhaps seven or eight years old, wringing his hands and looking to her with earnest, petrified eyes.

In Debienne's one remaining eye, Alison saw surprise and understanding as he realised the situation for what it was, and just as his swollen lips began to form a viscous grin of victory, she shot him twice in the face, feeling brains and tiny sharp edges of bone splatter across her forehead and cheeks. In sheer rage, holding his dead weight by his lapel in one hand, she shot him an unnecessary third time, and then motioned for silence from Frédéric, listened to the unmasked sound of boots climbing the loft stairs...

By six, the kitchen is a furnace. Stockpots, pots of soup, potatoes and pasta, the ovens, the pans and the body heat of Tom, Viola, Nigel, Charlie, three commis chefs and a pair of frantic pot-washers, scurrying like ammunition men in a battlefield, produce tremendous heat that the kiln-like cellar holds captive.

The dance itself is not complex. For instance, table five is presently a nine-top - a table of nine people - who each chef can tell by a glance up to his or her personal plasma screen have finished their starters. Tom carries the weight this time and therefore leads, beginning the step with:

'Five, brothers!'

Or, when he feels particularly enthusiastic, as he does now:

'Cinque, fratelli!'

Either way, he plates up a whole roasted pigeon with claret gravy, two pork cheeks with prunes and anise, and two Châteaubriands, one with oyster sauce and the other with Béarnaise, pouring over the sauces straight from simmering pans with deftness. Finally, from the oven, unable to resist a smile, he adds to the order one of his kidney and heart bridies that now in their third day are becoming something of a cult classic. The plates go to Nigel for finishing and the dirty pans he throws, literally lobs, towards one of the pot-washers or straight through to the washroom door depending on which opportunity presents itself in the moment. Once Nigel has added the appropriate accompaniments - red cabbage and roasted chestnuts for the pigeon, Brussels sprouts and carrots for the pork, roasted root vegetables for the steaks - he passes the plates under Charlie's steely grey eyes for inspection. So respected in Charlie's kitchen is the humble potato that she has a dedicated commis churning out a constant line of dauphinoise, boulangère, fondant, mashed, croquette and rösti potatoes, as well as gnocchi, stovies, hash browns, wedge and straw-cut chips and even the occasional potato scone. Viola has a single plate for table five, a mushroom and mascarpone lasagne with a salad bowl for the table, which Charlie does not need to check. Viola also has pastas ready, a simple double tap - table for two - and these plates go as well. Likewise, Nigel has the starters for table eleven ready - mussels, a kale-wrapped salmon terrine with sautéed foie gras and two bowls of his own variation on Potage à la Reine, the 'fashionable white soup'. Charlie completes the order for table five with sole soufflés and a grilled whole trout served simply with a few chips and a generous sorrel and rocket salad. The plates - table five, Viola's double-tap and Nigel's table eleven starters - are loaded into the service lifts by commis chefs, along with oeuf à la neige, two of his famous meringue Snowmen and basket of fresh rolls from Arthur in the cold kitchen, and after brief communiqué with Gavin by intercom, the food is gone, the order forgotten. The entire performance takes less than seven seconds and requires no communication at all other than Tom's initial signal.

The difficulty in the dance is keeping in step. The tide is relentless.

Charlie prepares her usual barrage of sole soufflés, monkfish risottos, parcelled baby mackerels, crappit heids, spicy salmon broth, oysters, mussels, lobster and, of course, her ever popular pan-fried scallops with spaghetti and kale, caper and scallop roe sauce. Her special tonight is seafood cassoulet. Chunks of salmon, sole and sea bass are sautéed in oil for three minutes with peeled langoustines and scallops, which she then removes to an individual-portion casserole dish. In the same pan, she sautés bacon, chopped onion and fennel until coloured before adding and cooking off dry white wine. Chopped peeled tomatoes and shredded kale go in and then after a moment haricot beans, fish stock and seasoning, particularly black pepper. To taste, she adds a finely chopped black truffle. After boiling, Charlie adds double cream and pours the mixture into the casserole dish with the seafood, which is finally cooked in the oven for eight minutes.

With no respite in sight, time has lost all perspective, reduced to multiple, overlapping arrival-times for the sixty-five meals delegated throughout the kitchen. Every hour brings a fresh wave of hungry bellies, made worse by the fact that it is almost Christmas. However, gone are the days of George Orwell's 'clanging inferno' kitchens, at least at Reserve. The computerized order system displays all pending orders on plasma-screens attached to the red-brick ceiling above each cook, eliminating the barrage of old-school banter.

Above the constantly squawking intercom and the humming air-vent system there is a light chatter.

'So how long have we got, chef,' Tom asks, 'before I need to shave and go and find another job? How long will it take Vincent to sell the restaurant?'

'He isnae selling the restaurant,' Viola corrects, dunking ravioli. 'He's selling the building.'

'What'll happen to the restaurant?'

'What restaurant?' Charlie explains.

'Ah, I see. Well, either way,' the butcher declares, 'this is bad shit, baby. It's crisis time. I need to pay rent at the hostel for another month and I've spent all my savings on my plane ticket home.' A thought illuminates his face. 'What about the Logie?' he muses. 'Vincent'll gimme work there, huh? It would mean travelling every day, but think of all that blood! No, hang on, Eva and I could move there, yeah!'

'Already sold,' Charlie says, mixing a simple aïoli for lobster.

'What is?'

'The farm. And the fish farm.'

'Cunt. Well, I suppose a change is as good as a rest,' he philosophises dryly. 'I'll just fry mars bars for a living. Hardly sounds disheartening at all.'

The Australian is a matter different from the precision of Viola and Tony entirely. Greasy and bloodstained, he slams his way around the kitchen with vigorous expertise, pounding meat, sautéing, searing, throwing handfuls of ingredients into his collection of sizzling pans while gulping pints of water to replace lost body fluid and smearing the icy glass across his forehead. Tom's true passion, however, is to flambé. The incandescent colours of the flames make him grin every time.

Red meats are naturally the butcher's area of expertise and he is an excellent saucier, and as much as his ability in these fields Charlie values Tom's workhorse mentality. The Australian rightly takes pride in his ability to bare an enormous workload for immense periods, losing neither his levity nor his finesse. His special tonight is a Florentine pork pie, caramelised with milk.

Charlie's apprenticeship into professional cooking, that is to say her romance with it, just as Tom's is beginning now, came six years ago, after three years of working the unmemorable kitchens of Leith, Stockbridge, Southbridge, George Street, Lothian Road and the Royal Balmoral and Caledonian Hilton hotels while simultaneously attended dance classes, boxing lessons and working every shift she could manage in a culinary bookshop on the Grass market that was at the time owned by Clarissa Dickson Wright of Two Fat Ladies fame. During these early years, as Tom does now, Charlie learned daily, firstly how to cook properly and secondly how to overcome her physical smallness. Then things really took off.

Charlie's career has become a matter of folklore in the city trade underbelly, never quite believed by those who do not know her personally. In 1996, she won her first chef's position in a Stockbridge fish restaurant, the

Oyster Tavern, and for her efforts there received the City Chef Award. The following year, at the age of twenty-three, she won the noted Bib Gourmand for a modest establishment on the High Street. The year after that, two weeks before her twenty-fourth birthday, Charlie became Britain's first female Michelin approved chef and simultaneously the youngest Michelin star winner in the world. Her achievement made all the national newspapers and indeed some of the international ones, inspiring a BBC documentary and a book. It also inspired bitter grumbling from the establishment that to this day persists. Not that Charlie concerns herself.

Less well known is that just prior to the turn of the millennium Charlie was raped. Walking home down Leith Walk, she was dragged kicking and screaming into a car. She was bound,beaten,sodomized and choked to the point of unconsciousness by a petrol-soaked rag, and her remarkable strength could do nothing to prevent it. Her assailant, a certified lunatic released from incarceration on the ground of the useless Mental Health Act only two days previous, committed suicide days after the attack by downing in the Water of Leith, ending the chance of any kind of reprisal and any lingering anger on Charlie's part. It was, she tells herself, just one of those things.

Two months after returning to work, the great chef Vincent Dussollier invited her to run Reserve, which still in its first year, had just lost its chef, the now Mrs Amanda Dussollier. Since then, Charlie has won two more Michelin stars and turns down job offers every week.

'Table two!'

Within seconds, a monkfish risotto, two truffle cannelloni's, a chateaubriand, a lobster, a roasted pigeon, pan-fried scallops and a crappit heid are gone from sight.

'Tony, what about you, bawbag?' Tom converses with Nigel because nobody else does. 'What will you do when the restaurant shuts? College ends pretty soon, huh?'

Without lifting his hooked nose, Nigel remarks:

'Couldnae gie two fucks. I have exams soon and I never liked this kitchen anyway. It's claustrophobic.'

Charlie has to remind herself than in his youth, his faultless naivety, though a more able cook than she was at twenty, Nigel is still very much unaware of the practicalities of his chosen trade, that when he finishes college and Reserve is closed, he will never again in Edinburgh find such a professional, civilised and particularly highly paid job, poor little spoiled bastard. Viola feels the same and indeed, judging by her taut expression, is about to say something particularly nasty when as if by extrasensory perception, Arthur saves her the bother.

With a puff of flour, the cold kitchen doors fly open. The cold kitchen is in effect a bakery. From scratch Arthur bakes breads, scones, buns, puddings and tartlets, cakes, fruit pies, cheesecakes, profiteroles and trays of tablet, fudge, macaroon and treacle. It is to Charlie, who resists sweet things, a gar-

142

den of temptation to be avoided as much as possible. A small man in a neat polo shirt and apron, no bigger than Charlie, with thick-rimmed spectacles, Arthur is seventy-three years old but physically firm from a life of lifting heavy flour sacks, loading hot ovens, and balling and kneading dough. Presently, steam seems to come from his ears.

A teacher at Le Cordon Bleu in Paris in the 1950s, the name of Art McAlister in Manhattan in the 60s and 70s held more sway than the name Vincent Dussollier ever held in London throughout the 1980s. Arthur provided most of the desserts in Vincent's book. The privilege of Arthur's long career: he has lived to witness his reputation fade and all his contemporaries die. Indeed, he had retired to a tiny, obscure Caribbean island before returning to his hometown at the request of Chef Vincent Dussollier to begin Reserve. Arthur, although no longer a famous man by any means, is as much as Vincent the ideal, the goal, to which Charlie has propelled herself these last ten years. He is probably more so. He has spent his years quietly working as a professional chef all over the world. He marches straight to Nigel, stopping less than an inch from him, and on tiptoes spits:

'Where's ma fuckin sieve?'

'What sieve?' Nigel's expression is that of a holy man who has just seen the devil.

'What die yie fuckin mean what sieve, yie sleekit wee dirty cum-suckin cunt! The fine one with the yellow...that one!' He reaches past Nigel - Nigel flinches - and retrieves his sieve from a magnetic rack.

'Let the kirk staun,' the ancient baker hisses through grit teeth, his eyes magnified huge by his lenses, 'in the kirk yaird!'

And at that, with more words than he has spoken in the main kitchen for possibly six months, he is gone again, leaving Nigel shaken and furious.

The dance continues.

'Table twelve!'

'Table one!'

'Table three and fourteen!'

'Awwwwwwwch!'

Although his colleagues expect a degree of clumsiness from Tom, the sight of him suddenly pale and stock-still with his eyes screwed shut raises a few eyebrows around the kitchen.

'What happened?' Viola asks.

'Oh shit, brothers.'

'What?'

'Tommy?' Charlie's concern is evident. 'What the matter?'

'I've cut my finger off,' Tom explains.

Silence, until Nigel remarks under his breath:

'Arsehole.'

Swallowing a deep breath, Tom opens his eyes. Still clutching the chicken carcass he was in the process of halving with his cleaver, his hand is not immediately visible. There is certainly blood. Reluctantly he pulls the append-age free and breaths a deep sigh when he sees that there are still five fingers! What for a moment he thinks is a piece of bone is actually a piece of chopped onion. He inspects the wound, careful not to bleed in his pans, and reaching for his sticky plasters, smiles:

'Nah, brothers. Sorry. È benissimo. Who's got chewing gum?'

After eight o'clock, conversation dies in the kitchen. The workload peaks. The mood becomes absorbed and even introspective. Tom sings quietly to himself.

An hour later, a disconcerting event occurs. Gavin's voice comes through the intercom, piercing all other sound:

'Upstairs, please, chef!'

Annoyed by both the request itself and the fact that Gavin knows better than to ask, Charlie jabs her finger over the intercom button and pronounces:

'Not now!'

'Aye, chef,' is the exited response. 'Definitely fuckin now!'

Furious, Charlie barrels up the stairwell, managing half a cigarette on the journey. She composes herself, pulls off her headscarf, fixes a smile and then enters into the dinning room as if onto a stage from the theatre's wings.

Lighting is low; flickering polished candlesticks glow in the yellows and oranges, highlighting the metalwork and the faces of contented guests, knives and forks clicking at an always-surprising rate. The impression is of gratifica-tion. Floor-staff glide gracefully between the filled tables. Fanny shares a joke with guests. The paintings look splendid. Charlie meets eyes with Brian Taylor, political analyst, and he raises his glass in greeting. Gavin is talking with the actor Brian Cox and he lifts half an eye to Charlie. She makes impa-tient eyes to her manager and...

Then she sees all too clearly:

A garish bunch of roses, thrust almost into her face.

'The great chef Brown in person,' smiles the fellow brandishing them. 'I'm the envy of the room.'

Charlie studies the man. No older than herself, though at least a good foot and a half taller, he has blonde hair and blue eyes and no distinguishing fea-tures at all. His cheeks are plush from the gin Charlie's professional nose can smell on his breath even from three feet. He is not altogether unsightly. But there is something about him.A vague memory stirs in the back of Charlie's mind as smiling curiously, she offers:

'Hello.'

'We're here for a friend's birthday.' His voice is false, attempting to be more genteel that it is naturally. 'I can see that you're busy, but I wanted to give you these. I've been thinking about you.'

Charlie is about to plead embarrassing ignorance when recognition hits her like food poisoning. Her stomach tightens into a piece of coal and her mouth fills with the bitter phantom taste of semen. Horrified, she is vaguely aware of herself affecting a polite, flattered smile over clenched teeth as Stan's mocking words fill her ears:

'I've been wondering all day whose cock that was yie swallowed last night? Had yie ever met that man before, Charlotte?'

'Thank you,' Charlie says, accepting the flowers as she might the rotting corpse of dead cat.

'You're welcome.' His smile reveals hellish teeth. 'Actually, I was wondering...'

'I'm afraid I've left something on the stove,' Charlie says.

He laughs politely. 'Yes, on the stove, ha ha! Well, then. You have my number?'

'Aye,' Charlie lies conclusively, smiling still. 'Enjoy your meal.'

And so the evening passes. Respite comes only after ten o'clock, by which time the back alley sparkles with a skin of frost. Stripped to a sweaty vest, her hair without her headscarf resting in its natural shape and smelling fiercely, Charlie perches atop the industrial refuge bin, holding a single buckwheat blin with crème fraîche, dill and salmon roe that she is slowly building herself up to eat. An unavoidable truth of the trade is that the busier one is today, the more one must do in order to be ready for tomorrow, and this is what awaits inside. She is exhausted, unusually so. The sky is clear, the stars bright.

Gavin, sitting on his usual milk crate, his waistcoat hung up safely on a hanger, is in foul fettle, although always the professional he is careful to maintain personal presentation because there are still customers on the shop floor. Like Charlie, he has spent the day closing various housekeeping accounts. The news of impending unemployment was not well received by his staff and he has bore the brunt of their discontent. He licks along the glue of a joint and rolls it into shape.

'What were the flowers for?' he asks, lighting up.

Utterly still, Charlie's gaze is vacant and imprecise. Her grey eyes reflect pure white, as does her skin. 'An especially good blowjob and, I assume, the hope of a repeat performance,' she says.

'Ah, another satisfied customer. What did yie dae with them?'

'Cooked then in liquid nitrogen and then Tom ate them.'

The manager smiles, sipping a small glass of Château Pieddé *L'Obscurité* and listening to the gentle sound of the surrounding city spill over the alley walls. Five minutes pass without conversation, during which Gavin's joint passes several times between him and Charlie. But then, as he begins to drift off into a pleasant desert island fantasy, Charlie startles him by saying with a stark intensity that seems completely out of place for this time of night:

'I'll be glad, Gus.'

'When?'

'When we shut!'

So surprising is the statement that Gavin asks:

'Eh, yie dinnae mean that?'

It is with Vincent that Charlie considers she truly matured as a chef and as a restaurant leader. In the early years, he would come in just to watch her work, lecturing endlessly and patiently, quoting not only himself but also all the great chefs of history, keen to help her understand not just the effect but also the cause. Now, his restaurant has become her life. There is nothing to distinguish from Charlie's personal routine and that of Reserve. She falls asleep with stock orders in mind. And although for the opportunity to shine Charlie is more grateful to Vincent and indeed fonder of him than she can express, now, as he so nonchalantly sells her restaurant - that to which she has given her soul - Charlie is sorely tempted to feel disposable.

This is just sour grapes. The closure of the restaurant is hardly a problem. It is merely a nuisance. The fact of the matter is that Reserve has engaged more of Charlie's time and effort than any other job she has had. She is, all be it to her own agenda, institutionalised. Put simply, she is spoiled. Perhaps she is even a little frightened. Yet, the legend of Charlie Brown speaks for itself. She is in demand. She is coveted. The future is bright, limitless.

And she is wholly uninspired.

'I dunno,' she confesses in a hollow voice, lifting her blin to study it before deciding against putting it in her mouth. 'Yie've worked for Vincent longer than I have. Will yie miss it?'

Not for a second can Gavin pretend he will miss Vincent. He smiles, hoping that this silent admission will cause Charlie no offence, which of course it does not. Sipping his Pieddé and passing her his joint, he looks wistfully into the night sky.

'Dinnae get me wrong, man, I appreciated this is a good gig. There's the money, tae. Vincent's always paid us well. But mibbae we've have been around long enough to know that it's too good. And to tell you the truth, even from the heady heights we are now,' he gestures around the stinking alley, 'I still feel like a bar man. I've been thinking for a while that it's time for a change. Think of it: a desk job at Standard Life!' He laughs. 'Or travelling around Europe like Tom and Eva? Or working at the Dungeon dressed up in a cannibal costume scaring the life out of wee bairns? There's a whole new world out there, chef. Mibbae we're deprived.'

Charlie's lips form a half-smile as she exhales smoke into the misty night. 'Can yie imagine travelling around Europe? Living in hostels and sharing a filthy shower.'

'Hmmm. I'd rather work for Standard Life and hang myself wae my tie in boredom.'

With a loud crack, the fire-door opens and into the nippy northern-European winter, wrapped in a woolly poncho, her lean legs bare, Evelyn emerges with a smell of aniseed. She is freezing and disorientated. Coming out into the cold stillness after so many hours on the shop floor is to her like coming up from a deep-sea dive without properly decompressing. She squeezes her eyes shut and ruffles her honey-coloured hair.

'Gus, who's doing Friday morning?' she asks. 'Fanny says that it's me. It had better fucking not be me.'

'It is you, Eva,' Gavin laments. 'Sorry. I've no got anyone else.'

Clenching her fists in the air almost as if in religious devotion, the Australian screams:

'I hate this fucking country! I hate the weather and I hate bloody Billy Connolly and I fucking hate you, Gavin! We're supposed to be friends but you're a sadistic, wicked bastard. I hope you burn in hell. Anyway, what's the fucking point now? I'm leaving this freezing, Godforsaken, shitty continent in a month. Fuck it. Fuck all of it. But most of all, Gavin,' she spits, 'fuck you!'

Immediately cognisant and appropriately guilty of this redundant outburst, she stamps a boot heal in frustration and settling against the wall, lights a cigarette. Her breathing is the only sound.

'Well,' Gavin muses, gathering up his wine and his hash tin and slipping on his waistcoat, quoting Charlie's words, 'nae rest for the wicked.'

'Good night, Gus.' Charlie smiles.

'Catch yies in the mornin, guys. Eva, go'n dinnae be long, eh? There are still two more tables coming in.'

'Fuck off.'

As the fire-door closes behind Gavin, echoing along the empty alley, Evelyn exhales smoke into the night air and smiling mischievously now, lifts her long eyelashes to Charlie. Something of her usual elegance returns. Her cheeks flush. Her glittery, inviting lips open slightly.

Charlie studies her for a moment, devours her pancake in a single bite, smearing cream around her lips and chin, and asks with typical frankness and a puff of smoke:

'Fancy a quick dance somewhere?'

147

12

Retching, her entire frame shuddering, Alison Gorry struggled for breath and from the foetal position, stretched out her legs and rolled onto her back. She concentrated all of her efforts on the seemingly simple task of focusing on the unchanging stars. Her limbs burned. From Rue La Fayette, she had run at full speed, winding through alleys and over gardens for what she correctly estimated to be almost four miles to the Bois de Vincennes. From where she lay on the forest floor, looking up past the treetops, dizziness and disorientation overcame her. She turned her head to the side and vomited, convulsing like a rag doll as she did, her fingers clutching repeatedly at thin air.

She lay motionless, breathing in sharp stabs and listening to the interest all around her of wild animals.

A voice startled her:

Well, it taunted, this is a fine situation to be in. Splendid. Why not just sleep here tonight in the mud and squirrel shit and bleed slowly to death?

'Yes,' Alison whispered.

No! The voice roared. Get up!

Resignedly, with what was almost an infuriated sigh, Alison sat up, wiped her mouth and face clean of vomit and Debienne's brains, and only then realised her injury.

She had been shot in the shoulder.

Poetic, eh? John remarked.

It was only a flesh wound. She could feel the bullet lodged between muscle tissue and the top of her right humerus, which she suspected was cracked, just below the cartilage. She wound not bleed to death, but neither would the arm support the weight of a gun in the immediate future. It was particularly fortunate, Alison thought, that she was not right-handed.

With clenched teeth, she pressed with her preferred thumb and index finger past the opening in her flesh, tearing the wound open further. Moving her right arm loosened the bullet and after four or five minutes of excruciating pain, she was able to grip it with her fingers and pull it free. She removed one of her boots and then the sock, with which she bound the wound as tightly as possible.

She sat below the moonlight holding the blood-covered bullet in her fingers, her face set in an expression of incredulity. But the impression was deceiving. It was not the first bullet she had removed from her body.

Calm flooded over Alison. She caught her breath, inhaling deeply the smells of the forest and lying back down, surrendering momentarily to the pain.

I wish I was with you, said the voice.

'You are.'

The stars were clear and bright. The world seemed still, a dangerous illusion.

Alison could remember that seconds after murdering Abbé Debienne, the door to the loft had crashed open and a hale of bullets had rained in, smashing the single tiny window and Jesus clean off the wall. She remembered seeing three different faces, three different pairs of eyes. She remembered firing shots herself. But after that point there were no clear memories, which Alison knew meant that what she thought of as her natural skills had engaged, focusing entirely upon the practicalities of survival with a detachment that spared no time for burning memories.

She had understood at once, before the firing of a single shot, that she had nobody to blame for the trap but herself. As revenge for the hanging of Madeleine, in arrogant foolishness, the body of Franz Wetzler had been left unconcealed and mutilated. The corpse had led somehow - probably by the simple means of his personal logbook - to the traitorous profiteer Blancpain, and Claude Blancpain, Alison knew instinctively, had spilled every secret in his head, hoping that the Nazis would find Alison before she got to his family in Switzerland, which of course she had never had any intention of doing. In the silence of the forest, she berated herself viciously for allowing the old bastard to live. She had done so believing that he might be of further use; all useful resources in occupied Paris were to be treasured. But she was in no doubt that the Nazis had murdered Blancpain soon after he told them exactly the same things he had told Alison less than a week ago, of the resourceful communist, Abbé Debienne. Tailing Debienne, the Schutzstaffel had only to come across the street from their sanctuary, putting down their drinks only briefly.

Fury at her own stupid mistake had fuelled the strength to flee, but the manner by which it had been achieved eluded her. She remembered physically wrestling with one man and killing another with her bare hands. She remembered crashing through glass and thinking as she hit the pavement below that her back was broken. She did not remembering getting up. Of only one thing was she sure.

Frédéric had not escaped.

You did what you had to do, John said.

Turning her head, Alison vomited...

Concentration is impossible. Curled into her armchair in her kimono, her hair resting in its natural shape and smelling of anti-bacterial shampoo, Charlie rolls and lights her eleventh joint of the day. The lamp variation creates an unusual light, angular and stark. Incense burns. Passively stoned, Snoopy sprawls across the back of the armchair, throbbing, his purring resonates in the stillness.

As keen as she is to continue reading - and she is keen; Charlie has followed the Alison Gorry chronicles for fifteen years and has waited two and a half years for the latest volume - her attention at present, sharpened by cannabis and exhaustion, is compromised by the niggling memory of dancing last night with Stan. She tries to focus on her book, manages a sentence and a half and then exhaling smoke, pitches it across the room. Her mind reels.

There is, at times like these, only one thing for it. She clears the piano lid of books, sits, feeling the leather stool cold on her bare bottom, and cracks her knuckles.

Charlie was not the musical prodigy her mother was. Charlie is naturally clumsy. Her musical ability was lengthily taught. But she is, now, just as capable as her mother. With her joint burning on her lip and without a conscious decision, she rips into Chopin's *Prelude in Bb minor*, barely able to keep up with herself, her small fingers floating nimbly and rapidly across the keys like dancing spiders. She plays quietly, perverting the feel of the piece for the sake of her neighbours. She leans into the instrument, absorbing its vibration, wrestling and refusing to be beaten. The joy of playing the piano for Charlie has always been physical rather than cerebral.

The last enormous, rising credenza she plays with wide eyes, resisting the urge to increase the volume, and...

The telephone rings.

Charlie's heart stops. Guilt and drug-fuelled paranoia mingle into a gut-wrenching, ridiculous fear. But this lasts only a second and as she lifts the receiver, she already knows who it is.

She hears Dean Martin crooning *Dream a Little Dream* and when the voice comes, it is altered by the acoustics of its new environment.

'Good evening, Brown.'

Stan sleeps little when he is under a deadline, which has much to do with disorganisation. He will commonly work or read until three or four in the morning and still be successfully in the office, if not bright and breezy, at least on time. Detached from his unlit lounge and kitchen by a large and luminous aquarium, he works at his desk, sculpting for a meeting with reptilian Janet at Leith Furnishings and Upholstery in less than twelve hours time a two-page glossy marketing plan, the action plan for implementing the marketing strategy he is simultaneously creating. While it is far from common practice to conceive a marketing strategy in two days, Stan is driven by his own motives. He wears his kaftan and his thick-rimmed glasses. Leaning back in his chair, he lifts his feet up onto his new attractive filing cabinet, which, while also heading the investigation into the disappearance of Megan Gilles, Stuart Mackenzie found the time to deliver earlier tonight. In the darkened lounge, the yellow of the Rothko seems to hang unsupported in the air.

He is mortally miserable. Perspective has vanished. To mention nothing of Janet's sheer incomprehension of the concept of marketing, the principal hindrance facing Stan is myopia, Janet's inability to look ahead and make decisions based on, rather than current circumstances, long-term objectives. Developing a marketing strategy is typically a case of understanding a business' internal strengths and weaknesses and its external opportunities and threats, then integrating a thorough understanding of the business' own ambitions and policies. The first question Stan asks a client is always: What do you want to achieve? But Janet's only ambition is to survive. Stan, on the other hand, knows exactly what he wants. His selfish desire fuels him to clarity.

Having lived opposite Leith Furnishings and Upholstery's showroom for ten years, he had until today never ventured inside, which in itself speaks volumes about the exterior of the shop. The challenge with the account is not as initially expected to improve Rose's strategy, which was never anything more than an article in appeasement, but rather to improve Janet's whole business approach, to inspire her. For the development of his strategy, Stan has gone back to the basics of marketing, the Four P's - Product, Pricing, Promotion and Placement - and the specifics are beginning to emerge.

'Any more gobbled up fish?' Charlie wonders.

His bottom lip projects mulishly. 'Nah, nae more casualties. I cleaned the tank out and there were nae bones either, which is strange. I fed the little bastards well, but I dinnae expect that tae do any good. I suspect cannibalism is less a matter of hunger than of sheer intent. Did yie have a busy night?'

'Yes.'

'Did yie see the news at all? It said that…'

Charlie is amazed to hear herself ask, sharply:

'What dae yie want, Stan?'

Silence, other than the sound of Stan's bubbling aquariums and Charlie's sleeping cat.

'I'm sorry, Charlotte. Am I interrupting something? I didnae think…'

'No, of course not.'

'You're tired. I'm sorry.'

'Stan, I'm sorry. I'm knackered and grumpy and stoned.' Charlie exhales smoke. 'I'm sorry.'

'Nae bother.'

Stan wants to say more. He wants to know how she has passed her day. He wants to know how she feels. He wants to tell her about his day. But it is the middle of the night and she has worked hard all day, and so to detain her would be, Stan considers, selfish. And besides, Stan has work to do, none of which he expects her to be interested in.

'Are you going to go to bed soon?' he asks.

Charlie thinks of her old, broken bed and the effort of contorting her supple body around stray, piercing spring, and lies:

'Aye. I'm gaun now.'

'Okay.'

'Goodnight, Stanley.'

'Goodnight.'

Charlie regards the re-cradled telephone for some minutes before beginning the business of the rolling a fresh joint.

13

Well-publicised in the world of jazz is that Jean-Luc Dussollier, whether performing or recording, played the same three trombones for the majority of his remarkable career. New York's Metropolitan Museum of Art permanently exhibits his Bach alto horn while his two Olds tenors remain in France, one a piece in Maison Dussollier and the Cité de la Musique in Paris. Less well known is that Jean-Luc's favourite trombone, a 1903 Gautier alto that he played neither on stage nor for recording purposes but rather for his son in the bath, now lies around his son's office gathering bashes, its brass slowly turning a handsome century brown. Vincent, indeed, is apt to play the Gautier. He does this now, lain in his silk suit on one of the couches with Chloé, a Baby Dior cherub with eyes like magnets, rising and falling upon his chest with each controlled breath. He blows Berlin's *Blue Skies*, softly but in a high range.

The office is nearly bare. Gone are the paintings, the soft furnishings and much of the furniture. Leisurely, more for fun than anything else, Amanda busies around packing travel chests with photographs and books, humming in counterpoint to her husband's melody. To her ears, even taking into account the night Vincent played *What A Wonderful World* after proposing to her, the old Gautier has never sounded finer, but this has nothing to do with the undressed stone walls altering the acoustics of the room to produce a harder, more resonate sound, nor is it because of the heart-warming sight of father and daughter together, eyes magically locked, joined by the music. The glorious sound results because today is simply the last time her husband will play his father's trombone in not only this particular room but in this particular country.

Not that Amanda is unpatriotic. Far from it. She is proud of her heritage, proud that she has lived her life in a fair variety of her homeland's towns and cities and even villages, proud of the reputation she gained as a chef before retiring. Indeed, Scotland has been good to her. But this is not to say that she wants her daughter raised here.

The melody stops as Vincent cranes his neck over his shoulder, steadying Chloé with his long fingers.

'Sweetheart,' he says, 'I remember that you asked me to do something today. I just dinnae remember for the life of me what it was. Nothing important, eh?'

'No, love, just that yie offered to take my mother shopping.'

'Hells bells!' Vincent exhales a heavy, tortured sigh. 'I dinnae have tae, do I?'

'There's nobody to blame but yirsel, Vinny,' Amanda smiles. 'Yie did offer.'

'Aye, only because she bloody intimidates me so much. Old Dot isnae any
older or unfit than me.'

'Ah, but yie can drive, sweetheart. That makes yie a prime resource to the
woman. And it's the last time, and then she'll be forced to trouble her beloved sons for such menial tasks, though I suspect that she'd rather hobble
than be a nuisance to them. And if yie take Chloé, I willnae have to see her
before we leave the country at all. What do you want for dinner tonight?'

The Great chef blows an improvised downward blues scale as he considers
the weighty issue, finally deciding:

'Stovies and cabbage.'

'Yummy.' Packing a photograph of Vincent and Roy Schneider, Amanda
resists the inclination to hum the theme from Jaws. 'You and Chloé deal with
Dot and I'll make dinner. But now I think about it, sweetheart, mother might
have said something about going to Ikea again.'

'Hells bells, Amanda! We went five days ago!'

Despite his protest, there is no question that Vincent will not take Dorothy
shopping, not least because he is more than pleased to do anything his wife
asks, but also because these last days in Scotland represent to both him and
Amanda, sadly, the very last days with any sense of normality in their lives.
They are about to inherit the ninth largest fortune in France. And this is not
without is stresses. The Dussollier estate requires not only an heir but a leader
as well. By selling his restaurant and both of his farms in Scotland, Vincent is
in fact gaining a country estate, a mansion, a multitude of smallholdings and
property throughout France, a leading fine art museum, a haulage business
and two charities. For years the Great chef has lived by a strict policy of non-
anxiety, and he finds now that the change is circumstance ahead of his family
is not a thing about which he is entirely comfortable. The quiet life, he has
come to appreciate, suits him well.

Amanda plucks this notion from her husband's eyes, leaving her packing
boxes to sit with him. 'Thank you.' She curls her arms around him. 'I'll come
with yie to Ikea, and I'll pay you back later,' she says with a mischievous
twinkle in her eyes. 'Charlie?'

Amid the Dussollier's, in her favourite armchair, Charlie is trying to work,
but she is unaccustomed to having more than one Dussollier with her at any
one time and the distraction is significant; she has listened to them bicker and
banter for nearly two hours about practically nothing. Her fettle is not good.
She rolls a joint on her closed laptop, using both cannabis and marijuana, and
at the mention of her name lifts her eyes only reluctantly.

'Yes, Amanda?'

Madame Dussollier, in Charlie's opinion, is a remarkable-looking woman,
in the prime of her life, not at all like the pretensions bourgeois portrait occasionally painted by the media. Her tall and athletic figure completely restored

154

from the ravage of pregnancy, except for enormous, milk-swollen boobs, Amanda conveys strength combined with a stark femininity, her bird-boned features set with the nuance of mischief, her blonde hair beautifully braided. She wears, nearly all the time, khaki combat clothes.

'I'm completely sure Vinny's forgotten to say,' Amanda says, 'but we're leaving on Saturday morning for France.'

'This Saturday?'

'Aye,' Vincent agrees. 'And we shallnae be back. Yie'll be on your own next week, which is nothing new. I dinnae like to think of my mother rattling around in that big house all alone at Christmas. So I'll only a have a few sherry's at the party on Friday night since I'm driving early in the morning.'

This is wit. Vincent is a recovering alcoholic. Lighting her completed joint, mindful of her hair, Charlie smiles thinly without mentioning that Vincent's mother, since the death of Jean-Luc, has already spent two Christmas's winters alone in 'that big house', during which she produced the best selling novel Charlie is currently reading. Nor is she alone; a massive medical and service staff tends her every need. More accurately, Megan Poe is about to die, and Charlie finds this lack of clarity distasteful.

Vincent continues:

'I've arranged for my personal things from upstairs, the paintings, some furniture and some other bits and pieces, to be packed and shipped on the seventh of the new year, but we're not taking everything. For the remainder, I suppose an auction would be best, and the proceeds can go to charity or something. Needless to say, Gavin, Morris and yirsel are welcome to take what you want beforehand. The building must be empty and all the keys must go to Morris by...eh...'

'February the third,' Amanda says.

'As for the details of next week, chef, I leave entirely to you. In my own mind, I dinnae think yie should work past Christmas Eve, which is...eh...Amanda?'

'Next Wednesday.'

'Have yie anything in mind?'

Charlie exhales. 'We shant work next week at all,' she says. 'I'll shut tomorrow night after the party. There isnae anything to be gained by working next week. The staff are all more than happy with their severance so they're no going to grumble about the loss of income, and they'll certainly no mind the time off. There willnae be any announcements. Gavin and I will come in over the weekend and possibly some of next week to tidy up the paperwork and do whatever needs to be done. We havnae placed any orders for next week,and I'm sure we can finish off everything tomorrow night at the party. And then that'll be that.'

With a comical glissando for Chloé's benefit, Vincent drops the Gautier on the stone floor.

'Good girl,' he grins. 'I completely agree. I'm sure you'll be glad as we are to see the back of this place.'

Vincent bought No. 39-43 North Castle Street in the spring of 1996 for £479,000, quite impulsively. Upon viewing No. 39, the unit now occupied by Reserve, and then noticing both that the building's facia happened to be particularly beautiful and that the other four units in it were also independently for sale, Vincent bought the job lot on poetic principal. Seventy minutes ago, he sold the building to Barratt Homes for over four million pounds and the irony in this is still stuck in his throat. For most of his early life Vincent laboured to achieve such large profits to the point of personal injury and this five-hundred-percent return on his 'investment', which comes finally in a time in his life when money means absolutely nothing at all to him, nearly makes him smile, except that his earlier efforts cost him a heart attack and a great deal of his self-respect.

Again, Amanda soothes the notion by stroking Vincent's shiny head and silvery-stubbled chin. She also nudges her elbow into his ribs, and says, with wide eyes:

'Do you think yie'll stay here, Charlie? Yie used to hate the city. It is home now?'

The question strikes Charlie. And with it, her full concentration awakened, she suddenly has the feeling of being led. 'It isnae really a question of home, Amanda,' she says. 'It's more a question of work.'

'Exactly! Which brings me to my final point!' Vincent says. 'There's another matter I'd like to discuss, if yie can spare a couple of minutes of yir time. I know yie're busy, but I'd like yie to take a look. I have it here. Come and sit wae us.'

Annoyed, Charlie closes her laptop and crosses the office, bare feet cold on the slate floor, her joint on her lip. 'What is it?' she inhales.

Amanda gives Charlie a brown A4 envelope with a Paris post-stamp while Vincent says:

'Take a look.'

Inside the envelope she finds the glossy particulars from a Parisian property company acting on the behalf of Vincent and Amanda. The details are in French, which poses no problem.

In the seventh arrondissement on the Left Bank, No. 114 Boulevard Saint Germain is an ornate baroque townhouse spit into four modern apartments, enclosing a private courtyard and fountain, each with an exterior terrace. The building's exterior carvings include Joan of Arc. Interior photographs show that each apartment has two bedrooms, a reception room, a huge kitchen, a bathroom and windows that are as tall as Charlie has ever seen. Three of the apartments are fully furnished in indulgent, antique fashion - Japanese, Louis XIV and classic baroque - but one apartment is entirely empty. All have digital television and broadband internet access.

'The foundations date from seventeen-hundred but the house itself was completely ruined during the Revolutions and again by the Occupation,' Vincent says proudly. 'Father and mother rebuilt it after the war, before my Grandpapa Pierre passed. George Orwell rented one of the units for a spell. And of course it's the model of the townhouse in my Mother's books. She wrote her first book there. I lived there myself as a student, for a time.'

All of Charlie's self-control is required to prevent from looking up at the photograph of Vincent, Eugène Bouveret, and fated Bernard Spencer, which is not yet packed away. No. 114 Boulevard Saint Germain, she immediately realises, is the house in which Bernard Spencer committed suicide. Charlie does not know, however, that is was Vincent and Eugène who cut down Bernard's body, hung like a guinea fowl, trying in vain to breathe life back into his already cold lips. She sucks her joint deeply, exhales the tangy smoke away from Chloe.

'It's very pretty,' she says.

Vincent says nothing for the longest time, his hand finding his wife's leg, and he allows Charlie to see him cast a glace at both the photograph of Bernard and the stone gargoyle, which, because of the sheer difficulty involved in attempting to move the thing, remains in place. Attempting to move it without the proper help would most likely result in his own death.

And it has never been Vincent's wish to die. Even the years spent in the depths of drunken despair and depression were, for Vincent, still good years. His heart attack cemented his belief in life further, just as his daughter and his wife do today. But this is not to say that Vincent does not think about death. His first wife died, as did the infant. His mother is dying. But more poignantly, the great chef is, and has been for four years now, apt to think about death - specifically the gruesome task of hacking Bernard Spencer down with a carving knife - nearly every single time he looks at Charlie. Their similarity exists, he believes, beyond the fact that she has, as he had, grey eyes.

Because of lack of sleep or lack of nourishment or because of other reasons altogether, Charlie finds herself after only half a joint fast becoming stoned. She forgets to breathe and suddenly understands exactly what is about to occur.

From her very hands, startling her, Vincent snatches back one of the photographs and begins to sketch on its blank reverse a line, a curve, more lines, until a map of central Paris emerges, emphasising the left bank, from the Seine to Montparnasse to Chinatown, his long fingers working quickly in indicative, graceful strokes. For perception, he includes the Panthéon, the Musée d'Orsay and les Jardin du Luxembourg, but the ancient Île de la Cité and Île Saint-Louis, Vincent adds for his own personal satisfaction. He adds his own No. 114 Boulevard Saint Germain as a large X, another X in the Latin Quarter, and then captures the small distance between the two by a circle, only centimetres by illustration. Finally, inside the circle, Vincent adds three Métro stations and two further X's, with words Farmers Market and Fish Market. Complete, Vincent throws the map back to Charlie, leaving her no option but to catch it.

'Charlotte, Eugène is looking for a fish chef and a manager to begin on the first of February. I told him yie'd go. He's expecting yie the last week of January.'

Eugène Bouveret and Charlie Brown have met several times. A professor at Le Cordon Bleu, Eugène's only restaurant on Rue Mouffetard, a feathers and sequins type gig, seating two hundred souls and open until two in the morning – represented by Vincent's X in the Latin Quarter – is the centre of the avant-garde culinary scene in France. Eugène has never written a book or cooked on television. He has been married to the same woman for thirty years, has seven children and four grandchildren, and he never been compromised by any kind of breakdown.

'Pardon me?' Charlie asks, her grey eyes black, her expressions frank.

'Dinnae look at me like that! And dinnae dare play coy with me, either. It isnae becoming of yie. Think. Just listen to me and think. Go to Paris, Charlotte, and work for Eugène. Lease out your home, because you'd be mad to sell it in this market, and I'll lease you mine for a very reasonable rate. Take yir pick which flat yie want.' He winks. 'All four are soon to be empty.'

Gripping the map with both her small hands, the joint on her lip nearly trembling, Charlie asks, simply:

'Why?'

Vincent shrugs. 'Because I'm a nice guy. Because I owe yie. Because having yie here has allowed me to enjoy the family life I never expected to have. Because yie, inadvertently, have made me a better man. But let us not get mushy, eh? Here me now, Charlotte: the best decision I have ever made, apart from marrying Amanda...' - this remark earns him a kiss - '...was leaving Paris and going to London as a young man. I cannot explain tae yie the sense of freedom it gave me. Old Arthur the Alchemist'll tell yie the same about America.'

Amanda adds:

'Not that we think for a second yie'd ever go to London or New York, Charlie. But Paris! Dinnae try to tell us yie've never imagined it, we've known each other too long.'

Vincent again: 'Yie speak the language. Yie cook the food. Consider what a woman like you could become in a place like Paris. The city would hold you to her swollen tit. She would suckle you and fill you fat and she would only be grateful. She would ask nothing of you. Far be it from me to tell you what's best. Just consider it.'

This said, and rather pleased with it, Vincent relaxes in the knowledge that his suggestion has been properly received. To push further would be to waste breath. His closing statement the Great chef delivers as he eases down to the floor all fours - coming down on Chloe gracefully, tickling her, like a feeding jackal - in a calm voice, somewhat nonchalantly, yet like a bullet:

'After my heart attack, Charlie, I chose to live in Edinburgh, from all the places in the wide world, for a quiet life. Think about that.'

14

In 1876, Alfred Wallace, a construction tycoon in and around the city of Aberdeen, and influential in the first public attempt to bring trams to the city, celebrated with his wife, Ethel, the birth of their first son, Angus, with the construction of a new family home. Modest it was not. Built in local granite by Alexander Marshall Mackenzie in the neoclassical style of the day, boasting a compliment of fifty-two rooms centred around a pair of grand staircases and halls, Wallace House sat deep in the seclusion of the Kemnay forest, twenty miles north and to the west of Aberdeen. It stands there still.

The Wallace's, however, lived happily in their new home for only twenty-three years, until in 1899 the building's timbers were ravaged by fire on account of Alfred setting his bed alight with his pipe. Hereafter, Alfred and Ethel opted for a smaller home closer to town, one with the new electric lighting, and left the empty granite shell of Wallace House, quite remarkably, to the wild deer.

In 1946, young Angus Wallace, by then an elderly man living with his own family in Holland, was finally traced by a group of six youths from Aberdeen, one of whom was a man with only one arm, claiming to have a proposal regarding the dilapidated and dangerous shell of a building for which, it was generally agreed, Angus was accountable.

The proposal was elegant and simple: the six youths obtained permanent tenancy of the building - if you could call it a building - and would maintain it as they saw fit. Wallace House would simply become their property. Angus, for whom the home was originally fashioned, was overjoyed to release himself and his family from his father's legacy and signed happily on the line.

Three years prior to this, Jack Blithe, like most fit and unskilled men of his day, had been conscripted into the Royal Gordon Highlanders where in six short weeks he was cultured into an artillery engineer capable of serving his King bravely for two years on French battlefields, passing the time by finding some small amount of logic in repairing broken mechanisms amongst the stench of death. Discharge from service came early for Jack in late 1944, at the cost of his left arm.

Rosie, Jack's fiancée, passed the war years as a typist in a legal office in Aberdeen's Union Street, in a granite building originally fashioned by Wallace Construction, and it was there she first heard the story of old-man Wallace and the decrepit, deserted natural reserve. It was Rosie who prepared the legal papers and it was she who dealt finally, and in person, with Angus Wallace.

The resurrection of Wallace House took less than two years. Funds and materials were achieved by engineering work done by the three male members of the projects, who also did all of the building themselves, though of course one-armed Jack was not much use. Credit, however, truly belongs to their wives, who coordinated the project completely, engineering an assortment of deals with local power-companies, water-boards, farmers and insurance companies. This activity was all the while accompanied by furious whispers from town - whispers made all the louder by the fact that two of the six people were Indian - of the wild folks living in the woods, scavenging the countryside like wolves in a pack.

The alternative community or commune has become synonymous in the modern society with the ideals of the 'hippie', of abandoning society and even with attempting to transform it. However, this was not the case in postwar Aberdeenshire. The term 'tree-hugger' did not apply. Communal living may be simply described as an environment in which people share aspects of accommodation, material possessions, finances, domestic duties and childcare. Indeed, the outside world was much discussed at Wallace House, over breakfast perhaps, as was discussed an excellent, flourishing tomato plant in the vegetable garden.

In 1956, Rosie and Jack Blithe, who never officially married, proudly produced to the commune, now grown to seven couples, in the resurrected Grand Hall a beautiful baby girl whom her father insisted take her mother's name.

Rosemary was a thoughtful child, a dreamer, happy to lose herself in the enormousness of Wallace House and her own thoughts. But by the age of ten, she wanted books. Books cost money and money was tight. Rosemary paid for her books by sewing buttons and, eventually, making dresses to sell in local markets. By her twelfth birthday Rosemary brought into the community as much money as any of her seniors. The haberdashery she began still exists today, as does the library.

A schoolteacher who came to live in the commune after losing his wife to cancer and his son to a road traffic accident provided education for the Wallace House children, of whom Rosemary was the first. Radios and televisions were considered both gateways and important educational tools, but each evening the children would congregate in the Grand Hall as the elders debated, in much the fashion of modern-day political television programmes, with their varied view-points, 'the world today'. Perception was all-important, the benefit of seeing a thing from all sides.

Rosemary Blithe left Wallace House in 1973. She was the first person ever to do so. There was, she had come to realise, as well as a lush environment in which to examine her own attitudes towards self and sexuality, a particular safety in the house, a security and a future that could not be forsaken. But she had realised also that her own time was up. She announced her intentions boldly to her parents, strutting around the Grand Hall with her hand on her hip and pointing wildly: first, a solitary year in France, to search for her father's arm, she had joked, and then upon her return to Scotland, it was Rosemary's intention to enter into society at Edinburgh University and study the history of art. Money would be her own concern. Jack and Rosie said little during the conversation, smiling softly.

Rose blinks, feeling cold air on her face, and suddenly thirty years have past. She finds herself and her Harvey Nichols' shopping bags locked with Stan inside a capsule, one of thirty such capsules attached to the monstrous Edinburgh Wheel, propelled by clunky mechanism high into the air. The capsule, which with a skeletal structure is more like a cage, lurches to a crashing halt as other punters are barred in below, and then begins to rise again, higher and higher, swaying with the wind. Further swaying Stan incites as he settles his briefcase, a bundle of mock-ups and two bags of groceries.

'I'm exited,' he confesses, wrapped in a duffle coat, scarf and gloves. 'What about you? Rosemary? Rose, what's the matter?'

By sheer panic, nothing less than a primal terror, Rose is gripped. She is also gripped to the cage itself, her knuckles marble white.

'Holy fucking fuck!' Her yell is shrill, piercing. 'Stan, tell the man tae stop, quickly, get us off before it starts properly. You fucking bastard, Stan, do something! Help!'

But to protest is futile. The wheel is moving steadily now, creaking dubiously as it descends at speed upon the terrible traffic of Princes Street, swooping past the throng of tourists happily overpaying at the wooden Christmas Euro-market huts, before rising again. Stan takes the opportunity to enjoy a long, hard look at Rose, petrified in her polka-dot rubber raincoat, boots and hat, and fixes the image - the final viewing - into his mind. Her copper hair seems longer than normal, hanging below her screwed-shut eyes, and it occurs to him suddenly, and rightly, that she has decided to let it grow.

'See here, Rosemary,' he says, firmly. 'I really dinnae want to have to remind yie that this was your own idea, because yie'll sure no like that. Yie have, mind, always taught me to be enthusiastic about my own ideas, no?'

'Yie're a fucking cunt, Stan!'

At this, her dire lack of composure, Rose is shamed and deems to get a grip of herself. With a deep breath, letting out a sincere squeal of utter terror, she simultaneously opens her eyes and her grip.

The sensation is like falling.

A dreich morning has mellowed into a pleasant afternoon, the air not disagreeably moist. At the crest of the capsule's cycle, the Edinburgh Wheel reaches almost to the top of the Scott Monument beside it, over one hundred and seventy feet into the sky, high enough to see shoppers inside the fifth floor windows of Jenners across Princes Street. From the West End to the East, from the New Town to the Old, from Arthur's Seat to the Gardens and Castle Rock, the city spreads out before her from an entirely new perspective.

She thinks of her fallen property empire, glad in her heart to be rid of it, allowing the thought to take her mind off the more serious issue of the Wheel's structural integrity.

Only briefly do her sterile Mannerist eyes linger on the galleries, Playfair's enormous neoclassical sandstone Royal Academy and National, both compromised by ugly scaffolding and construction builders, and advertising on huge banners an exhibition of Degas café scenes. Rose has never been a lover of Degas. A million memories flood her mind. She remembers sketching as a student and as the years past, visiting simply for pleasure, the last few years with Stan for company.

'Quite a view, eh?' Stan says.

'It's quite beautiful.' Rose meets his eyes. 'But yie stop looking after a while because all yie see is the traffic. Stan, do you think yie'll ever leave Edinburgh?'

'Why the smile?'

'Because you've only just got here.'

'I've been here for ten years.'

'Aye, and even after ten years, yie're only just settled. Yie've just arrived! You and yir big house by the beach. I bet that Edinburgh has never felt as much like home to yie as it does now. Forget I asked. It's silly to talk of leaving.'

'You're leaving. And I have a gift, for Stuart as well.' Stan moves his shopping bags, causing the cage to rock, and produces a package that appears to be A2 size mock-ups. 'A wee something to hang in Wales. For the filing cabinet and the house and for much more besides. But dinnae worry, it wasnae dear.'

'Stan, yie shouldn't have.'

Rose cannot hide her pleasure. There is plainly nothing Rose likes more in life than to receive an unexpected parcel. More than curl, her lips form into complete and beautiful smile as she rips away the brown, string-tied wrapping paper and the protective bubble-wrap, mindful all the while not to remove too much because whatever it is still has to be carried back to the car on Market Street.

Underneath the wrapping, an attractive wooden frame, and beneath the glass, mounted flawlessly, a drawing in black ink coloured over in acrylics, a parody of Nasmyth's *Edinburgh from Princes Street with the Royal Institution Under Construction.*

Born into the Scottish Enlightenment and educated by Ramsey, Alexander Nasmyth is remembered as more than just a Scottish landscape painter; he is the genre's father. The angular symmetry of the drawing, its perspective from the Mound on Princes Street eastward toward Calton Hill, is true to Nasmyth's neoclassical original of 1825, displayed in the National. But the drawing is contemporary, incorporating the Edinburgh Wheel, and reality twists into caricature. The detail of the work is both spectacular and engrossing. Each of the hundreds of faces is a charm.

Under Stan's gaze, Rose stiffens. She frowns, eyes narrowing, breath held. There is something wrong, something peculiar in the tiny world. All of the billposters are advertisements that until tomorrow are controlled on behalf of G. W. F. Associates by Rose herself. And then she sees it.

Stan is in the picture. In the bottom right of the image, standing by the road in the forefront, by the Degas Exhibition, he is just one person in a street of hundreds, illustrated in his usual tweed jacket and t-shirt ensemble. But Stan is the only person looking out to the viewer and the device is such that, once noticed, it becomes difficult to notice anything else.

Only Rose's copper hair moves in the breeze. She examines every inch of the drawing as the real world rushes past, the cage rising and falling, until she says finally:

'My father only had one arm. He lost the other in France. Have I told yie that before, Stanley?'

Of course she has not. It is the ability of Rose Mackenzie - like nobody else Stan has ever met - to be friends with everybody she meets but to keep the details of her personal life to herself. At work, only Dave and Stan know of the property she owned and of her future plans. And so to be here, to be the person Rose asked to come on the wheel with her today, terrified as she was, and receive such personal information, pleased Stan.

He looks across Princes Street to Jenners, remembering back twenty years to the crêpe paper-wrapped piece of marbled glass bought for his mother that still sits on her mantelpiece, and he feels no sadness, only a vague longing that he is accustomed to and a sense of wonder that so much time has passed. That freezing cold day of the shopping expedition remains in his mind as fresh as the air filling his lungs. As the wheel spins, Stan's twin brother, Henry, died twenty years ago almost to the hour.

'Did you know,' he asks, 'that Dave only has one foot?'

'Dave! David Quinn! But... I mean....' This to Rose is no less than amazing. Her eyes dilate. 'Dave only has one foot? Since when?'

'Since he was born. Congenital amputation. What about yir father, how did he cope?'

Replacing the brown wrapping over the drawing and laying it carefully away, Rose says:

'Forget it, Stan. He's dead now.'

The one o'clock gun sounds and the capsule stops mid-air as people below begin dismounting. These are the closing minutes now. For a week, aware that this moment would eventually come, Stan has tried very hard indeed to think of something fitting to say, some appropriate expression of gratitude for his wondrous new home. Rose has been his professional mentor and his art vent. She has shown him the importance of perception. But in the here and the now, Stan's mind is a blank canvas.

Watching him fumble for expression, Rose's lips curl, and to ease his burden she confesses:

'I'm worried, Stan.'

'I can understand that. Wales it a long way away and it's a big cha...'

'No, idiot. I'm worried about you, Stan. Yie're only a wee, young thing and it's, well, difficult for me. After tomorrow, we'll probably never see each other again.'

The weight of these words hangs heavy.

'So I want to say something, Stan. Mibbae it isnae any of my business, but I'm older, a lot older, and I know things. And if I may be so bold, mibbae I think yie look up to me, so it'll be advice well given. It will be, in exchange for this beautiful drawing, and for things yie know nothing of, a succinct tutorial based on the accumulated benefit of my own somewhat tainted and bitter experience. It will be my leaving gift. Are you ready? Because I dinnae want yie to fuck this up, Stanley. I know what yie're like.'

Absolutely caught by the moment, it is all Stan can do to nod assent.

'Are yie sure yie're ready?'

'I am.'

'Then here it is.' Rose licks her index finger and reaching across the cage, removes an eyelash from one of Stan's pale green eyes. 'Get the girl, Stan. Dinnae be such an arse.'

The capsule is moving again, jerking. Of course, Stan fully understands her meaning. Rather than surprise at the notion, the words merely take him by surprise. Yet, despite this, in simply shock, he asks:

'Pardon me?'

'Are yie so fucking dumb, Stanley, that I'm sitting here telling yie this and all yie can think tae say is tae ask me tae repeat myself? Well I will tell yie again. Lean closer.'

Stan does lean closer, but before he realises her intention, Rose takes the back of his head in her hands and then her tongue is in his mouth, warm and muscular, sending shivers into his belly and rendering him helpless.

Releasing him finally, Rose sits back into her seat, somewhat sheepishly, although by no means apologetic, and smacks her lips together as she might after a delicious segment of orange.

'Yie'll lose her, idiot,' she says. 'I would also tell yie that everything else is inconsequential but that would only be my own tainted opinion. I'm right, though.'

15

'This time next week it'll a' be over.'

Dave says this from a corner table by the glazed brick wall, straightening out his patchwork jacket, and then to complete the sentiment:

'Thank fuck.'

'What will?' Charlie asks.

'Christmas. This time next week we'll be back tae reality.' Christmas has brought Dave from his office across into town this afternoon. He has free time and presents to buy. On the table, a thick diary sits open at pages of enormous lists. Half a dozen bags of presents lie at his feet. 'This time next week, you and I will be up to our necks in dirty dishes and turkey grease and all the panic will be past.'

Again, Charlie seems distracted for a moment. 'How many is it now?' she asks.

'Including Larry and Ruby-doobie, who have yet tae confirm, by the way,' Dave consults his lists, 'yir mother makes twenty-seven, which is an awfy lot of people even for Stan's new place. It seems to me that if the restaurant is at your disposal next week, and since the groceries are being delivered here anyway, Charlie, and since there are nearly fucking thirty people coming, then it would be so much easier just tae huv the party here instead of shifting everything tae Stan's place and then squeezing everybody in wae a shoehorn, no?'

'Ah, but that would defeat the point, David, which is for Stanley to show off his new quarter-villa.'

The sheer unpleasant manner of this statement hangs in the air.

'Well, it seems unnecessarily difficult tae me,' Dave deems. 'But at least we can use the restaurant's plates and cutlery and such. Can yie think of anything else that needs done?'

Pretending to think for a moment, but in truth only passing her eyes across the busy dinning room, seeing Fanny chat with an American film actor by the Freud under the stern gaze of Gavin, who is in a foul mood, Charlie concludes:

'Nah, man. It'll be fine.'

Dave remains dubious. 'What's the matter?' he asks.

'What dae yie mean?'

Crossing his legs, Dave resists the urge to touch the new prosthesis that after six days is still something of a miracle, and instead studies Charlie with a keen eye, noting her unusually pasty-white skin, her bloodshot eyes and the blackness around them, and that she is both biting her fingernails and gums.

She has several knife cuts on her fingers, and as a rule, Charlie does not cut herself. Condensing all this, he diagnoses plainly:

'Yie look appalling, Charlotte, and yie're poe-faced, even more than usual. What's up wae yie?'

'I'm fine. I'm just sleepy. I suppose I shouldnae complain, though. After next week I have an extended holiday.'

'Which isnae necessarily a bad thing, buddy. When was the last time yie had more than one day off? Before the bloody millennium, I suspect.'

While others would never dream of saying such a thing, Dave says this unapologetically, referring to the fortnight Charlie took off after she was raped, three and a half years ago.

Charlie merely nods agreement and in the silence that follows thinks of living and working in Paris as she has dreamed of for many years, now for the first time as a practical possibility. She thinks of Elizabeth M. Brown B.D.S and her long years as a widow, finding pleasure when she can like Alison Gorry herself. She thinks of Stan, of dancing to Moon River on Tuesday night, and she thinks of Jock and Jim clinging to their upturned boat in the North Sea, Jock swearing to change his ways for one last chance. She thinks of the rape. Charlie's mind runs wild and only as Gavin arrives with two of Arthur's meringue snowmen and a pot of cinnamon tea do her eyes snap shut with acid remembrance. She watches Dave and Gavin banter for a few minutes, silently cursing her own self-absorption, her egotism, and then when her manager is gone says gravely, apologetically:

'David, I'm thoughtless and horrible. I havnae even asked about Victoria. Ignore that I'm such a selfish cow and tell me how she is? It must be difficult.'

Only now does Charlie take Dave's full measure. Reclining easily in the elegant Mackintosh chair, one elbow on the table, he tries very hard to look natural, composed, and to all intent and purpose succeeds. He returns the usual smiles attracted from passing women. But he does not fool Charlie. The cracks are beginning to show.

'It breaks my heart,' he says. 'Megan's disappearance is too much for a little girl to try to reason. She's too caught up in the scandal of it to be really aware of what's happening. And the child's parents, imagine! I must have smiled at Megan a thousand times in the playground and now she's probably been murdered. I hope not, but given the alternatives I think that might be the kindest thing tae wish.'

Dave has lived his entire thirty-three years in the city - the first nineteen in Glasgow's Rutherglenn, the last fourteen in Edinburgh's Leith - and he does not need the abduction of his daughter's school friend to exemplify the horrors of society to him. Suddenly, with no warning at all, the damn breaks.

There is no dramatic change in Dave, but Charlie sees it clearly. She can feel it, breathe it. She pours the tea, watching him delicately crack his snowman with a spoon, straight through the head, releasing cream and the smell of cinnamon.

Arthur's trademark snowmen are petite works of art, made with the culmination of fifty years' learning. They are, for their slightly flippant appearance, serious adventures in gastronomy, engineered to taunt the palette with a delicate mix of flavours in a very specific order. The wee old man is a true sensualist, his food nothing short of sexy. Although the use of liquid nitrogen in the professional kitchen is now commonplace and, in Charlie's opinion, somewhat passé, and although the term Molecular Gastronomy was not coined until the eighties by an Oxford physicist, Arthur has been a pioneer in the field for thirty years. Known in New York as the Scottish Alchemists, his sea-urchin mousse was a worldwide standard before Charlie was born, his nitrogen-frozen cucumber sorbet equally so. But this is not to say that he, like Charlie and Vincent, is above basic cookery. He makes a mean bannoffee cheesecake.

'I'm sorry I said that, about Megan being deid,' Dave says. 'That was terrible. Truth is I'm no really coping. I'm finding it difficult tae be sad for somebody else's bairn because I'm so pleased it wasnae mine. It's horrendous. There really isnae any other word for it. There were police at the school this morning. Everyone was staring at everyone else, and the looks, not of horror but of suspicion, everyone en garde, me worst of all. And Victorian's mother, even she looked at me last night from the corner of her eye like I snatched poor Megan myself.'

He sips tea. 'Yie work hard all yir life tae achieve a sense of security, Charlie, but yie never do. Never. There's always the unknown, and that's the bastard of the thing. I dinnae need tae tell you that, surely, think of yir parents, or Stan's brother, or the man who attacked you. Mibbae it's me, man, mibbae I'm just a slow learner.'

Charlie is amazed to hear such cynical words from Dave, who is usually so buoyant, so cheerful. Overcome now, he says no more for a while, his head tilted slightly as if listening to a far away conversation.

Then, tonelessly, near-despairingly, he says:

'I think in the summer I'll be feared tae let Victoria oot the house. I've lived my entire life in the city and I went out every single night as a bairn. And I only had one foot. Imagine not going out to play! She's only a bairn, Charlie, one in heels admittedly, but a bairn still. She needs tae be out in life, no feared of it, intimidated by it, suspicious and paranoid.'

Charlie is moved. 'When I was a child,' she says with glassy eyes, 'I hardly ever went out to play.'

Dave smiles bitterly, and before he can stop himself, remarks with uncharacteristic nastiness:

'Aye, yie'll forgive me, Charlotte, if that doesnae make me feel any better.'

16

At the beginning of his European tour, some forty-six months ago, backpacking was a sour disappointment to Tom. Through Austria and Greece he lived very comfortably on the savings earned by three years hard graft before leaving Sydney in 1999, but his cash reserve in the tourist throng of Europe lasted only a matter of months. Soon enough, reality landed with a thud.

Florence will always be to Tom synonymous with poverty. Amid a million tourists, steady work even for an experienced and enthusiastic butcher had not been easy to find. He did many jobs, saw many kitchens, went hungry many a night. And so it was from sheer necessity amongst the back street betting houses of old Italy that Tom's gambling skills were honed. Yet, to this day he knows surprisingly little about horses, by nature not a man to leave things to chance. His skills lie, rather, in his ability to listen and his patience, to converse with the wee old drunken old men, to gleam the rewards of their hard-earned knowledge. That this approach has worked so well for such a long time - over thirty months - amazes Tom, and he lives in the knowledge and perpetual fear that one day his luck will simply run out.

Presently, underneath the never-changing stars, Tom stands alone in Reserve's alley counting the day's winnings, the stink of the drains not unlike that of the Arno coursing through old Florence. Sleeping in a room with five other people, in a building with a communal washroom for sixty, the Australian finds himself rarely alone, and the stillness of the moment is no less than magnificent. He is filthy. His blistered hands ache with the long, hard day he has worked. He has a greasy meat bridie and a litre bottle of Irn Bru, the amber nectar. A cigarette waits amongst his blonde curls. He is as happy as a pig in shit.

In strict contrast to dark days of Italy, however, the Australian no longer finds himself a man without means. His blossoming reputation under the great chefs Dussollier and Brown, to name but a few across Europe, is worth more than money. But there is money as well. Tom's savings have become quite phenomenal, easily enough to secure a mortgage on a small Australian home. Furthermore, for the first time in his life, and infinitely more important than the funds, Tom is a cauldron, a red-hot furnace of ideas.

Finishing his bridie, he lights the cigarette, blowing a single smoke rings into the twilight European stillness, just as the fire-door tears the stillness of the moment.

In clicking heels, a long black cardigan covering her uniform, Evelyn strides out into the darkness, marble eyes glistening. She has a lily in her new purple-cropped hair and nothing of her usual spark. Settling with Tom against the wall, she takes the cigarette from his mouth and the stillness, the darkness, and the nicotine stun her.

A moment passes. Then another.

More than exhausted, Evelyn is sick. For seven hours today she has served food and at least four more hours of labour yet remains. Since Monday she has worked more hours than any of the other floor-staff, some sixty-nine hours in total, all for an equal share of the tips. Twelve-thousand hours serving food since she saw her family last, all with a smile on her face.

Her face aches.

In a few years from now Evelyn will become Dr Evelyn Ramsey MD, and she is nearly confident that she will look back on these days of her European adventure with the fondness and appreciation they do deserve. But she is for now, body and soul, broken, smashed. She is the Venus di Milo.

Her head falls wordlessly onto Tom's shoulder and she sobs.

It was in Florence, too, below the shadow of the Dummo of St Maria del Fiore that the two Australians, halfway round the world from home, collided. Eighteen months they remained in Italy, making it their indulgence to make love under the gaze of as many angels and dying Christ's in the churches of the town as possible, managing eleven without ever being caught. Of three of these events they have excellent photographs.

'I'm so tired, sweetheart,' she whispers. 'I'm weak. I can't take it anymore. What the fuck made us buy tickets for January? So stupid. Why not now! I want to sleep in a normal bed like a normal person, not bunk beds.'

Tom cannot help but agree. 'You smell wonderful,' he says.

'I smell like a dead dog, Tom. Don't tease me. I can't take it today.'

'Do I ever tease you?' Tom steals back his cigarette. 'Filthy or clean, hunny-bun, it's still you. I love your smell.'

'I love you,' Evelyn says, wiping her eyes.

Home in Australia, in less than a month, it is undeniable that having worked for the great chef Dussollier will do well for Tom. But in truth, except for a formidable knowledge of butchery, Tom has never been all that impressed by Vincent. Instead, all of his respect is reserved for Charlie. The bruiser cooks, so abundant worldwide, whom he so respected once, have paled by comparison and seem almost childish against Charlie's cool precision. Tom has learned from her more than any other cook he has worked with. During his six-months with her, he has come to aspire to her example. Indeed, he is very fond of her.

But Tom is not as gullible as he likes people to think.

'The wee one was looking terribly guilty today,' he says, hoping to cheer Evelyn up. 'She looked hellish, her eyes were red. I felt like asking her what was wrong, just to see her pale face burn. It makes my cock hard to see her guilty. Not that I would fucking dare, though. She'd... I was going to say she'd gobble me up, but that would be too good to be true, eh?'

Evelyn does smile at this, though sadly.

'I don't know if she likes men. She's never suggested so, but I don't know. I don't know anything about her.'

'I feel quite sorry for her,' Tom says. 'But she brings it on herself.'

Evelyn loves Tom's compassion. He has the heart, she believes, of every beast he has butchered, and it grows all the while. Not that Evelyn is without compassion herself, of course. She does, after all, intend to become a doctor.

'I feel sorry for her, too. It would devastate her to know that you know all about her and I, sweetheart. She likes her secrecy. She would be mortified. She would turn the colour of her hair.'

'I wish I could bring myself to touch her hair,' Tom muses. 'I'll build up my courage before we leave and try to steal a piece from her headscarf. Just as a souvenir.'

'It's like wire,' Evelyn says. 'Barbed wire. It cuts my fingers.'

'I'll miss her,' Tom admits.

'Fuck her,' Evelyn says flatly.

Tom scratches the heat-rash under his blond curls. 'I'll leave that to you, m'lady.'

Together they laugh and Evelyn's belly eases, the knot loosening. Tom loves Evelyn's laugh, musical and rich.

Together they have been half-way around the world, nearly all the way around Europe, and in less than a month they will both be home in Australia, but this brings no comfort at all. Tom is from Sydney, Evelyn Melbourne. A thousand kilometres divides their fate. There has been much discussion of the future but little in the way of resolution. No agreement. No vision. The future is uncertain. Tom intends to change that presently.

'Marry me,' he grins.

Believing she has misheard, Evelyn says nothing and her smile remains for a time. But not a long time. Unseen, an ambulance screams past. Then Evelyn screams and slaps Tom's face as hard as she can.

'How dare you? How fucking dare you ask me that now?' she hisses, her face a mask of horror. She is raging, but the will drifts from her. She trembles. 'You ask me that question, of all times, now! You had better fucking mean it, you bastard! You can't play with me. I'm weak.'

'Weak?' Tom scoffs. 'You're not weak, Eva. You're as strong as an ox. And anyway have I ever played games with you? I am serious. I'm never been more serous. I want to be your husband. I want us to have a house, a wee house to begin with and then an enormous one. I want us to breed like rabbits. Sweetheart, do you remember the person you were when you left home? I can't. I can barely remember Australia. I don't think I'm the same person anyway. But doesn't it terrify you? Mortgages and interest rates and health cover and which school is the best, there's no getting away from this stuff now. I don't understand any of it, but I'm ready for it. I'm hungry for it. And I'm sure that you're a part of it. I'll come to Melbourne. Sydney, well,' he muses 'it's all very well if you like that sort of thing.'

171

'But what about your family, your friends? So much had happened, Tom. Don't you just want to get home?'

Tom takes a step towards Evelyn and cupping her oval face in his hands, looks deep into her eyes.

'I'm home now, love,' he says.

And at this, Evelyn entirely buckles.

During the two years spent in Florence it was Tom's achievement, his attention focused on survival, to never once visit a museum or art gallery. He has never seen a Renaissance painting. However, the same is not true of Evelyn. Evelyn has a passion, as her lover has a passion for bridies and all meats, for sculpture. She has learned to identify the work of nearly all of Europe's principal sculptures by the merest glance, Rodin being her obsession. In Australia she intends to take lessons.

To her semi-professional eye, Tom is Michelangelo's *David*. Even to the layman the similarities are obvious. The muscles, the cool marble's size, the assurance, that same facial expression as if to say:

Yeah, it's me. Yeah, I've just slain Goliath. What of it? Gimme a cigarette.

Poverty had been so bad in Italy that Evelyn has wished at the time not to be rich but just to be comfortable. And now, looking into the eyes of her David, it occurs to her, quite without looking for it, that never before in her lifetime has she felt so comfortable as she does right now. From a chrysalis, before Tom's eyes, Evelyn emerges a butterfly.

'I love you, Tommy,' she says, struggling for composure.

'Enough to marry me?'

Evelyn hesitates. But not in doubt. It is simply her nature to tease. Her face speaks a hundred words and Tom smiles with her.

But suddenly there is a noise, a rustling, possibly a rat, and they both turn, forced from their embrace by the action of turning to look.

Charlie appears.

'Excuse me,' she says, eyes lowered, pretending not to have heard every word.

17

A genuine pine Christmas tree, eight feet tall and tastefully decorated in gleaming baubles, tinsel and lights, stands in the living room of No. 24B Lee Crescent, Portobello, reflecting hundred of points of light in the surrounding aquariums and dark windows. In jeans, a thick woolly jumper and bare feet, Stan is finishing the remains of a small roasted chicken with potatoes and carrots at the black slate dinning table, admiring the tree, the job well done, which including the time it took to lug the heavy bastard home from Portobello high street on his back, has taken several hours to complete. But he has more than the tree to be pleased about tonight.

Stan's finances, the position unaided by the reneged promise of his wages and commissions from work in time for Christmas, are dire. Scarcely has he enough money in the bank to cover his monthly expenses, a few scanty Christmas gifts, and food. Never does he remembering being as he is now so literally penniless, even during his years as a student, which is the direct consequence and indeed compromise of the purchase of his new home and contents. The saving grace, for which he is grateful beyond words, is that he has no mortgage to pay, no rent, never again rent to pay. And yet, even though he anticipated his current poverty, while not to this extent, Stan had quite some time ago fixed his sights on a new bed for Christmas.

Charlie's bed is the blight of her life, a broken, lumpy, poking monstrosity that causes her endless pain and irritation. He knows this indirectly, of course, via Charlie herself; Stan has never been in Charlie's bed. What he does know for certain is that left to her own devices, she - she who has pushed herself always to excel, who strived in her youth to get out of shared leased and rented accommodation, who has risen by sheer will to the pinnacle of her profession - will never in a million years get around to the simple act of buying a new bed. This is typical of Charlie. Despite her remarkable salary, Charlie rarely buys herself anything other than books and cannabis. Her house has not changed since the night Stan helped her move in four years ago, the cinnamon dress she bought at the weekend her first new purchase in years. Furthermore, and not to be overlooked, the symbolic not to mention masochistic nature of this particular item - the broken bed - does not escape Stan.

Void of currency, Stan's only available resource was his wit, limited though he considers it to be. Since the initial idea of asking Dave for the appalling Leith Furnishings and Upholstery contract he has spent most of the last ten days thinking about the matter, the last two actually doing it. Earlier today, after meeting Rose on the Edinburgh wheel and then a quick stop at the Kirkgate cemetery with some flowers, Stan met Janet in her premises on Manderston Street across from his old flat.

Until today, Leith Furnishings and Upholstery's marketing strategy consisted of a not ineffective radio advert that cost nearly Janet's entire budget. Radio, of course, is an excellent medium by which to advertise. But so too is the visual, so Stan included in his glossy proposal a choices of billboard graphics as well as several different sized bus and taxi boards that will run all across Edinburgh for six months with no cost to Janet. 'Pardon me?' she asked at that point. Stan achieved this by engineering a deal with a man he went to university with who works now for a company controlling a wealth of static and trilateral billboards as well as the bus and taxi boards. Stan's payoff, deflecting the cost from Janet, was agreeing to DJ for his thirtieth birthday party in February at the Venue.

But such things, ultimately, are window-dressing and would have been useless without a deeper assessment of Janet's fundamental practises. Indeed, the resurrection of Janet's failing business was no easy thing to conceive. The solution came hard to Stan at about twenty to three this morning, although in hindsight, as with all truly excellent ideas, it seems an obvious initiative now. Unlike his famous ancestor, Stan thinks on paper rather than cerebrally, scribbling, scrawling, narrowing and then finally arriving at something that will eventually become an idea. Last night he covered several sheets of recycled paper. The details took a further few hours to accomplish, five more sheets of paper. In fact, Stan did not sleep at all last night.

Think small is the essence, not big. The local factor is Stan's point of attack, the valuable community aspect, the sustainable competitive advantage Janet so badly needs. Stock, as chef Charlotte Brown so often says, is key. Janet's stock is presently tat, but by the beginning of next week she will have an innovative, uniformed and most importantly local line of beautiful furniture exclusive to Leith Furnishings and Upholsteries. The stock will come from Jules, resident DJ at Hubba Bubba and creator of Stan's new coffee table. Jules needs an outlet. Janet has an outlet and nothing of worth to sell. It is the perfect compliment. It is, Stan reflects, a remarkable idea.

For Stan's services, he explained three times under the purposefully thin guise that all of his new accounts receive such special attention, Leith Furnishings and Upholsteries will incur no additional fee for his efforts. Janet's next and subsequent invoices will be for the same amount as last month, and she had, Stan was sure by this point, gotten the message, but he believes in building to a climax.

A thoughtful silence occurred as the small, round woman looked over the glossy proposal, and it was then that he slid a pair of tickets to the Great chef Dussollier's invite-only Christmas party tomorrow night across her desk. Her beady eyes – those which looked so lustily upon Vincent in the restaurant - peered up to Stan, and barely a second before he was about to broach the subject of the new bed he just happened to be looking for, Janet took the initiative.

'I wish,' she said, 'there was something I could do for you in return, Mr Hume. You've given me so much.'

After finishing his dinner, Stan spends a while washing and drying the dishes and tiding the kitchen. For soup, a bowl of broth mix has soaked since morning and he leaves the remains of the chicken carcass in the fridge to deal with later, although he cannot resist picking at the meat now. Back in the living room he dims the lamps, lights incense and switches on the flat screen television, selecting the Channel Four evening news and muting the volume. He puts another log on the fire, feeling the heat on his face. More than anything else in the house it is the comfortable level of heat the building maintains that amazes Stan, so unlike his Gordon Street leased residence that no amount of central heating and electric fires in December could make anything but bitter. He removes his jumper, smiling without realising, to reveal a grungy t-shirt.

Easing himself down onto a couch by the fire, lifting his long legs up, Stan's pale-green, seemingly transparent eyes return to his Christmas tree.

But as comfortable as he is, enjoying the gentle popping and bubbling of his many aquariums, and even forgiving his fish their cannibalistic tendencies, Stan is not yet settled for the evening. Further effort is required. And he is by no means keen.

He scratches his sideburns, reaches for the cordless landline telephone, shrinks back, and then reaches again only to recoil for a second time…

About two hundred miles from Portobello as the crow flies, in the kitchen of a small, detached bungalow on the outskirts of Stornoway, Niamh Hume sits at the kitchen table selecting felt-tipped pens from a huge box as a joiner might just the right chisel for the job, her olive green eyes scrutinizing the four Encyclopaedia Britannica volumes open before her. Niamh's mother, Doris, has always encouraged her children to make gifts rather than buy them - 'create rather than consume' - and this is exactly what she is doing. She is working on an illustrated map of the Outer Hebrides for her big brother, to match her Egypt, which she is assured hangs in his new house in Edinburgh. She intends to check this fact at Christmas. Of course, none of the Encyclopaedia's text makes much sense to Niamh, being as she is only seven years-old, but she is able to copy illustrations with an ardent sense of imitation. Finally deciding on the proper light brown pen with a suitable tapered nib, she is, however, interrupted by the ringing telephone.

'Hume residence.' She hides her annoyance well.

'Good evening, Mrs Hume. This is the Stornoway orphanage calling. I apologies for bothering you so late, but I believe you have a horrible little girl for us to collect.'

'Funny.' Niamh says this dryly, although with an enormous smile. 'You're in big trouble, Stan. Mum says she's never going to speak to you again.'

'Ah, Niamh, have you left your sense of humour under your pillow again? How are you? What are you doing?'

'I'm very well, thank you. I'm making your Christmas present, but I'm not telling you want it is.'

'Is it a picture?' Stan asks hopefully.

'Stanley!'

'Sorry.'

'What are you doing?' Niamh wonders.

'Not much as usual, just watching the news. I've just had my dinner and I'm full up with chicken and potatoes. I'm going to make soup in a minute.'

An avid soup fan, Niamh declares:

'Yummy in my tummy! We had chicken, too, and Dad's gone out to catch something for supper, but I think it's going to ra...'

The conversation is rudely interrupted as the kitchen door slams open on its hinges to reveal, fifty years of age in a cashmere cardigan, expression stern, green eyes ablaze, Doris Hume.

'Is that yir brother?' she asks. She knows it is. Doris's natural Leith accent, after twenty years, remains. 'Go'n say goodbye, love, and away and watch the television for a few minutes. I'll give yie back the phone when I'm done.'

She waits until Niamh is gone and then finds in the hidden heights of the pantry an ashtray, a packet of cigarettes and a lighter. Slowly, in her own time, she opens the backdoor to let the smoke out and settles in Niamh's warm seat, her eyes passing with amazement across her daughter's remarkable drawing. The cigarette is her first in days. She inhales deeply, enjoying both the instant dizziness and the taste, and picks up the receiver to a sheepish voice:

'Hullo, Doris.'

Henry Hume was killed at the age his sister is now, twenty years ago to the day, and Doris still has nightmares. On an afternoon with a warm breeze, she and her husband, Archie, were shopping for Christmas presents with their identical tiny boys, when, at the junction off Leith Walk onto Pilrig Street, they watched with horror as Henry was bluntly nudged out of the way - ripped from his father's hand - by a drunken man in a Hibernian football top who had apparently no time to wait for the traffic to stop. Landing on the road, Henry stood absolutely no chance at all, and as well as the bus that killed him, the ensuing crash involved another three cars and four more deaths. The Hibernian fan survived the incident, albeit with the use of neither his legs nor his eyes.

Just to hear the sheepish voice is a tonic. But Doris resists the instinct in her belly to weep and crumple into a hysterical mess on the floor. Instead, she straightens her shoulders, inhales sharply and exhaling slowly, says calmly:

'You inconsiderate... untrustworthy... ignorant... spoiled... horrible thoughtless bastard, Stan. Yie're a fucking weasel.'

'Mum...' Sheepishness becomes an audible sense of torture. 'I know. Yie're right. I dinnae ken what...'

'At the very least, Stanley, yie might've picked up the telephone. That's no too much to ask, eh? Obviously yie never bothered to check the weather report, because if yie had, yie'd have known we had snowstorms up here all day Sunday and that the coastguard was on full alert. I had to physically stop yir father going out to look for crashed aeroplanes and dead bodies bobbing about in the sea! On his fucking birthday, Stan!'

This is a blatant lie, a true moment of inspired genius by Doris, and she sucks her cigarette with a satisfied grin, enjoying every second of tortured silence.

'Mum, I'm so, so very sorry. I...' But words fail Stan. He swallows hard, feeling like not only the worst son in the world but also the worst person in the world. '*Sann orm tha naire*,' he says: I'm quite ashamed.

The silence is hell.

But then, spanning the huge distance between his new home and that in which he grew up, Stan hears a sound so strange that his brain takes a few second to recognise it.

Laughter.

'Oh, for fuck sake, Stan,' Doris hoots, 'go and lighten up, eh. You dinnae think we really expected yie, did yie? It isnae every week a person buys their first house!'

'Eh?'

'And to tell you the truth, son, we didnae even make enough food for yie, so it's a very good thing you didnae come. Ease up, son. Yie bleed too much.'

She hoots with laughter as a relieved smile eases across her son's face.

'Mo Chreach! I was panicking there,' he admits.

More hoots. 'Good. Have yie decided what yie want Santa to bring? I'm making my lists now.'

'Pants and vests are always good, mum. Tell auld Archie to bring some trout.'

The great weight lifted, Stan takes what feels like his first easy breath of the week, sinking further into the couch. But then quite without realising he is on his feet, and as he begins to tell his mother about his week of work and its rewards, he crosses the warm room, past the Christmas tree and casts a glance up to the Rothko. In fact, as Doris listens she might tell her son that as a girl she actually knew Janet and her late husband from a pub darts team, but she has certainly no wish to be reminded of her younger days whoring about Leith.

Instead, she asks about the house. She has seen digital photographs sent by email and has a niggling memory of being at a party at Lee Crescent years ago, but she is dying to see the place with her own eyes.

'Have yie finished paining yet?' she asks.

The second bedroom of No. 24B Lee Crescent is equivalent in size to the room Stan has lived the last ten years in, and is now his studio. Stan considers himself an amateur artist only on the grounds that he neither works for money nor exhibits. It is simply an indulgence, a way to pass the time. But this is not to say that he is without talent. Strewn throughout the room, some crudely mounted, some stacked on the floor or merely lent against the walls, is a multitude of paintings, mostly on canvas and in oil, though there are watercolours and drawings as well.

Principally, Stan replicates. The quality of his work is astounding, including copies of work done originally by Hooper, Dhurmer, Hockney, Lowry and Van Gogh, all to correct scale. There are Giotto's, Bosh's, Spencer's, di Vinci's, Dalí's, Gauguin's, Canaletto's, Bruegel's and a range of Picasso's. Wilkie, McTaggart, Melville, Dyce, Faed, Eardley, Bellany and Guthrie as well as a dozen Glasgow Boys works represent Scottish art. There are old Venetian and Florentine religious works, the Crucifixion, the Lamentation, Halo-rimmed Madonnas and the particularly Christmassy Procession of the Magi being Stan's favourite themes, all executed in the correct egg tempera mix of their day. He also has a fetish for ink drawings of pterodactyls, Islamic architecture, Japanese rural scenes, vampires, most kinds of whales and the Lewis Calanais Standing Stones.

While landscapes and still-life's, ensemble scenes and abstract art all offer their own challenges, Stan's true passion is for the human face, and with the exception of a single self-portrait, his are exclusively of the female form; more specifically, without exception Stan's portraits are of Charlie. Her crimson web of wiry curls, her grey eyes, her pensive frankness unmistakable rendered, she is Manet's *Bargirl at Folies-Bergére*; she is Singer Sergeant's *Madame X*; she is Meredith Frampton's *Portrait of a Young Woman*; she is Frida Kahlo's *Self-Portrait*; she is Botticelli's *Venus*; she is William Waterhouse's *Pandora*; she is Ingres's *Odalisque*; she is Gainsbourgh's *Mrs R. B. Sheridan*; she is Nattier's *Princesse de Condé as Diana*. She is all of the *Primavera* women. Repeatedly, shrilly, Charlie is Ophelia, Cleopatra, the Madonna and Medusa. But most perfect for likeness, lending themselves effortlessly, are the sallow and melancholic works of Stan's favourite painter, Gustav Klimt: *Allegory of Sculpture, Danae, Hope I* and *II*, and *Lady with Hat and Feather Boa*. Of course, Charlie has personally inspected all of the paintings, and approves. In his previous residence there was simply nowhere to hide them. Not that he would hide them.

His own self-portrait is not so immediately beautiful. But it is an original work, harsh, uncompromising, grotesquely distorted, verging on abstract. With his arms folded, his expression stern, his eyes full of what is clearly horror, Stan Hume looks out from the work irately, yet with a contradictory devilish smile. It is a constant work in progress.

In Stan's own opinion his best work is his present work, which is literally a present for his parents. Doris Hume has always taught her children to make Christmas presents rather than buy them, and on this year's tight budget Stan is doing just that. Fuelled by the enlightened insights of Age of Reason, the Romantic's pushed past the objective, reason-based Neoclassical style of the day for a more dramatic, personal and emotional approach, a rejection of physical materialism, a turning in upon the self for a deeper assessment of the human temperament. But Stan's is merely a landscape. Turner's *Rain, Steam, Speed; the Great Eastern Railway* of 1844 is one of his favourite painting; that is to say, it is his parents' favourite painting. A print has hung in their hallway for years. But the reproduction is a dreary one. Stepping over a semi-unpacked mass of paint tubes, brushes, jars of varnishes and solvents, loose frame timber and rolls of fresh canvas, Stan rips the protective dustsheet from the easel by the window. His Turner, reproduced exactly like the original, 91cm by 112cm, is five fifths complete and perfect, accurate to the direction and angle of the dirty dabs of putty-like paint.

He allows himself a smile at the effort, and to answer Doris, says:

'I'm nearly finished. I only have one wall in the bathroom and the skirting in my bedroom to finish, but I need to get more gloss. I hate glossing. I put flowers on Hen's grave today, Mum.'

Doris's eyes snap shut.

'Thank you, son.'

'Nae bother. I got some for granny and papa, too. I got Dad flying lessons.'

'Pardon me?'

'Flying lessons for his birthday. He has to come to the mainland, though.'

'Wow. Good present, Stan. I only got him a Star Trek DVD.'

As Doris talks - Doris is apt to talk lengthily - about Niamh's Christmas presents, Stan crosses back across the flat into the kitchen for a beaker of water and some rags. As he nibbles a piece of meat from the chicken carcass, he can sense the inevitable question even before it comes:

'Anyway, Stan, how's Charlotte?'

No response comes.

'Stan?'

More silence.

'Stanley, hello, are you still there?'

Struck dumb, Stan stands unmoving. Having opened a cupboard in search of something to put some water in for painting, he has found something entirely different.

Inside a glass fishbowl, circling safely if darkly, swims his 'eaten' male fighting fish. Stan's face is still and thoughtful, and then he smiles, wholly amused and moved. A note in Charlie's distinctive italic scrawl reads:

EXPECT THE UNEXPECTED

'Stan? Hello?'

'I'm here, Doris.'

'What's the matter?'

'Nothing's the matter,' he says, smiling. 'Everything's absolutely fine.'

18

Stuart is hungry and berates himself for neglecting both breakfast and lunch. Withered by caffeine and sugar overdose, his body badly requires carbohydrates, the cramp in his belly worsened by the knowledge than his wife's delicious and nutritious stew is waiting for him at home. Nothing in the world Stuart can imagine would come close to the feeling of slipping off his shoes, sliding down onto the couch beside his wife with a bowlful of her mutton stew and putting his feet up to watch the news. But Stuart is unable to watch the news, because he is about to be on the news. And besides, the couch is probably half-way to Wales by now.

Detective Inspector Stuart Mackenzie was, so the First Minister repeated several times on Saturday night, the youngest Detective Inspector the city of Edinburgh has ever had. He has spent the last ten years shunning further promotion, and has worked with dedication and purpose to convict drug dealers, paedophiles, corporate thieves, people-traffickers, murderers and rapists. Yet, the search for Megan Gillies is the highest-profile investigation he has ever led. Only twice before in his distinguished career has he been involved in missing children cases - once in uniform and once in his second year in CID - and both of those children turned up unharmed in a matter of hours. Megan has so far been missing for ninety-seven hours.

Tonight's press conference in Gayfield Station is a spectacularly depressing event. Facing a mass of media all buzzing with talk of Ian Huntley's conviction today and of police error and blame, D.I. Mackenzie sits at the top table with Assistant Chief Constable Desmond Manish in full uniform and Councillor Brenda Marshall in a solemn work suit. Stuart wears a striking grey suit with a purple, open-collar shirt, appearing on the raised stage almost like a film actor doing promotional work. Erected behind the table and the three grave faces, the enlarged public image of Megan Gillies asks:
Have You Seen This Girl?

The hunger persists. Painfully, Stuart's belly grumbles, attracting the unsympathetic attention of the A.C.C., who gives a sharp nod down the table, a nod perhaps of *Good Luck*, or *Courage, Man*, but certainly *Do Your Job, Sunshine*.

Stuart does not bother to look round as behind him a door opens and the electric air is filled with whispers of *Now!* And *Go Live!* Then, except for the whirr of cameras, there is silence, a suffocating calm, as Jack and Sarah Gillies, accompanied by a young female officer, make their grim way towards the stage. Desmond and Brenda rise to whisper words of comfort as the tragic guests of honour take their seats, awkwardly, clinging together, but the Inspector says nothing.

Sitting forward, the Assistant Chief Constable immediately takes control, regarding the press with a blatant distain, his eyebrows joined. 'Mr and Mrs Gillies will give a short statement,' he decrees, 'which will be followed by a statement from Detective Inspector Stuart Mackenzie, who is in charge of the investigation.' He folds his fingers together and sits back into his chair, concluding:

'There will be no questions.'

Immediately, Sarah musters the strength to speak. She is thirty-seven, a primary school teacher, and under normal circumstances a beautiful woman. Today, she is a wreck, a husk of a person, swallowing down pained sobs and fighting collapse with every choke.

'Maggie,' her voice is a rattle, 'is a happy girl, always smiling and always so very full of... life. We chose the photograph behind us because in it she is smiling and laughing. You would know Maggie if you seen her because you say to yourself, there... is a happy child!'

She can manage no more. Drained completely, she folds into tears, wincing as the flashbulbs blind her eyes.

Beside Sarah, Jack Gillies is a self-employed painter and decorator in the prime of his life ruined by the effort of the last week, and although not by nature a cynical man, he is certainly a realist. All too well he knows that three-quarters of all missing children are murdered within six hours of their disappearance. His strong voice, under the circumstances, deserves respect.

'We just huv tae ken,' he says, 'because the not knowing is worse than imagining the worst. I would appeal to anyone who might have any information,' wincing, he swallows hard, 'good or bad, that would make this easier for us, tae come forward. I would also like tae say that my wife, myself and our family huv full confidence in the police, especially Inspector Mackenzie. They have our deepest gratitude.' He is fighting back the tears now, but he has promised himself he will not cry; he will not give that satisfaction to the creature who took his child, so he swallows down his rage. 'And tae Meg... our baby... the most extraordinary daughter a man could want, if yie can hear me now, Mum and I love yie very much. And we will see yie soon.'

Robbed entirely of his resolve, he cries hysterically, burying his face into his wife's breast, making an excellent photo opportunity for the press.

Keeping his face a mask, Stuart fights the urge to jump the table and smash every single lens in the room. That the press conference was indeed his own design tortures him further.

He thinks of his nieces. He has three nieces, two by his big brother, the other by his little sister who is now divorced. The youngest, Scarlet, is the same age as Megan Gilles, although from the other end of the city. The girls are the closest thing Stuart and Rose have known to raising children; they are the principal negative aspect to leaving Edinburgh, and they are, indeed, eventual heirs to Stuart and Rose's assets. He tries to push them out of mind, unsuccessfully, and although he has nothing at all fit for press release, says with the phantom taste of stew in his mouth:

'We are treating Megan's disappearance as a chance abduction. I would reiterate Mr Gillies's words and implore anyone who may have information to come forward. On behalf of my team and myself, I would like to thank the good people of Leith and the children of Megan's school for their excellent and invaluable support through these last few days. That's all. Thank you ladies and gentleman. I bid yie good evening.'

And so it finishes. Upon Stuart's command, the same female officer whisks away the Gillies's. The press quickly disperse. The Assistant Chief Constable leaves with the Councillor, but Stuart remains.

His mind is racing. Bitterness burns him. It seems to him that the press release image of Megan Gillies looks, even down to the missing-toothed smile, exactly like that of eight-year-old Sarah Payne, who was abducted and murdered by Roy Whiting in 2000. It was later revealed that Anglia police knew Whiting beforehand as a dangerous paedophile, just as Ian Huntley, the school janitor today charged for the abduction and murder of Jessica Chapman and Holly Wells in 2002, was also known by the police to be dangerous. Whiting's and Huntley's rights, it can therefore be surmised, were more important than the rights of the children they murdered. Whiting's conviction was followed by a heated UK-wide campaign for 'Sarah's Law', whereby all parents would be informed when a convicted paedophile moved into their community - irregardless of the Data Protection Act - but the idea was quickly discouraged by the government in Scotland, who claimed, via then Justice Minister, Jim Wallace, that implementing 'Sarah's Law' would be counter-productive, driving sex offenders underground. Stuart headed that particular committee of advisors to the government and has never forgiven their decision. Ironically, today the Home Secretary, David Blunkett, ordered just such an inquiry.

However, this violent thought is entirely irrelevant to his present investigation. Contrary to the mechanics of a police investigation, Detective Inspector Mackenzie has learned across the years to trust his instincts. And his instincts are tingling now to the point of overwhelming his hunger. He has the idea, which his staff are working furiously to prove, that Sarah Gillies murdered her own daughter. She did this, Stuart believes, and then disposed on the body, leaving her shoes in a litterbin, for reasons known only to herself. Even more tragically, Stuart believes that Jack Gillies has not an inkling of this.

Tomorrow, the truth will out.

Rising to his feet, the Inspector finds a lump in his throat. But not because he feels for the poor man and his child, although he certainly does - Stuart has never been able to work without involving his personal emotions - but for reasons altogether more selfish:

Because Megan Gillies, dead or alive, is Stuart's last such job; because after today he will be an anti-global terrorism analyst lodged fast behind a desk in a sleepy, unassuming country town in Wales; because tomorrow - a tear comes now - is The Last Day.

19

Dusk fell across the cold May night at five minutes to eleven, coating the clouds with a magnificent amethyst glow. Twenty minutes later, a heavy darkness engulfed even the stars.

Amid the shadows and the rats, watching with liquid eyes the glowing windows of the Hôtel Saint Marie and the Schutzstaffel clerks moving around inside, the assassin stood alone. An hour of patient study had drained her hip flask, but it seemed that no amount of drinking would ease the dull throb of the bullet wound in her shoulder.

Although since the attendance of the Reichführer the hotel had returned to its principal function as a 'paper plant', processing a multitude of paperwork twenty-four hours a day, she knew keenly that she had been baited here tonight by a prisoner who under normal circumstances would have been transferred immediately to either the Foch or Fresnes prison, neither of which was possible to breach. But the obvious trap was not a concern; the assassin had decided that nothing short of death would stop her this night.

Naturally, she had taken precautions. Fifteen minutes ago, more than twenty individuals, the majority of the hotel's staff officers, mostly Gestapo, left the hotel with obvious urgency, piled into Citroën cars and left rubber marks on the road as they speed away. They were responding to a call for help from another SS paper factory across the river that was under siege. Alison knew this because she was responsible. It was her distraction. While many Parisian résistance fighters loyal to de Gaulle and the Allied Expeditionary Force would not act without the proper authorisation, therefore saving ammunition and men from unnecessary risks, an equal number of fighters, many of whom were Jewish, relished any opportunity to slay Nazis. And that was precisely what they were doing as the assassin watched the Citroëns disappear. Indeed, the effectiveness with which her blunt preparations had worked amazed the assassin, and gave her insight into the particularly panicked Nazi state of mind. She suspected that the Germans were preparing to lose the war and wondered if their priority was to save their men or destroy their meticulous paperwork.

Either way, the Hôtel Saint Marie was devoid of officers and except for the movement of a prostitute silhouetted by the streetlights of Rue La Fayette - a tall, elegant figure whose taut strut implied, rather than drunkenness, soreness - the dark alley was completely empty.

The assassin touched the revolver and knives in her belt, but remembered just in time not to bother with the empty flask.

Are you waiting patiently for an invitation? the voice inside her head asked.

'I'm scared.'

You should be.

'I wish I could see the stars.'

I can see them for both of us.

'Johnny?'

I'm here.

'I wish I could see you.'

If you stand here much longer, Ali-bally-bee, you'll see me sooner than you think. Shift!

To delay any longer was indeed folly. She cupped her hands over her mouth and made a noise that sounded like a shrieking fox, watching as seconds later the 'prostitute', who looked in a flash of moonlight exactly like Marlene Dietrich, disappeared from view.

'As I walk through the valley of the shadow of death,' Alison was surprised to hear herself whisper, 'I fear no evil. Except of course my own.'

'Amen.'

Startled by the voice, Alison denied the pain in her shoulder, shifted her weight and spun, her knives drawn to kill.

'Jesus Christ, you gave me a heart attack, sir. I nearly stabbed you!'

'I'm aware of that.' Major Philip Scott of the British Army dropped his eyes to the knife pressing into his stomach, and shifted his weight on his cane. 'Has Juliette gone?'

'Yes, she…how…what the fuck… how?'

'The wheel was here before your generation, Violette,' the Major remarked. 'I'm not useless yet.'

'You can't be here.' Alison's voice was steady and sincere. 'You mustn't be risked, sir. Think of Overlord. You're needed!'

'As are you! I wish you would accept that. Our number is already too few. I know that I cannot stop you going in there tonight, but perhaps I can help get you back out alive, Alison.'

Although unconvinced of the sentiment, the shock of hearing her own name spoken in relation to herself, after fully two years, hit Alison like a bullet.

The major continued:

'I have during these last four years lost nearly seventy men and women who were following orders given by me, and in the last war over two hundred. I am fast approaching the notion, to mention nothing of the tactical loss of a soldier, that each one is to be taken personally. Highly unprofessional, I realise, but that seems to be another sentiment your generation has claimed. What's your plan?'

'Plan?' The assassin repressed a laugh. 'I've come this far on adrenaline, alcohol and arrogance, sir. You?'

'The same.'

'Do you have anything to drink?'

'Not anymore,' the Major said.

As it turned out, it was not a particularly thorny matter to gain access to the Hôtel Saint Marie. Nor was it bloodless or merciful. Entering through the front courtyard and main entrance, Alison Gorry and Philip Scott moved silently, and by the time they stood in the second floor dining room, a grand space mostly untouched since the days of the Ancien Régime, complete with table of hastily-left meals, a dozen corpses lay in their wake. Two lay at their feet. The Major had impressed his junior with surprising swiftness and a lack of hesitation so essential in the trade, so often absent in the younger agents. More amazingly, not only did the Major move without a cane, he walked without a limp. Neither of them had yet drawn their gun. The Major's tool of choice was the garrotte, a crude device made of what looked to Alison like a halved piano stool leg and one of the instrument's thinner strings. It was mortally effective and surprisingly charming.

Amid the wall-mounted tapestries and oil portraits of the hallway, a uniformed clerk passed three feet from the spies without sensing their presence. With difficulty he carried two crates of paperwork. He had a lush head of blonde curls and was at the most twenty years of age. The Major took him from behind, slipping the lethal wire around his meagre neck with sufficient pressure to make his point.

'Où est le prisonnier?' Alison hissed, noting the fallen files pertained to 'transport' and 'processed' numbers, each marked with the word: Drancy.

The clerk's voice came in a petrified wheeze.

'La cave.'

Alison supported his body down to the floor soundlessly and as she watched his last breath escape and his eyes fix in that lifeless stare, she felt nothing at all.

The spies crept down a carpeted staircase, meeting only meagre resistance on the ground floor, and continued down an uncarpeted service stairwell.

Coming out into darkness, they froze. A voice was audible and although she had never heard it before, Alison was able to put a face to it immediately.

'I can hear something.' The Major whispered the obvious. 'There, that door.'

Drawing her revolver, Alison nodded - a futile gesture in the dark - and restrained herself against kicking down the door. Instead, she put her ear to it.

The voice from within, surprisingly, was a petition:

'Il n'y a aucun besoin de ceci!' it said. 'Je n'aime pas faire ceci.'

'Damn you!'

The second voice, so familiar to her, caused Alison's blood to run cold despite its high alcohol content.

Patience, sweetheart, John's voice said in her head. Patience is a weapon as good as any bullet. Try the door.

The door was unlocked and yielded to her touch. Silently, with her breath held, Alison opened a crack wide enough for the Major and herself to slip through into a wine cellar racked for hundreds of bottles. The tart smell of spoiled wine met them. The racks provided the intruders decent cover.

The sight of Frédéric Trépont in the centre of the room forced a low exhalation from Alison that was the remnants of a suppressed scream. From a rope tied to piping on the ceiling, the schoolteacher hung by his bound wrists. But the position was unnatural, his arms twisted behind his back, pulling the weight of his entire body down on the reversed joints of his shoulders. He was naked and trembling with cold. He was battered and bleeding; blood dripped and pooled on the ground below his feet. One of Frédéric's eyes, conjuring in Alison's mind images of the late Abbé Debienne, was missing.

Yet, remarkably, even under the extraordinary circumstances, the young teacher refused to yield. His lips, swollen as they were, fashioned a bitter, obstinate smile. He seemed triumphant.

Guilt choked Alison. Almost as heavy as the fact that Frédéric was missing an eye because she had asked him to be present at the loft, weighed the knowledge that there were over a dozen other Special Operations Executive agents in custody throughout the city, most of them held at the notorious Fresnes prison, and it was a safe bet that they would not survive, that nobody would attempt to rescue them. But Alison did not know any of the other detained agents. Her motivation was that simple. The only agents she had known well during her six months in Paris and her twenty-five months in France were Frédéric, the Major, Madeleine and Juliette. Madeleine's capture and subsequent hanging, Alison believed, had much to do with her friend committing the cardinal sin: she fell in love with a local.

Nor were the other agents blameless in their arrests. Not often did Alison think in such judgemental terms, but the game was not, after all, played for conkers. True, there had been various inside betrayals, but she knew that some of her younger colleagues, both men and women often as young as Frederic but without the insight brought by the murder of ones entire non-combatant family, had gone so far as to meet in cafés and music halls, not to work but purely to socialise. To gossip. But even still, the matter weighed heavily on her.

She pulled her eyes away from the schoolteacher and forced herself to examine the cellar itself. Electric lit, the only point of access was the one she and the Major had just used. There were pipes overhead. There were crates of papers on the floor. With the exception of the wine racks, the room provided neither help nor hindrance; it was merely a backdrop. Two Nazi guards, each with an automatic machinegun, chatted quietly, smoking, having noticed nothing of the entry.

The vital point of interest in the room, the figure pacing before the prisoner, talking in poor French, did not surprise Alison. She had seen him before. It was her man, her mark. It was the Latino assassin commissioned with the death of de Gaulle.

'Je sais que tu sais,' the Latino said. 'Je ne veux pas te blesser plus loin. Je suis un gentil type quand tu finis par me connaître. M'aider à t'aider. Parler!'

'More!' Frédéric roared, a rude and barbaric sound. 'Hurt me more! Take my other eye. I've seen enough of this life, believe me. Do it in the name of my baby sister snatched away while she played with her toys, and then…'

'Stop!' The interrogator was horrified at this remark. 'Why say such a thing? I am not an animal. Help me to…'

'…When I look down upon you with my heavenly eyes,' Frédéric spat venomously, 'with generations of my family at my side, and make no mistake that will be the case, I shall be the victor. So fuck you, Nazi. Kiss my ass.'

'Nazi?' The Latino considered the statement. 'Those two up there, my bulldogs, yes, as you see they wear the uniform, but not I, my friend. The accusation is offensive. I am freelance.'

The Latino lit an American cigarette and removed his red leather gloves.

Alison swallowed down a gasp as she saw what was, in hindsight, blatantly obvious to her two nights ago. It was the fabled left hand, a hand with only four deformed fingers that formed a claw.

The most successful political executioner under the control of the Third Reich was neither Germanic, a soldier nor a member of the National Socialist party, though he had enjoyed a glass of finest port with the Fürher. Even before the war, every government official and intelligence officer throughout the modern world knew the rumour of Antonio Juan, reputed for professionalism, accuracy and sheer nerve despite his handicap, although more people considered him fiction than fact.

His art polished in Sicily during the 1930s, Juan had by his twenty-third birthday ended the careers of Gabon's, Chile's and New Guinea's presidents, as well as numerous parliamentarians and military generals worldwide. The achievement Juan himself was most proud of, which was simultaneously the most profitable, was the assassination of Don Luigi Versi of the New York Versi crime family.

As he paced the wine cellar glaring at Frédéric, he had reached at thirty-seven years of age the prime of his life. Like a cat he moved, constantly in motion, circling Frédéric, at all times poised to pounce.

The world war did not interest Antonio Juan. War in general he considered a blunt tool applied by clumsy and unnecessarily greedy amateurs. He worked for the Nazis simply because nobody from the other side, whom he secretly favoured, had bothered to ask him. He was not fond of Hitler. The Nazi Death Camps sickened him. But being in a business that never relied on written contracts, Juan's word was his bond. He would execute his commission with his usual excellence. Besides, he had already been paid.

Juan's large eyes were ink black and despite the bulb overhead, reflected no light. He exhaled smoke and asked in a matter-of-fact voice, in perfect English:

'Tell me. Who is he? Where can I find him? I cannot stand these mind-numbing questions any longer so speak up! You can die quickly or you can die horrible. Decide.'

'I will tell you nothing. And I will die with the knowledge that you will be next.'

'I will not! Who is he?'

'He's coming for you.' Frédéric smiled. 'You know what happened to your cohorts, Wetzler and Debienne. You saw them both.'

'They were hardly my cohorts. I never even met the Frenchman while he was alive. What's your point?'

'My point is they're dead now. And you're next.'

'I very much doubt it.' Juan smiled.

Alison's expression was grave, understanding that Frédéric had resigned his eye and his life to protect her identity.

Without looking, Alison could feel the Major lift his gun, which had a crude silencing device attached. Motionless, she held her breath for what felt like an hour, and then as if from far away or deep underwater she heard one sharp report followed quickly by a second. She watched both of the uni-formed Nazis collapse, one bleeding from his neck, the other missing half of his face, but still with his cigarette in his mouth.

Alison burst out from her position behind the rack and advanced with domineering poise towards Juan, her boot heels tramping loudly, her gun aimed. She could taste blood in the air. She could smell sweat. She could feel the shifting air.

'Hola.' Her voice sounded distant in her ears.

Calmly, Juan turned and his eyes met Alison. Silently, they faced each other with the trained gun keeping the peace, allowing the Major to begin the task of liberating Frédéric, which, because of his position, was not an easy one.

Tangible disbelief filled the cellar. Antonio Juan regarded Alison Gorry as if she had just landed from outer space; the lean, cropped-haired woman dressed in black aiming a gun at his head with the most disturbing set of eyes that he had ever been witness to. The stare was not the empty one Juan had so often faced but nor was it the familiar cold, calculating gaze. It was some-thing altogether different. The eyes burning into the back of his skull, as his intuition could best appreciate, portrayed a state of absolute serenity.

'It's a woman!' he said amazedly.

'It was once,' Alison replied. 'Hands in the air, Nazi.'

'Holy Mother.' Juan meant to cross himself but thought better of it, instead raising his hands.

'Frédéric's shoulder is broken,' Major Scott said, grappling with a mass of ropes. 'And I think his wrist.'

Alison's eyes never left Antonio Juan's. 'Can he walk?' she asked.

'You don't have to speak about me as if I'm not here!' Frédéric said.

'Can you walk?'

'Yes, I can fucking walk! I could dance a fucking tango if it meant getting out of here. Be carefully, he had guns and knives on him.'

Alison saw that Juan's spell was broken. He was thinking, calculating, looking with hawk eyes. He was also smiling. The atmosphere in the cellar made each of the tiny hairs on her body rise.

Shoot him, said the voice in her head.

'What's so funny,' she asked.

'You're not who they've sent for me, are you?' Juan laughed. 'I don't believe it. A woman?'

Alison laughed, too. 'I know, it is funny, I think. Not very long ago I spent my evenings tending my vegetable garden in Scotland, and my neighbours came everyday to see if I was managing all right while my husband was gone. I grew carrots, cabbages and potatoes to sell at market, but I lost much of my produce because I couldn't bring myself to shoot the foxes. It is kind of a joke.'

Stop the drama, Gorry, the silent voice said. No heroics. Shoot the bastard before he shoots you!

'What happens now?' Antonio Juan asked.

'You die.'

'Not before de Gaulle.' The words came with a startling confidence and a sincere smile. 'I've already been paid, my friend. If you kill me before I satisfy my contract, I'll never work again!'

'Get Frédéric out.' As Alison said this to the Major, she turned her head slightly, wincing at the pain in her shoulder and at the brutal state of the schoolteacher.

She realised her shocking mistake too late.

Antonio Juan was a professional with many more years under his belt than anyone Alison Gorry had faced before. It was simply a matter of experience. A split-second was all it took. In the instant his captor's head was turned, Juan acted. He did not attempt to reach for one of his two guns and did not attempt to fight; face-to-face confrontation, he knew, even when facing a wounded foe - as this one clearly was - had never been his forte. His left hand, deformed since birth, had prevented such a thing. The claw could hold a gun, yes, but the bones inside were brittle and vulnerable. He considered it, somewhat loftily, his Achilles Heal.

What Juan did do was flee. Leaping with the grace of a wildcat, he clutched at the overhead pipe with his good hand and smashed the single light bulb with his feet. The last thing Alison saw was his contorted body about to propel himself… somewhere. She fired two shots but simply could not shoot what she could not see. The Major also fired vainly.

In an instant, Juan's footfalls thumped on the boards above, growing fainter. The Major made a move to follow but Alison grabbed his arm.

'Let him go,' she said.

'But… de Gaulle, we cannot allow…'

'Let him go. It's begun now.'

Outside on the pavement, amazed to see the back door of an idling Citroën car fly open, Alison went as far as to lift her gun before the Major stopped her.

'We aren't all young idiots,' he said. 'Some of us have gammy knees. Get in.'

From the Citroën's back seat, Claude Lemaître commanded Juliette in the driver's seat and the car, like the Nazi ones earlier, left rubber on the road as it raced towards the streetlights. Alison watched the haze of the alley become the brighter haze of Rue Lafayette, her eyes wide, her breathing perfectly calm.

Frédéric, too, sat frighteningly composed. He ran his fingers through his hair and winced at the pain in his shoulder. The other arm was obviously useless. The oozing black hole of his socket was horrendous to look at, but Alison forced herself, and then forced a smile. She was amazed to see the smile reciprocated.

'About time,' he said. 'My patience was beginning to wane.'

'Better than any bullet.' Alison laughed in spite of herself and Frédéric joined her.

The Major took a bottle of whiskey from Lemaître with grateful eyes and trembling hands, swallowed a deep draught followed by two more, then passed the bottle on.

'That,' he exclaimed dryly, 'was quite exciting.'

192

20

Perched by the herbs on the sill, his purring resonate in the stillness, Snoopy watches with fascination the three-quarter moon high in the night sky, the only source of light, until his reverie is broken by the sound of the front door opening and then slamming shut. He turns his head at the sound of approaching footsteps to see Charlie come into the kitchen, wrapped in her duffel coat, scarf and toory, and flick on the harsh electric ceiling light. He appropriately adjusts his vision and approaches her across the bunker to offer his chin for a brief stroke before hopping down to the floorboards and curling through her legs, watching with eager eyes as from a greaseproof paper parcel she unwraps a fresh pair of fish heads. Feral by nature, Snoopy prefers to hunt his food, but he is certainly willing to make allowances.

Charlie plates the meal on the floor and the cat, predictably, looses all interest in her. She throws her keys with the morning post onto the breakfast table by the frescoed wall and slowly uncurls her scarf, unbuttons her coat and pulls off her toory, releasing her hair into its natural shape. Next, she kicks off her boots, sheds her coat straight onto the floor, then her jeans, shirt, vest and finally her underwear so that she stands entirely naked, feeling the delicious, basil-scented breeze from the window tightening her dark nipples. Unshowered, she feels to her very bones foul. Her pale skin is gaunt and badly in need of moisturiser, but she has not the will for such things tonight.

She fills the kettle with water and places it on the hot aga, more pleased than ever before in her life to be home.

Her eyes, lined in red, fix on her own reflection in the darkened window. But she shuts them, holding her breath, and with trembling fingers pushes against her clammy eyelids.

Charlie's bedroom is an unashamed state. Chaos replaces her usual orderliness; it is simply the accumulation of her life, her private sanctuary, familiar and safe. But so unexpected is the sight awaiting her as she pushes open the door that she curses with fright and her eyes dilated. The room is not a mess; it is sparkling clean. Most noticeably, however, her old, ruined single bed is gone, replaced by a beautiful, ornate cast-iron frame with a thick double mattress already made with her favourite silk linen. She stands motionless and takes in the scene. But she does not smile. Indeed, her expression hardens as she sees attached to the frame, by means of handcuffs though the metal bars, her own handwritten note:

EXPECT THE UNEXPECTED

In the green bathroom, naked still, she curses in fright for a second time at the sight of Stan lying sound asleep in the bath, his hands clasped over his thin belly like an otter, the pages of his Scotsman floating in the water. Snoopy arrives at Charlie's feet, purring gently, and together they regard the sight in silence as moonlight throws tainted light from the stained window across the tiles. She does not wake him. She lets him sleep, closing the door gently.

Charlie selects a stark, angular lamp combination in the living room and slips down into her armchair with her hair held tightly back in a band. She does not curl into the seat as is her habit, but rather sits upright, composed, braced, fingers clenched, jaws clenched, too. Music plays quietly, the second movement - the *tranquillissimo* - of Henryk Górecki's third symphony, *Symfonia Piesni Zalosnych*, commonly translated though not entirely accurately as *Symphony of Sorrowful Songs*. The solo soprano voice in unison with the strings, leaping the major third against the hollow, sublime harmony, and then falling slightly with a sense of hopeless longing, sends shivers up and down her spine.

But she does not allow herself the moment. Resolve is requires, perhaps more resolve than she has ever needed to muster before. She thinks of all the achievements of her life, her career. She looks around at the room at her beloved books, her piano, her home, her private place in the world and feels... nothing. Meaning has left her.

Carefully, taking all the time she needs and thinking of Paris, she rolls a potent joint with her dwindling piece of her hash. Lighting it, she is mindful of her hair and holds the smoke deep inside her body, causing a silent convulsion. Stillness comes suddenly, a heavy calm, clear and listless.

Then she takes the deepest breath of her life.

And picks up her mobile telephone. After pressing a few buttons, she hears from over her shoulder the sound of splashing as Stan's mobile telephone begins to ring in the bathroom. After an audible curse, he answers:

'Good evening, Brown.'

'Hume' Charlie exhales brusquely. 'Where are yie?'

'I'm watching television at your place,' Stan says, trying not to splash. 'What time is it?'

'It's late. It's after midnight.'

'Where are yie? Are yie coming home? I want tae see yie.'

'Why?'

'I have a Christmas surprise for yie.'

'I'm driving home, Stan,' Charlie says. 'And I have a surprise, too.'

'Oh?' The commas in the corner of Stan's mouth expand to a smile. 'Is it a nice surprise?'

Charlie smiles bitterly. 'Understand, Stan, that I cannae face you, and that I'm ashamed of myself. And understand that the few minutes we spent dancing to Moon River were the happiest I've had in...a long time. Stan, I love to dance with you. I remember that you were shaking.'

'We were shaking together.'

'Yes, but understand, Stan, before I look into your beautiful green eyes, that none of the words we said then matter anymore. Everything has changed. I've fucked it up.'

Softly, Stan says:

'Whatever's wrong, Charlotte, we can fix it together. We always have.'

'But that's just it, Stan.' A tear falls from Charlie's eye. 'This has nothing to do with you. I'm pregnant.'

The Last Day

This gigantic ordeal has shown that the danger threatening existence does not come solely from outside, and that victory without courageous and thorough internal reconstruction would not be real victory.

Charles de Gaulle

1

She imagines herself driving the boulevards of Paris, cruising from the maisonette in St-Germain to Eugène's restaurant in the Latin Quarter. She imagines herself immersed in the nightlife, the locals, the sex, browsing fish markets, fois gras factories and designer boutiques alike. But the fantasy is somewhat impressionistic and brief. Silently she laments its passing, closing her eyes and pushing against her tender eyelids with fingers smelling of garlic and fish scales.

Behind the obtrusive, tubular green and white structure of Easter Road Football Stadium, in the fetid wasteland adjoining Lochend Park, Stan and Charlie amble together amongst weeds, abandoned white goods and supermarket trolleys. They often walk here as a matter of habit. But not for much longer. A huge billboard advertises the fact that the construction of flats is imminent.

Both wrapped in duffle coats, scarves and gloves, neither has slept. There is no wind. There is barely air. All of Leith hangs in the panoramic horizon, down to the dock cranes and the hazy Forth, and as the rising sun turns the multitude of rooftops from purple to grey, it is merely a nuisance, a pain on tender eyes.

With her toory pulled down low, Charlie is stronger today. Gloom has settled and with it comes detachment. She feels filthy, unwashed since work last night. Charlie has long imagined herself soiled and now that she truly is, there is a strange relief in the submission. The tangled, filthy web underneath her toory she can only imagine.

The faint, tinny smell of blood hangs in the air, although it is certainly not coming from her.

Charlie's period was due on Sunday night. Obviously, it did not arrive. More evident than the lack of her usual first-day clot, and more telling, was the lack of pain in the preceding days. Charlie's period is often late, but the pain never is. And so at a quarter past eight on Tuesday morning, only hours before having a tooth pulled without anaesthetic, Charlie barrelled through the doors to her GP's surgery, provided a urine sample and demanded tests. An hour later, midway between Edinburgh and Kirkcudbright, a pharmacy pregnancy test kit showed positive in a public lavatory in Moffat. Official conformation would not come until yesterday, by telephone.

The matter of paternity is unpleasant. There are, humiliatingly, two suspects. Both are deplorable. The first is a married man, a well-proportioned cook from the Southside, with a wife and three daughters, one the same age as Charlie. The other was anonymous, a typical sloppy and nameless brief encounter that she can barely remember.

But there are matters more unpleasant. For the second time in her life, the first being after her rape, Charlie submitted blood for HIV/AIDS and Hepatitis B and C tests. She has long feared this act. Although every morning she takes a contraceptive pill, Charlie's level of sexual protection is atrocious, shameful.

There are matters even more unpleasant. Chemically speaking, Charlie fully confessed her sins to her aging physician, who had been blatantly horrified to learn of her fifteen joints a day habit. He had taken quite some convincing and even then eyed her suspiciously. But apparently having swallowed six ecstasy tables since her last menstruation and subsequent impregnation, and snorted two large lines of cocaine, Charlie is not uncommon.

'I imagine the baby will be blind,' she says suddenly, still smelling blood in her keen nostrils. 'And that it'll grow up to resent me without ever seeing me. Doctor Wilkie said there's no way to determine if and how much damage I've caused because the foetus is too tiny. It and I are equally helpless. And if not physically damaged, then it might be mentally damaged and helpless, premature and feeble, spat out into the world without the strength even to breathe.'

Gaunt, his hands deep in his coat pockets, his collar turned up high, Stan casts a long shadow on the uneven ground.

'Let's not be melodramatic,' he says. 'The first thing we need...'

'Stan, we dinnae have tae dae anything. Understand, idiot, that we arenae pregnant. I am. You are unaccountable.' Her face sets frankly. 'It's me who's fucked.'

In spite of himself, Stan laughs at the choice of words. And that does it. Piercingly, disturbingly, pale face turning maroon, Charlie screams at the top of her lungs, rips off her toory, her scarlet curls springing free like snakes, throws it at Stan and irrefutably stamps her boot heel.

'Well, there's always an abortion,' Stan snaps, surprisingly nastily, though his transparent eyes wide with melancholy cannot hide his contempt for the notion. 'That would surely ease the inconvenience. Yie could go to Paris entirely at liberty from responsibility and reclaim your beloved freedom.'

To his horror, Charlie says nothing to this, seeming lost deep inside herself.

They walk for a while in silence, until she lifts her eyes sharply, followed immediately by her professional nose.

More than blood now, an altogether more distinctive smell both pierces the stale air and her own stink like vinegar, and she finds herself strangely alarmed by the look on Stan's face. Nostrils flaring, he inhales a deep whiff. For a moment, she does not understand her own concern, her increased pulse, her apprehension. Not until she places the smell.

Rotting meat.

Decomposition.

Megan Gillies is Charlie's immediate thought. Stan gestures grimly by nod towards a discarded car door in the overgrown bush, the source of the reek, and then he begins slowly towards it. Upon reaching the door, however, he finds himself not so keen to lift it. From every angle he examines the door, debating, scratching his head, chewing his lips, until he finally hunkers down and tentatively lifts it to the side.

Although gruesome, he cannot tear his eyes from the spectacle. He returns to his full six feet as Charlie pulls her scarf over her nose, likewise without averting her eyes.

Rotting and rank, the corpse of a dead dog still seems very much alive with flies, its tongue protruding grotesquely, its ribs visible.

'It's what yie've always wanted, I think.' Stan says this without spite. 'Paris, living and working there, I remember hearing yie say such things years ago. Yie should be pleased.'

'I only feel shame,' Charlie says. 'For all this, Stanley, I'm truly sorry and truly ashamed. I dinnae deserve to… have you here.'

Stan scoffs. 'Where else would I be?'

Charlie lowers to her knees beside the carcass and for the briefest of seconds, Stan thinks she is about to pray. But instead she sits cross-legged on the ground and with the tiny nugget of hashish she has left, begins the process of rolling a joint. This action, more than any of her words, hits Stan hard. He is speechless. His eyes close. The words *Mo Chreach!* form in his mouth but he keeps them in.

When finally he opens his eyes, Charlie is standing before him, lighting the joint with a typical tilt of the head to reduce the risk of igniting her hair. Daylight has fully emerged now, a dull, dour light. Exhaling with a cough as she reapplies her toory, she seems to Stan a frail creature, pathetic and exposed.

He asks, agreeably, as if none of this has really happened:

'Are you going to work today?'

'I'm not sick. It's the last day. Will I see yie tonight?'

'Aye, if Vincent doesnae mind me falling drunk into his party.'

This, clearly, is not what she wanted to hear and Stan winces at his own stupidity.

'Vincent leaves tomorrow,' Charlie smiles bitterly. 'I dinnae suppose he'll gie two fucks, Stanley.' She turns and begins to walk away. 'Dae what yie want.'

Stan wants to protest, to apologise, to take her in his arms, but the effort is futile. She is already gone from him.

2

No. 34 the Shore, a plain cottage built in the seventeenth century as the harbour master's dwelling, is not visible from the modern streets, but from the crack in the terrace that conceals it, Rose emerges in her sleek winter coat, carrying in one hand a suit-bag and her briefcase, and in the other, her husband. Scarcely have they walked ten yards when Stuart stops, thrusts his hands deep into his trousers pockets, slouches and declares:

'I'm no gaun. It's my stomach, Rosie. I'm sick.'

'Move it, Rebus! We're late.'

But halfway across the bridge the Detective Inspector again detains his wife as he stops to looks down into the cloudy brown Water of Leith, his hands back in his pockets. He wears no police officer's clichéd raincoat, but rather a smart, vintage brown leather one. A scarf hangs neatly. His shoes are pointy and heeled.

Giving him the moment, Rose takes in the landscape, feeling a delightful breeze across her face and through her copper hair. Tall, shiny office buildings and 'executive' flats, contrasting with the old stone tenements, surround the calm landscaped reservoir that was once the principal waterway to Scotland. Suited office workers rush past. Milkmen and noisy vans deliver to the neighbouring restaurants and bars. Two police technicians in overalls at the quayside, loading up a white transit van with the last of the equipment used to dredge for the body of Megan Gillies, wave in acknowledgement to Stuart.

From behind, Rose slips her free hand around his belly, nuzzling her lips into his neck, whispering:

'Tick tock tick tock.'

'Phone in for me,' Stuart says gravely. 'Tell them I'm sick. Tell them I'm weary, Rosemary, and that I'm sick to death.'

'No.'

Stuart turns to face his wife. 'Then let me tell yie that this will be a very grim day indeed, my love, my lover. Likely the worst.' He kisses Rose's head, her nose and finally her lips. 'But everything will be over by tonight, and then I'll talk, sheriff.'

She smiles. 'Fine. Then we'll have sex, we'll go to sleep, and in the morning we'll go'n live in Wales. How does that sound, my little deputy, my cherub?'

'As good as a pink grapefruit with sugar on top.' Stuart's hands come out from his trouser pockets and join around Rose's waist.

'What's today?' she asks. 'Tell me.'

'I know what it is, love, but it doesnae make it easier.'

'Tell me anyway.'

'Today,' Stuart affirms, 'is the last day.'

'The what?'

'The last day.'

'Tell me again.'

'Today is the last day. But this may be the day I snap. Yie hear about that kind of thing.' However, to resist a smile, even in the face of the horrendous tasks awaiting him, seems impossible, and Stuart does smile, full and warm.

Rose's lips curl but she is stern. 'That's right, today is the last day.' She takes his head with her free hand, feeling him pull her close as her sterile eyes burn unblinking into his gentle brown eyes until she feels the spark that means she is fully occupying his consciousness. 'For this day, my love, and for all the days to come, we have waited and worked and sacrificed for twenty-five years. Yie should try to enjoy this day, sweetheart, whatever it brings. We've earned it. Now shift yir fuckin arse or it'll cane it.'

She is already walking away. Stuart lets her go, unmoving, watching until she spins on her heels, free hand on her hip, eyes ablaze.

'Move it!'

Other than to slip his hands back into his trouser pockets, Stuart does not move. 'Remember the Great Waldo Pepper?' he asks.

So unexpected are these words that all of Rose's self-control is required to prevent from falling limp onto the pavement. Instead, she advances three long, slow clicking paces, drops her case and suit-bag on the pavement and throws her arms around Stuart's neck, kissing him as hard and as deeply as she is able, pushing him back against the bridge until he is almost chocking for breath. She is vaguely conscious of a wolf-whistle.

In truth, Rose is not particularly keen to get to work either. The effort is futile. She would much rather spend the day reading or paying a last visit to Harvey Nichols, but the party arranged in her honour this afternoon by her colleagues has forced her into a work suit and out onto the cold bridge. Not that Rose enjoys parties.

'D'yie know,' she asks, licking Stuart's chin, 'how I know that you love me?'

'How?'

'Because I feel strong. You make me strong.' Rose's lips curl into a more savage contortion and her hand is suddenly between his legs. 'Now drag me home by the roots of my hair and do dirty nasty things to me!'

The Detective Inspector needs no second request. He bends, face lifted to receive the morning sun, to gather his wife's dropped case and then begins to lead her by the hand back the way came.

At least, he tries to. Impact prevents it. There is a clatter as a small comely creature in a toory collides with Rose. Stuart's personality changes utterly, although not noticeably, as he represses years of habit, resisting the urge to

201

topple the assailant, and simply steadies his wife with a single, gentle hand on the small of her back.

'I'm sorry,' Rose says instinctively.

For a long and silent moment, the two women regard one another with the hint of recognition.

'You're…'

'Go and watch where you're going, eh?' Charlie hisses, and is already gone.

Rose watches her for a moment, and then straightens her coat with a dramatic gesture, exclaims:

'Young people!'

'Aye, hen,' Stuart says dryly, lifting an eyebrow, 'you were never like that.'

Together, clasping their fingers together, they laugh. And although they are only a few steps from their car, an imported 2003 Jaguar limited edition hatchback, lilac, by Stuart's reckoning certainly the coolest car on the busy street and possibly the entire city of Edinburgh, instead they head back the way they came with a noticeable spring in their step.

3

Her feet thrashed as her fingers clawed at the noose. Above the pain in her spine and lungs she felt the strange sensation of nothing below her feet, her weight curiously held, which in no way detracted from the sheer terror of actually hanging by a rope around her neck. She felt a tiny snap in her back followed by another and felt numb below the strangling rope. Numbness, she gladly found, brought relief, mostly because she could no longer feel what she could see: her own bowels spilling out through the slit in her belly. Such detachment, although Alison had often cursed it in the past, was in the circumstance a blessing.

Alison Gorry opened her eyes, surprised to find her bathwater freezing cold, and swallowed down a draught of warming rum from a half-empty bottle. The flat was dark and even though it was the middle of the night, the voice of Maurice Chevalier floated in through the open Baroque terrace doors from a music hall down on the boulevard, presumably full of drunken Nazis. From where she lay in the bath, Alison could see the stars appearing from behind the clouds.

The Major and Lemaître had gone on to take Frédéric to an underground Allied Forces hospital for treatment. She could not shake the image of him smiling defiantly at Juan. Nor could she forget the confidence in Juan's voice as he pronounced the words:

Not before de Gaulle.

She drank. Heavily.

Three hours had passed since Juan's escape. It was feasible that he was on an aeroplane or a boat heading towards his mark, panicked by his recent narrow escape. Alison knew that the General of the Free French, the Great Hope of France, was travelling from Algiers by sea to England, landing on either the third or the fourth, but she had no idea when or where the assassin planned to strike. The third of July was two weeks away. It left plenty of space for Alison's mind to wander.

But she knew Juan would not flee immediately. There was no need to pursue him. He would come to her. She would draw him as a putrid corpse draws flies. Better, she told herself, just to lie still and drink.

She strained to hear John's voice in her head, but since meeting Juan there had been nothing.

She drank. The feeling of hanging by the neck clung to her. She could picture her stomach torn open; she could smell her own fluids escaping her, she could feel... nothing.

Alison slid down in the bath, letting the freezing, numbing water swathe and completely submerge her.

4

'African Republic bordering Togo and Nigeria? Five letters.'

'Benin.'

'Is anyone interesting coming tonight, chef?' Viola asks, filling in twelve down.

'Alistair Forsyth, Ian Rankin, John Belleny, Lord Frazer, Brian Stewart, Alison Elliot from the general assembly of the church of Scotland, Jamie Byng, Lord Prov...'

'Byng who?'

Scratching at a broadsheet crossword in a comfortable-looking woolly poncho, Viola faces Charlie in the white classical third-floor dinning space of The Waterhole, alone expect for Luca, who is four and contentedly negotiating two toy cars between the thirty tables. While it is fair to say that both women have curly ginger hair, it is not truly an accurate comparison. While Charlie's wiry, wilful curls are shocking scarlet, Viola's mane is lush, soft and deeper in tone.

The Waterhole is nothing like Reserve. Reserve is a basement; the Waterhole's principal dining space is a converted loft, light and airy. While Reserve is rich with antiques and art, the Waterhole is stark and uncluttered. Unlike Reserve's multitude of paintings, the Waterhole has only one, frescoed onto the wide gable wall following the arch of the ceiling, depicting a window view out over Leith Harbour of the nineteenth century. Portrayed are a multitude of merchants and ships. It is the only piece ever commissioned from the hand of Stan Hume. On the opposite wall, a similar floor-to-ceiling arched window reveals the genuine and less spectacular view.

'Jamie Byng,' Charlie reiterates. 'The publisher. Yie've met him before, Vi.'

Viola shrugs, trying hard to keep her eyes on the crossword rather than look at Charlie wringing her hands. 'Aztec god of war and sun, usually portrayed artistically as a hummingbird?'

'Letters?'

'Fifteen. Second one is U and the fifth is Z.'

'Huitzilopochtli.'

'Eh?'

Charlie repeats the word and spells it, explaining that Huitzilopochtli's mother was an earth goddess, his brother's stars in the sky and his sister a moon goddess.

'Hmmm. Anyone else?' Viola asks.

'Lord Provost Hinds, Anna Gregor, Brian McMaster and the of course the McConnell's.'

'J.K.?'

'Free food, isn't there?'

Alfredo appears with a steaming cheese omelette that he proceeds to devour, as he does all his meals, pacing on his feet. More than a handsome man, thirty-six and Arab-Greek, his body-fat ratio precise to his five foot nine inches, Alfredo is in Charlie's opinion nothing short of beautiful, and although still generally addressed as Freddy Four Eyes he now prefers contact lenses. He begins to say something but stops suddenly, disgustedly, and coming to a sharp halt by Charlie, offers a forkful of pungent, stringy goop.

'Egg, little one?'

Viola and Alfredo Ritsos are legendary in the cities culinary underbelly. Commonly said is that Alfredo has owned more restaurants than Viola has cooked pastas. From nothing, they have carved a niche in the city restaurant market for themselves and are only now beginning to enjoy the financial fruits of their labour. They have three restaurants across the city, none of which have achieved any kind of major establishment awards but all of which are filled with stuffed happy bellies seven days a week. Charlie has worked for Alfredo and Viola three times in the past. And now she is back again.

'Poison,' she says, meaning the omelette.

'Yie're skinny as a scheemy,' Alfredo protests. 'Each time I see yie, yie're thinner. It's no right, man.' He gives his offering to his son.

Charlie pulls herself up.

'It's only fair to tell you now,' she states, 'that if I come and work here, it could only be a temporary gig. I know I'm already making demands but that would have to be clear.'

'I told yie, Vi,' Alfredo scoffs with a mouthful, 'the little one thinks we're animals now, brutes serving up muck for the scum of Leith. And we are! But we're proud of it. She's forgotten us, Vi, forgotten her own pedigree!'

'Shut up, Freddy,' Viola says, and then to Charlie:

'We understand, chef. I'm no too thrilled about being back here myself, eh? Say what yie will about Vincent, but he always paid well.'

'That's for sure!' Alfredo misses his mouth and dribbles egg down his jumper. 'The point is, little one,' he says, and, fork pointed, suddenly the small man is utterly commanding, 'you come to us for what yie need. Yie might have forgotten us but we havnae forgotten you. A week, a year, dinnae concern yirsel. But take some omelette. Yie're obviously meant to be bigger.'

'I will be soon,' Charlie says. 'I'm going to have a baby.'

'A baby,' Luca repeats from the floor, crashing his cars together.

Silence.

Charlie waits for what feels no less than an age for any kind of reaction. Mr and Mrs Ritsos simply stare at her bemused. And then in a flash, Viola is out of her chair, round the table, and wraps her arms tightly, with force, around Charlie's neck.

'Thank God,' she sobs, crying now. 'Thank God!'

Alfredo wipes his smiling mouth with a napkin and kisses Charlie's forehead, and then his wife. 'Yie're eating for two now, little one,' he beams. 'What does the boy Hume say? I'll bet he's over the moon! Viola, we've still got the Silver Cro...' Before the words even leave his mouth, Alfredo realises his mistake. Charlie's looks at him with glassy eyes and in reaction to this, Viola, still clinging to her, look at Alfredo as if she is about to rip out his windpipe with her fingernails.

'Oh,' is all he manages to say before Marie and Helen come in, bickering already, school bags over their shoulders. Never in his life has Alfredo felt so pleased to see his daughters, or more specifically the subsequent justification to leave to building.

Helen is eight, slightly overweight, with thick glasses and the pretty uniform of Holyrood Primary School. She rarely speaks more that a few words. Marie, however, is another matter altogether. In her own unique version of Leith Academy's uniform, she is fourteen but looks twenty-five, and a model at that. She is as beautiful as Viola, with her father's darker skin, her black hair sculpted into a hard, curly shape that reminds Charlie of Betty Boop. She casts her eyes across Charlie and her sobbing mother, and then to her four-year-old brother on the floor, who seems the only lucid party present, and asks out the corner of her lip-glossed mouth:

'Luca, what's the score here?'

'A baby,' Luca repeats.

'Mum, not again!' Helen protests. 'You promised after Luca! Dad!'

Viola laughs through her tears, wiping her eyes with the back of her hands. 'Not me! Aunty Charlie is having a baby.' She takes Helen in her arms.

'Then why are yie crying, mum?'

'Can I not cry when I'm happy!'

As is her nature, Marie is more reserved, looking with a cool eye.

'Congratulations,' she offers with a kiss.

While Charlie loves and feels protective of the entire Ritsos family and has several times fired staff for insulting the good name of Freddy Four-Eyes, Marie in particular charms her. This is not only because as the oldest of the children, already four when Charlie met her parents, she is the easiest with which to communicate. It is purely and simply because Marie, Charlie believes, is exactly like she was at fourteen.

From her schoolbag, Marie hands Charlie an old dog-eared Penguin paperback edition of *The Mouse's Tail*. 'I've finished your book, Aunty C.'

'Did yie like it?'

'What dae yie think? It was rude and gory. I loved it. They dinnae gie us that at school.'

Written nearly forty years ago during the summer Vincent left Maison Dussollier to study at Le Cordon Bleu in Paris, Megan Poe's *The Mouse's Tail* won her amongst other things a Pulitzer Prize. It was the first of the now-famous Alison Gorry chronicles, episode one of what would become thirty-six, marking Alison's first months as a Special Operations Executive agent and her transition from Scotland to France, from civilian to combatant, and from wife to widow.

'Keep it. I hear yie're getting a tattoo,' Charlie smiles.

Alfredo's face turns three shades of blue as he chokes on his omelette, but before he can comment, Marie says, glancing to the paperback:

'And I hear yie're moving to France, Aunty C.'

'How dae yie know that!' Charlie is amazed.

Alfredo shrugs, his hand on his wife's shoulder. 'Freddy Four-Eyes sees all, little one. Only eejits forget that.' He gathers up Luca and his toy cars. 'Right, ladies, Luca and I'll take the girls up to school and drop him at nursery, and I might go and try some work, eh?'

And with this, and a barrage of kisses and cuddles, the school party is gone.

Alone again, Viola faces Charlie, settling back, her arms folded under her poncho, her large hazel eyes sparkling after her tears, unblinking. She is waiting.

She does not wait long.

Charlie's serine expression contorts, cheeks flushed with blood, shoulders heaving, and she bursts into howls of tears.

'I've lost him,' she says through sniffs and snotters. 'So stupid! So fucking typical, Viola. The only thing that makes me feel... joyful, and I've lost him! And worse, I deserve it.'

'Have yie lost him?'

It seems to Charlie that Viola is speaking Japanese. 'What do yie mean?'

'Basic social unit consisting of persons united by affinity or consanguinity. Six letters. Begins with F.'

5

A master carpenter by day and something of a society man, Deacon Brodie was by the light of the eighteenth-century moon an unscrupulous thief, a thrill-seeker. Finally caught, the 'notorious scoundrel' was executed publicly on gallows of his own design, becoming the inspiration of Robert Lewis Stevenson's novel of the hidden-self, *The Strange Case of Dr. Jekyll and Mr. Hyde*. Years later, Muriel Spark coined the name for her novel, *The Prime of Miss Jean Brodie*, which was also a novel about freedom of thought. A pub on the Royal Mile now coins Brodie's famous name, and at three in the afternoon, on the Friday the multitude of city centre offices break early for Christmas, it heaves with a writhing mass of GAP and Gucci work-suits and Santa hats, allowing Rose and Stan to slip in quietly.

Removing her sleek winter coat to reveal a silk cinnamon dress and stiletto heels, Rose is suddenly self-conscious. Like herself, the dress is older than initially supposed, an anniversary gift from her husband in 1983, bought for a pound in a Leith Walk charity shop. Her brown buckled Vuitton handbag is more reassuring, procured three hours ago for just over five hundred pounds. From it, she produces a packet of tobacco and begins the effort of rolling a cigarette.

'I want tae leave already,' she says.

'Is there a payphone in here?' Stan's head spins. He is clean-shaven and respectable in his usual tweed jacket and a cinnamon t-shirt bearing the words *Everything You Know Is Wrong*.

'Stan, dinnae leave me.'

'I'll only be a minute.'

'Bastard!' Watching Stan disappear into the throng quite disproportionate to the size of the bar, her aesthete's eyes instinctively examining her dreary surroundings, Rose lights her cigarette.

Deacon Brodie's is not a large bar and is fashioned in the typical, tacky and non-specific 'old style' for the tourists. Shiny festive decorations blink sparks of light. BBC News 24 plays silently on the big-screen television, showing Christmassy images of death, destruction and violation in Iraq, Israel and Africa. The noise level is noxious, an omni-directional rasp of pretensions conversation competing with the traditional and hellish sound of Slade from the jukebox. She can see that High Street Adverts have already laid claim to the far corner of the pub, bullying their way to supremacy. Sue flirts with a politician, the creative team huddle in a tight group. Interestingly, Rose watches Dave Quinn and John Whirrel conduct a private and muted liaison in the corner, their backs turned.

Feeling awkward, not yet ready to delve into the multitude of goodbyes awaiting her in the far corner, Rose buys a whole bottle of Beaujolais from the bar. Retired at forty-six and shed of the burden of property, she pours a large glass, sinks it in one and then pours another. She would rather go home.

Rose turns to see Dave beside her and notes, amongst other things, a faint glow of guilt.

'Yie look wonderful,' he says. 'That dress!'

Another gulp of wine brings an immediate flush of colour to Rose's cheeks. 'Thank you.' She looks the boss up and down. In a patchwork suit, his round belly sitting on his belt, Dave has none of his usual cheer about him, though he does smile. His sleepy eyes are heavy. He drinks fresh orange juice and lemonade.

'In the corner just now with John?' Rose extinguishes her cigarette under foot. 'What were you doing?'

Dave rubs his nose, then his eyebrow, and then to prevent any further rubbing, secures his hand in his trouser pocket. 'I…ah…'

'Dae yie think I came doon the Dee on a digestive, David. Truth.'

'I was making an arrangement,' Dave confesses, unable to resist a grin.

'What kind of arrangement? Be clear.'

Dave merely smiles. 'Yie'll see.'

Frowning, Rose refills her glass as Stan returns, smiling courteously, still wearing his duffle coat over his tweed jacket.

Stan is distracted. More specifically, Stan is having an idea, which manifests itself as a distinct glazing of the eyes hidden behind thick-rimmed glasses. For Stan, despite his famous pedigree, having an idea is hard work indeed, an arduous, laborious and often maddening undertaking. All of his philosophy is purely aesthetic. So-called deep thinking is to him no more real than the Loch Ness Monster, nothing more than a thing written about in books. Of course, even basic thinking sometimes presents its challenges; he is forgetful and often taken unawares. Rather, practical matters are Stan's forte. He is able to deftly blend two records to create new music. He can paint in oil and watercolours with the aptitude of any of the great artists or forgers. In his professional life, too, his most successful marketing strategies have invariably been those conceived in practicality and necessity rather than in theory, which was exactly the case with Leith Furnishings and Upholstery and Charlie's new bed.

Yet, the promise of an idea persists in his mind. Torturously, he has no clues as to what it might finally be or if it will come at all, only that something is niggling, distracting, annoying. It is, finally, a nuisance.

'Stan, what time are we eating?' Dave asks, rubbing belly. 'I'm starving already.'

'Stanley?' Rose physically pokes him.

From far off into the distance, Stan turns his eyes to Dave and then Rose somewhat vacantly.

210

'Pardon me?'

'I asked where and what time are we eating?'

Stan shrugs. 'Dunno. Why?'

'Because you said you'd arrange it,' Rose says. 'Idiot.'

'I forgot.'

'Table five, please! And three and fourteen! And also eleven, please!'

Reserve's arched stone kitchen is as hot as an oven and as busy as it has ever been. A barrage of bookings placed in response to Gavin's closure announcements in yesterday's late edition Evening News and today's Scotsman fill the dinning room to capacity.

Final closure occurs in forty minutes, at half-past three, after which preparation for Vincent's soirée will occupy the kitchen staff until eight. Neither a menu nor set courses are planned, but rather a kind of lavish self-service, medieval buffet, the principal benefit of which is that as soon as food goes upstairs, in a single, enormous effort, the kitchen will close. Not only for the evening, of course. Forever.

But for now there is controlled chaos. Charlie cooks intensely, wide-eyed, engaging herself with the consistent fare of sole soufflés, monkfish risottos, parcelled baby mackerels, nippy salmon broth, and crappit heids, to mention nothing of the oysters, lobsters, mussels and of course her signature dish of pan-fried scallops with spaghetti. There is no fish special, per say; since all the customers today are hardcore regulars, Charlie has agreed, rather magnanimously she feels, to make almost anything asked of her.

Ten years ago, to keep afloat in a busy kitchen was for Charlie extremely difficult, and the contrast now, as she not only survives but flourishes, while simultaneously leading a crew at the very pinnacle of the game, is surprisingly reassuring. To a civilian, her graceful, swift and precise movements would seem like modern dance, and although she does not know it, she wears a small, curious smile on her thin lips.

She keeps half an eye on Viola and Tom as they twist and turn around one another, lobbing used pans through to the washroom and slamming finished plates of food into the lifts, muttering all the while to the commis chefs and dishwashers. Their humour is good; they are both obviously enjoying themselves.

'Table three, please!'

The plates arrive even before the acknowledgment. 'Chef.'

Partially responsible for the good cheer is that Nigel, sometimes known as Tony but regarded today as the Traitorous Fucker, is absent. When he failed to arrive for his shift this morning, it took Charlie only one telephone call to learn that he has already taken a job at Oloroso, across George Street on North Castle Street with his hero, Tony Singh.

Vincent works in place of the Traitorous Fucker, in stiff whites, toiling with speed and sureness that to everyone including Charlie is nothing less that a revelation, his trademark lack of pretension amplified. For this, his farewell to the industry that has occupied the majority of his life, as it were his serenade, his head nods rhythmically, as if to a funky jazz beat audible only to him. He appears to his colleagues, as he never has before, the genuine great Chef Dussollier.

That Vincent is concentrating so intensely, however, is not to say that he is quiet. Somewhat loquacious in fact, although certainly not nostalgic, he has entertained the kitchen for the better part of three hours with yarns and anecdotes from what he terms 'the old days,' or occasionally 'the dark days', and even once, 'the lost time'. His chronicles find keen ears, too. For a man who has lived the majority of his life in the public eye, and spent a great deal of that time as a drunken idiot, very little personal fact is known about the great chef. The conversation has encompassed his education at Le Cordon Bleu in 70's Paris, his early years in London, and his slide into various addictions. He has discussed the effort of sobering up and the business of writing his masterpiece manuscript, *Leçons dans la Cuisine*. He has even told his favourite story, his most treasured remembrance from the Dark Days that never fails to bring a not-quite-guilty smile to his face: the tale of vomiting over Nancy Regan's nice two-thousand-dollar frock in No. 10 Downing Street. Even after three hours, he has many more stories left in reserve.

'This one time,' he recalls, 'it was just after Gillian died so it must have been eighty-two or eighty-three, I worked in Highgate for a man who made millions in cocaine imported from Columbia and even had the cheek to call his restaurant Blow. We were busy as hell this particular night and it was noisy, too. At one point, I went through because the noise was so bad and it turned out that the entire company of Evita was in because someone was getting married. There were about sixty of the bastards, including Lloyd Webber himself. But at the opposite side of the restaurant... it was a horrendous South American style place, gave me a headache every time I was sober enough to pay attention... anyway, at the other side of the room was the Prime Minster with her husband, Dennis, some friends and a small army of Secret Service agents who...'

Charlie deals with table nine alone, sending up a lobster and a roasted whole trout as soon as the plasma screen shows the starters are cleared. She also has a great deal of single-sitters who invariably want her scallops and spaghetti, which she is able to do in her own time. All the while, desserts, breads and pastries come past from Arthur's cold kitchen while a pair of dishwashers scurry around like trapped rats, replacing clean pans and utensils and grabbing anything for washing.

'...Anyway, about half an hour later the noise started again so I went back through and there was Maggie Thatcher up on a table, accompanied by Andrew Lloyd Webber at the piano and the entire cast of Evita, singing *Don't cry for me Argentina*! Someone took a photograph but the Secret Serve confiscated the camera on account of the war in the Falklands. Which reminds me, Tom, did I hear properly upstairs… are you and Eva getting married?'

'Surely!' Tom beams. His station is laden with pans of bubbling sauces and sizzling meat cuts, many of which he is flambéing, giving his cheeks a rosy glow. Further blush comes from the fact that his ovens are loaded with - now in their fifth successful day - his own heart and kidney bridies.

'Hopefully as soon as we get back home, brother. February, probably. We don't want a big church service or anything, just something nice and simple.'

'Good for you.' Vincent thinks of both his weddings. His first only slightly more than a year before Gillian's death, was a white-church event extraordinaire, heavily covered by the media, as apposed to his marriage to Amanda three years ago, which was a small service in the grounds of Maison Dussollier with only immediate family. The memories of both days make him smile. 'I mean it, Tom. I wish yie both the very best of luck.'

'I agree.' Viola fires three pastas to the commis for dressing. 'You're made for each other. Listen, I hope yie dinnae think I'm a cow for asking, but how old's Eva?'

'Twenty. Four years younger than me.'

'What'll yir parents say? Will there be sparks? They've never met her, have they? You and Eva met in Italy, eh?'

'My folks are cool, Vi. They're old hippies. They speak on the phone more to Eva that they do to me. Eva doesn't have parents.'

'Eh?'

'She's an orphan, like Gus. She grew up in a Catholic institution in Melbourne after her parents died in a terrorist attack holidaying in Spain. Does that look in your eyes, Viola, mean you think that she's too young for marriage?' Tom asks this sincerely, without hostility. 'I'm hardly an old man myself, remember. No offence, Vincent.'

'None taken.'

'Tommy, I married Freddy when I was seventeen,' Viola says. 'Twenty's plenty old. Make sure you get her knocked up as soon as yie can.' She looks directly at Charlie. 'I myself am currently compromised by an overwhelming urge to get pregnant again.'

Tom laughs. 'I'll try my best, brothers.'

'But not tonight,' Vincent says. 'I intend to fill yie so full of drink that yie'll both be incapable. No that I encourage such behaviour, of course. If yir race comes in tonight you can buy her the Hope diamond as an engagement ring.'

At this, the warm glow from Tom's cheeks disappears. 'Let's not think about the race yet, please. My sphincter may loosen. Table eleven, please.' For table eleven he has ready a roasted pigeon with red cabbage and claret gravy, two steaks and beef ribs with oyster sauce. He needs spaghetti scallops from Charlie, a mushroom and mascarpone lasagne and a salad bowl from Viola, and a range of accompaniments from the commis'.

Just about to launch into the anecdote of the time he cooked for the Royal Family of Monaco, something catches in the corner of Vincent's vision. His Jackal's eyes lowered and narrowing still, he speaks in a confidential voice.

'What is it wae yie today?' he asks.

'What's what?'

'You look funny. What's the matter?'

'There isnae anything the matter,' Charlie snaps. 'I'm fine. Watch your pans!'

'Dinnae take the hump, I mean it as a compliment. I meant tae say that yie look very well indeed,' the great chef smiles. 'Yie've a kind of bloom about yie today, an aura as we used to say in the eighties. Have yie a big date lined up tonight?'

'Certainly have, Vincent. With Alison Gorry. I'm almost finished the book. Tell your mother when you see her that I expect more books.'

'Tell her yourself when you come across next month,' Vincent watches her hard.

'How is she?'

'She's fine. We spoke this morning. She's looking forward to seeing us.'

Vincent winces. Megan Poe, of course, cannot see anything at all.

Around midmorning, Violette Rodin walked the quieter streets from the Left Bank to the Right, stopping at Pont Royal a while to look down into the water. Abandoning her customary red and green scheme for mild browns, Violette wore a distracting summer suit, clicking heels and a small leather handbag. Her outfit concealed two guns and her knives. She was asked twice for her papers without incident. The morning was bright and clear, the sky cloudless.

From the bridge, through a panorama of swastikas, rising eagles and barricades, she made her way past the Louvre and crossed the Tuileries gardens. Written on a wall in paint, which a young Nazi was furiously trying to remove, the well-known Flaubert quote:

'What an awful thing life is. It's like soup with lots of hairs floating on the surface. You have to eat it nevertheless.'

After Rue de Rivoli, via Place de la Concorde, Alison came finally upon Rue Royale.

Known simply as the Madeline, L'église Sainte Marie Madeleine, an enormous Romanesque temple commissioned by Napoleon as a Temple de la Gloire de la Grande Armée, stood ominously at the end of Rue Royale, seemingly supported by its fifty-two, twenty-meter-high Corinthian columns from one of which Special Operations Executive agent Madeleine was hung naked by the neck. Violette climbed the steps, feeling Lemaire's sculpted *Last*

Judgement pediment bearing down on her and by way of distraction recalled her long-deceased grandmother explaining that the Polish composer Frédéric Chopin had received in 1849 his funeral at the Madeleine to the sound of Mozart's *Requiem*.

The bronze doors showing the Ten Commandments were open for business. Unlike its stark exterior, the interior of the Madeleine was lavish is its Renaissance-inspired gilt decoration. Violette walked through the nave, into the particular stillness of the church and resisted the urge to shudder. She saw people praying and heard the occasional echo of footsteps across the stone floor. She smelled burning wax.

Although baptised a catholic, Alison Gorry had never been a believer. Her last church visit, she realised as she switched from Violette's thoughts to her own, was her wedding day eleven years ago. Her stillborn daughter had been buried without a service, and similarly her husband went without proper religious observation because there had been no body to inter. A service had seemed superficial. Alison built a small memorial in their garden instead.

Memories came fast and hard. She remembered the texture of her silk moiré wedding dress, the smell of her long hair braided with lavender, her first married sex. She remembered John's gentle father weeping at the wedding and then, years later, weeping horribly as he learned of the unsuccessful pregnancy. She remembered the hopeful movements in her swollen belly and later the pointless milk seeping from her swollen nipples with clarity of recollection that hit her like a grenade.

She could hardly breathe. She could hear the Requiem.

Breath came finally, as it always did, and Alison smiled as she met eyes with an elderly, shuffling woman. As a child, visiting her grandparents, Alison had been inside the Madeleine many times and it pleased her, made her strangely proud, that the church still functioned, that it had not been packed away, reinforced and fortified. Above the altar, Marochetti's white marble *Magdalene* stood just as she remembered it, propelled with open arms heavenward by angels. Above the statue, the half-dome fresco by Ziegler illustrated the History of Christianity, the principal figure, of course, Emperor Napoleon himself.

At the altar, Alison knelt and closed her eyes. But rather than God, she thought of Louise.

Louise had always been a more accurate title for the woman than 'mother' had. Alison wrote to her often and always without a return address. Not that she would have expected replies. Relations with Louise had never been stable. It was understandable that the relationship had all but snapped after her decided to fight.

Louise Bouvier left Paris in 1901 at the age of twenty to marry her sweetheart, Alan Carmichael, a Scottish soldier returned from duty in India whom she met in the Louvre. After establishing a life for themselves in Alan's hometown of Gourock, Scotland, they produced in the space of six years two sons, Claude and Maurice, and a daughter, Alison. In 1917, Alan died in the trenches of the Great War inhaling hydrogen cyanide. Claude and Maurice Carmichael were killed during the first year of World War Two, Claude burning to death in his spitfire, Maurice drowning in his ship. Mortar shrapnel claimed Louise's son-in-law, John Gorry, not too long after.

In her letters home, Alison wrote of anything but the war. She spoke of the city and vaguely of herself, mentioning nothing of the devastation incurred by either.

Noise broke the reverie, the approaching sound of footsteps behind her. Without looking, Alison knew whose feet they were. The sound was of expensive, hard-edged shoes, not boots. The tread was light and considered. Without lifting her bowed head, she felt the air move as the presence knelt silently on the step beside her.

When the voice came, it suggested a sincere reverence that startled Alison and brought to mind, curiously, a penny-dreadful horror paperback she had read about vampires who were unable to set foot on consecrated ground. The sound of wrung rosary beads turned her head.

'Blessed mother,' came the whisper, 'forgive my sins with compassion and show me the light of your eternity. And also bless my sister and her family. They are slow but well-meaning, as you can see, Holy Mother.'

When the prayer ended, the figure crossed himself, kissed his rosary and stood to find Alison already standing, and as their eyes met the assassins shared a peculiar smile.

'Hello,' the renowned Antonio Juan said...

Although Dave, Rose and Stan attempt no movement from their standing spot at the bar, it is clear that a small commotion occurs amongst the G. W. F. Associates crowd in the corner. The Accounts Manager, John Whirrel, is the centre of attention, speaking into his mobile phone, plugging his other ear with a finger.

'I expect that'll be the London office,' Dave says, looking at Rose over the rim of his orange juice glass with sleepy eyes.

Rose's eyes narrow. 'To declare the winner of the Christmas raffle I expect.'

Absent-mindedly, without lifting his eyes from a particularly potent gin martini, Stan remarks:

'I wish I'd bought more tickets. The hamper would have come in handy for feeding the fifty-thousand.'

Dave shrugs, and as she sees John Whirrel end his call, Rose understands exactly what he is about to say:

'And the winner,' John Whirrel says in his usual booming voice, clearly audible over the pub's noisy ambience, 'of the 2003 Christmas hamper...' He pauses for dramatic effect, 'is our very own Mr David Quinn!'

Sleepy eyes wide, Dave feigns complete surprise. 'Fantastic,' he declares, shaking the congratulating hands of his thwarted subordinates. 'I'm sure it'll come in handy.'

'Fix!' Rose's protest is good-humoured.

Stan, had he truly appreciated these goings-on, might have thought it odd that Dave has won the raffle since Stan alone knows that Dave, convinced that the charity chosen by head office as the beneficiary are crooks, did not buy any tickets. Indeed, Stan might have even returned the wink offered him by his friend. But Stan is simply not paying attention. He is removed, disconnected. The itch of his prospective idea persists, and resisting the urge to scratch his head, he tried to force the idea either to completion or to the back of his mind. Neither is possible. A headache comes instead. He silently curses the useless Hume DNA.

He watches, unseeing, Dave receive a small chocolate cake with a sparkling candle from the barman, which he then presents to Rose. As a student in Glasgow, it is probable that Dave and his three chemist flatmates might have starved to death if not for Dave's ability to bake, which he learned from his grandmother. Rose's cake is a rich treacle sponge, layered with almonds and allspice flavoured chocolate cream. Dave's biggest downfall in life is by far treacle; hence, his round belly. The effort of baking the cake, however, slightly guiltily, was in fact less for Rose's benefit than his own. It kept he and his daughter's mind off the Megan Gillies situation, if only for an hour.

'Congratulations, Mrs Mackenzie,' he pronounces, 'on yir retirement. We shall both miss you.' Unselfishly, he includes Stan.

Draining her wine and then replenishing her glass from the bottle, lips curling, Rose toasts in a soft but frank tone:

'Allow me tae tell yies, boys, that in this my last day in Scotland I am wholly without sadness. Nostalgic I admit, but not saddened. I will miss neither the tourists nor the festival nor the Scottish Government, for which I once longed but which now disappoints me, nor the Holyrood Parliament Project, which I have supported from my ivory tower these past six years. I shall especially not miss the Socialist Party or Margo McDonald. Nor do I lament the bigotry and the Buckfast culture of my nation. I shall not miss the property that has ruled both my own and my husband's life for too long, and no offence, boys, I doubt I'll pine long for the job either. In fact, to be candid, I struggle to think of a single thing in this city that I will miss. Except mibbae the Evening News and you pair.' She licks a finger full of chocolate cream, and in her best Welsh twang, says:

'Here's to getting ol…'

Her mouth snaps shut. Elegant in her cinnamon dress and her Jimmy Choo stilettos, clutching her buckled Vuitton handbag, she appears like a statue, a photograph in a fashion magazine, moving only to brush the copper fringe from her eyes.

217

More sensing that actually seeing the change, as if emerging from a dream, Stan lifts his gaze and sees that Dave, too, has turned as white as a sheet. Deacon Brodie's in its entirety becomes stiff with silence. There is not even music.

Silence; at least until the volume on the television rises.

In 1976, a century after the construction of Wallace House, Rosemary Blithe was the most well tailored art student at Edinburgh University, noted for her dissertational and verbal skills, if not her paintings. Already she had published an article on medieval paint pigments in a university textbook and was beginning to favour, upon the counsel of her lectures, a career of academia.

Three years earlier, she has intended a staggered transition from Wallace House into university life by travelling rural France for a year, alone, where her social difficulties might charitably be confused with the language barrier. But the transition came more as a thud. Her train from Aberdeen to London derailed shy of Edinburgh's Waverly Station, causing nothing more serious than an eleven-hour delay. Eleven hours in Edinburgh, as it happened, were enough. By the time the passengers reboarded, Rosemary had had already achieved employment as a tailor's assistant on George Street and had secured lodgings in the West End. When she did begin her student life the following autumn, rather than moving into university accommodation, she was able to maintain her shared-flat by continuing her job part-time.

To mix with like-minded peers finally, to join society! Rosemary was certainly sociable, playing the carefree nymph with panache, Aphrodite herself, managing by no more than sheer luck to avoid either catching diseases or falling pregnant. In her limited free time, away from her peers, she prostituted herself in the city's grand hotels for no more reason than she wanted to, having been fascinated by the idea since reading novels of Venetian and Ancient Greek courtesans in her youth. The money was certainly useful, but it was, in hindsight, perhaps not the best way to carry on.

The Great Waldo Pepper would mark a different approach.

Stuart Mackenzie, by the age of twenty a failed novelist, although he had never actually attempted to sell his work, was a criminal. He sold marijuana in Leith, and when Rosemary thinks back to this time, she remembers a particularly hopeless individual still living with his parents, neither physically dramatic nor socially proficient, whose mop of filthy, matted hair completely covered his eyes. She pictures him wearing a long Crombie coat two sizes too big with Bay City Roller-style denim bellbottoms, white above the knee, tartan below. Peace and CND badges were essential. His pride and joy was his velvet top hat. Although Stuart now denies such accusations, photographic evidence exists.

Silence was his redemption. Rather than talk, it was Stuart's preference to listen, and in a city that even after three years still seemed so noisy, so full of people speaking all at the same time, arrogantly, myopically, seemingly igno-rant of one another and competing constantly for notice, Rosemary quickly found herself charmed. He was the first person she talked to at length about her atypical upbringing. Not that Wallace House embarrassed her; on the few past occasions she mentioned it to friends, the matter simply provoked an onslaught of too many questions that she was unwilling to answer, all asked in a subtly derisive tone that was to her deathly tiresome. With Stuart, she had, and found, no such qualms.

But it was more than just curiosity. Rose believes that Stuart was and still is blessed with an unnatural capacity for empathy, which often leaves him emotionally vulnerable. He asked no blunt questions because he could al-ready, somehow, *imagine* the answers.

Their first social outing confirmed this. They had originally planned to see Laurence Oliver and Dustin Hoffman in *Marathon Man*, which they failed to accomplish because Stuart's car broke down on North Bridge, holding up almost the entire city of Edinburgh. The next night, they saw instead *The Great Waldo Pepper* with Robert Redford and Susan Sarandon, following the escapades of a Second World War fighter pilot making ends meet as a dare-devil air stuntman.

After an hour of what Rosemary considered unremarkable and sometimes-puerile drama blended uncomfortably with comedy, Susan Sarandon's char-acter, while rehearsing a stunt, fell quite predictably off the wing of Red-ford's - Waldo Pepper's - plane. Rose can clearly recall her lips curling in delight. Turning to Stuart, however, she was amazed. Open-mouthed, tears stood in his eyes. A silly reaction some might say, embarrassing, to be apolo-gised for and forgotten. To Rosemary, it was nothing less than wonderful. She still thinks of it often.

The courtship lasted slightly less than a week more. Then they married. The service was a plain registrar's ceremony witnessed by Stuart's two older brothers, and instead of a honeymoon they invested their collective wealth, which was not unimpressive due to Stuart's marijuana dealing and Rose-mary's past whoring, in a painting by an unknown local artist who died three years later and achieved phenomenal posthumous success. The profits from the sale of this painting paid for their first house a month after Rosemary's graduation.

In 1977, the year Stuart gave up his criminal career for one in the police force, Rosemary's first job after graduation was as a studio assistant to John Bellany, preferring to spend her days mixing paint and cleaning brushes then furthering an academic career. The same year, Rose made her first suit for Stuart and this habit has sustained to the present day. Compulsively, joyfully, she makes all her husbands suits with her own hands, using skills she taught herself long before moving to Edinburgh.

The world lay at their feet.

And then, just shy of her twenty-third birthday, Rosemary developed cancer in both her ovaries. Similar complaints in distant relatives were offered in explanation and hysterectomy presented as the cure. As so with the removal of her ruined ovaries, fallopian tubes, uterus and cervix, came the horrendous truth that Rosemary and Stuart would never conceive.

Worse than cancer itself and the consequences of it was her mental decline. Reason was difficult to find. Had she contracted syphilis during her vivacious days and therefore ruined her own body by her own actions, she might have been able to find some amount of peace. As it was, she was inconsolable. Her deterioration occurred slowly at first and then more rapidly until the day came when she could no longer structure a cohesive thought in her head. Knowing now that the same thing happens to hundreds of women every year, she looks back on this period of her life ashamedly, with horror and resentment at the dreadful way she chose to deal with it.

One day, a particularly cold December day in 1980 that for its entirety threatened to snow but never did, Stuart came home and found Rose in the bath, bleeding heavily from her cut wrists.

That day, and for many of those afterwards, all that remained for her to do was to hold, in a very literal sense, to her husband. Near catatonic, unable to offer even hope, she did hold on. And whenever necessary, which was often, Stuart found enough strength for two.

Adoption, of course, has presented itself as an option at various times during the last twenty years, but in the end, because of his career and her various and numerous careers, Mr and Mr Mackenzie decided against it. In truth, their hearts were simply not in it. Instead, they chose to release their energy in fruitless sex and the property market.

A scar remained, of course, and as they built, it has always been with splinters in their fingers. Twenty-five years after the fact, the lack of a child in their life is often overwhelming, and both Rosemary and Stuart would happily give the one-point-nine million pounds they have accumulated in wealth and moveable assents, after tax, to conceive.

'You can speak English,' Juan said helpfully. 'I learned it very well in America, the land of the free, as you heard last night. I want you to feel comfortable.'

The seats were wooden and wicker-covered, simple and quite comfortable, and for the first time in the two years of her new life, Alison sat not as the valuable Allied Forces killer, Special Operations Executive agent Violette Rodin, nor as Violette's finest creation, the late Edith Thiéry. She sat as herself, the woman who in the last five years had lost her brothers, her husband, her child and possibly her mind. She sat entirely at ease.

She took the measure of the man. His face was striking and handsome, but his splendid suit was crumpled and stale. She saw on the jacket's lapel a tiny stain of Frédéric's blood. He smelled of sweat and cigarettes and it was clear to Alison that his lack of freshness obviously bothered Juan. She saw the claw-like left hand with fascination, all the while fighting a desire to confess her sins to Juan, who would surely understand better than any God.

She asked, already knowing the answer:

'You followed me?'

'Yes, since last night. You fascinate me. I've never met a woman like you before,' Juan smiled almost shyly. 'I think perhaps I'm in love with you.'

'I think you're crazy.' Alison's voice was not unfriendly.

'You have to be halfway crazy in this business. Madness begets an indispensable viewpoint.'

'You followed only me?'

Juan's face changed immediately, indicating that he had grown bored of the line. 'Yes, as I told you. I have no interest in your colleagues. Not anymore. After the car dropped you at the bridge, I let it go.' He pronounced these words in his best English, hoping to draw an end to the subject.

'And Violette?'

'Violette?' Juan seemed confused. 'The Marlene Dietrich double who got out before you?'

Alison nodded, lying.

'As I said, and I will not say again, your colleagues are safe from me. They are useless and mean nothing, although I admit the older man moved quickly for his age. I'm sorry about your friend's eye,' Juan relaxed back into the chair. 'I assume he's your friend, because otherwise you would have chased me out of there. He's strong. I think he'll be fine.'

'My name is Alison.'

Juan's face opened with a charming smile but he did not offer his hand. 'It's a pleasure to meet you, Alison. Antonio is my name.'

'I know who you are,' Alison sighed. 'I've heard of your exploits since my beginning in this game. You're a legend. Everyone knows about Chile's president and Don Versi. But at the same time, nobody really believes you are real. I doubted you myself.'

'I'm just a man.' Opening his good palm, Juan lifted his eyebrows. 'Onc not as young as he often thinks. And I'm sure that given your situation here you can appreciate how difficult it has been to maintain such subterfuge, the sacrifices I've made, the missed... opportunities. It's hard work.'

'I admit that while the tiny part of me which is still human deplores you and I,' Alison said. 'I find myself very much in professional awe.'

During her 'career' Alison had caused, excluding what she considered peripheral causalities, the deaths of seventeen men and two women, mostly political enemies of the Allied Force and conspirators against the Free French. Most of the nineteen had died at close range. She could remember the smells of each of the bodies, living and dead, and the look in their eyes as

221

they expired. She wondered how many smells lingered in Antonio Juan's nostrils.

She purposefully conjured an image of Frédéric's new face, the sucking, bleeding hole where his eye had been, expecting to feel a deep loathing fill her. She braced herself against the flood, but it did not come. Instead, she felt only like an amateur.

'I liked what you did with Wetzler, making him eat his own penis,' Juan nearly giggled. 'It certainly confused everyone. Nice touch.'

'I'm not proud of it. But I cannot honestly say that I'm ashamed either. I'm at odds.'

Juan considered this and turning slightly to Alison, laid his arm on the back of her chair.

'I think I understand. It's the same with my niece. She's an opera singer, a soprano. I have never told anyone that before. She was singing for an audience by the time she was eight and filling the grandest halls by ten. She was a lucrative business for my sister and her husband. But by the time she reached... what's the word... puberty, people were tired of hearing the same songs time after time. She needed a new trick, so my sister had her up there singing Bizet and other lusting songs. She was only a child. It was simply too much too soon.' He smiled. 'And so it is with you, my friend. Too much too soon. Speaking of opera, I saw you with Wetzler last week but of course, I didn't remember your face until his body was discovered and even then it didn't truly connect until I saw you last night, without the wig. And so here we are.'

Alison allowed Juan to stroke her shoulder with his only thumb.

'Antonio, may I ask you a question?'

'Speak freely. I want you to be comfortable.'

'Do you care about this job?'

Juan scoffed. 'De Gaulle? I care not in the slightest. The man means nothing to me. Why? Do you think the son of Spanish emigrates might understand the evils of fascism and communism and be persuaded to change sides and go after Hitler instead? As a matter of fact, Alison, I'm sure together we could do that, you and I. Think what a team we would make! But I don't work for free. I'm a professional in the true sense of the word, my friend. I work only for money and the Nazis have oodles.'

Nodding, Alison seemed satisfied with the answer.

'Now I'll ask you a question?' Juan said.

'Anything you like.'

'Can you sleep after you do it?'

'After the kill?'

Appreciating the idiom, its predatory hint and lack of pretence, Juan conformed:

'Yes. After the kill.'

'I sleep eight hours a night, every night, kill or not.'

Juan was obviously impressed. In fact, he was somewhat amazed. 'I rarely sleep,' he admitted. 'I haven't slept in two days. I doubt I've had a good night's sleep for fifteen years. I've adapted. My reality is simply different to those of everyone else, as are my principles.'

'I sleep every night because I drink myself unconscious,' Alison said. 'And I have nightmares even then. I dream of my father who died in battle, along with my brothers and my husband. Everything is a nightmare, really.'

'I myself do not drink,' Juan said rather distastefully. 'So I shall continue to sleep little.'

A silence descended over the assassins, pierced only by echoing footstep around the church. The change in Juan was noticeable. His body seemed to harden. His smile became fixed.

Alison broke the silence with a sharp intake of air, as if pulling herself back from a dream. 'What happens now?' Her voice was acquiescent. She could hear Mozart.

'I regret that you don't seem like a woman who gives up easily, Alison. Of course, I'm clinging to the hope that we could leave together and live happily ever after. But I doubt that strongly.'

'Only one of us will leave here alive.'

'Obviously.' The Latino smiled at this truth but his eyes did not smile. They were as black as ink.

'And you're saying that it won't be me,' Alison said.

Nodding slowly but heavily, Juan's expression grew thunderous.

'I regret such a thing,' he admitted gravely. 'I believe there is much we might have talked about, lessons we might have shared. But your job is to slay me and that I'm afraid I cannot allow. Forgive me.'

'There's really no need for forgiveness,' Alison smiled weakly. 'I don't think you understand.'

She was silent for a moment, thinking. When she did speak, her voice was no more than a whisper, a hollow, distant sound.

'I surrender,' she said. 'I yield. I want you to take my life. I don't want to be like you.'

In a suit made by his wife, Detective Inspector Stuart Mackenzie exits No. 127 Easter Road accompanied by three other detectives, who take a supporting position behind him under the full glare of the media. Photographers flash repeatedly in the hush

Stuart's thoughts are of Wallace House. He can smell the oak trees that surround it, protect it from the world. He has felt since his first visit a profound love for its ideals, which have outlived both of Rose's founding parents. It is a community without crime. There is neither child kidnap nor murder. Reason is law. There is rarely a harsh word spoken in Wallace House. The last time he and Rose travelled to Aberdeenshire was to bury his dear one-armed father-in-law, and even that was a relatively uplifting experience.

Not like this.

Focus comes to Stuart only by the fact that there are two dozen members of the press, marshalled by uniformed officers and complemented by onlookers, gawking at him hard. Many of the faces are recognisable from last night's television appeal; many he has seen for innumerable years. The discovery itself is less than forty-five minutes old and the fact that the press have already arrived means that some enterprising officer at the station has made a few extra quid today by selling information. Although such things are known to occur, the Detective Inspector makes a metal note that his last duty on this his last day will be to make all efforts, using his considerable sway, to have the guilty officer suspended.

National television crews are still unloading, irately humping equipment to the scene outside a nondescript terrace front, but Stuart has no intention of waiting. Furious beyond expression, his face remains a mask. He fixes his hands behind his back.

'I can confirm to you now,' he says curtly, 'that the body of Megan Gilles was recovered from this building earlier today. Mr and Mrs Gillies have been informed and we are confident that in light of today's new information that an arrest will follow soon. That's all. Thank you.'

Flanked by his colleagues, the Detective Inspector leaves the reporters standing.

All of Reserve's afternoon customers have left, but the elegant art nouveau dinning room is far from calm. Gavin coordinates a bedlam of furiously prepping floor-staff, roaring and cursing at the top of his voice to nobody in particular. He does this from a sitting position, with his waistcoat loosened as Fanny rubs his shoulders. The altered floor plan fashions a single, huge banquet arrangement, leaving room for dancing and the equipment of a ceilidh quintet that so far consists of a small set of drums with shimmering cymbals and an upright piano.

Ignoring the commotion, the family Dussollier recline with a pot of tea, and Charlie, by the fire. Still in good spirits and his soiled kitchen whites, Vincent's earlier burst of enthusiasm has left him exhausted. He stirs his tea vacantly for possibly the tenth time, while Amanda, in her brown and green combats, her bare, manicured toes on the marble hearth, reads the Scotsman, feeding Chloe from her breast.

'Yie look about eighty-five stone in this one,' she says, her face set in an expression of equal delight and wonder. 'When was this? I havnae see this picture before.'

'Eighty-six, mibbae, or eighty-five,' Vincent decides, investigating the pertaining article. 'Look at the colour of my nose, it's nearly purple. I could pull

Santa's sleigh with that.' He points to the second, more recent photograph featured. 'Look at us, we're such a handsome couple.'

'Aye, the pram suits you.'

'As do you, chéri.'

This earns Vincent a kiss. But as she withdraws, cradling Chloe, Amanda's eyes narrow. 'Are yie okay, Vinny? You look peaky. Knackered?'

'I am. I'm pooped. That was the hardest I've worked in years. I enjoyed it, though. I only hope I get a second wind before tonight otherwise everybody'll be out early doors.'

Neither is Amanda shinning with enthusiasm, although the excitement of her last day as a British Citizen sustains her. She and Vincent were up all night packing their life into travel cases, and then dispatching the cases to France. Their antique furniture and painting, however, as with those in the restaurant remain, requiring specialist attention. This morning they donated seven paintings by Scottish artists to the National Galleries, worth in all a seven-figure sum, including the Wilkie in the dinning room.

'I forgot to say,' Amanda smiles over her teacup. 'I told Dorothy you would go and fetch her.'

'Hells bells, Amanda!'

'And take her home later.'

A long sigh escapes Vincent's lips, although he is happy to oblige. After all, they are moving to a country far away from his mother-in-law in the morning.

'Want your daughter?' Amanda folds away her newspaper. 'She's sucked my nipple numb.'

'Lucky her.'

Seeing her father's smile, the Baby Dior cherub opens her arms wide for the transfer, telling a long-winded story in her own language and dribbling milk. Amanda rolls her khaki top back over her stomach and stands up to stretch her legs and poke the fire a bit.

Amid the Dussollier's, with her hair tied tightly back, Charlie finishes her paperwork. Having already completed the accounts for Morris and written the combined wages and severance cheques that she plans to distribute tonight, she now signs the last of the hired equipment contract cancellations, incurring with every pen stroke scandalous short-notice penalties. Not that such a thing matters. Nor particularly does tonight's food matter. Vincent's guests are not customers, and by definition easy to please. The free bar will receive more attention than will the food. Downstairs, Viola and Tom have the operation under control.

But she realises now, feeling a heavy silence envelop her, that Vincent, Amanda and even little Chloe Dussollier are watching her intently. They are waiting.

225

Charlie closes her folder for the last time, feeling no nostalgia. She feels only an urge to play the upright piano. She swallows a deep breath and straightens her spine.

'Vincent,' she begins, 'I want to say thank...'

'There's no need.'

'Yes, I think there is. Please listen to me, I want to say...'

'No, you listen to me, Charlie Brown.' Vincent speaks with Chloe's fingers exploring his mouth. 'And hear me good, my friend.'

At this, Amanda is amazed to see the change in Charlie. She is like a scolded child, sitting back in her chair and - Amanda's eyes narrow at the sight - wringing her hands.

'I suppose you want to thank me for...I dunno,' the great chef says, almost mockingly, waving his hand as if at a bothersome fly, 'for the opportunity to run this restaurant almost without supervision, for the faith I've shown in you, for... for all the rest of the shite. And of course, you want to thank me for the offer of Paris.'

'Yes.' Charlie finally lifts her eyes.

'But you're not going to Paris.'

'No.'

Vincent nods with understanding and he and his wife share a tiny smile.

'I'm sorry,' Charlie says. 'I feel ungrateful. It's...'

'It's because you're in love.' Amanda's expression invites defiance. 'No?'

Charlie opens her mouth to speak but the ability to do so fails her. Vincent also tries to speak, thinking of Eugène Bouveret and fated Bernard Spencer, but his nostrils suddenly flare and he says to Chloe, whose face is decidedly purple:

'Jesus, sweetie, that's a bit ripe.'

He removes his chef's jacket to reveal a white vest and his potbelly. He carefully lays the jacket down clean side up on the tabletop and lays his daughter on the jacket. Changing nappies is an indispensable part of the great chef's day and he draws immense pleasure from the act.

'Dinnae thank me,' he says. 'It is I who thanks you. Over the years, chef, I havnae had to thank many people, and that's the truth. But I am grateful to you. And I want yie tae promise me something right now...' In a quick, fluid motion, his arms and Chloe's legs flailing, Vincent has the reeking nappy off and a fresh one on in a matter of seconds. He rolls up the old one and, without thinking, throws it into the fire.

'Vincent!' Amanda is horrified.

'Sorry. Charlie, I want you to promise me that the first person you dance with tonight, once you've taken a shower of course, will be me.'

Charlie smiles. 'If Madam Dussollier doesn't object.'

'Charlie, he has a pair of left feet. He's all yours. I'll take Stan.' Again, Amanda smiles challengingly. 'He is coming, I assume.'

226

With his back against the sandstone support of David Hume's greened-bronze effigy outside Edinburgh High Court of Justice, Stan stands as sober as a judge, his tweed jacket and t-shirt ensemble smelling ferociously of cigarette smoke. He has fled the noisy confines of Deacon Brodie's, fled his friends and colleagues, fled the dampened jovialities. He cannot flee himself, though, as much as he would like to.

Clarity avoids him. Extending down the ancient volcanic rock from the Castle to the Palace, Old Edinburgh's backbone, the Royal Mile, channels a sea of distraction. Underscoring the rapt tourists, barrelling drinkers and party groups, a busker strums to a small crowd by St. Giles' Cathedral, her Christmas song floating in the frosty night air, mingling with the sound of two American's with Starbucks coffees passing Stan, discussing the slaying of Megan Gilles the week before the anniversary of Christ as if they are discussing a play they have just seen. The neoclassical frontages of Parliament House and the City Chambers, to say nothing of the gothic cathedral, add further unwanted distraction, to mention nothing of the vile exhaust fumes.

Above aesthetic disturbance, however, Stan's half-idea, as it has for hours now, persists, round and round, dizzying, like a fish in a bowl, no more specific than before, like a dull toothache. He feels, as he so often is called, an idiot.

Turning his head to look up at the slight, fixed smile of his ancestor, Stan feels mocked. Rendered in perhaps his fortieth year, attired bizarrely in a Grecian toga, the great thinker offers no insight at all, prompts no inspiration. But this is hardly a surprise considering that David Hume, while talking the talk, spent the majority of his career rewriting his very first work, the Treatise, and, in fact, never in his lifetime dared to attempt long-term companionship. He was, at bottom, an empty and unfulfilled man. This thought, although vaguely implying that Stan is pondering his relationship with Charlie, brings no clarification.

'You look thoughtful.'

Hazily aware that this statement is directed at him, Stan turns to see Dave approaching. His overcoat is buttoned up high. His sleepy eyes appear black and cold, but his usual smile remains.

'No really.' Stan says softly. 'Just trying to find some fresh air in this polluted city.' Remembering his embarrassing blunder at the weekend, he asks without further delay, 'Howz yir foot, buddy?'

'I feel like Ali McCoist.' He mimics a goal. 'Perfect, as you can see,' he says. 'If pride really is a sin then I'm damned.' He positions himself at Stan's side against the monument, shorter and rounder, sturdier, and lights a cigarette, carefully blowing his smoke away from Stan.

'How did yie win the hamper?' Stan smiles.

'I've worked for the company for nearly ten years, Stan. Such an investment is no without it's benefits, even if some rules do get broken. They're no my rules. And the hamper'll come in handy, eh? Did you get Charlie's new bed?'

'I did' Stan appreciates that Dave is reminding him that he has already broken the company rules this week by giving him the account necessary to achieve the new bed. 'Cheers, buddy. I got it last night. I also got the Christmas tree last night.'

'Fake?'

'Nah, man. The fucker's shedding needles already.'

'Good man, Stan.'

Above the gentle ambience of the people and vehicles on the street, the busker's song, seemingly coming from the monstrous cathedral itself, fills the night air, resonate yet gentle. And for a moment, Stan doubts his senses. He thinks he is dreaming again, lost deep within his thoughts. But the realisation that he is not comes to him like indigestion.

The music, lapping gently across the atmosphere, is Henry Mancini's *Moon River*. Stan thinks of Princess Diana. He remembers waltzing with Charlie and at this, something in his mind unfurls. But now is the wrong time for such selfish thoughts.

Cringing, guiltily, not wanting to cause distress, Stan turns his face to his friend for the first time and asks in a breath that crystallises in the cold:

'Are yie gaun to collect Victoria?'

Dave nods and blows his cold nose in a linen handkerchief. For the briefest moment, a flash of pain lights his eyes, but the lights of passing traffic quickly replace it. Since learning of the discovery of the dead body of Megan Gillies an hour ago, he has experienced an intense calm, almost like a drug high. He is detached. He is stronger. The cold fact is that he has cried all the tears he is willing to shed for someone else's child. In truth, although he does not realise it, he is in a deep state of shock. Even expecting the terrible news, it is not an easy thing to hear.

'Aye, she's at her music lesson 'til six,' he says, his voice strong and clear. 'I'm gaun tae see her mother now so we can decide what tae tell her and how. I cannae imagine how she'll take it.'

'I wish I could do something to help,' Stan says. 'I know that I cannae. I know that it's silly to say…' Stan's seemingly transparent, pale green, melancholic eyes appear nothing less than wounded. 'What I mean, man, is that I'm thinking of yies.'

'I ken, Stan. Thanks. But listen, let's no be dour. We have nothing tae worry about, Stan. It's Christmas, after all, and I won the hamper.'

Stan laughs, and slowly and sparsely it begins to snow.

'Charlie finishes up tonight, eh?' Dave asks, lifting his face into the falling flakes. 'After the big party.'

'Surely.'

'Howz she? I saw her yesterday but I didnae ask. I was a bit of a mess myself. Beside, one gets accustomed to not asking Charlie anything.'

'The change'll be good for her.'

'Will she change?' Dave scoffs these words, though not unkindly. 'Yie're coming to mine for dinner tomorrow, did she tell yie?'

'She didnae.' Stan pulls an exaggerated face of distain. 'Yie're no cooking, eh?'

'Cheeky fuckin cock, of course I am. I'll do a beef stew.'

'Then I'll look forward tae it.'

'Good.' Dave stands on his cigarette. 'I'm away. What a lift someplace? I've got the car. Yie'll catch yir death oot here.'

'I'm gaun over to Reserve, but I'll walk.'

'Sure?'

'Surely.'

'Dinner at six the morra. Go'n dinnae be late.'

And with this, Dave Quinn is gone, walking confidently in his new prosthetic appendage despite the slippery snow.

Stan listens to the busker for a while, breathing nauseating exhaust reeks, feeling snow on his face, closing his eyes.

He needs to build the strength to go back inside and say goodbye to Rose, and he is not sure he can do such a thing with composure. And then, later, he must say goodbye to Vincent and Amanda, who, like Rose, have indulged his love of...

Stan's eyes snap open, clear and fierce, and suddenly, like a revelation, his idea emerges full and complete from the haze of his mind. A smile buds. Under the gaze of his great ancestor, he clasps his hands over his belly and lets his head rest back against the cold stone.

The idea, after everything, is simply this:

Tonight is about to become the most remarkable night of his life.

'I expect you to have enough professional respect for me to be merciful. I did sneak up on you last night, after all. One in the back of my head should suffice.'

Alison said the words matter-of-factly and in the silence that preceded them, heard Juan's chair creak as he shifted position, lifting one leg over the other and clasping his hands over his stomach. Meeting eyes with a passing worshiper, Juan smiled candidly and then said to Alison, calmly:

'What in the name of God are you talking about? What kind of trick is this? I won't be tricked, I assure you. I came here to kill you, yes, but I expected a fight.'

'No trick. I won't fight you. I doubt it's in me to fight.'

'Explain yourself, then.'

'My reasons are personal.'

'I don't give a fuck.'

Alison looked at the Latino for a moment, and then up towards the marble Magdalene.

'I don't want to remember the things I've done or the person I've become, and more than anything I don't want to be a drunk for the rest of my life. It's as simple as that.'

'I've seen drunks before.' Juan eyes narrowed with suspicion. 'They aren't like you.'

Alison shrugged. 'Freedom is a powerful thing. I've become a murderer and a maniac and I do not trust myself anymore. I'm going to give you my guns now. I have two.'

'Slowly.' Juan looked disbelieving.

From her coat pocket and her handbag, Alison handed Juan her revolver and a smaller black pistol, both loaded, and then wiped her hands on her dress. Juan put the black pistol in the inside pocket of his coat. The revolver, he held in his good hand, feeling the comfortable grip agreeable.

'I like this,' he said. 'It's the gun you aimed at me last night. I wondered what it was. It's like something from the American wild west.'

'I think it is.' Alison looked away. The few people who had seen the gun and lived were invariably curious about it. 'It was my husband's. His father gave it to him.'

'It's heavy. It must be laborious. Do you always use this weapon?'

'Not anymore.'

Juan hid the revolver in his coat pocket and kept his hand in with it. The click as he cocked the trigger was clearly audible.

'Come with me, Alison.' Juan began to rise.

'It's beautiful here, don't you think? It's a perfect place to die,' Alison said. 'I can think of nowhere better. Do it here. It'll have to be a bullet, because I'm afraid of knives.'

Alison's face was unreadable, but there were plenty others for Juan to read. He counted eleven souls within the walls praying or meditating, eleven potential witnesses. To consider them victims, he knew was simply not practical. The main exit was only feet away and he could see several more doors. He could not hope to shoot all eleven worshipers before at least some managed to flee, no matter how good a shot he was. Having fled, they became witnesses, able to identify him by his South American countenance. To leave witnesses, Juan mused, would be an altogether bad job. Witnesses would further the cause of neither Antonio Juan nor his employers, who were already struggling to control a population that, not withstanding several deplorable stupidities of collaboration, generally despised them. Indeed, the Nazis, furious for such sloppiness, would themselves attempt to ruin the reputation Juan had worked a lifetime to construct. They might even want their money back. Witnesses would be a very bad job indeed.

But he was reluctant for another reason. Antonio Juan was, somewhere in his black heart, a deeply religious Catholic. If not fearful, he was certainly

cautious of the Almighty. Usually his faith and his vocation separated themselves easily - he was a professional, after all - but to commit murder in the
very house of God... well, it would not look good to Saint Peter.

'No,' he decided. 'Not here.'

'Because of the vampires?'

'What?'

'Never mind. Where then?'

'Not far. I saw a place. I'll make it easy, don't worry.'

'Can we sit for a few minute so I can clear my head?'

'Of course.' Juan nodded towards a marble bust. 'Is that Saint Joan of
Arc?'

'Jeanne d'Arc. Yes, it is.'

'I love it. She also thought herself indestructible in a world of men. I think
I'll come back and take it.'

After fully fifteen minutes of silence, Alison exhaled deeply. Then they
were on their feet, walking, her slightly ahead, knowing without looking that
Juan still had his hand on her revolver in his pocket.

They had walked almost to the nave when Juan said:

'Wait.'

Alison turned. Face to face, separated by less than six feet, or as Juan
counted, three and a half slabs of floor marble. She lifted her eyes and Juan
was gripped like never before in his lifetime. He was afraid she would try
something and catch him unawares. He felt sweat break on his brow. He
squeezed the trigger of the revolver in his coat pocket just enough for
comfort.

But he need not have worried. Alison did nothing more than smile wistfully. She seemed to look past him into space. There were tears in her eyes.

'It's a sin to do this thing, I think,' he muttered. 'Maybe I... no, no of
course not...'

He crossed himself, demanding:

'Say something!'

'What should I say?' Alison was calm.

'I... how should... anything!'

There was, in fact, something Alison wanted to know. Nearly sure of the
facts in her mind, she desired final confirmation, asking without need of
trickery or slyness, as cleanly as she could:

'Do you know the name of Violette Rodin?'

'What? What did you say?'

'Violette Rodin, Antonio. I asked if you know her. Have you told the Nazis
about her? I don't think you have.'

Confirming his ignorance, Juan's eyes shone with suspicion. 'Why ask
such a thing now? What difference does it make?'

'All the difference in the world.'

'Tell me why or I'll flay you wide open. Who is she?'

231

Alison shrugged. 'She's hundreds of miles away.'

'Then why... the Dietrich double... or do you mean someone else?'

'Do you ever wonder, Antonio,' Alison said, 'if there will be a day of reckoning? And do you worry that on such a day you will not find the words necessary to explain your actions? Those are my worries.'

'Do not play games with me, woman, I warn you, I'll...

Alison's voice, startling in the stillness, was sharp and without tone as she said:

'Better think of some answers fast, Nazi.'

'I am not a Nazi!'

Seeing Juan's temper break, Alison made her move.

It had been Juan's practise, because of his powerless left hand, to kill his victims from afar, as a matter of policy preferring a detached sniper shot. He had not performed a face-to-face killing since his teenage years, expect for those victims tightly bound.

Time slowed. With his professional detachment, Juan saw that Alison was moving, reaching, and he instinctively lifted his good hand from his coat pocket and fired the revolver it held.

Juan had not inspected the revolver. If he had, it would have been obvious to such a professional that the barrel of the gun had been altered, skilfully jammed. It was an amateur's mistake. Instead of firing its projectile forward, the revolver exploded with an almighty burst of colour and released its round through the back of itself, straight into Juan's shoulder. The ignition shredded his good hand.

While Antonio Juan was reluctant to take life under sacrosanct timber, Alison Gorry made no such distinction. As shock and scorching pain filled the Latino, he felt the first sharp impact in his chest. The second knife struck one of his eyes, lodging firmly to the hilt, ending all sensation of pain.

For a moment or two - the witnesses later claimed it was much longer - the body of Antonio Juan, the most successful assassin under the control of the Third Reich, stood erect, somehow balanced in a pool of its own blood. Then it collapsed forward onto the cold marble with an audible thump and a final exhalation. Contacting with the floor, the knife in the eye socket pushed deeper and burst the head open like a piece of fruit. It was quite a sight.

Belated panic flared like a mortar explosion. People were screaming, running, crying.

From Juan's remains, Alison retrieved her knives and as a matter of habit, wiped them clean. As the last of the screaming witnesses fled, she tore off her suit to reveal a dress in red and green. The stuffed handbag containing the blood-spattered brown suit she deposited down a sewer drain on Rue Royale, and as Violette Rodin made her way causally back across the city, showing her papers whenever necessary, she found herself hungry and stopped off to buy some bread for lunch.

And so the end comes. Reserve's dinning room is, with an hour to spare, finally ready to receive its guests. The floor-staff congregate by the bar, exhaustedly sipping tea while Gavin and Fanny, in splendid matching dark Armani suits, sip champagne as they arrange a few final festive decorations. Below the mistletoe, they share a small, lovely kiss.

Still in her kitchen whites, hands on hips, Charlie stands alone, running her grey eyes carefully across the space. The restaurant looks splendid, sparkling by candlelight, its metal and glasswork reflecting glimmering light. The band's equipment waits for its players. A harsh-looking woman in her forties, Vincent's private conserver who is also a National Gallery director gives the painting frames a final, careful polish. Asleep in a couch with his daughter sleeping in his arms, the great chef's snoring is the principal sound in the room. Amanda stretches her toes before the open fire, reading, her face set in a curious smile.

Charlie lets her hair out into its natural position. It is her intention to descend downstairs into the kitchen where Viola, Tom, Arthur and her commis chefs are no doubt engaged in pandemonium. She is uninspired. She needs a shower. Her hands find her stomach. She needs, in her own opinion, showered in bleach. Not that it would do any good.

At times like this, she knows, there is only one thing to do.

She plays Beethoven, the second movement of his eighth sonata, the Pathétique. The piano keys are a little heavy for her taste, the stool slightly uncomfortable and high, but she manages admirably well. The sound, too, is peculiar, louder and more resonate that her upright or her mother's grand. More familiar are the particular harmonics of the key of C# minor, her favourite. All heads in the restaurant turn not only to listen but to watch as well.

The Beethoven, exceptionally blending the Classical and the Romantic, represents to Charlie a time in her life that was simple, when there was only her widowed mother telling her to practise, practise, practise, even when her fingers were too small to manoeuvre the keys, practise and practise more. Now, years later, she gives a virtuoso performance worthy of Beethoven himself or even Elizabeth M. Brown B.D.S., charged with passion, freedom and dignity. The more sombre middle section she repeats twice for her own pleasure, once softly and then even more so before moving back into the main refrain.

The final chord Charlie sustains until the notes die naturally, and then she closes the lid. There is no garish applause or crass whistles, although such things considering the performance would not be entirely inappropriate. Instead, there is simply a respectful silence of Charlie's private moment.

Awake now, Vincent gives his still-sleeping daughter to Amanda in exchange for the thick book she is reading and a kiss, and he takes the book to Charlie, his silk suit creating a slight shushing noise as he moves.

'May I sit?' he asks, looming over her, rubbing his eyes.

Charlie budges over on the piano stool and as he does sit with her, Vincent places the book, the first edition *L'Art De La Cuisine Français Au Dix-Neavième Siècle* by Antonin Carême, on the piano lid.

'Is anything the matter?' he asks.

'No.'

'But yie've been crying. Yir cheeks are wet.'

'Things are changing too fast, that's all.'

Vincent nods, studying his elegant hands, finding several pieces of rough and broken skin from his earlier culinary efforts. 'I understand, chef,' he says. 'Believe me, I do. My life has shifted gear more times than I care or am able to remember. And always it happens without warning, or perhaps I just didnae see the clues, I dunno. I do know that invariably things have a way of working out fine in the end. I think yie shouldnae worry so much. I ken what yie're like. Take a deep breath, eh?'

Suspecting that he means this metaphorically, Charlie takes the advice literally and swallows down a deep lungful of air that does much to clear her head.

'Are yie exited?' Charlie feels the immaturity of her question immediately. 'Yie'll be in France this time tomorrow.'

Vincent smiles his handsome and famous smile. 'It's bittersweet. My mother shant see out the winter, I know, and as much as that truly breaks my heart, I have my own family to think about now. And, if I'm honest, as much as I know she loves me, I think her life ended the day my father died. So to answer yir question, Charlie Brown, I think that I couldnae tell yie how exited I am if I spoke for a hundred years. But enough about me.' He gestures towards the Carême. 'I want you to have this.'

'Vincent…'

'Charlotte, if yie'll no go to Paris then at least take my book. It's only a book.' To pre-empt further protest he says, 'I owe you something. Yie know it. I owe a damn sight more than this measly book, too, but this is all I have to give.'

Despite the fact that the collector in Charlie covets the book very much, there is no way on earth she will accept such a thing; it is worth a small fortune. Not, that is, until she lifts her sparkling grey eyes and sees Vincent's expression, pleading and at the same time demanding. He will not force the book on her, but at the same time, clearly, he will not be satisfied until she accepts.

'Thank you,' she says. 'I want you to know that it's been an honour working with you. Everything they say about you is true. Yie're a gentleman. And I wish you and Amanda all the best, Vincent, I truly do. If Chloe grows up to be anything like her mother or her father, she'll be fine.'

The compliment is well received. Vincent looks as if he may say more, but finally says merely:

'Goodbye, chef.'

234

And only after he says this does Charlie truly realise, after four years, how much of a father figure Vincent has been to her, and that he is exactly the age her own father, Dr Charles Brown, would have been had he lived. She feels her eyes well.

'Adieu.'

'And listen, I meant what I said about dancing with me later. We've never danced.'

'I know.' Charlie thinks, of all things, of Princess Diana dying. 'I promise.'

Vincent wipes away a tear from Charlie's eye and then, standing and scratching his potbelly, says:

'Right, I'm away back to sleep. I'm fucking shagged, man. Yie ken the worst thing about moving back to France, dae yie not?'

Charlie knows full well, but humours him. 'What's that?'

Vincent rubs his bald head, frowning. 'I'm gonna huvtae no speak like this any more, man, eh?'

However, before Vincent reaches the swing doors, he is almost barrelled out of the way by Tom, Viola and the entire kitchen staff marching past him, tramping the peace under foot. Even Arthur is with them, moving with a speed surprising of his age.

'Gus, Radio! Now!' Filthy, bloody, bellowing, Tom's eyes blaze. 'It's time.'

The butcher's bet today, or to be specific his combination bets, is like no other bet he has ever made. Reserve's collective staff stake, inspired by both management's generous severance package and his own engagement, is larger than he has ever before dared to risk in Scotland. More than pride, three and a half thousand pounds rest on this evening's final house race at Mussel-burgh racecourse. The winnings... he cannot bare to contemplate yet.

'Who did we bet on?' Fanny wonders.

'Shut the fuck up!' Tom's eyeballs are like boiled eggs. 'Please.'

Reserve's radio, contrasting with its surroundings, is a battered thing that Gavin pulls out from behind the bar, extending the telescopic aerial almost into Fanny's eye. Manual turning proves a nightmare. Maximum volume is pitiful and distorted, and the entire restaurant staff with the exception of Charlie gathers in a tight bundle, breath held.

Tom quickly realises to his horror that, in fact, the sixteen-fence class C race has already begun. Only three furlongs remain. Like a live stock auctioneer, the commentator reaches fever pitch. The Australian begins to mutter to himself:

'Come-on-baby, come-on-Jakari, come-on-baby, come-on-Kock de la Vesvre...'

The cadence spreads to his entire body; enacting something of a skiing mime, he becomes a jockey riding the last furlongs.

'Come-on-baby, come-on-Jakari, *come-on-baby, COME-ON-KOCK DE LA VESVRE...*'

Although he very much regrets it now, Tom has bet the entire collective stake on two French horses, Jakari to finish first and Kock de la Vesvre second. Both places are essential for a return. One result will not do. Despite Jakari being a safe bet, the inclusion of Kock de la Vesvre, a lesser racehorse not expected to be placed, is a bold move that increases the odds significantly to 18:1. It is, in hindsight, perhaps too bold.

The race has ended. Completely carried away and muttering still, Tom realises that he has no idea what happened. Still bent over in the jockey position, his hands find his brow, and it does not escape him that every eye in the restaurant trains expectantly on him.

'What happened?' Fanny shrieks, all composure gone.

'Fanny, shut the fuck up, man!' At least four people simultaneously make this exclamation.

Tom concentrates on the radio.

'...so it's first place to Jakari, second to Kock de la Vesvre and third to...'

The words do not register immediately, but rather dance around Tom's consciousness for a while like butterflies. The squawking electric box is telling him that he has just won, for the common good, sixty-three thousand pounds, just shy of three grand for every soul in the room. But his mind resists. His good sense defies.

Chewing a piece of shortbread, Arthur breaks the silence:

'That means we won, eh?'

Tom nods. 'It does, Art, aye.' He says the words in such a manner that his colleagues take a further moment to register. But as the facts settle, Tom's eyes become distinctively clear. 'We won,' he repeats, now with conviction. 'We fucking won! Holy sweet baby Jesus, I won!'

Near-hysteria ensues, exhaustion forgotten. Waitresses who usually make a professional point of looking as frosty as ice now jump in the air, screaming childishly, but their jubilance is nothing compared to that of the pot-washers. Two thousand eight hundred and sixty-three pounds in cash each the week before Christmas on top of a healthy three-month severance cheque is not to be sniffed at. Such is the occasion, even Gavin smiles.

In a single, elegant movement, Evelyn advances to Tom and throws her arm around him, locking tightly against his filthy whites. Inaudible to everyone else in the room, she says into his shoulder:

'I told you.'

She is crying. Tom, too, for lack of words, bursts into tears, and howling, they cling to each other, the entire world forgotten.

Rising finally from the piano, clutching her new book to her breast, Charlie merely watches. Yesterday she felt bitterness and anger towards them both for using her as a sexual pawn, as Charlie herself has used many people, but now she feels for them only hope. As they stand weeping, locked together, she is deeply moved. She remembers waltzing with Stan on Tuesday night and thinks again of Princess Diana. But noise breaks the pleasant reverie.

236

Charlie's head snaps round on her shoulders but for a second she does not understand what she is seeing, so amazing is it.

Then she understands all too clearly.

She dilates.

Vincent yanks a tablecloth, displacing the entire setting to the floor with a loud, harsh clatter. His face is a mauve mask of horror. His eyeballs swell, his teeth gnash as he claws alarmingly at his chest and then, more horrendously, his neck, drawing blood. His colour returns and he seems to relax into a more natural bearing, catching a deep breath and righting his balance, but then he coughs and the effort releases a tangled clot of crimson blood down his front and onto the mosaic floor. Seeing this, his eyes become desperate. Then his entire body falls forward onto the mosaic floor, taking the Christmas tree with it.

There is no stunned silence. Charlie's staff are professionals. Tom and Viola are immediately on the great chef, yanking limbs, clearing his airway and beginning the business of resuscitation. Gavin is summoning an ambulance. Amanda is silent, clutching her daughter in her arms with an expression of tangible dismay.

Throughout this, however, Charlie does not move. It is as clear to her as it is to Arthur, who other than respectfully removing his cap also stands still, that the great chef Vincent Dussollier, friend, husband, father and teacher, is already as dead as a doornail.

The Christmas Party is cancelled.

6

Charlie and Gavin arm the formidable restaurant security systems and lock the door, waiting until the warning bleeps stop before mounting the worn steps to North Castle Street, which but for Gavin's taxi and the noise spilling down from George Street is gravely still. Fanny the maître d' is waiting, her back to the railings, wrapped in a furry coat and a woolly toory.

'Yie gaun out?' Charlie asks.

'There isnae any work in the morning.' Gavin slugs from a £93 bottle of 2001 Pieddé. 'And I've got three grand in my back pocket. I'm certainly no gaun for an early night, chef.'

'I've a bag of coke as big as a bag o' Tate and Lyle,' Fanny says, wrapping her fingers around Gavin's and huddling up to him for heat. Such a public display of affection is not like them, so much so that it is easy to forget that they have been a couple for fourteen years. 'And I've got three grand, too.'

'Come wae us,' Gavin says. 'Yie look like yie need it.'

'I'm weary, Gus.' Charlie shivers with cold. 'I need my bed. I'm broken.'

She watches him fastening his coat buttons over his waistcoat, half-expecting him to say something entirely inappropriate, an attempt to defuse the gruesome and hellish day by ill-timed humour. But he says:

'Eh, the castle looks good?'

Surprised, Charlie turns her eyes. Up the hill, framed by Pink Fashions, Starbucks and a huge council Christmas tree on George Street, Edinburgh Castle looks splendid indeed, high on its hazy rock, sparkling with frost. Years ago, during her service on Rose Street, it was Charlie's habit to correspond her breaks with Stan's, who at the time worked as a maître d' around the New Town, and they would sit together on a bench looking up to the castle, Charlie smoking joints as Stan talked Scottish history, of perhaps Charles Edward Stuart and his Jacobites, or of the tattooed Picts, or the semi-conquering Roman general Gnaeus Julius.

'It's beautiful,' she agrees, wistfully.

Gavin slugs his wine. 'Wouldnae go that far.'

Impatiently, severely, the taxi's horn blasts, resonating across the quite street. Fanny kisses Charlie cheek, smiles, and makes her way to pacify the driver.

Gavin extends his hand and says simply:

'Thanks, chef.'

Standing on her tiptoes, Charlie wraps her arms around his neck hard.

'Thank you, Gavin. Yie're spectacular. We're a pretty good team, eh?'

'Number one, baby.'

They break with an affectionate kiss.

'Take care, Gus.'

'And you.' Gavin rubs the neatness of out his raven-black hair, obviously relishing the act. 'Until the next time, chef: goodnight.'

'Bye.'

Jogging up the hill a few paces, Gavin gives his two-thirds full bottle of Pieddé to a huddled-up beggar Charlie had not even seen, and then without a glance back to the restaurant that has occupied the last five years of his life, climbs into his taxi, pulls the door closed and in a haze of exhaust smoke is gone.

Alone, Charlie closes her eyes. In one hand she holds the Carême and with the fingers of the other hand, she presses gentle on her eyelids, thinking of the Dussollier women; Amanda, who has just become sole heir to the ninth largest fortune in France, and at the same time, a widow and a single parent; Megan, who has outlived her husband, her first daughter-in-law and grandchild, and now her only offspring; Chloé, poor Chloé, who will not remember her father at all.

Allowing the soothing freezing air to seep through her jumper and contract her skin, she leaves her duffel coat unbuttoned. Her hair, without her toory, rests freely in its natural shape, luminous fire-red in the moonlight.

She opens her grey eyes and, leaving Reserve, begins up the hill past the beggar, one boot heel echoing on the pavement after the other.

George Street is a different matter. Heaving with clubbers and tourists and people just out to walk their dogs, the street is alive. The buildings and Christmas lights create a miasma of colour that Charlie's eyes absorb and refract like fleeting sparks. Taxis, cars and busses roar past. Charlie feels the usual semi-recognising glances and hears the customary whisper:

'She's famous, eh?'

Parked on Hanover Street, it takes only a moment to negotiate the Cortina down onto Queen Street and past the Portrait Gallery. From Picardi Place, Charlie hurtles down through Leith Street, craning her neck as a matter of habit to see into the windows of the restaurants. Shifting down a gear, past Gayfield police station and her own home, she thinks of her new, unused, virginal bed. She has not slept since Wednesday and imagines with almost a smile the sensation of slipping between the fresh sheets.

But it is not possible to go home yet.

There is an addiction to face, and the stark and terrible practicalities of it.

Off Leith Walk, Charlie parks the Cortina on Pilrig Street and walks up Spey Street, coming finally to the enormous, rising structure of Inchkeith House.

The tiny metallic elevator is particularly nasty, made worse by Charlie's co-traveller, an old woman of at least eighty, hunched and wrapped in what seems to be a dozen layers of urine-soaked woollens.

The door opens finally onto the open-air landing of the eighth floor. The view is of all of Leith, nearly the same view as offered by the wasteland this morning, though from a different perspective.

Buying hashish and marijuana in Edinburgh is often more difficult than is commonly assumed. It is true that one can procure almost every variety of narcotic on nearly every street corner, but finding the quality Charlie desires in her drugs is somewhat more taxing. Of course, she knows a great deal of reliable 'high-class' drug dealers but, generally speaking, smoking cannabis makes people talkative and Charlie, as a matter of both privacy and security, does not like her habits discussed. She therefore buys her regular supply from a trivial, insular dealer in Leith, Jimmy, who is both ignorant of Charlie's surname and her celebrity. Naturally, all drug dealers pose something of a risk - cannabis, lest we forget, is illegal - but Jimmy's risk is more a worry of police surveillance rather than, and preferable to, being discussed irresponsibly.

Somehow eligible for full disability benefits and therefore relieved from such boring matters as working for a living or paying rent and council tax, Jimmy is at forty an obese mass of saturated fat with the mean look of a genuinely nasty bastard. His eyes are small and ugly. Jewellery covers his fingers and neck. Plaque covers his teeth. He leads Charlie through into the living room, managing to touch her three times, and as he disappears into the kitchen, leers:

'Have a seat.'

Although there is nowhere to sit, Charlie would be reluctant anyway. The small living room is, as is the rest of the flat, bare and dirty and smells foul. Smoke hangs thick. There is an enormous plasma-screen television but no books in sight apart from for a tabloid television supplement. The window offers a view across Leith Walk and up to Calton Hill that is not too bad. On the only couch, a twitchy-looking specimen of a woman with a heroin-complexion listens to music on headphones, rolling a joint with languid movements, her foggy eyes dancing in the sockets like marbles, while beside her, a man of perhaps fifty-five, an old hippy type who Charlie establishes as the primary source of the foul odour, plucks harshly at a battered acoustic guitar that is missing two strings. Taking position at the unused gas fire, her back against the wall, Charlie affects no pretence of a smile.

'What are yie listening tae?' she asks.

'What? What did yie say?' The woman's eyes snap into focus.

'I asked what you are listening to.'

'The *Wall*, man. Floyd.'

Charlie resists the urge to roll her eyes as squeezing back through the kitchen doorway, Jimmy says:

'What can I do yie for the night?'

'I want some hash,' Charlie says obviously, laying the accent on thick.

'H'much, like?'

'A bar.'

Jimmy whistles. A bar, also known as a nine-bar, is literally a slab of hashish weighing nine ounces, usually the unit of production.

'Yie want it the night, like?'

'I want it right now, Jim. Can yie dae it or no?'

Rubbing the folds of fat around the back of greasy his neck, Jimmy decides after heavy deliberation:

'Mibbae.'

'Mibbae aye or mibbae no?'

'Depends on the price, like.'

In the doorway leading back into the hallway, a tiny figure emerges. Beautiful, like an angel in a nightdress, the girl is perhaps five or six and rubs her eyes in sleepy confusion. Both Charlie and the other woman are equally horrified by the vision, though for different reasons.

'Mummy?' The voice is like a tiny bell.

'Yie're really starting to piss me off now!' Mummy barks. She places her joint carefully in her ashtray and drags the child roughly, screaming now, by the wrist, back to bed. Charlie hears the sound of a door slamming and hysterical crying.

'Jimmy, I'm no here tae fuckin negotiate wae yie, man,' she says, watching Mummy re-appear. 'I'm rushed. I've no had a good night. I'll gie yie a hundred and fifty notes and yie'll be thankful for it, eh?'

The fat man scoffs. 'Nae danger! Yie're a guid customer, aye, but if I sold the same bar in half-o's I could make five-fifty. Twice as much if I sold quarters, as I'm sure yie ken, hen. I need two-fifty.'

'One fifty, James, take it or dinnae.'

'Course I'll take it,' Jimmy smiles grotesquely to the sound of unrelenting hysterics. 'I'm only makin conversation. Since yir here, eh, I could dae yie a tidy Christmas hamper. Yie ken what it's like been left short over the festivities.'

Obviously taking some idiotic pleasure in the action, Jimmy presents his merchandise in a large fishing tackle box like something from Hunter Thompson's *Fear and Loathing in Las Vegas*, and just as surreal. Collapsible trays display pills, prescription capsules, amyl nitrate poppers and measured bags of various powers. In the belly of the case sit pieces of hashish and plastic Bank of Scotland moneybags of marijuana in various weight-denominations. The box represents, if nothing else, ten-year's imprisonment.

There is not need to weigh the bar; it maintains its original distinct 'factory' shape, like a huge slab of chocolate. Charlie tears a piece of its wrapping and after a sniff, seems happy enough.

Jimmy's tiny black holes for eyes sharpen as he takes a few gram bags of brown power in fat hands. 'I've got some smack,' he says. 'It's cheap as chips these days, heroin. It is, after all, Christmas, my friend.'

At this, a bubble burst inside Charlie's head and she sees herself with detachment, standing in Jimmy's disgusting house looking into a fishing tackle box full of heroin and date-rape drugs. Somewhere in the flat, the child is crying. She sees in her mind Vincent, not as she has so often seen him swanning around in his silk suit, or as she saw tonight, dead, but rather as a young man in his prime, revered by his contemporaries, world-famous, yet still snuffing ashamedly around Soho is search of an opium fix like a deranged pig hunting sour truffles. Charlie has heard these stories but has never, until now, fully appreciated their sheer ugliness. In fact, Charlie has listened to Vincent talk for years of his earlier career in tones of shame and sorrow, and she realises now that those feelings are not at all alien to her.

Slowly her grey eyes meet Jimmy's fat face. She looks for a moment, frankly, as if she might physically attack him. But she does not. She says nothing. She simply takes her drugs, pays him, and leaves.

Sitting in the Cortina on Pilrig Street, behind tinted windows and tired eyes, Charlie rolls a joint straight off the bar, using grass instead of tobacco, and after lighting it and rolling down her window a crack, she is on her way again. Back onto Leith Walk, she heads towards the city centre, working the gear stick with the joint in her hand, pressing buttons on her mobile telephone with her steering hand.

'Hello?' Stan's voice seems different in his new house, the acoustics more rounded and mature. He sounds, contrasting with the last time they spoke, entirely agreeable and calm.

Indeed, Stan is calm. He is perfectly at ease. He is smiling, reclining in his new couch in his new house staring at his new corner-tank marine aquarium.

'Yie're home early,' Charlie says.

'An early night never hurt anyone.' Stan tosses away the book he was reading.

'I want to say, Stanley,' Charlie says, 'that I'm so very truly sorry for this situation. I'm a cow.'

'Yie're nae such thing.'

'What more can I say? How was your party?'

'Sombre. Charlotte, it sounds to me like yie're driving. It's only just past nine. What's the matter?'

'Vincent died.' Idling at the Brunswick Road traffic lights beside a maroon double-decker bus that advertises one of Stan's strategies, she exhales, knocking ash from her joint out the window. 'Stan, I assume yie're alone?'

'Except for my fishes. Charlotte, what happened to Vincent?'

'He's dead. Heart attack and a bleeding lung.'

Stan speaks, after a moment, in a low and mournful voice, lamenting simply:

'Poor Amanda and Chloé.'

'Tomorrow'll be soon enough to grieve, Stan. Tonight, I want us to talk.'

'Talk, then.'

'I don't really know what to say.'

'Liar. Try harder.' These words are spoken in the same calm tone, confusing Charlie.

She frowns. 'What I mean is that I don't know what to do.'

'That's better, Charlotte,' Stan muses, 'but I suspect equally untrue.'

Anger flushes in Charlie. She grips the steering wheel tight and says, harshly, metallically:

'I'm afraid, Stan. I'm scared.'

The difficulty in saying such a thing for Charlie is obvious. Silence falls, through which Charlie listens to the sounds of Stan's bubbling fish tanks and Stan listens to the sound of Charlie's revving engine.

Stan breaks the quiet, remarking in an agreeable tone:

'I'm no gaun tae give yie this for free, Charlotte. Yie'll need to work for it. Yie have to earn it.'

'What dae yie mean?'

'Dinnae gimme it. You said that yie dinnae know what to say or what to do, Charlotte, but I think yie ken fine well. I want to hear it.'

'What I want, Stan,' Charlie sighs, 'yie know I have no longer the right to ask for.'

'I want yie tae ask.'

'You already know.'

'I don't know, Charlie. I try to understand, but I am not a mind reader.'

Charlie swallows a deep breath and says, more afraid that she has even been in her life:

'I want you to be the baby's father, Stan. I want it to be your baby.'

'Whose baby?'

'Our baby.'

'I won't have an open relationship,' Stan's voice is harder now.

'I don't want that either.'

'Ah, but there are other things as well, Charlotte. Yie dinnae come to me after this long and expect to make demands.'

'What things?' Charlie exhales cannabis-tainted smoke.

'Yes or no, Charlotte?'

'Yes.'

'Yes, what?'

'Yes, Stan, I'll do whatever you say.'

'Tempting, but be more concise.'

'I want to have a family with you. I want to be a family with you. I want to get into bed every night for the rest of my life beside you.'

'Why?' Stan asks, maddeningly calm.

'For the reasons we discussed while we danced to Moon River.'

'Tell me again.'

Charlie realises now what Stan realised earlier tonight.

'Not yet. I want to tell you as I show you. I'm coming round,' she says. 'Be ready.'

'Ready how?' For the first time, there is uncertainty in Stan's voice.

'Hard, Stanley, idiot. Be hard for me.'

'Well,' Stan muses, 'if yie want cocoa, which I know yie will, yie'll need tae bring some milk.'

Charlie smiles to herself, throwing her phone into the back seat.

Past Elm Row, the traffic is bumper to bumper and she waits again at a red light. She tokes her joint deeply, holding the smoke in her lungs and resisting the urge to think about Vincent, and switches on the radio to the ten o'clock bulletin.

The female newsreader, who is a woman Charlie once slept with, states:

'...who led the investigation, had this to say only ten minutes ago.'

'Ladies and Gentlemen,' the Detective Inspector's recorded voice, underscored by a bustle of reporters around him, says, 'thank you for coming. I can confirm to you than following the discovery of Megan's body earlier today ...'

Charlie is moving again, turning right onto London Road, where acceleration is possible.

'...Sarah Gillies has now been charged with the murder of her daughter. Megan's father, Jack Gillies, was also arrested but was released soon afterwards without charge. That's all.'

Charlie inhales her joint. But Charlie is not a fool. She has long suspected that a crash is inevitable. Unhappiness and cannabis, after all, do not constitute a balanced diet. As fate would have it, when the crash finally comes, she just happens to be driving her car. Lost inside her thoughts, smoking and driving, thinking of Amanda Dussollier and of Jack Gillies and mostly of Stan Hume, she simply fails to notice that further along London Road a crash has already occurred...

So loud and so unexpected are the series of impacts that onlookers at the Easter Road-London Road junction think for a moment a bomb has exploded, and many hit the pavement. Then a true explosion lights up the sky, plumps of smoke disappearing into the night. But by now the initial astonishment has passed.

An electric-blue 1997 Vauxhall Corsa, clearly identifiable to the layperson as the cause of the scene, sits embedded into the corner grocery shop, fully ablaze, its back wheels still spinning. In the middle of the crossroad, a black taxi lies partly crushed, inside which, despite the raging fire, trapped passenger are trying vainly to smash their way out. Two pedestrians lying on the road in their Friday Night Best are clearly dead.

The scene is truly hellish, and to the onlookers so accustomed to seeing such things on their television screens, somewhat surreal. The smells come as a shock.

By the time the first police car arrives from Easter Road, followed by the sound of more approaching sirens, the taxi's passengers are dead. The officers jump from the still-moving car, one restraining the crowd, the other trying to asses and prioritise the duties of the scene.

'He went straight though the lights,' an elderly man with a dog volunteers, trying to be of use, pointing at the blue Corsa. 'Just ploughed straight through, he did.'

'Thank you, sir. We'll speak to you as soon as get a chance. Step back now, please,' the young officer says, as he realises there are more vehicles involved.

Further back along London Road, three more cars, trying to avoid the crash, have been compromised: a silver BMW, a Mimi Cooper and a red Cortina, which is burning.

Waking Up

'Welcome aboard, Mr. Pilgrim,' said the loudspeaker. 'Any questions?'

Billy licked his lips, thought a while, inquired at last: 'Why me?'

'That is a very Earthling question to ask, Mr. Pilgrim. Why you? Why us for that matter? Why anything? Because this moment simply is. Have you ever seen bugs trapped in amber?'

'Yes.' Billy, in fact, had a paperweight in his office which was a blob of polished amber with three lady-bugs embedded in it.

'Well, here we are, Mr. Pilgrim, trapped in the amber of this moment. There is no why.'

Kurt Vonnegut

'Do you want to dance with me, stupid?'

'No, I dinnae fuckin want to dance,' Charlie hisses without lifting her eyes.
'I'm reading! Leave me be. Please.'

*'I finished that last night. Shall I tell you what happens and save you the
bother? I know how little time you get to read.'*

'Fuck off, Stanley.'

Charlie is faintly aware of footsteps as Stan crosses the room, but continues to read as she inhales smoke. The footsteps are followed by several indeterminable clicks and noises, but she does not concern herself, except to be annoyed. But by the particular hiss at the start of the recording, she recognises the music before it even begins, and she forgets to be annoyed, forgets even to breathe: the comical strumming squeezebox introduction to Moon River, Charlie's favourite interpretation of Charlie's favourite song, wordless and tender, recorded in 1976 by Jean-Luc Dussollier.

'Bastard,' she smiles.

But as the waves of the river lap against her face, it is too late. She falls helpless, drowning, and almost without realising, she is on her feet.

Maintaining her virginity until the age of nineteen, Charlie came to sex late in life. Afterwards, her first experiences were tentative to say the least. Her experimental sex pursuit began in earnest with Stan on the night Princess Diana died in Paris, and yet despite this, and at the same time quite probably because of it, Charlie and Stan have never been lovers. On August 31st, 1997, after falling out with her then boyfriend, Stan performed what would be the most erotic and incredible experience of Charlie's life, the encounter to which she still holds all others to account.

On his acoustic guitar, singing in a cavernous voice that Charlie never suspected would come from him, Stan performed for her Moon River. But there was more to it than sound. It was a matter of vibration. Stan sat at one end of a reclaimed church bench made of solid oak he once owned while, facing him, Charlie sat at the other end. Upon his request, slightly reluctantly and wholly self-consciously, she was naked, straddling the soft, polished wood, her legs gripping tight, her ankles twisted together underneath. Her hair offered nowhere to hide because it was, at the time, cropped short. The guitar was and still is deep-bellied, with twelve strings rather than six, and he placed the instrument, rather than on his knee, on the bench itself, which Charlie would soon understand caused its sound to resonate through the wood like an electric currant.

An orgasm came in a matter of moments, quite unexpectedly and fiercely, her face a glowering red, her back wet with sweat. The moan was magnificent.

Since that night almost seven years ago, physical contact has been all but eliminated. Charlie does not remember the last time she touched Stan. Now, however, with her chest against him, feeling her hand in his, his other hand *pressing the small of her back, and his glorious natural smell filling her lungs, she almost faints. But she does not. She grips him with all her strength, berating herself for not putting down her joint before she got up. Smoke curls around them but Stan seems unbothered. Of course, Stan is much taller, but the contours of his body seem to complete her own perfectly. She can feel him hard in his trousers.*

'I liked your dress at the weekend.' Stan speaks softly in his natural voice. 'I confess it's been on my mind.'

'Has it?'

'It has. I saw you with your waitress friend in the club's lounge. She seemed to like the dress, too. Larry filled me in on the rest.'

'I knew she would.'

'She's very pretty, your friend. She's very young.'

Charlie's eyes are closed, her voice small as she says:

'She's an entertainment.'

Stan smiles and abruptly manoeuvres the slow, swaying waltz into something of a brief tango. It is all Charlie can do just to hold on until the natural rhythm returns.

'Ah, but tell me this, Charlie Brown,' he says, in a notably peculiar tone, 'when will you be entertained enough with your silly wee lassies? Are you not fed to the teeth? Is it not time for something... harder? I grow weary, woman.'

The sheer audacity of this takes Charlie quite by surprise. She says nothing, merely waltzing, so Stan continues:

'You asked me to wait, Charlotte. I can't remember why you asked such a thing, but I'm sure you had your reasons... fear, perhaps...and so I have waited.' His voice is calm, measured. 'I've waited for years, but I will not wait any more.'

Charlie's heart stops, her grey eyes open wide but she does not lift them to see Stan. To feel and smell him is already more that she can tolerate.

'I understand,' she says.

Stan scoffs. 'Nah, I do not believe so.' He speaks in his Edinburgh voice now. 'I dinnae think yie understand at all. Sell your flat. I mean, obviously dinnae sell it if yie dinnae want tae, but dinnae live in it. I forbid it from this night onwards. Live here. This is yir home. I bought it for us, Charlotte. There's too much space here and my life is too small.'

Dizzy now, Charlie stumbles and almost loses her balance. She brakes from him and they face each other, her grey eyes burning into his green transparent ones as she says as clearly as she is able:

'No.'

Stan's shoulders fall. 'Why not?' He appears not only confused but also furious. 'Explain yourself.'

Her mouth opens to speak but Charlie finds herself wordless. And breathless. She listens to the soft, luscious sound of Jean-Luc Dussollier's trombone and the rougher cello that follows a heartbreaking third below the melody, wishing that she could somehow find the strength to tell Stan that she was, at the end of the day, correct. It has long been Charlie's belief that she is simply not good enough for Stan, that she would unavoidably let him down, hurt him, betray his trust. And now, allowing a stranger to impregnate her, she has proven herself correct.

The future hastens. Charlie believes that she will quietly become a single working family, which after all is hardly a new concept to her. It has been her mortal fear her entire life: to be just like her mother. Worse, she will be forced to watch Stan, eventually, settle down with some other girl. Jealously burns at the very thought of such a thing, bringing a flush to her face. But there is no one else to blame. Charlie, she has come to understand, is her own worst enemy.

'Just dance,' she says, reconnecting with him.

As difficult as this is to accept, Stan does just that. Acceptance has become a matter of habit.

'Tell me,' he says, still smiling.

'Tell you what?'

'I need to hear it.'

She speaks now with a sincerity that break her own heart, looking deep inside his eyes, and her toes almost curl at the pleasure of saying the words.

'Stan. I love you.'

'I love you, too.'

Broken hearted and without further discussion, they waltz, unaware that the music has stopped.

'Why should we try to hide our emotion which we all of us here, men and women, feel? We are back home in Paris which is on its feet to liberate itself and which has been able to achieve it single-handed. No, we should not try to conceal this profound and sacred emotion. We are living through moments which transcend each of our poor lives.'

Charles de Gaulle stood tall in full uniform, eyes like steel, while the whole world listened. In the far corner of the crowded room, Major Philip Scott of the British Army, also in uniform, held the weight of his body on his cane, happy to distance himself from the action.

Earlier in the day, only hours before the General entered Paris, Philip had stood in the corner of a different room, one in the Préfecture de Police, watching with tear-filled eyes Colonel Rol and Général Leclerc of the Free French Army receive the Nazi surrender. It had been an exhausting day of tears for many people.

'Paris!' de Gaulle declared. 'Outraged Paris! Broken Paris! Martyred Paris, but liberated Paris! Liberated by the people of Paris with help from the armies of France, with the help and support of the whole of France, of France which is fighting, of the only France, the real France, eternal France.'

The Major smiled dryly to himself.

Less than an hour ago, as the General and his entourage entered the hotel, a sniper had opened fire, but the attempt was made by an amateur and failed to hit anything but pavement. More danger was in store the next day. It was Philip's task to arrange a parade, even though the city still crawled with Nazis. Along with Leclerc's Second Armoured Division, De Gaulle intended to walk the Champs Elysées, and Philip already could see that the march, unfairly, would be the sole event the world remembered as the Liberation of Paris, despite the incalculable tiny battles of the last three years.

De Gaulle was still talking and Philip felt it was drawing out a bit. He had never liked speeches, no matter who was speaking. He shifted his weight on his cane and yawned, thinking that because of his position at the back of the room filled with the British and Free French finest he had gotten away with the monstrous offence. But he had not. One man had seen.

Young, tall and lean, stiff with the air of propriety, the new Advisory on Jewish Affairs to the Interior stood amongst the small throng on the stage, three bodies from the General. Upon seeing the yawn, he met Philip's guilty gaze and repressing a smile, winked his good eye.

Although he did not know for sure, Philip assumed that Alison Gorry was still in Paris. Indeed, he doubted that she would ever leave the city. Since her release from duty, he had not and did not expect to hear from her.

'Vive la France!' concluded Charles de Gaulle, and for the second time that day, Major Philip Scott, a hero of both the Great War and the Second World War, thinking of his own bed in his own bedroom in which he would feel his wife pressing naked against him, gave way to a near-hysterical floods of tears.

No. 24B Lee Crescent, Portobello, is packed to capacity. More than people, however, Charlie's furniture takes up a lot of space. Tinsel lines each of Stan's aquariums, one of which sits atop Charlie upright piano. Below the huge replica Rothko, an enormous chain of tables circles the living room, some of them from Reserve. Inside the circle stands the seven-foot Christmas tree.

Dinner is served. Amid Dave, her mother and all of her grandparents, Victoria talks with Doris and Archie Hume and Margot, who has brought Kirkcudbright's handsome new dentist. Dave's three younger sisters flirt unashamedly with Gavin, while Tom and Evelyn feed one another. Fanny and Lorraine from the Doonhaimer, who are sisters, both listen rapt as Rubydoobie, in her fifth year, talks to everybody and nobody about everything and nothing. Stan and Niamh Hume, both wearing paper party hats, discuss the intricacies of felt tipped pens, Stan all the while using hand gestures to help explain his ideas.

Watching all of this, her hair loose in its natural position smelling of turkey fat, Charlie takes in the scene. For a second the idea of a cigarette flashes in her mind. But effortlessly, she waves away the craving. Charlie has not smoked since she got out of hospital three days ago. She intends never to smoke again.

Despite her broken foot, her three broken ribs and her fractured collarbone, to mention nothing of the multiple bruises and swelling, the baby is alive.

Looking around the table, she thinks of Vincent. She thinks of Amanda and Chloé. She thinks of the missed opportunity of Paris. She thinks of Reserve. But all she sees is Stan, and her own furniture blending, with the exception of Snoopy eyeing the fish, perfectly with his.

Painfully, ignoring her crutch, she rises to her feet and taps her Irn-Bru flute with her fork.

'I'll have your attentions for a moment, ladies and gentlemen. Particularly you, mother. Stan and I have an announcement to make.'

Meeting eyes with Stan, Charlie finds her stomach with her hand, and ignoring the pain in her bruised face, she smiles.

Permissions

We would like to thank the following for their kind permission.

Matt McGinn's 'The Wee Kirkcudbright Centipede' (1972) used by kind permission of Janette McGinn.

Ani Di'franco's 'Gray', 1999 Righteous Babe Records, used by kind permission of Ani Di'franco.

Translated Victor Hugo extract from Les Misérables of 1862 used by kind permission of Wordsworth Classics.

David Hume extract from a personal draft letter of 1734 used by kind permission of the National Library of Scotland and the Royal Society of Edinburgh.

Kurt Vonnegut quote from Slaughterhouse-Five (1969), used by kind permission of Donald C. Farber, Esq.

Lipstick Publishing
www.lipstickpublishing.com